ENTWINED

Emma Jensen

D0038031

BALLANTINE BOOKS • NEW YORK

Copyright © 1997 by Emma Jensen

All rights reserved under International and Pan-American Copyright Conventions. Published in the United States by Ballantine Books, a division of Random House, Inc., New York, and simultaneously in Canada by Random House of Canada Limited, Toronto.

http://www.randomhouse.com

Library of Congress Catalog Card Number: 97-93814

ISBN 0-345-41659-0

Manufactured in the United States of America

First Edition: November 1997

10 9 8 7 6 5 4

For my grandmother, Maxine Brown,
who first explained to me the magic of the rose

PROLOGUE

Lisbon, 1810

The night air smelled of roses. Nathan Paget, Marquess of Oriel, stood just outside the wharfside tavern and inhaled deeply. "Hail the caprices of war," he commented dryly. "Our soldiers can't get food, but the ladies of Lisbon will have their roses."

"Whatever happened to your romantic soul, man?" his companion chided. "Think of the beds that will be strewn with petals later."

Nathan grunted. "My romantic soul is back in London, with the ghost of the last decent meal I ate."

"Yes, well, you'll be reunited soon enough with your fiancée, so you can cease whining," Gabriel Loudon, Lord Rievaulx said cheerfully, as he propped his long form against the tavern wall and regarded his friend. "By this time tomorrow, you'll be well on your way home."

"So I will. You know if it were up to me, I would stay to see this damned war through, and we would go home together."

"I know, but if our intrepid leader had had his way, you would have been on a ship weeks ago."

"Gerard should understand better than anyone why I

needed to stay." Nathan thought of their superior officer, no doubt wearing tracks in his carpet while waiting for news from the Peninsular campaign. "I am a rat catcher," he grumbled, "not a messenger."

Rievaulx chuckled. "You caught your rat, Nathan. Go home, gloat to Gerard about having ferreted out one more of Napoleon's spies. Reacquaint yourself with your fiancée's lovely blue eyes. If all goes as planned, I will be back in time for the wedding. Ah, I suppose I'll have to bring a gift. What do you think Cecily would say to some Portuguese crockery?"

"Gabriel . . ."

"No, I suppose you're right. Too heavy. Some Madeira, then?"

Nathan sighed. "Gabriel, you know how much it would mean to me if you were there, but I would understand—"

"Now don't you start with that again! Cecily and I would never have suited each other in the end. She had her sights set on you, and I daresay she knew from the onset that you were the better bet all around. You, my friend, are the one with the heart inclined to love."

Nathan raised an eyebrow. "And you?"

"I have a heart inclined to quick leaps and quicker retreats, rather like the little Corsican's army these days."

True, Nathan mused. Gabriel did have the reputation with women of striking hot and fast, then trotting off before the sheets were cool. For his friends, however, his affection and generosity were boundless. "You really don't try to make me feel guilty, do you?" he muttered wryly.

"On the contrary. I intend for you to feel vastly sorry for me, abandoned in this dismal place without so much as a cross-eyed spinster longing for my return." Gabriel's easy grin flashed in the faint light. "Oh, Nathan, stop lashing yourself for imagined sins. Cecily made her decision; Gerard made his. You are naught but a sorry pawn in their clever strategies."

"Well, thank you very much for that kind observation. Would you like to kick me now?"

"I think not," Gabriel replied, chuckling. "The last time I tried, we were twelve, and despite the fact that you had yet to grow into the great, hulking beast you are, you had my face in the mud in seconds."

"So I did." Nathan was smiling, too, as he recalled the countless childhood scuffles in which only the best of friends could have indulged. "You know, it really isn't too late for me to ignore Gerard's summons. There's no reason Brooke shouldn't go, or St. Wulfstan."

"Brooke, I believe, is busy chasing Napoleon's rats in Salamanca, and, as usual, no one seems to know where Wulf is."

"Dennison, then."

Gabriel snorted. "Dennison is a toad. Besides, one of the Ten bucking protocol is enough to send poor Gerard into an apoplectic fit."

Poor Gerard had never, to Nathan's knowledge, suffered a fit of anything. He had earned his position as the head of one of England's most elite intelligence corps by being as cool as ice in a crisis and damned smart at all times. He was soft-hearted, however, when it came to his "Ten" and would no doubt forgive them this lapse in heeding his orders.

Nathan was late in obeying the summons to return because he'd had one more French rat to catch. Now that the job was completed he had no other excuse to delay returning.

As for Gabriel, he was nowhere near where he was supposed to be. He should have been in Ponte de Mucella, some two hundred miles away, with Wellington. Instead, he was risking, at the very least, a stinging dressing down by the general in order to wave good-bye to Nathan from

the Lisbon dock. The damned hardheaded fool should
have left him behind days ago, Nathan thought, and not
spared a backward glance. But Gabriel had remained in
Lisbon because no matter how hard Nathan had tried, he
had not been able to fool his oldest friend into believing
he wanted him to go.

There was no telling when Gabriel would be called
home. Nathan could only hope it wouldn't be too long.
They had torn up the playing fields of Eton together, cut
a youthful swathe through London together, and had
walked through Matthew Gerard's door side by side.
Nathan knew his wedding to the lovely, blue-eyed Cecily
would not be the same if Gabriel was not there to stand
up for him.

"We'll find you a cross-eyed spinster," he offered
solemnly, "just to be sure you don't lose your heart to
some sloe-eyed señorita and decide to stay."

"You're confusing us again, old boy," Gabriel scolded.
"I'm the one who believes in strategic strike and retreat.
You accept the legshackles."

"Charming analogy to toss at a man who is eagerly
anticipating his wedding."

"Oh, I daresay you'll be happy enough clanking along.
It's all part of that romantic nature, you know. Now I
believe I just spied a rather luscious barmaid through the
window. We have plenty of time before we have to get
you to the docks."

Nathan gazed down toward where the ship waited and
caught another whiff of flowers. "Roses," he muttered.

"Better than the gun smoke I will no doubt be inhaling
in Wellington's compound," Rievaulx said cheerfully.
He peered into the tavern again. "Now stop sniffing and
move. I am beginning to envision a glorious future for
myself."

Nathan, for his part, envisioned himself being quite
drunkenly seasick when his ship set sail in the morning.

CHAPTER 1

Gie him strong drink until he wink,
That's sinking in despair;
An' liquor guid to fire his bluid,
That's prest wi' grief an' care:
There let him bowse, and deep carouse,
Wi' bumpers flowing o'er,
Till he forgets his loves or debts,
An' minds his griefs no more.
                              —Robert Burns

Hertfordshire, 1811

Armed with nothing more than a glare, Isobel Mac-Leod shoved open the inn's massive door and prepared to battle dragons. She was chilled to the bone, exhausted, and still rattling from an hour's ride on the swaybacked, mean-tempered beast that masqueraded as a horse. It was proving to be an utterly miserable night.

The innkeeper's wife was bustling down the hallway, a tray of pasties balanced in one hand, a hefty, knobbed walking stick in the other. On seeing Isobel, her broad, homely face creased into a smile.

"Told 'em you'd be along, dear," she said, giving a raspy laugh, "but they just set my heart a-thumping with those smiles and settled right in."

Isobel untied her cloak but did not remove it; she did not plan on staying long. "I don't suppose it would do much good to ask you to turn them away," she said wryly, and earned another laugh.

"Not a bit, I'm afraid. Those boys could sweet-talk Saint Peter himself into opening the Pearly Gates."

Aye, the dragons were of the incomparably charming variety, Isobel thought, but she could not take that into

5

account when facing them. She eyed the older woman's cane. "Are you thinking to hasten them on their way with that stick, then?"

"Oh, just being prepared, dear. The squire's sons have dug in for the night, it seems, and there's no telling what might erupt with all that hot young blood about. Now, will you have a cup of tea? The wind's rattled every window in the place tonight."

"I haven't the time for tea, Mrs. Harris, but thank you." Isobel was already stalking ahead of the woman toward the taproom. Geordie and Rob had no call to be spending money they did not have on ale, even less so to do it when the Pattons were around. As young and thick-headed as her brothers, Squire Patton's sons never missed a chance to let fly a few choice comments about Scots penny-pinching.

Despite the fact that they were the least frugal creatures imaginable, Isobel knew that her brothers could not possibly let such a heinous slight pass. They were the most proud of their Scottish blood when it was slandered, and they were required to defend it.

Vowing that their soft-hearted sister Maggie would not be bandaging any split knuckles that night, Isobel quickened her stride.

"Oh, not to worry, dear," Mrs. Harris called after her. "Your brothers have bought three rounds since they arrived."

Isobel skidded to a halt. "With what? Sweet words?"

"A sovereign young Rob had. Shiny as my husband's pate, too."

It was all Isobel needed to hear. Resisting the urge to commandeer the walking stick and set it smartly over two auburn heads, she stormed into the pub. However her brothers had come into a sovereign, they had no right to be squandering it on liquor. Not with meals to be put on the table and their father's wretched hunter eating sack after sack of fine oats that would be far better served as breakfast porridge.

She heard Rob's booming laugh well before spying a tuft of artfully contrived curls just visible above the edge of a far table. Geordie was nowhere to be seen, but Rob was, for some reason, sitting on the floor. He glanced up as she approached, his handsome face made all the more so by the broad grin and ale-bright eyes. He made a token effort to get to his feet but only got halfway up before sliding cheerfully back onto his rump.

"Why, 'tis my favorite sister! And looking fine as a May morn. Have you come to join us, Izzy? A glass of something would do you good. Here, Harris! A pint for my sister—" He yelped as she smacked his waving hand. "Why'd you do that?"

"For shame, Robbie MacLeod. 'Tis your sister I am, not your crony. Offering to buy me ale!"

Eyes narrowed, she scanned the room and found her other brother. Geordie, looking nearly identical to Robbie with mussed hair and rumpled, padded coat, was gazing dreamily into the fire, his chin propped on the hearth. One of the Patton boys was sprawled facedown over another table, his jaw resting on a bent playing card.

"All right, lad. How much did you lose?" Isobel prodded the closer brother with the toe of her boot. "How much, Rob?"

The aroma of liquor was so strong, she found herself holding her breath. Clearly her brothers had spent most of the evening drinking themselves right out of their chairs. She fervently hoped that meant they could not have managed too many hands of cards.

Instead of answering, Rob began humming a cheerful if tuneless melody. No angel could look so innocent, Isobel thought, as he peered up at her through a shock of auburn hair, his green eyes as guileless as could be. She was hard put not to take a swing at the clefted chin.

Her brothers were pure MacLeod in looks, temperament, and sheer irresponsibility. Isobel alone of the five siblings had inherited heir mother's flaming red hair— and the temper that came with it. It had been Muire Gordon MacLeod, with that temper, and unflagging humor, who had kept the three MacLeod men in line. But she had died six years earlier of the fever, and her eldest daughter had been fighting ever since to keep a roof over their heads.

"Well?" Temper roused and humor shredded, Isobel prodded again.

"*Och*, Izzy. 'Twasn't so bad. I lost but ten pounds, and Geordie won two. So we're out but eight. We'll have it back in no time at all."

Isobel gaped at him. "Eight pounds, Rob! We haven't two to rub together most times, and you know that!"

"Oh, leave off, love. I studied my mathematics. The odds—"

"Mathematics, is it? Odds? You must have paid less attention to your lessons than I thought if you think you can wager with air. You're a grown man, Rob. Act like one!"

Rather than shaming him into any semblance of humility, she only set Rob to grinning anew. "I'm but one-and-twenty, Izzy. I've four years yet to grow as pinched and serious as you." Finding that excessively amusing, he heaved a mutton bone at his brother. "Now you, Geordie lad, will be three-and-twenty soon. Best drink and be merry while ye may!"

Geordie mumbled something incoherent and waved his empty tankard in their direction.

Crouching down, Isobel pushed her face near to Rob's and, trying not to inhale, demanded, "Where did you get the sovereign?"

"Hmm?" He was busy comparing another stripped bone to the bleached buttons of his waistcoat.

"The money, Rob! Where did it come from?"

Apparently the buttons won, for he tossed the bone away and met her gaze as squarely as he could manage in his condition. "From Father's pocket, of course. Would've taken more, but he rolled over. Bloody flush he was, too."

Flush? Jamie MacLeod? The man never had more than a shilling to his name—Isobel and Maggie saw to that. What little he was paid as secretary to the marquess went straight to Maggie who then hid it in the bottom of her herb basket.

Isobel's jaw tightened. If he was hoarding coins, there would be hell to pay. She did her best to allow for small luxuries in the family budget. The MacLeod men, after all, fancied themselves gentlemen, and she did what she could to humor them. Unfortunately, it seemed their foremost gentlemanly trait was a basic inability to live within their means. Just that morning, Isobel had found a bill from the village tailor. Apparently the boys had taken a fancy to silk brocade waistcoats—as if they had any place to wear them.

"Enough," Isobel got a firm grip on Rob's curls. He yelped as she pulled, but he came unsteadily to his feet. "Home for you, lad."

Perhaps he would have protested, but the second Patton chose that moment to stumble through the back entryway. Isobel regarded him with distaste. Never an attractive specimen, the younger of the squire's sons now resembled nothing so much as a great, unripe fig. His face was the same color as his tight green coat.

"You've taken my money, MacLeod!" he bellowed, heading for the prostrate Geordie. "Two pounds, and I'll have it back!"

He did not make it to the hearth, however, for he

stumbled on a chair leg and went sprawling across the wooden floor. His brother, roused somewhat by the resulting tremor, raised bleary eyes and echoed, "Two pounds!" Then his forehead hit the table again.

The party was over.

With a bit of help from Harris, Isobel got her brothers outside. She was forced to wait while Geordie stuck his head into a bush and retched, but at last she managed to help both boys onto her horse, while she rode the hunter that had carried them to the inn. Chances were, should either brother take a tumble, his drunkenness would keep him pliant enough to prevent any serious damage. But it still seemed prudent to have them on the slower, wide-backed horse.

The weather had not improved, and her cloak was little protection against the dampness. Isobel knew with the certainty of experience that her brothers would make it home eventually. So, waiting only long enough to see that they were reasonably steady in the saddle, she kicked her mount into a canter. The lads might well take it into their heads to turn back for another go at the Patton pockets, but she knew that the horse would have none of that. He had seen the path home, and nothing short of lightning in his face would deter him.

Lights were bright in the cottage windows when she arrived. So Tessa had woken Maggie after all. Trying not to think of the oil her sister was wasting, Isobel settled the hunter in the stable, then headed toward the warmth of the cottage. She would be outside again soon enough to see to her brothers. For the moment, though, she was looking forward to the hot tea Maggie would have waiting and a seat by the kitchen fire.

Margaret, like the boys, was almost painfully beautiful, with her MacLeod auburn hair and sea green eyes. " 'Tis Rob and Geordie again, isn't it?" she asked as Isobel entered the cottage. "Tessa woke me."

She was moving through the kitchen as she spoke, collecting mugs and testing the water, efficient even half asleep. Isobel sank gratefully into a chair.

"Aye, she came flying out the door after me, bare feet and all. I told her not to wake you."

"Mmm." Maggie measured leaves into the teapot. "She said you were off on another moonlight ride and wouldn't let her come."

As if on cue, the youngest MacLeod popped into the room, holding unruly auburn curls away from her face with one hand and gripping an unlit candle like a dagger in the other. The girl was barefoot, as she frequently was, and wide awake as always.

The elder two looked at the young girl's feet, sighed, and, in unison, muttered, "Slippers!"

Tessa wiggled her bare toes and shrugged. Then, seeing Isobel's cloak, she asked, " 'Tis the princelings, isn't it? They've gone and done it again."

"Go back to bed," Isobel said sternly. " 'Tis well past time for you to be asleep, and I don't want you becoming ill."

"I am never ill."

True enough, Isobel conceded. Tessa had the constitution of a wild goat. "Only because you have older sisters to see to it that you get enough rest. Now off with you."

Tessa did not budge. "Have you found them, then? I expect they were at the inn."

"How do you know?" Isobel sighed. "Nay. Don't tell me. Why can you not stay in bed like a proper twelve-year-old girl?"

"I am nearly thirteen. And I cannot sleep."

This time, Isobel smiled. "Of course. The sleep of the innocent would elude you." She raised a hand when Tessa made a move toward the table. "Ah! Not another step, lass. You will take yourself back to your chamber right now."

"But I cannot sleep."

"Unfortunate, that. Count sheep."

"Oh, do be serious, Izzy! I'll only be roused again when the wee highnesses come blundering in."

Trying to keep the girl either ignorant or quiet was as futile as trying to keep the male MacLeods from the bottle. Isobel loved all with a bone-deep fierceness, but she was not quite noble enough to refrain from wishing them to perdition on occasion. While Maggie helped with her tangled bootlaces, Isobel aimed what she hoped was a sufficiently stern glare in Tessa's direction.

"Go back to bed, *ribhinn*. And when you awake in the morning, you will tell yourself 'twas all a dream."

Tessa rolled her eyes. "Oh, Izzy. Really!"

"A dream," Isobel repeated firmly, rising to her feet. She propelled the girl into the hall. Tessa, muttering all the way, vanished in the direction of the stairs.

Margaret, fully awake now, peered out the window. "Did you find them at the inn?"

"Aye, drunk as bishops on alms day. They'll be along soon enough." Isobel gazed again toward the kettle, willing it to boil. "Rob had a sovereign, Maggie Líl. Do you know where Papa is?"

Margaret, being Margaret, merely gave a serene smile and nodded. "Aye. He's in the cellar in fair form, I'd say. And he's supposed to be attending the marquess tomorrow, too."

As if on cue, a rumbling snore drifted through the cellar door.

Isobel, being Isobel, would have liked to howl. Instead, she merely gave the steaming kettle another wistful look and sighed.

*   *   *

The greatest problem with receiving news of an acquaintance's death, Nathan decided, was that one must engage in the pretense of giving a damn.

"Unfortunate," he managed at last, "though not surprising. The only indication we were ever given that the man had a heart was the red-faced fits it set him to. I find it a wonder he didn't kick off far sooner."

Nathan stood facing his study window, brandy snifter in hand. There was a distressed rustling of paper from the desk behind him. Judging by the audible scratching, he could only assume Matthew Gerard, ranking officer of the War Department and his former superior, was jotting down frantic notes—with a nearly dry pen. Nathan allowed himself a wry smile. Brilliant as the man was, Gerard tended to forget such practical things as employing the inkwell regularly.

"I said the *surgeon* cited a fit of the heart," Gerard muttered, and scratched harder. "I do not believe it."

"No? Well, perhaps he did not have one after all."

"Really, Oriel, this is no time for levity."

In truth, Nathan could not agree. There were so few times for levity, and Dennison's death seemed as good an occasion as any. But he had no desire to further agitate his companion. Gerard was flustered enough as it was.

"If not his heart, then what?"

"Poison."

Nathan nearly choked on the brandy. "You are not serious."

"Didn't see the body myself, but it seems the most likely scenario."

Again, Nathan disagreed. It seemed the most dramatic scenario. "No one saw or heard anything?"

"No one we've found as yet. Dennison died sometime between leaving White's around two in the morning and five, when the steward found him in the alley off

Saint James. I have to take this very seriously, Oriel, very seriously."

Nathan had been uneasy from the moment Gerard had arrived unannounced and at such a late hour. Now he knew precisely what was coming next. "I want no part of it, Matthew."

"I know I had promised to let you go, but damn it, man, this one has me rattled!"

Nathan stared out into the darkness, seeing nothing but deep shadows. He did not want to be involved, did not want to feel even the smallest share of Gerard's disquiet. True, the man had just lost one of his agents, but it was far from the first time, and Dennison did not merit such a response. Better men had gone before him, their deaths unavenged.

"Find someone else," Nathan said quietly.

"Who?"

"Brooke . . . St. Wulfstan. Anyone."

"Brooke is in Spain," Gerard replied. "And, as usual, no one knows exactly where St. Wulfstan is." Nathan found no amusement in the familiar lament. "There is no one else available."

"Use someone who was not among the Ten, then."

"I cannot do that." There was the sound of a glass being refilled, and Nathan found himself hoping the man would drink himself senseless. Then he could be bundled into a carriage and sent elsewhere, preferably all the way back to London. "This could involve the . . . occurrence in Lisbon."

It took all of Nathan's willpower to keep his head from snapping back around. "Explain."

"In the days before his death, Dennison was in possession of some documents." At his host's curse, Gerard hastened to assure him, "Nothing crucial, and he delivered them."

Nathan tamped down his rising ire. "Dennison was a toad, and his performance on the Continent disgraceful. What was he doing carrying anything but snuff?"

"I know you never liked the man—"

"I detested him. But that had nothing to do with my opinions of his work. He was a pompous, preening fool. Worse, he was incompetent."

"Perhaps after the fort at Almeida fell . . ." Gerard cleared his throat. "He was useful, though, at the beginning of the campaign."

"Very well," Nathan said. "I will concede that he had his small merits—once upon some fairy-tale time. But I can't even begin to imagine how his demise in Saint James alley could possibly be connected to—how did you phrase it?— the occurrence in Lisbon. It was an ambush, Matthew; you may say the word. Rievaulx and I walked out of the tavern and straight into an ambush."

"Well, Dennison was at White's the night he died, mumbling something about Portugal. And about being pursued."

"By?"

"We don't know. But apparently he was damned cocky about it. Kept repeating that the matter was more than an ordinary man could handle, but he would win out in the end."

Nathan's patience was wearing thin. "Good God, man, he could have been speaking of a bill collector."

"Bill collectors don't dispatch their debtors," Gerard insisted.

"You've obviously never refused to honor a debt!" Nathan snapped back.

"Listen to me, Oriel. Dennison was still communicating with Brooke. And for him to die so, even after all these months . . . . Think of Harlow, Witherspoon, Rievaulx, all dead. It is too much to be a coincidence."

Nathan carefully set his glass aside before he could snap the fragile stem. "Do not list Rievaulx's name with theirs."

"Oriel . . ."

"Not in my home, Matthew." Nathan kept his face averted. His leg was aching fiercely, but he did not want to return to his seat. "Harlow and Witherspoon died doing what we were all sent to the Continent to do: intercepting French communiqués. Rievaulx—" His voice broke. "Rievaulx died because he followed me to Lisbon. He shouldn't have been there."

Behind him, Gerard sighed. "No, but he was with you willingly."

"And he lost his life for it." Nathan leaned his forehead against the cool glass. "Let me be, Matthew. For pity's sake, just let me be. I can be of no use to you. You know as well as anyone that I am not the man I once was."

"You are the *only* man who can be of any use, Oriel. Your wound . . . yes, I know. But I am not asking you to run anywhere. I am asking you to go to London to use your ears and eyes and brain, not your legs."

Nathan gave a harsh chuckle. "A comfort, that. Use sense, man. We are a country at war. Every unexplained shadow makes us wary. So Dennison had a tricky heart. That's all there is to it."

"I would be happy to think so. But I know better. Please, Oriel. It would simply be a matter of coming to London, going about your life as you always have there. I cannot move among the ton as you can."

"Rubbish."

"You are a marquess."

"That is merely a title."

"A title of great social importance. In London—"

"I am content here!"

Gerard ignored Nathan's snapped retort. "As I said before," he continued, "I have been in this line of work too long to believe in coincidence. There is *something* there, some connection to Almeida and the Busaco campaign. We simply need to find it."

"How can my returning to London possibly help? Rievaulx died in Lisbon, the others in France."

"Dennison—"

"Dennison is not connected!"

"I believe you know better. Think, man. There were ten of you in the company. You *were* the Ten. Now there are six, and it would have been five had you not survived the attack in Lisbon. Someone is coming after us, Oriel, one by one, and whoever it is had intimate knowledge of Dennison, of the circle in which he moved. Damn it, the man could have been at White's with Dennison and slipped something into his drink with no one the wiser."

"Supposition. No more."

"Oriel . . . Nathan." Gerard left his seat to stand beside him. "When you returned from the Continent and shut yourself up here, I did not press you. It has been more than five months, and I need you now. You will find whatever there is to find. You always do."

The ache in Nathan's chest far surpassed that in his thigh. "Ah, Matthew. Your confidence is misplaced. We're chasing shadows here."

"You have never let me down."

How very wrong he was, Nathan thought. He had failed everyone. "You are forgetting the most crucial issue. Beyond the fact that this is all conjecture, of course."

"And that is?"

Nathan's mouth twisted. "I am not whole, Matthew."

"I told you, I know—"

"You know *nothing!*" Nathan gripped the windowsill

and fought for control. He took a steadying breath, then said, "You will stay the night, of course."

"I will. Thank you. But I must return to Town early in the morning."

"Well, you will have to leave without satisfaction then. I have a rather annoying domestic matter to attend to in the morning."

"We have very little time, Oriel. We cannot afford to waste any of it."

"There is never enough time, Matthew, and most is wasted." Nathan gave a humorless chuckle. "But now you have me indulging in maudlin and idiotic philosophy. Leave me to think on it. You return to London in the morning. I will contact you there."

Long after the other man had retired, Nathan remained in the library, gazing sightlessly into the guttering fire. Sleep was as evasive as it was unappealing. There was no English linen, no matter how fine, immune to the sweat of nightmares.

"Ah, Gabriel." He sighed, finding the one-sided conversations that had become so common since Rievaulx's death no more crazed than any of the few he carried on with the living. "Remind me again just what sort of future you envisioned for us."

Nathan made no move to collect the notes Gerard had left for him. What good would it do to hold the papers in his hand? He had become singularly incapable of managing his own affairs, although he was reasonably adept at living with that truth.

At moments such as this, Rievaulx's ghost, so real sometimes that he could see the man's flashing grin, was welcome. "Let's go back, shall we, Gabriel? Don't be silly—of course we can. You shall have Cecily, I the Lisbon barmaid, and together we will drown Dennison in the Ebro."

Cursing, he picked up his glass and hurled it against

the hearth, where it shattered, sending the scent of brandy through the room. It really was a pity, he thought wearily, that he did not have the energy to crawl through the shards.

CHAPTER 2

Despite living in a fairly small house, Jamie Macleod was very good at being lost in it. In fact, Isobel decided as she reached the cellar door, he was rather good at being lost in general.

She found one of his tasseled slippers outside the door and picked it up. She opened the door and saw the second slipper. It was still attached to James MacLeod's foot, if only by an inch. He was sprawled contentedly on the landing, snoring with gusto, an empty claret bottle nestled against his cheek and a nearly empty one clutched in his hand. Isobel was amused, but not at all surprised, to see that her father was holding it securely against any possibility of spilling what drops remained. Even unconscious, he would see to that.

"Oh, Papa," she said, sighing as she sank down beside him, "could you not have made it even to the kitchen?"

Jamie MacLeod did not respond. Instead, he smacked his lips together and proceeded to snore in a different key. Isobel reached out and prodded his shoulder. She was not especially gentle, but she knew a soft touch would be of as much use as trying to move a mountain with a feather. She prodded again, to no avail.

"Aye, of course. 'Twas a two-bottle night, after all."
On two-bottle nights, more than a bit of poking was
required.

She got a grip on the bottle he held and tugged. No
response. Then she tugged harder. Still, James did not
relinquish his hold, but he did open one eye. "Eh? Whass
tha'?"

There was a bit of a struggle, but when it was over,
Isobel had the bottle, and her father had lost the other
slipper. "Come along now, time for bed," she coaxed. It
was clear there would be no coherent conversation with
him till morning.

"Isobel?" He had both eyes open now, the famous
MacLeod green made all the more vivid by the red surrounding it. "Did ye want me for somethin'?"

She sighed. Then, unable to help herself, she patted his
gray-whiskered cheek. "Not at all, Papa. I simply thought
you might be more comfortable sleeping in your bed
rather than on the stairs."

"Ye're a good lass, Izzy," he mumbled. "Ye're all
good lasses. I dinna deserve you, miserable wretch that
I am." A single tear slipped down the side of his red-
dened nose.

Isobel glanced down the stairs, scanning the shadows
for another empty bottle. She knew that her father's
Highland brogue thickened with the first bottle, but he
only lapsed into damp lamentations of his unworthiness
on three-bottle nights. Not that it mattered, she decided.
He had had enough wine to effectively prevent him from
being of any use when it came to answering questions.

"You really must try to move, darling," she said. " 'Tis
cold here."

"Och, aye, I'll see tae it . . ." He made a halfhearted
attempt to rise, then sank down again. "Just like the
waves," he announced thoughtfully. "Oop an' doon, oop
an' doon."

Isobel knew she could get him into his bed quickly enough. She was no weakling and had had a good deal of practice. But she had just heard the first shout from the yard and knew she had best rescue her brothers before they drowned themselves in the stable trough.

"I'll send Margaret," she promised, then dropped a kiss onto the top of her father's wild gray head.

"You're a good lass," he said again.

"Papa . . ."

"Nay, nay. I'll get meself to bed." He pushed himself up again. "Just like the waves . . ." As Isobel hurried away, she heard his fuzzy baritone beginning, "O row ye boat, ye mariners . . ."

She left him to getting Annie o' Loch Royale over the sea to Lord Gregory and himself up the stairs.

Maggie was by the rear door, pulling a cloak over her night rail, when Isobel reached her. "They've arrived."

"So I heard." Isobel commandeered the cloak. "I won't have you catching a chill because of them. You see to the drunken fool inside."

As if on cue, Jamie's voice drifted from the stair landing. "Izzy? That ye?"

"Aye, Papa."

"Izzy, lass, 'tis a lowly toad I am, an undeserving wretch—"

"Not *now*, Papa." Isobel sighed and reached for the door. "I'll be back soon enough."

Uncustomary anger sparked in Maggie's eyes. "One of these days, you'll not be there, and they'll find themselves left to face the devil."

"Aye, well, the devil would have to face them, too. Fair trade, I would say. Oh, don't fret, darling. All will be well."

It occurred to Isobel as she entered the yard that those last words had become something of a chant since their mother's death. The problem, of course, was that with each new challenge, it became harder and harder to believe them.

After a good dozen such moonlight rides, as Tessa called them, Isobel knew the routine well. This time, however, there had been neither moon nor light. As the dense night fog turned to an icy drizzle, she set her jaw and vowed this would be the last time she attempted to rescue her brothers. The next time those thoughtless, witless young men took it into their heads to court disaster, she would let them go right ahead and do it.

Even as she had this thought, she knew she didn't mean it. The two might have the consideration of gnats, but they were her brothers. No matter what, Isobel was determined to see them healthy and safe.

After she ascertained that her brothers had not gone headfirst into the trough, she went in search of them. She found Geordie easily enough as he was retching again behind the stable. She left him to it and went in search of Rob. It took a bit more effort to locate him as he, for some reason, had climbed into the loft. He was sprawled in the hay, snoring contentedly, and did not so much as twitch when Isobel tossed a horse blanket over him.

She would have another talk with Mr. Harris as soon as she could. Not that it was likely to do any good. She could threaten, cajole, and beg him not to serve the boys, but the simple truth was that they had, upon their arrival five months earlier, quite charmed the village. No one would refuse them anything.

Of course, matters had become a bit strained when the MacLeod men had taken to leaving bills unpaid. But Margaret's sweet nature and talent with healing herbs had soothed as many ruffled feathers as ailing stomachs, and it was utterly impossible to stay angry with either the young lads or the aged one. With their angels' faces and devils' tongues, they could soften even the hardest heart.

Isobel returned to the house, satisfied that the latest

situation was under control. What she needed was another cup or two of scalding hot tea and her sister's gentle presence.

Maggie was not alone. Their father was huddled at the kitchen table, looking rather like some pale, wizened woodland creature. His wild hair seemed but an extension of the graying herbs hanging above him, his skin a distressingly similar shade.

Annoyance forgotten, Isobel hurried to his side. "Papa?"

Margaret calmly took Isobel's cloak, then carried a steaming cup to the table. However, her lovely face was tight with strain. "Oh, he's well enough, Isobel, in body anyway. 'Tis a different sort of ailing. I've no faith in his wits at the moment."

"Maggie?" Startled by the sharp tone, Isobel's gaze moved from her father to her sister. "What is it?"

"You'd best hear it from him."

"But—"

"Ask him!" Maggie snapped. Then she folded into her own seat. " 'Tis bad, Izzy."

Frightened now, Isobel murmured, "Papa?"

"I'm a wretch of a man, Izzy. A snake, a lowly worm." Slowly he opened his hand, which had been clenched on the table. Several gold coins slid between his fingers to clink against the polished wood.

Her voice shaky now, Maggie said, "There's more, too. I found a pouch beneath him when I helped him from the stairs. It bears the crest of the Hall."

Isobel felt as if her heart had landed somewhere in the vicinity of her feet. "I don't suppose there's any chance his lordship was feeling generous."

Drunk or no, Jamie MacLeod knew better than to play dense with his eldest daughter. He dropped his head into his hands and, saying nothing, answered her with perfect clarity.

* * *

Isobel gritted her teeth as she stood and stretched cramped muscles. The marquess, assuming the light in the window had indeed been his, deserved every hushed word the villagers spoke of him. The man *was* inhuman if he kept such hours every night.

She had never met Lord Oriel, nor had she even gotten much of a look at him. As far as she knew, he had not left the estate since taking her father into his employ five months earlier, but neither had he appeared much inside its bounds. Her only view thus far had been of him careening wildly across the fields behind the cottage on an enormous gray stallion, the animal dodging boulders and leaping walls as if ridden by the devil himself.

Now, to the minimal knowledge that the marquess had night black hair, no apparent regard for the safety of his limbs, and appallingly poor luck in his choice of a secretary, Isobel could add that he did not sleep.

As far as she was concerned, the man could drink blood and howl at the moon. What mattered was that he had finally taken himself out of the library and she could take herself in. All she wanted was to return the marquess's money, then creep home and into bed.

First things first, however, and the library window beckoned. Oriel Hall was a monstrous place. It was not unattractive, really, with its rosy stone and legion of mullioned windows, but it was behemoth nonetheless. Isobel had managed to get the information out of her father that he had taken the money from the marquess's desk in the library, and he had given her reasonably clear directions on where to find the library among the countless windows. Now, after a miserable hour of lurking low among the spiny bushes that grew under the library window, she was frozen, aching, and weary.

Isobel slowly and quietly raised the sash, not wanting to alert any servant who might have the unfortunate duty of keeping hours with the master. As she pulled herself up over the sash the coins in the pouch clinked loudly, and she bit back a reflexive curse.

It was a moonless night, and the room was pitch-black. Jamie had said the desk was set in front of the window, and set in front of the window it was. At first, however, as Isobel slid her hands over the vast surface, she thought she had somehow ended up in the dining room—and began to curse her father for his miserable directions. But no, her fingers soon encountered a blotter and an inkwell. Like the Hall itself, the desk was crafted on massive lines.

Third drawer, left. Or had her father said right? Not that it mattered. If the lofty Lord Oriel had been so careless as to leave fifty pounds sitting in an unlocked drawer, he would most likely not notice should the money be in a different drawer.

With any luck, he would also be too careless to note that the fifty pounds had somehow become thirty-six.

Isobel gritted her teeth as the coins inside the pouch clinked again. Of course, the clinking ought to have been fourteen pounds louder, but that was hardly a comfort. Inwardly cursing her father, brothers, and even the marquess, just out of spite, she slid a drawer out—then shrieked as a massive hand closed around her wrist.

The next thing she knew, her cheek was flat against the desk and her right arm pinned painfully behind her back. She would have screamed again had there not been a crushing weight between her shoulders. The hood of her cloak slid forward, covering her face. When a hand swept roughly over her bottom and hip, she could do no more than gasp.

"Bloody hell!" The voice, coming from right above her ear, was deep enough to resonate and harsh enough to send her already thundering heart right into her throat. Then, to her astonishment, there came a sound that was somewhere between a growl and a weary sigh. "One of the Misses MacLeod, I presume."

She said nothing, more from shock than stubbornness. Instantly, the vise around her arm tightened, and she cried out. "Yes," she managed at last. "Yes. I came to—"

The hood was jerked away from her face. "Speak up! You are one of MacLeod's daughters, are you not?"

She thought she had just said so, but decided not to mention the fact. "I am." She drew a shaky breath, then another. "Isobel."

"Isobel. Ah, yes. The plain one."

This was no time to wonder how he knew, or to be offended. Nor was there any need to ask who he was. The clipped, arrogant, thoroughly *Sasunnach* voice told her in no uncertain terms that her arms and ribs were being crushed by none other than the marquess himself.

"I—I am here—"

"I did not ask why you are here, Miss MacLeod." Isobel heard a now-familiar clinking as he hefted the pouch. "I simply requested an introduction."

Which was, Isobel decided, just as well. Despite the hour spent waiting in the gardens, she had not bothered to devise a plausible excuse for being there. Quite simply, she had not expected to be caught.

Her shoulders burned, and she found herself wondering just how terrible jail would be. And whether she would be there alone, or with her entire family chained beside her. The boys, she was certain, would not like it much; it was hardly the best showplace for brocade waistcoats.

She very nearly giggled. Lying facedown across a field of a desk, with what had to be the better part of a gentleman's weight on her, and she was thinking of waistcoats. Madness. She wanted to laugh, then wail. Instead, she did what any intelligent woman would have done in her position: She let loose with a string of Gaelic curses, passed down through countless generations of Island MacLeods, and fervent enough to strip the fine lacquer from the desk.

Suddenly the marquess's weight lifted from her back. An instant later, he pulled her off the desk, around it, and into the dark depths of the room.

"Damn it, woman, be silent!"

Tongue stilled in the midst of her tirade, Isobel stumbled behind him. She heard a grunt as some part of his anatomy collided with some item of furniture, but he did not release her. Her own toes came up hard against a chair leg, followed immediately by her knee. She bit her tongue hard, harder still when he shoved her unceremoniously onto what turned out to be a divan.

Instantly she was on her feet, but before she could run, he sat down heavily beside her, grabbed a handful of her cloak, and jerked her right back. "If I ask you to be still, Miss MacLeod," he growled, "you will understand it is not a request."

Understanding was one matter; obeying was another, and Isobel edged defiantly away. Again, he pulled her back, and she found herself all but sitting in the lap of the man her father had robbed—a man who, if village gossip was to be believed, was not quite of the human race.

"I suppose I could try to convince you that I do not ravish virgins or sacrifice small animals, but somehow I don't feel I owe you the courtesy, Miss MacLeod. Besides, I doubt you would believe me."

Isobel started. Either the man read minds, or he took some interest in local gossip. Somehow, the latter seemed far less likely.

She herself had never formed an opinion about the marquess, but some of the villagers were convinced that he was perfectly capable of performing numerous atrocities. Several of the more foolish townsfolk had even gone so far as to ask Margaret for protective sachets. Maggie's gentle suggestion that perhaps such extremes were un-

warranted had gotten no response whatsoever. Tessa's
eager recommendation, involving hemlock, had been
much more popular.

No one seemed to know the marquess at all, but everyone seemed happy to pass harsh judgment on his character. Except Jamie, whose only useful description had
consisted of three words: *Sasunnach* and *bloody rich*.

As if reading her thoughts again, Oriel muttered,
"Your father, Miss MacLeod, is not a smart man."

"No," she replied, "he is not." She felt herself blushing
with the looseness of her tongue. "But he means well. I-I
can only apologize and hope—"

"That you will not see the blackguard dangling from
the nearest tree?"

Isobel shuddered. "Please, my lord. 'Twas but a foolish
impulse."

"That is certainly one way of looking at it. I might be
inclined to choose another. Base thievery, perhaps."

Behind the polished, nearly polite tone of his voice
was another tone, this one harsh and damning. It cut
through whatever bravado Isobel had left. "I did not
mean to insult you by implying the matter was not
serious, my lord. I only intended my words as a plea. I
am begging you—"

"Don't!" The word snapped like a lash, and she shrank
back still more. "You came boldly enough into my home.
I will not tolerate spineless groveling now."

Aye, she had been groveling and would do so on her
knees if it would make a difference. " 'Tis all I have to
give, my lord. My pleas."

That earned her a derisive snort, followed by something
that in another time and place, might have sounded like a
laugh. Then there was silence.

Her senses all but screaming in the darkness, Isobel
was far too aware of the hulking presence beside her. She
was aware, too, suddenly, of the faint aroma of brandy.

Growing up as she had, she knew she was smelling superior liquor. Countless occasions of helping her well-soaked father into bed had made her a connoisseur of sorts.

She considered making another dash for the door. But she did not know precisely where the door was, and even if she could find it and Lord Oriel was too drunk to catch her, he would know where to locate her later.

Better, she thought, to take her chances with the dark and ominous silence. If she was very quiet, Lord Oriel might just fall asleep where he sat. If she was very lucky, he might awaken to think it had been a dream. And if she was very, very stupid, she might convince herself that either could happen.

His movement was so sudden she nearly shrieked again. The divan creaked as he pushed himself to his feet, an awkward move that caused one of his knees to knock into hers.

"I beg your pardon, Miss MacLeod." Lord Oriel's voice, now coming from well above her, sounded mocking—and cruel. She was not certain which was worse.

"You—where are you . . ."

"Your father has called you an intelligent creature, Miss MacLeod, but your inability to complete a phrase is doing nothing to convince me of the fact."

She opened her mouth, but found no words past a halting *I*.

"It is fortunate that I manage to understand you nonetheless. Where I am going is to the mantel as it has occurred to me that you might stop rattling the furniture with your shaking if I light a candle."

Again he knocked into her, this time as he made his way around her feet. She swallowed her cry and wondered how he had managed to move so silently earlier. If only he had encountered an object or two while she was at the desk . . .

There was a scuffling at the hearth and something clattered against the tiles. A moment later, the marquess gave a guttural curse. Then the candle sparked, blackness turned to shadow, and Isobel's breath caught in her throat.

CHAPTER 3

Were't not for gold and women,
there would be no damnation.
                    —Cyril Tourneur

She promptly decided there was much to be said for
darkness.

Lord Oriel was real enough in the flickering light, but
no less terrifying than Isobel had imagined. He was taller
still than she had expected, with shoulders whose width
competed with the mantel. His hair, the unremitting
black of night, was swept back to reveal a high brow and
cheekbones so prominent that the hollows beneath them
seemed fleshless. There was no softness to his face, the
features bordering on savage.

He turned his head then, and a new tremor rippled
through Isobel as she lifted her gaze to his. His eyes were
the color of time-worn bronze, lion's eyes, cold and
predatory.

Shaken, unaware of her actions, she started to rise,
only to drop back when he snapped, "Sit *down*, Miss
MacLeod!"

By now, her knees would not allow her to do much
else. So she sat, hands clenched tightly in her lap, and
waited. The marquess did not return to the divan but
remained at the mantel, one massive hand wrapped
around the silver candlestick. Long fingers, broad palm, a
faint scar snaking along the thumb. It was, she thought

somewhat vaguely, a hand capable of rendering the sterling to a tarnished lump.

As she sat, silently watching, Isobel saw Oriel rub his other fist once, hard over the outside of his thigh. She heard the hiss of indrawn breath, and her eyes went again to his face. The grooves beside his wide mouth were etched deep. Suddenly she realized that he appeared much less brutal and far more pained.

She blinked in surprise. She ought to have seen it immediately—the loose fit of his expensive coat, as if cut for another form, and the gauntness of his face. Lord Oriel was not a well man.

"If you have completed your scrutiny, perhaps we can turn to the matter at hand."

Isobel felt her discomfort sliding into embarrassment. If Lord Oriel did not like the sensation of being examined, it was no wonder. No doubt he had once possessed a formidable, if unconventional beauty. Whatever plagued him had left its mark. His face was not ugly; it was simply unsettling in its harshness.

"I am sorry, my lord. I did not mean to be rude."

"No, I expect you did not. Nor did you mean to insult me earlier or vex me with begging. It seems you have difficulty reconciling intent with action, Miss MacLeod. Is it a family failing?"

"I-I do not . . ."

"Ah, and again with the stammering. You really must get hold of yourself if we are to get anywhere. Am I frightening you, perchance?"

She had, if anything, difficulty reconciling honest words with wise. "You are, and not without meaning it. 'Tis cruel and needless."

Nay, she thought, baiting the lion was not wise, but her wits were still scattered. The entire scene had spiraled so far from any she could have imagined that she could only wonder if she just ought to suffocate herself in her cloak and spare the marquess the effort.

"Aye," she muttered with a sigh, " 'tis a failing family I have, Lord Oriel. And I'll not expect anything I say on the matter to change your decision, whatever it may be."

"No more pleas?"

She lifted her chin. "Would it help?"

"Unlikely."

"Well, I'll swallow them then."

There was a long pause. Then, "Tell me, Miss MacLeod, are you finding this as unpleasant as I am?"

She could not stop the choked laugh. "There could not be a comparison."

"You really believe I am enjoying myself."

Again eyeing the taut features, Isobel replied, "I've no reason to expect otherwise, my lord. And you've every right to do as you will."

"Generous of you," he drawled.

Isobel moistened her lips, wishing for a return to darkness where she would not have to see that ravaged face and he would not be able to see her confusion. "What—what are you going to do?"

"I have not yet decided. Do you care to make a suggestion?"

Oddly, it seemed a genuine question, and Isobel could not have been more surprised had he asked her to advise him on matters of finance. Knowing she was standing on the shakiest of ground and desperate to choose the right words, she replied slowly, "I believe, my lord, that retribution should be dependent on more than just the crime."

"Yes? And what else ought to be considered, Miss MacLeod?"

"Motive. And circumstance."

The marquess lifted a dark brow. "Motive and circumstance. Is this Scots justice I am learning?"

"God's, I would say."

"Ah, interpretive scripture. What if I am a believer in an eye for an eye?"

Isobel cringed. "Then I have nothing with which to make reparation, my lord. My father is neither a noble thief nor a habitual one. He lost his way, taking the money because he had none."

"And just when I was beginning to believe I had brought a Robin Hood into my employ. 'Lost his way,' was it? Tell me, if you would, how much of my money would have found its way into your household coffers."

"Why—well . . ." *Lie!* Isobel told herself fiercely. "He would have— It would have been . . ."

"You will make yourself ill trying to prevaricate, Miss MacLeod. I have already come to the conclusion that honesty is a great strength of yours—or a great weakness." Oriel rubbed his thigh again, as if to push away a weakness of his own. "Were his circumstances so ill, then? I was under the impression that I was paying him a sufficient salary."

Sufficient perhaps for a man with better habits and fewer children. "You are, my lord."

"As I thought. Thus far, I see no reason for clemency."

"I do not suppose you would. But I do have one more heart-deep belief," Isobel said wearily.

"And it is?"

She took a breath. "I believe everyone deserves a second chance, my lord."

She did not flinch this time as his eyes passed, cold and unseeing, over her face. "Redemption, is it, Miss MacLeod? What a shame. I was beginning to think you were genuinely clever. That is what your father has said, you know."

"He spoke of redemption?" How very like James Mac-Leod to pave his own wretched way.

"No. He spoke of you."

"He— For God's sake, why?"

"I asked." Before Isobel could ponder that, he continued. "You are the bright one with the granite head, your sister the beauty with the impossibly soft heart. Together, you keep the family together."

Stunned that her father was so clear on the matter, and mortified that he would have spoken so to his employer, Isobel said nothing.

"You do not contradict me?" Oriel demanded.

"Nay."

"And you do not envy your sister who got all the beauty?"

Perhaps, had the entire night not been so bizarre, she might have found the question odd, or even resented it. Instead, she merely sighed. "We cannot all be beautiful, my lord. 'Tis like sense: its lack noted more by those with it than without."

"How true. Perhaps you are wise after all. You did try to return the money." He paused. "That is what you were doing, was it not?"

Isobel stiffened. "Aye, I was trying to return the money."

This time, when the marquess's brow went up, it was followed by the corner of his mouth. "You reproach me, Miss MacLeod."

"I do not—"

"And lie again. Curious turn of events, is it not? All of it. Your father steals from me, you creep into my home in the middle of the night with foolish honor, and then your tone reproaches me for catching you at it. How did I become the villain of this piece?"

If there was an answer to that, Isobel certainly did not have it.

"Go home, Isobel MacLeod."

"I-I beg your pardon?"

"Use the door—or window. I don't care which. Go home."

She shook her head, not sure she had heard correctly. "You're letting me go?"

"More than that. I am commanding you. And you will see to it that your father attends me in the morning as planned."

"Attends you?"

"Do not make me question your hearing as well. We have an appointment for nine. Make certain he is here." When Isobel did not move, the marquess ran a hand wearily over his brow. "Ah, yes. You wait for the voice of doom. Perhaps it is cruel of me to choose this method, Miss MacLeod. The indiscretion, after all, was not yours. But I am not feeling particularly kind, and I suggest that you do not allow your father to take flight. It would serve him ill, and your family worse."

Lord Oriel might indeed be cruel, Isobel mused, but he was no fool. If she told her father about this encounter, there was little doubt that he would take it into his head to make a run for Scotland. And less doubt that the results would bode ill indeed for them all.

"He will attend you in the morning, my lord."

"Good. Now go away."

Even as Isobel rose, she couldn't take her eyes off his forehead. Where he had run his hand across his brow was dark streak. "My lord—you are—"

"Cease stammering at me, damn it, and leave!" Oriel turned away from her to face the mantel. "Before I decide that the sins of the father should be visited upon the daughter after all."

It was good advice, certainly, but Isobel did not heed it. Instead, wondering where her last vestige of sense had gone, she made her way toward him, drawing her hand-kerchief from her pocket as she went. "You are bleeding."

He did not respond when she reached his side, nor did

he make any move to take the handkerchief from her hand. So she reached to place it in his.

The blood had seeped from his palm into a faint line around his thumb. "How? . . ." Isobel took a step closer, then stopped as glass crunched under her foot.

"Are you fond of tempting providence, Miss MacLeod?"

She ignored the growl, and the fact that, standing as close as she was to him, he all but filled her vision. "You've cut yourself, my lord."

"I was careless with a glass earlier and encountered it while trying to give you some light. Now, take yourself—"

But she already had his hand in hers. The sight of the barely protruding shard was distressing, not in itself, but in the fact that he had not removed it. She did not want to begin speculating on what sort of man would ignore such a wound.

Shaken anew, she removed the glass and pressed her handkerchief where it had been. Then she fled.

His voice stopped her in the doorway. "You did not answer me."

"I did not—?"

He gave an impatient snort. "Do you believe in tempting providence?"

"Nay," she managed weakly, and tried again to leave.

"I am not sure whether that is another lie." He shrugged. "No matter. Just remember, Miss MacLeod, no actions pass without consequence. Yours of tonight are no exception."

In the dark, Isobel made two wrong turns and spent a full minute tugging at what turned out to be a wall medallion rather than a doorknob before she finally located the massive front portal. At last, as she made her shaky way across the fields, she was able to think on the mar-

quess's final words. She decided they were far from
comforting.

Nathan was facing the gardens through the library
window again, this time in morning's light. He inhaled
deeply, knowing better than to think Isobel's scent had
lingered through the hours. It had filled his senses, a faint
aura of honey and rosemary, from the moment she had
climbed through the window. And it had taunted him
even after she left through the door.

Again he smelled her, Isobel MacLeod, and knew she
had returned.

It had crossed his mind that she might. He was not certain what she hoped to accomplish. Perhaps she would
try to dissuade him from throttling her father, not that he
had any intention of doing something so physical.

Jamie MacLeod was a weak man, and basically a
stupid one. Nathan had been perfectly aware of that when
he offered MacLeod the position. All Nathan had required
was someone who could read, write, and manage basic
sums. He had not wanted either a particularly clever secretary or a dedicated one.

The Scot had seemed a good choice. Overeducated to
the point that he thought in poetic meter, MacLeod was a
literate fool. And he was desperately in need of funds.
Being a gentleman on his native Skye had not put food
into his children's mouths. Neither, apparently, had his
stints in Edinburgh, Dumfries, or Manchester. From what
Nathan had been able to ascertain, MacLeod's charm had
made it simple enough for him to find three positions as a
schoolmaster; his passion for Burns and brandy had
made it impossible for him to keep any of them.

Irresponsibility aside, the man had seemed genuinely
devoted to his five children and willing to do whatever
was necessary to see them set well in life. Yes, Nathan
had expected MacLeod to blunder a bit in the job. And,

in five months, there had been distinct blundering but nothing serious. What Nathan had not expected was larceny.

It was a shame, really. Nathan had enjoyed the man's inept presence—the lilting brogue that deepened with drink, the unsolicited tales of his deceased fiery wife and lively daughters. The sons were not particularly interesting; Nathan detested hearing of yet another generation of young bucks growing into fools as great as the preceding. But the daughters ... Maggie with her angel's face and gentle ways, Tessa the frighteningly clever imp. And Isobel, unmarried at twenty-five, always battling her own romantic heart with her granite head as she tried to keep the family above water.

At first, Nathan had not wanted to hear these things about his secretary's family. Better, he had always believed, to keep such matters at a distance. But MacLeod prattled on whether Nathan listened or not, and before long, he had found himself wishing he could meet these vibrant characters and waiting for the next installment. He followed the tales as Tessa was pulled from trees and was caught listening at keyholes, as Maggie enacted one miracle cure for chilblains after another, and smiled to himself as Isobel took to bartering like a charwoman with the village merchants.

Sadly, as with most of life, it was now time to put practicality ahead of amusement. An inept secretary was one matter, a thieving one quite another.

Nathan recognized the smell of wine and some strong soap undoubtedly meant to remove the aroma of alcohol coming from Jamie MacLeod. Neither he nor his daughter had spoken.

Odd, how one could identify scents with so little effort, Nathan thought. It was not a skill he had ever thought to hone, but it aided him now, as he stood with his back to the room.

"Sit down," he commanded harshly. There was a faint scraping of chair legs. He waited several moments, then added, "You, too, Miss MacLeod."

Her indrawn breath was half surprise, half pique as she obeyed. So she did not want to be seated. He did not blame her. He imagined he made quite an imposing figure, deliberately turned away from them, towering dark against the sunlit window. She would know the advantage he held, not just by who he was, but by standing with the massive desk between them. It was a tactic he had learned as a boy from his father, and one he had used countless times through the succeeding decades.

He had added another touch. The coin pouch sat on the cleared desk, a blatant reminder of just why they were gathered. Idly he wondered if MacLeod's fingers itched with greed at the sight or trembled with apprehension.

"I find myself in a unique position here. To my knowledge, I have never had an employee steal from me before."

He heard Isobel's barely audible sniff and felt his mouth twitching. Yes, she was probably right. It was more than likely that he had been fleeced before, perhaps frequently, and simply remained ignorant. Smart girl. It really was a wonder that she had sprung from the loins of such a fool.

And fool MacLeod was. Instead of being silent as circumstance dictated, the man opened his mouth and promptly inserted his foot. "I haven't the foggiest idea what you mean, my lord. Have you been robbed?"

So it appeared Isobel had not informed him of the events of the night before. Curious, even as it made sense. MacLeod would no doubt have tried something foolish. Nathan wondered how the girl had explained her desire to attend this meeting. One thing he had learned after mere minutes in her company, something her father probably did not even know, was that she choked on dishonest words.

"Do not make matters worse for yourself, MacLeod. The evidence speaks for itself."

Still without looking at the seated pair, Nathan turned and reached for the pouch. His leg, stiff from the hours he had sat awake in a wing chair, nearly buckled as he made the turn. With one hand in his pocket, he had to drop the coins and steady himself against the desk. It was a minor stumble, but he was forced into the awkward and embarrassing task of retrieving the pouch from the floor.

He groped for the pouch, his damaged thigh protesting each motion. By the time he was upright again, he could feel the dull flush in his cheeks and knew some of his control over the situation had been lost.

The MacLeods would know better than to laugh, or even smirk; they were still very much at his mercy. But the weakness had shown. Jaw stiff, Nathan dropped the coins back onto the desk and spun again to face the window.

"Your father and I have matters to discuss, Miss MacLeod. I think it would be best if you were to leave us."

There was a long silence. Too long. Then he heard the rustle of her skirts as she rose. He waited for her to speak to her father, to leave. She did neither.

"Is there something you wish to say? In your father's defense, perhaps?" Nathan asked.

It seemed ages before she replied, "I do have something to say, aye."

"Speak, then. I don't have time to waste."

"No? Well, 'tis but a few words." He heard her draw a soft breath. "I've learned to trust what I feel over what I see. 'Tisn't as simple as one might think, my lord, is it?"

She did not wait for a response. There was another waft of rosemary and honey as she left the room.

It took Nathan a moment to comprehend her meaning,

but when he did, the significance slid like ice down his spine. By the time he turned, Isobel was gone, closing the library door behind her without another word.

Silence would have been advisable on her father's part. No, more than that, it was necessary. Nathan needed to think, needed to catch his breath and get his suddenly tumbled thoughts in order. But MacLeod, never more stupid, it seemed, than when insight was most important, took no heed of his employer's agitation.

"I would apologize, my lord, for my daughter's behavior. She's a sensible creature ordinarily, is Izzy, but at times I cannot fathom what she could possibly—"

A fierce glare from Nathan immediately silenced the man. Nathan's mind was spinning. Suddenly, his planned satisfaction against MacLeod no longer seemed important. He flexed the hand that Isobel had clumsily bandaged the night before.

"I have changed my mind as to your fate. Your daughter's sense, MacLeod, has done you a great service." Inwardly, he added, *Perhaps at her own great expense.*

Yes, Isobel MacLeod had changed everything by the simplest of revelations. He had to work quickly now to silence her. It would be unfortunate indeed if she was to spread what she knew.

It galled him, even as it amazed him that one young woman had, in the space of two fleeting encounters, realized what no one else had in half a year.

She knew he was blind.

CHAPTER 4

The strain of waiting for her father to return from the Hall was turning Isobel into a jittery mess. Up to her elbows in flour, she tried hard to concentrate on the simple, calming task of kneading dough and to ignore her brothers' cheerful blathering.

"Again, Izzy. What sort of cravat was he sporting?"

She bit back a more caustic retort and answered, "A white one, Robbie. I can tell you no more than that."

Visibly disappointed, her brother fingered his own messy Orientale and sighed. "Ain't fair, you know, being born into all that. If I had half his blunt, I would cut quite a dash in London. Wouldn't hole myself up in the country like some bloody recluse."

Geordie, busy with straightening the sleeve of his coat, chimed in, "White's, Bond Street . . . Manton's!"

The last was spoken in a reverent whisper, and Isobel rolled her eyes. Knowing her brothers, if they were allowed into Manton's, the elite London shooting gallery, they would most likely blow off their own toes. The only use Isobel could find for her brothers' shooting at gallery targets would be that they might be able, then, to take their meager skill outside to shoot something edible, like a grouse.

Of course, every bird within miles belonged to Lord Oriel. According to her father, the man had never forbidden hunting on his lands. No one in the area went hungry, nor had Isobel ever heard reports of anyone's being punished for poaching. The inevitable question was whether the marquess was truly charitable or just disinterested.

More than once during their months in residence, Isobel had caught herself speculating on how very much belonged to the man. He had land as far as the eye could see, herds of prime cattle, the monstrous house. He even owned the people insomuch as people could be owned.

And now, as surely as if they had been purchased on the block, he owned the MacLeods.

"What of his boots, Izzy? Were they Hessians? Do you suppose he polishes them with champagne froth like Brummell?"

Mired in her decidedly sour musings, Isobel did not have the energy to do more than gaze wearily in Rob's direction. Maggie came quickly to her aid, turning from the stove to flutter her apron at the boys, "Listen to yourself, Robbie MacLeod! Asking of the man's boots! Better that you take yours into the stable muck. The place won't become clean of its own effort."

Geordie and Rob all but upset their chairs in their haste to get out of them. Of course, Isobel knew, their rapid exit from the room would take them nowhere near the stable, but it did get them out from underfoot. She would be the one who would end up wielding the pitchfork. Rob and Geordie were heading toward the river as fast as their unglossed boots would carry them.

"There," Margaret announced with a sigh as the outer door slammed. "We'll be free of them 'til their stomachs bring them home."

"A fine thing to be grateful for," was Isobel's dry retort. "If they'd half the passion for honorable employ as they do for sport—"

"Oh, Izzy, leave them be. They'll be no help at all in the matter, so better to have them away."

True enough. At least Maggie had not gone so far as to absolve them of guilt in the mess. Their father had taken the money, certainly, and Jamie had taught his sons their wasteful ways, but neither Rob nor Geordie showed any inclination to improve themselves—and they were responsible for much of the depletion of the stolen funds.

Isobel's fists clenched in anger. Maggie, calm as ever, gently slid the earthenware bowl out from under her hands and set it aside. The dough was most likely ruined anyway. She had taken some small comfort from kneading with unnecessary force.

In the hours that had passed since her return home, Isobel had been restless, heartsick, certain she had sealed their fate through her impetuous words to the marquess. She had performed her tasks, poor as her efforts had been, out of habit. It was baking day, so she was baking, when she would have liked nothing better than to rush off to the river herself, scattering shoes and stockings as she went, and plunging in to her knees.

As if the clear, cool water could wash away her troubles.

Heedless of the flour coating her hands, she sank into a chair. "I could not tell you what sort of boots he was wearing if my life depended upon it, Maggie, but we're well under his heel. He was so . . . cold."

Perhaps she should have kept silent on the entire matter, but the strain had been too much. She had arrived home, chilled in more than body, and poured the miserable tale into her sister's lap.

Now, as Maggie tipped the too-stiff dough into a pan, she said exactly what she had then: "We'll panic when we must."

It seemed as good a time as any for a bit of well-deserved panic. No sense, Isobel thought, in waiting for better. Before she could say so, however, her sister continued, "Squire Patton would take the hunter. No doubt he'd cheat us out of half the fair price, but it would be something. We could repay Lord Oriel, and go—"

"Where?" Isobel's voice was sharper than she intended. "Papa has surely lost this position and has shredded any chance of finding another. Who would hire a man fool enough to steal from a marquess?"

"There must be a village or two where this particular marquess is unknown." Maggie replied, her smile strained.

"Aye, to be sure. And the boys will no doubt behave themselves perfectly in some distant corner of Wales or Cornwall."

It was a grim thought, that of Rob and Geordie truly rusticating. On Skye, the pair had been bored enough to create their own amusement, an admirable pursuit ordinarily, but taken to new lows by the male MacLeods.

It had been pure chance that a forgotten book of sermons had caused Reverend Biggs to return to the kirk on the night the boys had arranged for their mouse races. The good reverend, on finding his second-best altar cloth doubling as a track, had not murdered them on the spot. Not that his position as a man of God had stilled his gnarled hands. Nay, it was simply that he had taken such a fit that Lachlann MacDomhnall, whose mouse had been winning at the time, had been forced to toss the man over his massive shoulder and head for the MacLeod cottage at a dead run.

A dose of Maggie's Saint-John's-wort tea had turned Mr. Biggs from vivid red to a calmer pink; a stronger dose of her gentle coaxing had relaxed his grip on his walking stick. But the following week's sermon had included such a stinging and direct tirade against the boys that even Isobel's ears had rung with it. Less than a month later, the MacLeods had decamped for Edinburgh.

Everyone had been happy enough there, even Maggie, despite the fact that fresh herbs were near impossible to come by. Perhaps they would have been there still had not Jamie taken it upon himself to storm the Holyrood Castle gate after downing two bottles of brandy. And he might have gotten away with it had he not ended up wedged between wrought-iron bars too narrow for even his slight form. His employer at the time had been one of those required to get him unstuck.

In Dumfries, all three MacLeod men had decided Jamie's small school would look ever so much better if painted with green stripes. Their departure from Manchester had been precipitated by a foray to a distillery warehouse—on Christmas Sunday. That escapade, too, might have gone unnoticed had not Jamie been so overwhelmed with whiskey and bonhomie that he climbed to the roof, finding it the best possible location from which to regale the city with Burns's "Scotch Drink."

To date, he still insisted that he would not have been dismissed from his teaching position had he chosen an English poem.

Isobel could not fathom what had provoked the change from foolishness to larcenousness, but it was too late to speculate, and useless besides. The simple truth was that she was bone-weary and, now, at a complete loss as to what to do next. She had promised her mother that she would take care of her father and siblings. It had been a heavy burden for a girl of nineteen and was near crushing six years later.

How on earth could she, a harried young woman with too much brain and too little beauty to aid her, convince a ravaged and reclusive nobleman that he should not do precisely what was his right and boot them all out onto their posteriors? All things considered, few would censure him for demanding a great deal more retribution than that.

In trying to describe both meetings with the marquess to Maggie, Isobel had been unable to find words even close to expressing the man's cold resolve. All she had been capable of explaining was how thoroughly Jamie's folly had trapped them.

She had not mentioned the other matter at all. There had been no noble intent in refraining from exposing the lord's blindness, nor even a hope of later using it to bargain. No, she had simply decided to keep the knowledge to herself for the single reason that Lord Oriel would, she was sure, expect her to do just the opposite.

Isobel, after all, was a MacLeod. Doing the expected was more than her proud Scots blood would allow.

"Isobel?" Her sister's voice cut into her thoughts.

"Hmm?"

"We could go home."

Isobel's heart wrenched. Across the table, so adept at hiding her own sorrow that it appeared she might have forgotten it, Maggie sat with her serene Madonna's smile undimmed and clearly ached for Skye.

Home. Away from this impossible, cursed England. What a terrible shame, Isobel thought, that no matter how appealing the possibility, they could not return to Skye, at least for the present. It was just as great a shame that it was only the MacLeod women who seemed to comprehend that.

"Och, Mairghread Líl." Their hands met, linked. *"Nam b'urrainn dhomh, bheirrin mi dhut . . ."*

"I know, Izzy." Maggie's fingers tightened around Isobel's. "If you could, you would give me earth, sea, and Skye. And you must believe I am content wherever my family is."

"Aye, well, how do you feel about Australia, then?" Isobel knew it was a weak attempt at humor, but it was all she had to offer at the moment.

Maggie even managed a faint laugh. "I've heard there are animals there who resemble monstrous mice and actually box . . ."

"Kangaroos."

"Aye? Well, I daresay the boys could have a go at sparring with them."

With that, she slid her hand from Isobel's and went to remove a pan of shortbread from the oven. Calm, as always, Maggie would not indulge her sister with bitter and maudlin contemplations of their fate. Nor did she so much as flinch when Tessa leapt into the room, bearing a goodly amount of dirt and no footwear whatsoever.

"Shoes." Maggie sighed and deftly lifted the short-bread from the girl's grubby reach.

Tessa shrugged. " 'Tis spring. Shoes are for winter." She made a grab for a ginger biscuit on the table, but Isobel was quicker. "I should like to spar with a kangaroo, I think," she announced, doing her best to appear unconcerned about failing to snatch a single biscuit. "I daresay I could plant it a smashing facer!"

"Tessa, your language!" Maggie scolded.

Isobel scowled. "Listening at doorways again, were you? 'Tis a bad end you're aiming for, my lass."

"Pish. I'll simply trot off when word of danger comes through the keyhole."

Isobel tried her best to look severe, but it was difficult when all she could think about was how very special and how very lovely her young sister was—both of her sisters. Ill-fitting, outmoded gowns did nothing to diminish their startling beauty, nor had life dimmed their spirits. What a pair they were, different in character, perhaps, but near mirror images of each other and deserving of so much more than they had ever received.

Tessa squeaked as Maggie tried to twist her tangled auburn curls into some semblance of order. The girl was forever after her older sisters to let her crop her wild hair like the boys. But such beauty, Isobel could not help thinking, was best left untamed. As Tessa's eyes strayed in familiar longing toward Maggie's herb shears, Isobel sighed.

What sort of future did the child have? Their father was loving enough, and genuinely wanted the best for his offspring. But good intentions did not produce the necessary funds to give them a better life.

"How much did you overhear, *pigidh bheag?*"

"I am not a little pitcher, Izzy. And I heard enough."

Enough was a frightening concept when it came to Tessa. The girl missed nothing. "How much?"

"We are in some sort of trouble with the marquess. You went with Papa this morning, and it did not go well. Australia seems to be our next port of call." This time, neither sister was swift enough to protect the biscuits. Tessa shoved one into her mouth whole, liberally spraying Isobel with crumbs moments later when she demanded, "Shall we have to leave directly? There is a nest of robin's eggs in the apple tree, and I should very much like to see them hatch."

Perhaps Isobel could have ignored Tessa's very adult recitation of the recent chain of events had it not been accompanied by such a poignantly childlike desire. Tessa wanted to see the robins hatch. She was resigned to yet another upheaval, but she wanted to see the baby birds first.

Isobel's muttered curse caused Maggie to raise her eyebrows and Tessa to giggle. Silently vowing that she would pack up robin and nest and carry them along if necessary, Isobel pushed herself to her feet.

"Enough of this waiting!" She pulled her bonnet from its hook.

Maggie immediately blocked the door. "You are not thinking to go—"

"I'm half gone, so you may take your hand off the door."

"You cannot! Izzy, after all that's happened, what would Lord Oriel think if you were to barrel into his house again, and in such a temper!"

"Well, we'll find out, won't we? He was civil enough about the fact that I climbed through his window last night. After nearly suffocating me and crushing my bones, that is." When Maggie refused to move away from the door, Isobel let out her breath in an exasperated huff. "What would you have me do? Sit and wait patiently for our fate to be handed down from Above?"

"What I would like, Iseabail Ròis, is for you to do a bit of thinking before you do something rash!"

"Rash? The man has already caught me creeping about his house like a thief in the night; our father *was* a thief at some point yesterday; and you use the word *rash*?" Unable to help herself, Isobel laughed. "Oh, Maggie, I do love you. Now, get out of my way."

In truth, she had no intention of barreling into the Hall. Not yet, at least. She simply needed to think a bit, perhaps allow herself the ultimate luxury of dipping her toes in the stream while she did so.

As it turned out, there was no need for Maggie to move. Both sisters were forced to jump back as the door swung in. Jamie MacLeod, visibly confused sons in tow, appeared in the doorway. Without a word, he removed his coat and hat and headed straight toward the study, the image of the whiskey decanter all but blazing from his eyes.

"Papa?" Hot on his heels, Isobel pressed, "What happened?" All four of her siblings followed. "Papa!"

Having had years of practice, Maggie slipped past and reached the liquor first. She poured her father a miserly shot, then tucked the bottle tight against her chest when

Rob reached for it. Jamie tossed back the whiskey and held out the glass. Maggie shook her head.

"*Och*, lass, I need another wee dram after what I've just suffered!"

Isobel moved in front of him. "Not until you've told us what happened."

Jamie ran his free hand through his grizzled hair and darted a beseeching glance around her shoulder. Maggie ignored him. "Aye, if I must. But not with *an pigidh bheag* here."

Five pairs of eyes swung to Tessa, who promptly tried to make herself inconspicuous behind the wing chair. "Off with you, brat," Geordie ordered.

Tessa set her jaw. "I'm every bit as much a member of this family as you, you great lummox!"

"Aye, perhaps, but ten years younger and aeons dimmer."

"Debatable, that," Tessa muttered, but made a show of marching from the room. Maggie, for what it was worth, closed the door and did her best to block the keyhole with her skirts.

"Now, Da', suppose you tell us why you dragged Geordie and me away from our walk to town." Rob draped himself over a chair. "There's a regiment passing through, you know."

"Blues," his brother chimed in. "The officers are always good for a bit of news from Town—"

"*Cuist!*" Isobel hushed him, her patience shredded. "Well, Papa?"

"*Och*, Izzy . . ." Jamie, with all the drama of his sons and none of the elegance, dropped onto the divan. From his sagging hose to the glass dangling from his limp fingers, he was the very picture of woe. Isobel felt both an urge to embrace him and to smack him smartly atop his graying head. " 'Tis done for, we are. Sacked," he moaned.

"Given the boot. Deprived of my livelihood and the only means of supporting m'darlin' bairns!"

This brought Rob's head up. "What was that?"

Geordie gaped. "The marquess sacked you? Why?"

"A cruel man, he is. Heartless. Why, he hasn't a whit o' concern for aught but his own money. No thought of my family . . ."

"Papa!" Isobel closed her eyes and tried to count ten. She made it to three. "How can you say so? His lordship's concern for his money is right enough. 'Twas your sticky fingerprints all over it!"

"What was that?" Rob demanded.

Geordie's jaw swung as if on hinges. "You took money from the man?"

Isobel turned on them. "For shame, both of you! Where on earth did you think your shiny coins came from last night?"

"Well, I—" Rob stammered. "I thought—wages . . ."

Geordie said nothing.

"Oh!" Isobel threw up her hands. "God save us from the witless!" She looked back to her father, who now had his face in his hands. "I suppose we ought to be grateful he didn't have you tossed headfirst in jail!" Not surprisingly, there was no response to that. "Well, how long do we have to get out? Papa, *how long*?"

There was a lengthy silence. Then Jamie cleared his throat. "Actually, there is . . . We can . . ."

"We can what?" she demanded.

"We can stay."

Had he announced that the Archangel Gabriel himself had descended to their aid, Isobel could not have been more shocked. "What did you say?"

"Lord Oriel gave us an alternative. Can't take it, of course . . ."

"Papa!"

"*Och*, very well. The man is willing to let us keep the house. He even offered an allowance. If . . ."

"If what?"

"Nay, nay." Jamie lifted bleary eyes. " 'Twas a lifeline, but one not to be grabbed. Damn me if he wasn't generous, though."

"We'll be here a long time if you cannot manage to get the tale out, Papa."

"You'll not like it, Izzy lass."

"As if my liking for the way of things has stopped you in the past!" She ignored Maggie's hand, lifted in warning. "Out with it now."

Jamie shuffled for a moment, then announced, "He'll forget about my—er—lapse in judgement in exchange for . . ."

Suddenly the room grew very still. Isobel took a deep breath. "In exchange for what?"

"For you, Izzy. He'll trade his hold on me for you."

There was a quiet gasp from the other side of the room as Maggie nearly lost her grip on the decanter. Isobel's jaw was slack. For what seemed an eternity, the only sound in the room was the ticking of the mantel clock.

Then Rob's voice shattered the silence. "He wants *Isobel*? My God, is the man daft?"

"Deaf?" was his brother's contribution. "Blind? No offense, Izzy. You know we think you're a prime article, but you've a hell of a tongue on you, and, well, Maggie's the looker. Why didn't Oriel ask for her?"

"Geordie!" Maggie had clearly found her voice. "How dare you say such things?"

"Didn't mean anything by it. You've always been the pretty one."

"Oh, you idiot! I wasn't referring to your nasty insults, though you'd do well to take a bit of lye to *your* tongue. Nay How dare you be so glib about a devil's bargain?" She slammed the decanter onto the nearest table and rushed to Isobel's side. She wrapped one arm around her sister and, in uncharacteristic fury, shook her free fist at her father. "You told him what he could do with his offer, didn't you?"

There was another ominous silence. Isobel, roused from unfamiliar speechlessness by Maggie's equally unfamiliar shouting, managed, "What did you say to him, Papa?"

Their father could not have looked less impassioned if he had tried. "I refused, of course."

"And called him out on the spot, I trust," Maggie snapped.

"Called him out?" Geordie repeated.

"Are you daft now?" Rob demanded. "The fellow's no doubt had years at Manton's!"

"Madness," Geordie agreed. "Da' would only end up with a ball in the gut."

Jamie shuddered. "I know I ought to have. . . . Manton's. Aye, Manton's."

"I cannot believe I am hearing this!" Maggie was nearly spitting in her rage. "The man has the gall to bargain so, and you let him get away with it?"

"Don't see that he had a choice, Mags." Geordie was making his way stealthily toward the decanter. "Happens all the time. Local demigod, holed up on some ghastly country estate. I daresay he's gone through all his maids already."

"And the tavern wenches," Rob added, gesturing for a glass. "Be happy he hasn't had a look at you, Maggie Líl. You're the only one with hopes of marrying well, after all."

From his seat, their father was moaning again, this time something about being a miserable wretch of a man. Isobel felt her sister stiffen to the point of shattering.

"A curse on the three of you! " 'Tis ashamed I am to

share blood! Why, if I'd one of Manton's pistols right now—"

"Maggie," Isobel said gently.

"You'd what?" Rob laughed. "Have a go at Oriel? He might just let you shoot him if you'd but flash a smile first."

"Robert." Isobel's voice went up a notch.

" 'Tis right, Margaret is," their father mumbled. "Honor and my duty as a father, wretch of one though I am, demands no less. Find me some gloves, Geordie lad. Daresay the blackguard'll shoot me dead on the spot, but I'll have the satisfaction of slapping him like a proper gentleman."

"Both cheeks, Da'!" Geordie chuckled into his glass and made no move whatsoever to find the demanded gloves.

"I mean it, lad! Off with you now to m'wardrobe! And you can lay out my best black coat while you're at it. 'Tis fine enough for any man to be buried in."

That did it.

"Enough—all of you!" Isobel jerked from her sister's embrace and planted herself squarely in front of her father. She spoke very slowly. "You will tell me now, exactly what Lord Oriel demands. Is he looking for a bedmate?"

"Isobel!"

"Shh, Maggie. Well, Papa?"

Jamie shook his head. "What else am I to think, Izzy? Damned cool bugger. He claimed to want you as his secretary."

"Was there more?"

Now her father looked surprised. "Isn't that enough? His secretary. Hah!"

"Answer me. Was there more?"

"To be sure there was. Wants you to live at the Hall,

he does. A full time employ, he called it." Jamie gave a
halfhearted wave in his son's direction. "Gloves, Geordie!"

Isobel grabbed his hand. "And if I go, what do you
get?" Her father stared at her blankly for a moment
before his eyes sharpened. It was an expression part
hopeful and part wounded. "Tell me. Do we get to keep
the house?"

"Aye."

"And he would pay me your wages?"

"Aye. That, too."

Maggie's fingers clenched over hers. "Isobel, you
cannot."

"You're wrong, Mairghread Líl. I can." Turning her
back to her father and brothers, Isobel touched Maggie's
cheek. "I do not believe he will ask anything truly ill
of me."

"How can you know that?"

"Ah, well I cannot. But I can believe. And hope, You
will help me pack, won't you?"

Their eyes met, Maggie's concerned and loving, Isobel's
as certain as she could manage. "Aye," Maggie said after a
long moment. "I will. And I'm coming with you."

"So am I! I'll plant him a facer he'll feel for weeks!"
Tessa's voice came clearly through the keyhole.

Isobel spun back to face the door. Somehow, in the
midst of it all, she found the ability to laugh. "You'll do
no such thing, either of you. It's my affair, and I'll see
to it."

Minutes later, a reluctant Tessa dispatched upstairs to
search for a valise, Isobel rounded on her father again. "I
understand that you're a bit unclear as to my end of the
bargain, but I suggest you inform us of his in complete
detail." She shoved trembling hands into her apron
pockets. "If we're to accept his lordship's generosity, this
time I, for one, would like to know precisely what you're
to get."

"Izzy." Jamie struggled from his seat. "I don't think—"

"Nay You don't." She struggled to soften her words with a faint smile. "You dream. I suppose 'tis your legacy to all of us. We hope for the best."

Hoping for the best was all well and good, she decided as she walked away from the cottage several hours later, valise in hand. Expecting it, however, was dangerous. All things considered, perhaps her future was not so uncertain. There was no doubt in her mind that Lord Oriel would be perfectly clear on what he wanted from her; there would be no need for any expectations at all.

Behind her, she could feel Maggie's eyes, no doubt worried and grim. Somewhere behind her sister, the men's eyes, Isobel was sure, were beginning to glaze with drink. Disaster averted was the best excuse they had had for celebration in months.

CHAPTER 5

*It had been hard for him that spake it to have
put more truth and untruth together, in few
words, than in that speech: "Whosoever is
delighted in solitude is either a wild beast
or a god."*

—Francis Bacon

Isobel stood in front of the Hall's massive doors and
knocked again. She had been pounding the bronze knocker
for a good five minutes. Already nervous, she felt very
small and thoroughly insignificant as she waited to be
admitted, rather like a poor and unwanted relative. It did
not improve matters that the knocker itself, designed to
look like the face of a satyr, leered at her.

The possibility of turning around and heading straight
back home was tempting. Of course she would do no
such thing. The marquess had agreed to accept her in her
father's stead, and the least she could do was to speak
with him.

It would help a great deal if someone would let her
into the house.

Her ears were ringing from the steady assault on the
door, and she took a moment's rest. She turned about on
the step to survey the grand sweep of sparkling gravel
that completed the approach to Oriel Hall. Despite the
rather bedraggled appearance of the central flower bed
and the tired look of the Hall itself, the estate screamed
of old money and even older title. One day the Marquess
of Oriel would become the Duke of Abergele, and hence

would entertain some of the more illustrious personages of the Realm.

She assumed the architect had not had a poor, plain Scottish spinster in mind when he had designed either the circle or the sprawling Hall. No, the images would have been more along the line of regal ladies in farthingales and starched ruffs, visitors who would most certainly not be left standing on the steps with a single, worn valise beside their scuffed shoes.

Isobel had never paid much attention to the great house. The secretary's daughter, after all, was not likely to be invited for tea. Nor had she gained a clear impression of the place in the past day. One arrival had been in the dead of night, the other in nervous anticipation. She had left shakily both times. This visit promised nothing different, except that she had no idea when she would be leaving.

She was not going anywhere until she had seen Lord Oriel. Squaring her shoulders, she twisted her face into an imitation of the leering satyr and spun, determined to keep knocking until someone answered.

She found herself face-to-face with the butler.

She had seen the man once before, that very morning. Resembling nothing so much as a lichen-covered tree stump, stunted and whiskery, he had silently escorted her and her father toward the cavernous library, then disappeared just as quietly. Now he was regarding her from under hoary brows, only a single blink of his pale eyes to indicate that he was any more animate than the brass satyr.

Isobel hurriedly rearranged her features into a smile. "Good afternoon. Lord Oriel is expecting—"

She flinched when his shoulder jerked, thinking she was about to receive a faceful of brass-mounted wood. But the man pulled the door fully open and gestured her inside.

Rattled, she entered the hall. There was a tense moment as her worn valise caught on the massive latch, but she tugged it free and, red-faced, followed the clearly unconcerned butler across the marble foyer. He moved slowly, from age or inclination she could not tell. Either way, it gave Isobel an opportunity to study the massive entryway.

Her second daylight visit to the Hall confirmed her vague recollections. She had absorbed little in the way of decor earlier because there was little. The walls were filled with portraits, certainly: hawk-nosed men in various amounts of armor and pale women weighted down with gems. Past marquesses and their ornaments, no doubt.

There were marble pillars, too, fat enough that her arms would not reach around them, rising to the vaulted ceiling and first-floor gallery. Other than that, the place was impressively, vastly empty. The butler turned a corner, and Isobel craned her neck for a last look at the foyer. There were no tables, no nymph-topped pedestals, none of the assorted antique vases and other useless knickknacks she would have expected in such a grand house.

And, oddest of all, was the complete lack of people. There was no sign of so much as a footman. Save for the butler and the austere, disquieting marquess, Isobel had not seen another living being at Oriel Hall.

Thus, when she was finally standing in the library doorway, she did not so much as blink when the grim voice announced, "Good day, Miss MacLeod. Welcome to the netherworld."

The greeting was no more incongruous than the sight before her. The marquess was standing behind the desk, neat as a pin in his simply tied cravat and midnight coat. His ebony hair was perfectly combed, his collar points sharp. In fact, had it not been for his taut, ravaged face, he would have appeared the perfect gentleman. He certainly did not match Isobel's notion of a man set on dastardly conquest.

When she did not answer his unorthodox welcome, he continued, "Miss MacLeod will be staying for a time, Milch. Take whatever she has brought with her to the Blue Room."

There came a grunt from behind Isobel. It might have been some new variation of "yes, milord" or, just as likely, the aged butler's bones protesting a sudden move. She handed over her valise, not particularly concerned with burdening the man. He had done nothing to make her welcome and besides, there was little in the bag. Packing, she had found in the past few years, was a rather simple process when one possessed naught.

She waited for the door to close before speaking. "You've a fair pair of ears, Lord Oriel."

It was hardly more proper a greeting than his, but Isobel, never at her best when nervous, spoke without thinking.

"Why, thank you, Miss MacLeod. I've always thought them overlarge, myself."

She blinked at him. Coming from another man, it might have sounded like a jest. "I meant, my lord, that your hearing is to be commended."

"Yes, Miss MacLeod, I assumed that was what you meant." He raised an eyebrow. "I am not certain, however, why you said it."

"I—well, I thought . . ." Curse her tongue for floundering now. "Since you cannot—I assumed you did not—er—see me. You seemed to have detected my step."

"Ah. Now I comprehend." He appeared to ponder the matter for a moment. "No. I am afraid my hearing is no more acute than it ever was."

"Then, how . . ."

"Sorcery, Miss MacLeod. Would you care to sit down?"

She noticed he was gripping the handle of a walking stick tightly and realized his leg must be paining him. Sitting did seem like a good idea, since her own legs were not quite steady. She chose the nearest chair.

"I—this is all . . ."

He lowered himself slowly into his seat behind the desk. "Ah, the stammering again. Is this to characterize all our encounters? I assure you, our discourses will go much more smoothly should you complete your thoughts."

"This is madness, my lord. Why in God's name would you make such a bargain?" There, no stammering.

"Very good. Two sentences." Oriel rested his stick against the desk, then leaning forward, steepled his hands in front of his face. "Tell me this. Did you come of your own free will?"

"Aye, of course."

"Your father did not force you?"

"Nay—he would not . . ."

"A telling pause there, Miss MacLeod. He would not demand such sacrifice from you, but he offered no alternative? There *must* have been an alternative. You will recall that I am well acquainted with your father."

Isobel sighed. "He thought to challenge you to a duel, my lord."

"Did he really?" Oriel chuckled, but Isobel did not find it a heartening sound. "Perhaps you ought to have let him. I daresay, even two sheets to the wind, he could put a bullet in me. My aim, I am afraid, is not what it once was. Ah, but I have not answered your question. I expect you are interested in hearing what I am planning to do with you now that I have you in my clutches."

Interested did not even begin to describe her feelings at the moment. *Eager* would have been better, *frantic* quite apt. Isobel could not quash the sensation that her awkward step through the front door had somehow transported her into a place far removed from whatever reality existed elsewhere.

The marquess's disquieting calm was doing nothing to help. His words were polite, even easy, but something behind the genteel facade frightened her now, just as it had the night before. Letting one's guard down around a courteous Lord Oriel was, she found herself thinking, rather like trusting a purring cat. A pounce was sure to follow.

"I would make the most unsuitable of mistresses, my lord!" she blurted.

Lord Oriel was clearly not amused. Nor did he appear shocked. In fact, his expression did not change a whit. "Is that what you think I want of you?"

Humiliated, helpless, Isobel bit her lip. "I do not want to think it."

"Yes, the honest answer. I find I expect that of you." He paused. "And if it is such services I require? Will you accommodate me?"

Never in her wildest imaginings could Isobel have envisioned such a conversation. Her cheeks flamed as she considered, for the first time, how little she really knew of the ways of the world. "Nay, my lord. I would never—"

She jumped as his hand hit the desk, and she was even more startled when he gave a rough laugh. "Now you lie!"

"I do no such thing!" She was halfway to her feet before knowing it, the chair creaking with her sudden move. She returned only to the edge of her seat when Oriel impatiently waved her back.

"I am not impugning your honor, Miss MacLeod. Quite the contrary. It humbles me to know there is little you would not consider doing for your family." He leaned back then, a decidedly feline, unhumble smile on his face. "Trust me when I tell you I should have no trouble in finding a willing female body should that be my desire. What I want from you is what my gold will not buy."

More confused than ever, Isobel leaned forward warily. "I do not understand, my lord. 'Twas gold that brought this all about, and need of it that has me here now."

"Is it? I think not. I believe you are here for something far more important than money. You are here because I have offered your family freedom and comfort in exchange for yours. It is that part of your character I desire."

" 'Tis love, my lord. No more."

"And what if I wish you to love me?"

"Then you are daft!" The words hung heavily in the air. Gathering her wits, Isobel took a calming breath. "You are jesting with me again."

"I must say, your spirit is appealing. A bit hair-triggered, perhaps, but appealing nonetheless." His fingers slid along the empty surface of the desk. "I have a feeling what I require from you will change as we go along, but I'll phrase it as simply as I can: I need your silence, Miss MacLeod, and I need you to be my eyes."

"Your eyes?"

Gilded and unreadable, they rested somewhere in the vicinity of her top spencer button. Isobel could not resist lifting a hand to the spot. As if sensing the motion, Oriel gave another half smile.

"In case you have forgotten—and I feel compelled to inform you that you are the only person who was astute enough to notice—I cannot see. It is an inconvenience, I'm sure you will agree, but not an insurmountable one. In the past six months, I have managed to leave matters of importance to my solicitor, less important ones to your father. That, as you well know, ended badly."

Heat rose anew in Isobel's cheeks, and she resisted the urge to apologize yet again for her father's behavior.

Instead, she asked, "Why have you felt it necessary to conceal your . . . affliction?"

"Affliction." He snorted. "Interesting choice of words, though no worse than inconvenience, I expect. As to why I have chosen to conceal it . . . Pride, I suppose and simplicity. Your cleverness has put me in an awkward position, however.

Isobel was uncertain how she was meant to respond. "How so, my lord?"

"It was either employ you or have you killed for knowing my secret," he said smoothly.

Isobel's heart lodged in her throat before she realized he was teasing once more.

"Satisfy my curiosity, Miss MacLeod. How did you know I cannot see? Your father has been in my company for a number of months, and he never guessed. There is no satisfaction in fooling a fool, but I still considered it something of a feat."

Isobel did not bother to defend her father. Oriel had spoken no more than the truth. " 'Twas watching you grope for the pouch on the floor this morning that made me certain," she answered. "And even last night, there was something in your eyes . . ."

Oriel's bland expression did not change. "Your perceptiveness, Miss MacLeod, borders on dangerous."

Confused, Isobel hastened to assure him, "I would not have betrayed your secret."

He gazed toward her silently for a moment, as if not comprehending her words. Then he nodded. "Would not have. Well, it is the future I have in mind." Isobel thought she heard him sigh. "Now I beg you forgive me, for I am about to display the character so rightly attributed to me by the local populace."

He rose again to his feet and moved toward her, his uneven gait in evidence as he avoided the furniture. When he stopped, it was to tower over her. "All jesting and genial patter aside, I do not think I need to remind you what is at stake for your family should you decide you made the wrong choice in accepting my bargain."

"N-nay, my lord."

"Good. Because I would very much regret having to cause extreme discomfort to the one person I have met in quite some time who shows a vestige of heart. Now, I am going for a ride. At supper we will discuss the extent of your duties."

He was almost to the door before she found her voice again.

"Supper, my lord?"

"The last meal of the day, Miss MacLeod. Milch will show you to the dining room. I dine at eight."

"But I had thought I would take my meals with . . . your staff."

"You will take supper, at least, with me. Is that clear?"

"Aye, my lord. But I do not . . ."

He growled with impatience. *"What?"*

"My clothing is not—suited . . ."

His snort made her flinch. "Of course. It has been so long since I last dined in the company of a lady that I seem to have forgotten what an event it can be. Trust me, Miss MacLeod, what you wear does not matter in the least. Come in armor—or nothing at all if it suits you. I couldn't care less."

It would have taken a far thicker skin than Isobel possessed to ignore the sting of his dismissal. "As you wish, my lord," she muttered as the door swung shut behind him. "How gratifying to know your blindness serves some purpose."

Unable to help herself, she went to the window. She was afforded a fair view of the front of the house. The familiar gray stallion stood by the stairs, saddled and clearly ready for a bit of exercise. There was no groom in sight.

Oriel appeared moments later. Isobel watched him navigate the stone steps. Only someone who knew of the man's affliction would see that the walking stick was used as much to locate the steps as for support. Once he reached the massive horse, he swung with surprising ease into the saddle. Then, with the faintest touch of his stick to the horse's flank, they were off, careening down the drive.

Even as she wondered how he kept from breaking both his neck and his mount's, Isobel was impressed. She watched as the pair took a low fence leading to the fields. He was obviously a skilled horseman but it was just as obvious that he trusted the stallion would not refuse any command. She found it both odd and terribly sad that the only creature this man trusted implicitly was his horse.

Sighing, Isobel turned from the window. With several hours left until supper, she would do her best to compose herself and maybe do a bit of exploring. Perhaps if she were one of the ladies with whom the marquess had once been accustomed to dining, she would have spent most of the time dressing. As it was, she would need no more time than that necessary to change her gown and poke a few pins into her unruly hair.

He knew she was plain. Her father must have been thorough in his descriptions. True, Lord Oriel was blind, but Isobel knew enough of men to know that they had very vivid imaginations. Her brothers were forever speculating on the appearance of the dazzling ladies mentioned in day-old editions of the *Times*. They were convinced every last one was a ravishing beauty.

Lord Oriel would not even bother to speculate on how she looked.

The absurdity of the thought struck her, but too late. It hardly mattered what she looked like or whether or not her new employer cared. But she could not shake the fleeting conviction that, perhaps, she had lost her one chance at being thought a beauty: working for a blind man who might have assumed her pretty and never known otherwise.

Annoyed with herself, she tugged at the bell. " 'Tis preening you'll be at next, my lass," she muttered. "And howling at the moon."

Nathan reined his mount to a shuddering halt several miles from the house. Ordinarily, he would have pushed until both he and the horse were shaky and drenched with sweat. This time, however, he felt the urge to press his mind harder than his body.

She had come. And, from all he could gather, she had come willingly.

He could not deny the fact that Isobel MacLeod would most likely march into hell should her family need her to do so. He had never met someone more quick to act on another's behalf. Most people of his acquaintance did little that was not aimed for their benefit alone. Isobel, he had decided mere minutes after their unorthodox meeting, put her own well-being at the very bottom of a long list.

He wondered what she would say if she was to learn just how much he knew about her. For instance, would she be mortified that her father spoke of her passion for Highland ballads—or merely resigned to her sire's loose tongue? Would she respond at all if she knew MacLeod had mentioned her love of bright colors and fine fabric? Most likely, she would stiffen in her aged muslin and snap out some bit of Scottish wisdom on frugality.

Nathan found himself wondering just what Isobel had to say about other virtues. To be precise, he wondered what she had to say on the matter of her own virtue. Something in her voice and manner told him in no uncertain terms that she was innocent in the ways of the flesh. She had been quick enough, however, to comment on her capabilities as a mistress.

It would be at least mildly entertaining to hear her conception of a proper paramour. No doubt her description would be clever, decided, and quite unlike anything a real courtesan would admit.

Isobel would quite probably make a poor mistress indeed. She possessed none of the requisite traits, most notably those of complete self-interest and cunning. In her opinion, however, she would be lacking elsewhere. She would think beauty necessary, and sensual allure.

Nathan sighed. He was certainly finding himself allured by Isobel MacLeod, and he could not even see her face.

Now, sitting in a sheen of sweat atop an equally warm horse in the midst of a spring field, he could not free his senses of her smell. It taunted him just as it did in her presence, hovering at the edge of every breath he took. He had been hard pressed during those moments when he had loomed over her not to bend close and sniff at her neck like some rutting beast. In fact, only the knowledge that she would have taken flight had stilled the powerful impulse.

Perhaps it was madness, bringing her into his home. He was accustomed to solitude, had grown to appreciate the silence of empty rooms. Yet why, then, did he find himself eagerly awaiting each swell of that husky, musical Scottish voice?

All things considered, Isobel MacLeod could prove to be more thorn than rose. Already she pricked at his shell and registered under his skin. He remembered as a small boy rushing into the Hall's gardens to capture a rose for his mother. He had grasped eagerly at a crimson flower and ended up with a fistful of crushed petals—and briars.

It was the first time he had bled for a woman, and a sad lesson in acting on impulse.

Beneath him, the horse shifted impatiently, ready for a

wild gallop. Patting the massive neck, he murmured, "Ah, Chiron, I know precisely how you feel."

His hands nearly itched with the desire to touch Isobel. He knew from their encounter the night before that she was neither large nor petite. When standing, her head would perhaps reach his shoulder. He recalled, too, and smiled in the remembrance of his hand sliding warmly over the curve of her bottom. The lady, brief experience told him, was very pleasantly formed.

The thought of touching her so again was appealing. But he wanted more. He wanted to run his fingers over her face and through her hair, to sense just why she was considered plain and to ascertain the length and texture of what James MacLeod had called "de'il's fire." Isobel had the red hair to match her temper, it seemed. And it stood to reason that any pawing on his part would get him a blast of that temper at the very least. He would simply have to wait.

He had always hated waiting. He was a man of motion and deed by nature. The past months of helplessness had been hell. From the moment he and Rievaulx had walked out of the Lisbon tavern and into a silent, brutal ambush, he had been helpless—unable to fend off the savage blow to his head that had taken his sight, unable to save his friend's life. Since his return to England, holed up in the Hall like a wounded animal, he had been helpless to seek revenge.

Now, perhaps, he had been given a chance to live fully again—and to be useful. Isobel could help; she *would* help. He simply had to be careful and patient in his demands.

He did not want to be patient, damn it.

"You're finding this amusing, Gabriel, aren't you?" he muttered into the breeze. "Me, blind and bumbling, seeing salvation in a smart-mouthed Scottish spinster." Again, his mind filled with thoughts of Isobel. "You would like her, I think. She has a way of cutting right through the husk of things to the core."

There was a fundamental problem inherent in her perceptiveness. Nathan was, quite simply, concerned with what she would see when she looked closely at him. It was not physical. He knew he was not what he once was, but neither was she a beauty. Appearance meant nothing. No, there were other parts of himself he did not want uncovered.

Then, too, there was the worry that Isobel would balk at what he meant to propose. Nathan had no doubt she would be up to the demands he had made of her father. In fact, she could quite probably relieve his London solicitors of all their responsibilities and, in the process, make him an even wealthier man than he already was.

The question, of course, was whether or not she would accept the larger task he was to lay before her, and if he was making a terrible mistake in asking it.

CHAPTER 6

Dining with Lord Oriel was very much like sharing a meal with her brothers when they were well sotted, Isobel decided. She bit her lip as he missed yet again and spattered the linen tablecloth with soup. From her seat at the opposite end of the massive table, she could hear his growl of impatience.

All things considered, he managed very well for a man who could not see what he was doing, but the experience was still unsettling. Neither had spoken a word since the obligatory greeting. Oriel's complete attention was directed to getting the food from his plate to his mouth.

Isobel dragged her gaze from his efforts and surveyed the room. It was much like the rest of the Hall, at least what she had seen. The meager furnishings were of excellent quality but showed unmistakable signs of neglect. The silver was tarnished, the veneer of the sleek mahogany sideboard dulled. And over every surface was a faint coating of dust, as if the house's occupants had departed some short time before, leaving everything just as it was.

The chambers she had seen upstairs were clearly unused, the furniture draped with dustcloths. Even the windows were covered. With the exception of her room,

74

of course, which was beautifully appointed and blessedly dust-free.

"I trust your accommodations are satisfactory, Miss MacLeod," Oriel said, interrupting her thoughts.

Isobel's eyes flew back to his face. Mind readers, she thought, should not have soup on their chins. She blinked as he promptly lifted his napkin and wiped away the streak.

"I, ah, the room is lovely, my lord. Thank you."

And it was. She had wandered about the chamber, reverently stroking the lines of the blue silk chaise, the applewood writing desk. Having half expected quarters in the recesses of the attics with the other servants— assuming there were other servants besides Milch—she had found herself feeling like royalty in the richly appointed room.

"You have a beautiful home," she added.

"It comes with the title," was his terse reply.

She wanted very much to ask about the unnatural quiet, but sensed it was not a subject he would welcome discussing. She was spared the immediate necessity of finding a safe topic by the appearance of Milch, bearing the next course. Isobel had yet to see another person and was fast coming to the conclusion that the dour butler was Oriel's staff in its entirety. Hard as it was imagining the man cooking, it was harder still to see him in apron and mobcap, wielding a feather duster. Of course, considering the amount of dust in evidence, it would seem he had chosen to ignore that task.

An ominous clattering from the far end of the table told her that Oriel was having a bit of a problem with the fish. Isobel's own appetite was poor. Part had to do with the fact that the food was barely palatable. Still more was due to the knots in her stomach. They had twisted and tightened through the afternoon. If she did not rid herself of some of the tension soon, she would be likely to do something foolish.

"My lord." She stilled her fingers as they worried at a worn spot in her napkin. "If you would not mind, I should very much like to discuss my . . . duties here."

"Yes, I expect you would."

Instead of continuing, Oriel awkwardly speared another bite of the overdone trout. Isobel found her gaze centering on his mouth. When not twisted in cold amusement, it was rather nice—the upper lip wide and perfectly shaped. His face, with that mouth, sharp cheekbones, and near-gold eyes suddenly made her think of a cat. A large one, to be sure, and one not to be petted.

"If I am to assume my father's duties, perhaps we ought to work out a schedule. And"—she paused and drew a breath—"I really do not understand why it is necessary for me to stay here. I could arrive each morning and return to the cottage . . . ."

"No."

"Really, it would be—"

"I said no, Miss MacLeod. It was a very clear part of our deal that you reside here at the Hall. There will be no bargaining on the point."

She was fast coming to the conclusion that there was no bargaining at all with this man. He got precisely what he wanted. "I thought only to—"

"I have a very good idea what you thought. One does not need one's eyes to comprehend human nature."

Isobel had no reason to doubt that his comprehension was quite remarkable on many matters. He had his share of misses, however, when it came to her character.

"If I might ask—"

"I doubt I would give the answer you wanted."

Finally losing her temper, she slapped her palm hard against the table and had the satisfaction of watching the goblet jerk in his hand. So he could be startled. She had begun to wonder.

"If you would allow me to complete the question, you might surprise yourself with the answer!" she snapped. Then, "I do not mean to be impertinent, but you have—I mean—" She gave up and poked her nail through the napkin. "Oh, bother it!"

"No, by all means, continue."

She sighed. "I can only be bullied so much, my lord, before I lose my temper. Are you having yourself a wee game here, trying to make me do something I'll have cause to regret?"

Carefully he returned his glass to its place. "Trust me, Miss MacLeod, a wise man never plays games, wee or otherwise, with a woman's temper. And I might suggest that spitting at me is not your best option."

" 'Tisn't wise," she muttered, "I know. But I cannot seem to help it."

"You could try," he replied equably.

"Aye, and now you'll go all polite and condescending. If this is how you go about managing your employees, running hot then cold, 'tis no wonder my father . . ."

There was no need for him to interrupt her this time. Her tongue faltered on its own, of course too late.

"No wonder he stole from me? Now that, I must say, is perhaps the best excuse I've heard yet for his behavior. He was goaded into it by my personality. Tell me, Isobel, do you find liking your employer a necessary qualification for loyalty?"

"Liking isn't necessary, my lord," Isobel replied after a long moment. "Not when there is respect."

Nathan felt as if she had pricked something inside him, and he didn't like the sensation in the least. "You do not think you can respect me."

"To the contrary," she said softly. "I respect you, or rather what little I know of you, very much indeed. 'Tis a grand feat you've achieved. I cannot say how I'll feel once we're done with all this crazed circling and settle whatever there is to be settled, but I am impressed thus far."

"Well." Nathan sat back in his chair. "You humble me with your honesty."

"And you mock me with that tone!"

He could almost imagine her eyes sparking with annoyance. Green, he thought. Vivid and slightly tilted and every bit as telling of her mood as Jamie had once tipsily described. "I am not mocking you, Isobel. Honesty is to be prized as little else. I am genuinely awed by yours, even more so by the loyalty that accompanies it. Ah, but I daresay you do not believe me. What you know of me, as you say, is very limited. In fact, you know little more than the fact that I am blind and have managed to conceal it."

"A feat worthy of respect," she said firmly.

"Perhaps. But you are still not certain I am an honorable man."

"I wasn't thinking of honor, precisely, my lord. I was thinking of cruelty."

"You think me cruel."

"You can speak cruelly, my lord. The two are not necessarily the same."

"*Mmm*. I would venture to agree with you there." The sigh eased from his throat before he could stop it. "Has it ever occurred to you, Isobel MacLeod, that I might be every bit as nervous as you?"

Nay, it had not. And even when he said the words, it made no sense. Isobel frowned. "Why on earth would you be nervous?"

"A good question, certainly. By all appearances, I am the one in control."

It was not merely appearance. Isobel believed the man to be very much in control of both the situation and himself.

"You are a formidable presence," he continued. "Restless, disquieting and, I would say, volatile."

"I disquiet you?"

His lips twitched. "Ah, you like hearing that. Your pride takes odd sustenance, I see." He reached for his plate, then pushed it away. "God, I cannot stomach any more of this disgraceful food. That will be one of your duties."

"Cooking?" she asked, surprised.

"No. Simply overseeing the kitchens."

Well, at least they seemed to be getting down to important matters. "Not the usual task for a secretary, my lord, but I daresay I'll manage it."

"I daresay you will. As for the secretarial duties, I will require you to deal with such correspondence as still reaches me. Then there are various concerns of my tenants. And I will ask you to . . ."

"Yes?"

"I will ask you to read to me, Isobel."

"Letters? Estate business?"

"Sometimes." His face was turned away from her now. "But more than that, I should like to hear literature. Poetry. I have . . . missed such things."

Isobel was stunned, and unwillingly touched. How could she not be? This moody, damaged man wanted her to read poetry. "I can do that for you," she said softly.

"Good." With an abruptness that startled her, the breath of melancholy vanished, replaced once again by aristocratic crispness. "I will also expect you to accompany me to London in two weeks' time. I will have need of you both at home and at social functions."

"I beg your pardon?"

"Social functions, Isobel. Soirees, balls, evenings at the opera. You are not wholly unfamiliar, I think, with such matters."

"I'm not, nay, but, well, it hardly seems the province of a secretary."

"No more so than are the kitchens. I have somewhat of a revision to make to your title. I need you to be more than a secretary."

"You will pay me to be a companion, then?"

"In a manner of speaking." As she watched, his features took on the familiar, granite resoluteness. "Tell me, if you would, why you think you would make a poor mistress."

The question caused Isobel to choke on her wine. "Really, my lord. That is a highly improper question."

"Thus far, this is a highly improper arrangement. And you were the one who brought up the subject earlier."

It was, and she had. "Very well, then. I've no talent at toadying, my lord, nor at deception."

"*Mmm.* Helpful traits in a ladybird, to be sure. Is that all?"

"You seem to know I've neither the face nor form for such a position."

"True, I have not seen your face, but you seem to have all the requisite curves in the right places."

"How . . . ?" She felt herself blushing as she remembered their first contact. "Why are you doing this, my lord? Sporting with me."

"Interesting choice of words." Across the table, Oriel tapped his fingers in a slow rhythm on the tablecloth. His face was impassive, unreadable. "I am merely trying to ascertain just what you believe yourself capable of. Honesty, of course, and loyalty. Emotion and affection. Pride. Yes, there is a certain proud arrogance to you." He leaned forward. "What of vengeance, Isobel?"

"What?"

"Vengeance. If someone did you ill, would you strike back?"

"Nay." She thought of Maggie, of Tessa. "But I'd strike hard against anyone who harmed those I love."

He eased back in his chair, eyes sharp now, and said, "Marry me, Isobel."

The silence stretched longer than the table, long enough to make Nathan think she had not heard him, or did not believe what she had heard. "It is a serious proposal. I am asking you to marry me."

"*Dia s' Muire,* you've gone daft!"

It was not quite the response Nathan had expected, and it certainly was not what he would have chosen, but he was not really surprised. The possibility had occurred to him more than once in the last hours that he had, in fact, gone a bit daft. He considered validating her assertion but opted instead for cool assurance. "Not at all. Do you think only madness could prompt such an offer?"

"Aye, that or a very poor understanding of what an employer should be about."

"I'm about seeing to my needs, Isobel. And, though you might not believe me, yours as well."

"You don't know me well enough . . ."

"Well enough to what? To marry you, or to know what you need?"

"Oh—either!"

He could almost feel her agitation across the length of the table and it heartened him. It was the latter of the two possibilities that bothered her most: the concept that maybe, just maybe, he had an idea of what she needed.

"I know enough of both, I think. You will give me fealty." He raised his hand before she could say anything. "You cannot help it, not with your nature and certainly not with your family's future at stake. I am perfectly confident on that matter, so you need not waste your time arguing just for the sake of spiting me."

Her indignant hiss told him she had been prepared to do just that. He fought a smile as he continued. "Your intelligence will be invaluable as well. In fact, it was that which set me on this path to begin with." Not precisely true. Her attention to his bleeding hand had done as much, but that was not something he could tell her. "And I can provide what you need."

"What might that be, if I may be so bold as to inquire?"

Ah, she was piqued now. And frightened.

"I can give you my name, Isobel, and the title and wealth that come with it."

"*That* is what you think I need? 'Tisn't merely daft you are, Lord Oriel. 'Tis positively deluded if you think I see life in such terms." She shoved away from the table then, sending her chair thudding backward. "I'll not sit for another minute of this!"

Nathan waited until she had reached the door. "Think of Tessa."

It was low of him, he knew, but expedient.

It certainly stopped her in her tracks. "What do you know of Tessa?"

"Your father is a garrulous man. I hardly need to tell you that."

"What are you telling me, then? That you'll see my sister done ill if I refuse your . . . I cannot even call it a proposal!"

"It *is* a proposal, Isobel. A perfectly honorable one. And no, I would never be so callous as to harm the girl. On the contrary. I'm prepared to see to her future well-being. Margaret's as well."

She said nothing. Taking advantage of her silence, he pressed, "You'd do well to think about it. Will you be content to live out your life as a spinster in a small Hertfordshire village? Something tells me you want more than to wither like a rose left on the vine. You are un-likely to receive another offer of marriage. Certainly not one from a man able to give you what I can. You are twenty-five. Young, perhaps, in the scope of the world, but on the shelf as far as marriage is concerned. You are fiery of temper, too, and—"

"Plain. You may say it, my lord. 'Tis no secret." Head spinning, Isobel gripped at the door frame as if every ounce of her equilibrium depended on its support. "I might well not be a young man's dream bride, but 'tis the right of even a plain woman to refuse an offer from—"

"A man unwhole in body and mind? You may say it, Isobel. But I think we both know I am not truly unsound of mind. No, I am entirely sane and, I think, wiser than you."

"A wisdom that escapes me," she shot back.

"Yes, I am beginning to see that."

He was so calm. Even the trail of soup spots trailing down his lapel could not detract from the fact that he was every bit the lord of the manor. Nervous, he said. Aye nervous as a lion with a mouse beneath its paw, Isobel thought. His confidence set her teeth on edge. "I do not have to stay here," she managed.

"Yes, actually, you do. But I will certainly release you to the dubious safety of your chambers for now." She was halfway out the door when he added, "You will attend me in the library at nine tomorrow morning, Miss MacLeod. Your father left something of a mess."

Aye, he had indeed. "We are done with it, then? This marriage nonsense?"

His laugh did nothing to soothe either her turmoil or her frayed temper. "Not at all. I had to ask. And I will keep asking."

"I will keep refusing."

"That, of course, is your prerogative. I am a reasonably patient man. But hear me well: I intend to have you, Isobel MacLeod, and I do not necessarily play fair at getting what I want."

Shaken and speechless, Isobel fled the room.

* * *

She'd had scant sleep and restless dreams.

Breakfast the next morning did nothing to improve Isobel's spirits. The debris scattered at Lord Oriel's place told her he had already eaten. After a few bites of the porridge Milch all but tossed in front of her, Isobel, feeling vaguely nauseated, made her way toward the library. For the thousandth time since she had fled the dining room and Lord Oriel's crazed proposal the night before, his words played through her mind.

Think of Tessa.

I can provide what you need.

You want more than to wither like a rose left on the vine.

Of all he said, that had struck deepest. He could not have known, couldn't possibly have known how many times, as she tended the pitiful gardens she coaxed into whatever patch of earth their residence afforded, she had likened herself to the plants beneath her hands. Tough, resilient, but easily bruised. And the only certainty being that of eventually withering.

Now, as she crossed the hall, she did something she seldom allowed herself. She stopped in front of a tarnished mirror and took a long look. It was simply her face: pale, the nose a trifle too broad and dusted with freckles, the mouth a fraction too wide above the gently rounded chin. Her eyes, too, missed the elusive edge of beauty even though she knew they were her best feature: wide-spaced, slightly tilted, and vivid green beneath hair so bright that it rivaled new-wrought copper.

There was nothing subtle about her appearance, nothing delicate, and certainly nothing that would seem anything but a mockery of the various portraits stretching along the walls. Nay, she had no place among the marchionesses there, nor did Lord Oriel have call to thumb his very patrician nose at his ancestors by placing her among them.

How easy it was, reducing the matter to something so simple as a portrait. If only she had better reason for refusing, or any heartfelt reason at all to accept. For all her years of dreaming, this was not a path she could ever have imagined. Nor could she imagine taking it now.

A night spent tossing in the elegant bed had left her with the conclusion that Lord Oriel was not mad. In fact, at the most superficial level, his plan made perfect sense. Of course he would want to return to Society, and he certainly could not manage on his own, not if he wanted his blindness to remain a secret.

In Society, where being seen was more important than seeing, with a supporting arm to help him avoid obstacles and a soft voice to prompt him, he would manage perfectly well indeed.

The question was why he would consider tying himself to an arm and voice so far beneath what would be expected of him. Surely there was a lady in his social sphere who could be trusted with the secret of his blindness, perhaps even one who would be able to convince him that secrecy was unnecessary. After all, vision was the sense best deceived.

Isobel's own eyes were clear enough. She found no pleasure in viewing her face, less still in seeing the outmoded, faded blue gown whose tight bodice succeeded only in pressing her full breasts into unattractive and uncomfortable slopes. Sighing, she drew her mended shawl closer about her shoulders despite the fact that there was no one to see.

She had written countless scenes in her mind, changing and rearranging her words so she would be able to greet the marquess with some grace. Of course, all these thoughts fled when she reached the library door. She cursed silently, swallowed, and knocked.

There was no answer. She rapped again, then hesitantly entered, inexplicably relieved at finding the room empty. In the absence of its owner, the place seemed altogether different. Perhaps it was due to nothing more than the fact that the draperies were drawn fully back, allowing the morning sunlight to flood in. In another time, another place, she would have been delighted by the scene. The countless leather-bound books alone would have enchanted her.

As it was, her eyes flitted briefly over the very male, very expensive furnishings and seemingly endless, book-lined shelves before they were drawn to the massive desk. Rather than being cleared, as she had seen it the day before, the surface was now covered by ledgers. Atop them was a single sheet of paper. Still uncertain of the proper move, she crossed the thick carpet and took a quick peek. A single word was scrawled diagonally across the foolscap, written in a bold scrawl and liberally dotted with smeared ink: *Read.*

It was a command she could not possibly misunderstand. Opening the topmost ledger, she realized that Lord Oriel had left her the estate books for several years past. Sensible, she thought, and perhaps even courteous. Instead of being thrown into this part of her duties with no preparation, she would have the chance to familiarize herself with the basic running of the place.

With only the faintest of misgivings, she settled herself behind the desk. There was a chance the marquess would object to her use of his chair, of course, but she was certain she would hear his approach in enough time to move. He was most likely tearing through the fields on his monster horse and might well be gone for some time.

She opted first to skim, rather than read, each book. The entries were made in several hands, including one she recognized immediately as her father's. It was shaky in spots, and Isobel shook her head resignedly at the sight. It seemed Jamie had had no compunction against dipping into the crystal decanters across the room. He would have noted soon enough that his employer did not make a regular check of either the liquor supply or the books. Of course, he would have been completely fooled as to the reason why.

Isobel allowed herself a single sigh. At least it appeared her father had limited his sticky fingers to the decanters and his single attempt at petty thievery. There seemed to be nothing amiss with the records. It was a small blessing, perhaps, but a welcome one.

Interspersed infrequently among other hands was one she now knew belonged to the marquess. Cleaner then, but just as bold, it spoke of confidence, arrogance, and the best education money could buy. It stopped appearing altogether a year before. That must have been when he had gone off to the Peninsula, she decided, and felt a stab of pity. Whatever had happened there had taken the very control of his property from him. What a blow that must have been.

Isobel resolutely pushed all soft thoughts aside and turned to business. Yes, she would read. And she would learn. Whether she wanted it or not, she had a job to do, and she would do it better than any before her. She would not have it any other way.

Fifteen feet above, hidden in the shadowed recesses of a balcony alcove, Nathan sat still and patient. He could not explain, even to himself, why he was there. He had relegated himself to quiet discomfort, perhaps for hours, but he had been unable to resist the impulse.

Some twenty minutes into her reading, Isobel had begun humming. Nathan wondered if she was even aware she was doing it. It was, to his ears, a lovely sound, soft and lilting, but not a tune he recognized. And it seemed to change with each quiet slide of a new ledger. It was quick and airy, then low and melancholy, as if she were setting the estate's past years to music.

After perhaps an hour, he heard her rise and move through the library, most likely relieving cramped muscles. In those minutes, she stopped humming and sang instead. Nathan could not help smiling at her choice of songs. It was lively and undeniably bawdy, telling of a Highland lass whose love of morning dips in a secluded loch afforded the local men with the best of entertainment.

This was a side of Isobel MacLeod that Nathan had not expected, and it charmed him completely.

Well, there was no doubt about it now. He would bind her to him in any way possible. Somehow, in a brief two days, she had changed his future beyond imagining. A brief two days, and he could not imagine her gone.

He would go to London on Gerard's foolish errand, but even when that was over, he would have Isobel. As she returned to the desk and began humming again, he leaned back, more at peace than he could remember being in a very long time. She would read to him in that fluid voice, and sing. Music was a pleasure he had forgone, one whose return was poignantly sweet.

But there was more. Turning to face the sun-brightened room again, he smiled. It was not something he planned to tell Isobel just yet, but he got an even more stirring pleasure from seeing the fiery glory of her hair.

Oh, his eyes were useless, at least as far as the basic tasks of living were concerned. But in strong light he could perceive faint shapes and color. With the sunlight coming through the window, he could see the red of Isobel's hair. The rest of her was hazy, except in his imagination. But it didn't matter how little he could actually see. That fire was enough.

When he had awakened in the Portuguese field hospital, he had kept his near-total blindness to himself in the desperate hope that it was temporary. Later, only slightly improved and home in England, he had cursed the incompleteness of his ruin. He had been convinced there was nothing so cruel as to be taunted by the colors and faint shapes of life without being able to move easily among them.

Accepting the loss of sight as penance for Rievaulx's death had been simple enough. Living with that cross had been all but soul-crushing. Now, for the first time, Nathan gloried in what little sight had been left to him.

In all his thirty-two years, he had never thought anything as beautiful as the wavering, indistinct, sunlit halo of Isobel's hair.

CHAPTER 7

Wi' lightsome heart I pu'd a rose,
Fu' sweet upon its thorny tree!
And my fause luver staw my rose—
But ah! he left the thorn wi' me.
—Robert Burns

Isobel was used to sermons. Reverend Biggs on Skye had possessed a set of lungs worthy of competing with the famed MacCrimmon bagpipes. And the good reverend had been vastly pleased with the resonant sound of his voice, especially when he had a helpless target trapped in the pews below. The MacLeod brothers had once engendered a tirade so loud and eloquent that no doubt people would be talking of it for years to come.

Aye, Isobel thought, she was used to sermons, but seldom two in one day. The first, a fiery speech from the Reverend Mister Clarke of Lord Oriel's parish, had ended an hour ago. That diatribe against fallen women was now being continued by Frank Patton, a truly incongruous source for spiritual guidance.

"Luscious food for thought, ain't it?" the squire's elder son was asking, leaning down in the saddle to leer in her face. He was wearing the same coat he had been wearing the night Rob had deprived him of two pounds, and still resembled a great, green fig. "Daughters of Eve, one after the other, skipping merrily along their path. Can't help it, not a one of you."

Behind him, his brother Charles chuckled. "Ah, but

you forget the matter of guidance, man. With the proper male hand . . ."

Isobel and Maggie had been strolling from church, talking peacefully, when the Pattons had all but run them down in the road. The sisters had been liberally sprayed with dirt, and Isobel now made an exaggerated show of shaking it from her skirts. The motion disturbed the Pattons' horses enough that, for a moment, the brothers were forced to turn their attention from baiting her.

"Isobel." Maggie tugged at her arm. "Let's go."

Frank, having quickly warmed to his subject, blocked the path again before they went more than a few feet. "In such a hurry. And we haven't even gotten to important matters."

Isobel's neck ached from having kept her chin rigidly aloft during Reverend Clarke's sermon. Now, she raised it another notch and tried to walk around the horse. Charles immediately rode forward so she and Maggie were effectively boxed in.

"Yes. You see, we have a question, Miss MacLeod." He grinned broadly, displaying mossy teeth. It was not an attractive sight. When Isobel made no response, he simply shrugged. "Since it appears Oriel has let you out of his sight, what do you say to giving us a firsthand view of fallen virtue?"

"We have two pairs of the best guiding hands," his brother chimed in, aiming one of those hands at Isobel's bodice.

She jerked away, her own hands fisted at her sides. "Why, you clod-pated, foul-minded worm! I'd sooner lie with the devil!"

"Izzy." Maggie's hand moved to her shoulder in warning.

"Some say you have already," Charles jeered. "Why, you heard it yourself. Kind of Reverend Clarke not to call you by name, don't you think? Come now, Isobel, the entire village knows what's been going on up at the Hall these past days. We've a mind to see just what has Oriel so fascinated that he hasn't let you out of his sight until today. We'd even be willing to give you a coin or two, of course. More if you prove worthy of it."

Isobel cursed the heat she knew was coloring her face. Shaking now, and past clear thought, she let loose with a string of vivid oaths.

The brothers, clearly unimpressed by the Gaelic, merely laughed. "Spirit counts somewhat," Frank mocked, "though I daresay your mouth is far better used at other occupations."

"You will die and rot before you'll ever get more of me than curses," she shot back. Then, drawing a steadying breath, she muttered, "Come along, Maggie, before I lose my chance at heaven by going to violence." Tugging her now-sputtering sister behind her, she deliberately pushed past Frank's horse.

"Well, Charlie, I'd say Miss MacLeod means to turn us off." Frank gave a mocking tilt of his hat. "I daresay she won't be so grand next time." The pair rode in front of them again. "You might want to rethink your Sundays, Isobel. The Church of England is hardly a place for a Scottish whore."

There was another spray of dirt as they charged off.

Isobel stood, frozen in shock and fury. Her sister gently grasped her hand. "Pay them no mind, darling. They haven't half a brain between them, nor the morals of a pig."

"Nay, they haven't. But you cannot say that of the entire village, Maggie. The good folk there have made their opinion clear enough."

And they had.

Perhaps no one had said anything close to what the Pattons did, and perhaps some looks had been more curious than condemning, but there had been much whispering behind hands and long stares. There had been, too, unstifled repetitions of the various ghastly names by which the marquess was known in the village.

Reverend Clarke's sermon had been fuel for an already flaring fire. Taken haphazardly from Genesis and Luke, it had roved from the digressions of Eve to the penitence of Mary Magdalene. And the reverend's eyes had focused on Isobel through it all. By the time the service was over, she felt as if her skin was burning—or branded. Even her sister's loving presence had done little to diminish the sharp pain.

"I should have expected it, Maggie, should have known it would come about so."

"Rubbish! How could you, when you expect only the best of everyone?"

Isobel managed a sad smile. " 'Tis yourself you're thinking of, love. I hope for the best of folk, but expect the very worst. Of the boys, of Papa, of Lord Oriel. Aye, I should have known this would be the way of things."

"Izzy . . ." Maggie took a deep breath. "You said the marquess keeps mostly to himself. He truly hasn't asked anything . . . unseemly of you?"

"Truly."

But he has asked me to wed him. Six times. Once for each supper we've had together. Other than that, he is brusque, polite, and has me all but sure the earth is flat.

As much as it troubled her, Isobel could not tell her sister about the proposal. Not yet. Perhaps she would be able to tell the whole tale when this grim chapter of their life was past and they had moved on to wherever the wind took them.

"The fact that he hasn't touched me counts for naught now," she said wearily. "People see only what they wish to. They see I've been living under his roof and hence see a blemish large as the Hall on my reputation."

"Oh, Izzy."

" 'Tis all right, Maggie Líl. I daresay I'll survive."

"But it grieves me to see you hurt."

"I know it does." Isobel turned and rested her forehead against her sister's. They had had so little time together, just these fast-fleeing hours out of an entire seven days. " 'Tisn't real pain I'm feeling. I'll need some time to think on the matter before I know just what it is."

She forced herself to speak lightly, knowing even as she spoke that there would be no fooling Maggie. "I'll tell you what grieves me, lass—that rag you're wearing, and knowing it's your best."

Maggie's beautiful face hardened for a moment, and Isobel could see fierce love and understanding warring in the green eyes. Understanding won out, for Maggie gazed down at the moss gray muslin that had once been green and shrugged. " 'Tis clean, has no holes, and will do well enough 'til autumn. I'm thinking of buying some fabric for Tessa, though, with the money you've given me. She grows like a weed."

"Aye, and always seems just as green. Best buy black cloth to hide the grass stains." Isobel managed a smile and said firmly, "Choose something for yourself. You deserve it."

"I've all but decided on some new dishes," Maggie replied after a moment with far more resignation than enthusiasm, "and Thomas's has some lovely blue glass jars. The color will keep my herbs fresher."

Isobel rolled her eyes. "God forbid you take a fancy to blue silk."

"What use would I have for silk?"

"Of course. 'Twould only be gilding the lily. Och, Maggie. Go and buy your glass, then, if it makes you happy, and Tessa will have her dress." A new thought, bleak and sharp, flashed into her mind. "The merchants, they're not spurning you because of me?"

"Oh . . . nay. They're not."

"I heard that pause, Mairghread Líl. Out with it."

Maggie sighed and stared down at her work-roughened hands. "There was a bit of a to-do Thursday at the tailor's. Geordie wanted a new pair of breeches, and Mallon wouldn't see to it. But then, he's had bad enough luck with the boys. I'd say likely as not it has nothing to do with you."

"You're still not telling me something."

"Oh, Izzy. 'Tis nothing, really. Let it go."

"I'll do no such thing."

"You will." Maggie's soft voice held a thread of steel. "I'll see to the garden now. There's no need to be buying from the Kendalls what we can grow on our own."

So the righteous Mrs. Kendall was casting stones, was she? Even as she reminded herself that revenge was far more bitter than sweet, Isobel tried to recall if her grandmother had a spell for the evil eye. It was no use. Like Maggie, the woman had been more for healing than cursing.

"May her beans rot on the vine," Isobel muttered with some small satisfaction.

"Everything comes full circle eventually," Maggie said gently. "And we'll be due some comfort."

They walked on, Maggie's hand tight around Isobel's.

It was hard keeping silent, harder still for Isobel to say good-bye when it came time to part. So she gave her sister a hard, quick embrace, then turned and hurried up the drive to the Hall.

Unwilling to face the confines of the house, she headed instead for the rear gardens. There was solitude to be found even in the midst of the grand entry hall, but there was peace in the garden. She had discovered the roses several days before, and even their sorry state, overgrown with weeds, had done little to stifle the glorious burst of pleasure. Isobel loved plants, roses most of all. So it was only natural that she would seek their solace now.

Perhaps, had Maggie not been with her, Isobel would have been less pained by the morning's events. Naively, she had never thought her position with Lord Oriel would become a matter of public speculation. But of course it had, and her family was feeling the brunt of the scorn. Maggie, beautiful, kind Maggie, deserved only adulation. Tessa, even though she was, at times, insolent and a nuisance, deserved the brightest of futures. Instead, they had been saddled with a careless, selfish father and brothers, and now, a sister who had all but been publicly labeled a whore.

If she was to be objective, Isobel had to concede that the village had no way of knowing the truth about her presence in Lord Oriel's home. That, in itself, was a blessing of sorts. Everyone knew Jamie MacLeod to be habitually both a drunk and a fool. Matters would be far worse if it was also known that he was a thief.

Nor did anyone know of the marquess's blindness—or the fact that he treated her as he would any employee during the day, polite and distant, only to repeat his outrageous proposal each night.

Aye, if she was to be objective, she might forgive the villagers' cruelty. But the town knew her, knew her morals and pride. And at least a handful of Oriel's tenants knew something noteworthy of him, too. In reading the journals, Isobel had found something consistent, and so surprising that she had at first doubted the ink before her eyes.

Lord Oriel was—or at least had been—a man whose generosity should stand as an example to all. His tenants' rents had not been raised in years and had even been reduced on a scattering of occasions. In one case, a tenant did not pay at all. Maude Kendall had not paid rent on either her cottage or land in five years. She had an invalid husband and six young children. The marquess, it seemed, had known that.

This was the man about whom the village now whispered. The fact that he had become a recluse since returning from the war apparently gave ignorant minds leave to fear him. These people knew *nothing*, nothing but the glee of flapping tongues, now lashing at Isobel as well.

Weak-kneed, she sank onto one of the stone benches set against the garden wall. It was a sunny spot, away from the trellises and statues, with the warmth she needed. A tendril, bare but for thorns, snagged at her skirts, and she brushed it away. The rosebushes to each side of the bench had gone so long without care that their canes reached to curve over the stone.

Above on the wall, tendrils had crossed and twined about each other. Without blossoms, it was difficult to tell where one ended and the other began. The plants would not bloom for at least another month, but Isobel had a very good idea how they would appear when they did. She knew roses, and these were recognizable, even in their bareness.

She closed her eyes tightly, fighting the tears her pride had held back thus far, and tried to imagine the red and ivory blossoms that would come with summer.

Nathan found her there some time later. He had wandered through the house, book of poetry in hand, growing increasingly frustrated with each empty room he entered. He had given Isobel the morning to herself and had been impatient in his own company from the moment she stepped out the door. Odd, he thought, how quickly solitude grew undesirable.

He knew she was mystified by his cool, businesslike demeanor during the days and his single repeated proposal each night. In truth, he was doing no more than what prudence dictated. Gerard would wait; London would wait. Nathan's patience was stretched to the point of shattering, but he too would wait. No matter what it took.

Being close to Isobel, leaning in to hear every word she spoke, whether estate details or stammered rejection, was proving harder than expected. He'd had her reading Burns aloud the day before. Listening to her soft burr flowing over poetry was torture even as it was incomparably sweet.

Something more instinctive than logical had him quitting the house to navigate the uneven steps and overgrown paths of the gardens. It seemed right, somehow, that he would find Isobel waiting for him in his ruined Eden.

He found her in what had been his mother's quiet haven and his grandmother's before. He could just make out her bright curls as she rose to her feet and could not help wishing he'd been quieter in his approach. But when not in the familiar confines of the house, he moved with all the stealth of a drunken bull.

"M-my lord. I meant to have returned to the house before now. Did you have need of me?"

Her voice, with its velvety roughness, was shaky. Nathan, already attuned to his own dour mood and familiar enough with Isobel in a nervous state, knew this was something different. "You are unwell." It was not a question. He was certain of her distress, and equally certain she would deny it.

"Nay, I am fine."

He wanted to snap at her, to tell her how futile it was for her to try to lie. Instead, he pressed, "Your family is well?"

"My family is . . . fine. Truly, my lord, I am but drowsy from my time in the sun. Forgive me."

Nathan fought off the childish urge to glower at her. She was hardly likely to spill her woes simply to make him more comfortable. "Sit down, then. I don't want you drowsily falling off your feet."

She complied. Wishing he could sit and remove his weight from his cursed leg, Nathan tried to remember how long the bench was. Not long enough for him to share in comfort with this particular woman. He moved instead to the right of it, thinking to lean against the wall.

"How was the service?"

There was a distinct pause before she replied. "Illuminating."

Now there was hurt in her voice. Nathan had, in a sudden flash of bitter insight, a very good idea of what had put it there. He cursed himself for not thinking to warn her. "A village of fools," he muttered. "Damn them!"

"For what?"

"For subjecting you to whatever cruelty you experienced today."

"I do not know what you mean."

"Oh, for God's sake, Isobel! Don't bother. I am neither deaf nor stupid. I can hear the hurt and shame in your voice."

She gasped at that. "There's no shame, my lord! No one can shame me but myself."

His own temper drained away. "True. It was a poor choice of words." He fumbled with his cane as he tried to prop it against the wall. As expected, she was there in an instant to help. "Thank you. You are afraid your family will suffer."

This time, she let out her breath in an exasperated huff. " 'Tis a sorry thing when I cannot keep my business even from a blind man!"

"I have made it my business as well."

"Aye, and unasked. My life is my own to manage."

He felt his mouth curving wryly. "Damnation one way, hell the other."

"I beg your pardon?"

"Ignorant minds and vicious tongues will condemn you if you choose to leave matters as they are," he said. "Your alternative is marriage to a creature of darkness."

It was the first time he had mentioned the matter in daylight, and he cursed his loose tongue. It had seemed to make so much sense that if he asked her in her own darkness as well as his, she might someday accept.

" 'Tisn't so simple, my lord, nor so bleak."

"No? Are you a woman of epiphanies, Isobel?"

It seemed her temper had waned, too, for she gave a strained laugh. "Nothing so dramatic. But I have been thinking. You have offered six times, my lord. 'Tis time, I believe, to—oh!"

Nathan had tried to be smooth, first in dealing with the cane and now in leaning his arm against the wall. He had forgotten the roses.

A palmful of thorns caused him to draw his hand back and lose balance. Furious, resigned, he threw out one arm, and it came to land, hard, over Isobel's shoulder. She must have sprung from her seat to help him, for she was now supporting his weight, chest to chest. *Dear God* was his only coherent thought as her arms closed around him.

The sensation of Oriel's body against hers struck Isobel with the force of a summer storm. It had been instinctive, the leap to arrest his forward fall. He was still standing, or rather he was leaning against her. And she could feel every connected inch humming like a plucked bow.

Her hands trembled as she held him, and she was almost certain there was a tremor in the hand he had tight at her waist. She felt his breath at her temple, was certain she could feel his heartbeat through the warm silk of his waistcoat. Breathless, her heart pounding in her ears, she waited, with no idea what she was waiting for.

It seemed an eternity before he spoke, and when

he did, his voice resonated through her. "What did you say?"

"What? I said nothing, my lord." Her wits scattered, she tried to pull away. His arm only tightened. "C-can you stand on your own now?"

"Probably. You did say something, Isobel. That you have been thinking."

"Only that I do not . . . that I . . ." It was no use. She had to sit. So she slid downward from his embrace before he could tighten it further. "What I said was that I've been thinking on your proposal."

"And?"

He seemed steady enough. As a mountain, really. Isobel gazed up at him, past the unyielding jaw and aristocratic nose to the sharp, gold eyes that did not see. "Will you truly keep asking if I keep refusing?"

"I will."

"Why?"

"We've been through this, haven't we? Would it help if I was to spin a romantic tale for you?"

"Nay, of course not. But to keep at it . . ."

Her first impulse was to jerk away when he slowly lowered himself to sit beside her on the small bench. Something stronger than will, however, held her still, had her arm settling as if by its own volition next to his.

"No one has refused me before."

The words were spoken without arrogance. Isobel tilted her head, wondering if it really could have been resignation she had heard. "You've done this before, then?"

"Oh, yes." The laugh stuck in Nathan's throat. He had hoped, desperately hoped, her words would take a different path. "Twice."

"You've been married?"

"No. Neither betrothal made it that far." He did not want to explain but could not seem to stop the words. "I went off to the Peninsula with a fiancée. I sent home assurances of my survival from the field hospital. The return message was that she had changed her mind. She married another man a month later." Familiar bitterness swelled in his chest, but it was nothing compared to the sadness that swiftly engulfed it. "Before that was . . ." The pain had dimmed with the years, but still struck with enough force to make him close his eyes. "Anne. She died."

Isobel's hand slipped over his. He doubted she was even aware of the gesture. "Oh, I am sorry," she said.

"It was nearly ten years ago."

"We lose loved ones, my lord, not the love."

How simple it seemed, her quiet assertion. Yes, he had lost loved ones. Too many of them.

"The past does not concern me." *Liar.* "And I cannot seem to see into my future." He steeled himself, tried not to hope again. "What can you tell me of it, Isobel MacLeod?"

Her sigh settled like the breeze. "Tell me of the roses first."

"The roses?"

"Aye, the pair behind us. What do you know of them?"

He frowned. "My grandmother planted them, I believe. One red, one white."

"Why did she plant them here, away from the rest?"

"I have no idea."

"*Mmm.* Can you tell me more?"

"No, I'm afraid I can't."

Restless, Isobel stood and stepped away from the bench. It did not matter that he could not see her. She needed to speak her piece without looking into those disturbing eyes. "Nay, don't get up," she urged when he started to rise. "I'll tell you, about the roses. The red is a Gallica, the other an Alba."

"Alba, as in Scottish?"

She tilted her head back, felt the sun on her face. "As

in 'white,' most likely, as it came with the Romans. But they named Scotland Alba, so perhaps 'tis one and the same."

She envisioned the tendrils behind her. "You might not know, my lord, but they've reached out to each other, entwined. The Gallica is larger. 'Tis older, perhaps, or had a better start. But the Alba is stronger. I can already see where it will flare green. 'Twould be a sorry thing to separate them," she said softly, "when they balance each other so well."

"What are you saying, Isobel?"

She felt it again, that stirring, though he was far enough from her that even if he stretched out his arm, he could not touch her. " 'Tis a wondrous, mystical thing, the rose, each color and small part of it with meaning. A red rose is for sorrow—martyrdom if you follow the Church."

"I would have thought it for love."

"Aye. There is that, but 'tisn't the true province of the red."

"And the white?"

"Innocence," she answered, her voice softer still, "and silence." She turned then, her own gaze clear and direct as she stared into the ravaged, starkly captivating face. "There's my answer, then. Aye."

Something poignant and unfamiliar briefly sparked in his eyes, then was gone. "You are saying you will marry me."

"Aye."

"Be my support and my silence."

"Aye. That, too."

He nodded slowly. "Thank you." Then, after a moment, he asked, "Does it bother you a great deal, the idea of being tied to a blind man?"

"Well, that's an odd question, isn't it? I've just accepted a proposal from one."

"You didn't answer me." He paused, then frowned slightly when she said nothing. "Tell me, then, would you have accepted had I not been blind?"

Isobel was slowly becoming used to his strange twists of thought, but this one made no sense whatsoever. "Had you sight, my lord, you would never have asked."

"If I had?"

She rolled her eyes, knowing he could not see the gesture, and decided nonsense was best answered in kind. "Of course I would have refused you. I would have no use for you with sight, and you'd have none for me."

"Ah. Perhaps not."

Isobel glanced down at her hands and saw they were trembling. "Are we . . . done with this, then?"

"Yes, we're done." As if to prove he was, in fact, finished with the matter, he gestured toward where the Gallica and Alba entwined. "Tell me, Isobel, is there a rose in this garden for hope?"

Relieved to have a question she could answer, Isobel glanced around at the wild tangle. "Hope is in the leaves, my lord. We've but to wait to see what comes with the blooms."

CHAPTER 8

Either Nathan's vision was improving, or the Reverend Mr. Clarke was in danger of expiring on the spot. Nathan was fully convinced it was the latter, and while the bombastic old coot's demise would hardly be cause for sorrow, he would have preferred the former. But no, he could still see only wavering shapes and colors, so his certainty that the reverend's face was a dramatic shade of purple must have been nothing more than imagination. Of course, the pained wheezing which accompanied each line of the ceremony was telling enough.

True, the man was performing what must have been an odious task, joining a church-avoiding nobleman and proclaimed harlot in holy matrimony. The fact that Clarke had been commanded by his bishop, no less, to perform the ceremony immediately must have made it all the more unpalatable. No doubt he would have preferred to see the banns read three Sundays in a row, giving him fodder for some maniacal ranting. But heathen though he might well be, the Marquess of Oriel was a rich man. Rich men did not have to bother with banns. They simply bought special licenses and turned a library desk into a makeshift altar.

". . . if any man can show any just cause, why they

may not lawfully be joined together, let him now speak, or else hereafter forever hold his peace."

The reverend sounded hopeful. Nathan stiffened, waiting for a damning voice. There was a tiny gasp, like an indrawn breath. Margaret, probably. Of all the MacLeods, she was the one who had not been effusive in her well-wishes. Oh, she had said the words, in a soft, Highland voice much like Isobel's, but there had been wariness behind them. He could not blame her for it. MacLeod and his sons had no doubt seen their cup running over with his gold once Isobel married a nobleman. Maggie would have seen her sister sliding into the clutches of a beast.

The silence had all but become deafening by the time Reverend Clarke, obviously resigned to the fact that the wedding would go on, continued with the ceremony. Nathan glanced briefly toward Isobel, still and silent at his side, and knew at that moment he would have given everything he owned to see her face.

Would there be resignation in her eyes? Martyrdom? But no, his was the red Gallica rose. Hers was the white Alba, innocent and silent.

In the three days since she had accepted his proposal, she had not once complained. Not when he had all but dragged her from the garden, making them both stumble in his blind haste, nor when he dictated to her the terse, dispassionate request to the bishop. Not even when she had been forced to send a message to her sister, asking for her mother's wedding band as Nathan had none to give her.

And he knew she would not complain in an hour, when he would bundle her into a carriage, taking her from her family and into the midst of the cool, cliquish ton, where the best sport was had at the expense of others. Where nothing was sacred. Nothing at all.

". . . keep her, in sickness and in health; and forsaking all others, keep thee only unto her, so long as ye both shall live?"

"I will," Nathan answered, knowing without question that he had already gained far more in Isobel than their union could ever cause him to lose.

She answered as before, neither quickly nor with hesitation. If her voice was hardly light with joy, at least it was not laden with misery.

Reverend Clarke gained speed then, as if thinking that since there was nothing to be done to prevent the marriage, he might as well be done with it as soon as possible. It was simple enough, Nathan thought sardonically as he answered, short responses for perhaps the most ponderous questions ever put to man. Perhaps that was the point. Throw death, poverty, and sickness in rapid succession at a less-than-enthusiastic bridegroom, and he might well be out the chapel door before anyone could pronounce a bloody thing.

But he had never been reluctant to marry. How it pained him that he could not say the same of his intended brides.

He repeated the reverend's grunted words and slipped the ring on Isobel's finger. For a moment, her hand was pliant and warm in his, Then, as Clarke spoke again, her fingers clenched and, Nathan was convinced, turned cold.

"With my body," she repeated in turn, then drew an audible breath, "I thee worship."

And that was that. Nathan had a wife. A clever, warm-hearted, sharp-tongued wife, who had vowed before God and her family to give him everything and refuse him nothing. A pang of regret hit him hard and fast, right behind the surge of proud possession. No, she would refuse him nothing, but that certainty paled in the face of another thought: She was not going to come tripping merrily to his bed.

Not that he had expected her to feel any differently. After all, what could he seem to her but an oversize brute, sightless and clumsy? No, he had not expected, but, as had become so common since she entered his life, he had hoped.

Hope is in the leaves, my lord. We've but to wait to see what comes with the blooms.

With his new wife's arm tucked through his, as much in guidance as symbol, Nathan turned away from the makeshift altar.

Isobel tightened her grip on her husband's arm. *Her husband.* She had just pledged heart and soul to a man she scarcely knew, a man whom others believed possessed neither heart nor soul. She darted a glance at his face. It was tense with concentration as he tried to cross the library without leaning either on his cane or her arm.

Although she had only spent ten days in his company, she was already seeing less the ravaged shell and more the bone-deep aristocratic beauty. It was still a stretch to call him handsome, but the promise was there. Some regular and decent meals would fill the hollows below his cheekbones, time in the sun would relieve the pallor, and a pair of shears would tame the wildness of the thick, black hair.

A smile tugged at the corners of her mouth. Married less than five minutes and she was already thinking of ways to improve her husband. No doubt any other marquess would be thinking of ways to make *her* presentable. But, of course, the man she had just married could not see her outdated, worn yellow gown or her scuffed slippers.

There was little she could do with the rest of the package, but she imagined the wardrobe would be simple enough. Not that a few new gowns would make her any more a part of his world. Maggie in silk might well be a gilded lily; she herself would be a cloaked weed. Yet she could not bring herself to be bothered by the fact. There was no doubt she was a wholly unsuitable wife indeed for the Marquess of Oriel, but perhaps she would do well enough for Nathan Paget.

Once she got to know him, of course. In more than a week in his company, she had formed so many conflicting impressions that she could have been in the company of a dozen different men. He was alternately gentle and gruff, even-tempered, then showing flares of fury that frightened her. He was an utter mystery. And he was her husband.

"Congratulations, my lord, my lady."

Isobel started as her father, grinning broadly, popped in front of her. Aye, he was well pleased with this turn of events, too much so. Only her furious resolve had kept him from demanding a settlement from the marquess. It had apparently not occurred to him that a dowry might likewise be expected and that he was already in Oriel's debt.

Jamie was certainly playing the part of the proud papa to the hilt and had clearly begun celebrating early. "Good man!" he bellowed, giving them both a blast of liquor fumes and the marquess a hearty slap on the shoulder. Then, oblivious to his new son-in-law's annoyance, he jerked Isobel into his arms. "Ye're a good lass, ye are, Izzy. You'll be seeing to our future now. Daresay we'll all be cutting quite a swathe through London in weeks to come."

Still absorbing the fact that she was now Lady Oriel, Isobel was not quick enough with a response. Her husband was. "I would suggest you delay any plans to come to Town for the time being, MacLeod."

"Now why would I do that, with a daughter so well settled?"

Isobel felt Oriel's lean muscles cording beneath her hand. Had he been anyone else, she would have silently shushed, soothed. Here, now, she did not dare.

"You will remain here," the marquess replied, his tone all the more unyielding for its very evenness, "because we will not be receiving. And I would not recommend spending money on Town lodgings when you have a comfortable home here—at no expense to yourself."

Jamie did not even have the grace to blush. "I must say, sir, your lack of hospitality is surprising."

Oriel grunted. "I am afraid to say, MacLeod, your continued lack of sense is not." Then, moving his firm but gentle grip to Isobel's elbow, he announced, "We must move along, my dear, if we are to spend any time at our wedding luncheon."

Isobel managed a weak smile for her slack-jawed father as they moved away. "He'll undoubtedly find a reason to come to London regardless of your decree," she said softly, and sighed. "With every confidence of finding you hospitable."

"Is that a warning or an apology?"

"Well, 'tis both, I suppose. I *am* sorry you've seen so much poor behavior from him and so little gratitude. If I can, I will—"

"Isobel." He silenced her. "You will take no more of his transgressions upon your shoulders. Is that clear?"

"But after what he's done—"

"I am in earnest. We are beginning again, you and I, in a sense. What your father has or has not done is of no importance. I will see to your family because I can and because it is my duty as your husband. They shall want for nothing. But I will not tolerate his deliberate idiocy, and you will no longer take responsibility for it. Is that clear?"

"Aye, my lord." Torn between her own gratitude for his easy generosity and an equally strong loathing of being beholden to anyone, she bit her lip and said no more.

"Good. Now, shall we see what delicacies have been prepared for our nuptial feast?"

They remained at the table a very short time. The meal, such as it was, was somewhat less than appetizing, the company tense. Reverend Clarke, not so condemning, it seemed, as to refuse a seat at a marquess's table, muttered into his rubbery trout. The boys, when not gazing in envy at Oriel's blue Weston coat, amused themselves by flicking bits of hard bread at an unusually subdued Tessa. Jamie had dipped again into the wine. And Maggie, her lovely mouth set in a tense line, did no more than pick at her food.

Jamie managed an acceptable if brief toast to the future happiness of his daughter and son-in-law. Rob and Geordie followed with less grace but more enthusiasm, as toasting by nature involved the refilling of glasses. That done, all three subsided into contented drinking.

Isobel did her best to keep a cheerful conversation going, but it would have been a task above even the ton's most experienced hostess. Her husband sat, still and brooding, at her side, eyes fixed sightlessly on the ill-set table. When he abruptly rose to his feet, announcing in no uncertain terms that the meal was over, she joined him with relief.

Her meager baggage had already been loaded into the carriage. She had feared the moment when she would have to leave her family but had managed to hide her dread. Now, with the carriage door open and waiting, and her family standing in a wavering line beside it, she felt her stomach give a painful jolt. The sensation was mirrored on Maggie's face. With a sob, Isobel rushed into her sister's embrace.

"*Och*, Maggie, what will I do without you?"

"The same as I without you. You'll write, and plan for the next time we'll be together."

Isobel drew back, stared into her sister's beloved, beautiful face. "How it grieves, Maggie Líl."

"Aye, it does." Maggie reached up to touch Isobel's cheek gently. *"Dia bhi maille ribh, Iseabail Ròis."* Then she turned to Oriel. Suddenly she looked like an avenging fairy, with her flame-touched hair and flashing green eyes. "I'll say God bless you, too, my lord."

"Thank you, Miss MacLeod."

" 'Tis a blessing that comes with a curse, though. Cause my sister pain, and I'll see that you regret it as long as you live."

"Maggie—" Isobel broke off as her husband's hand curved around her arm.

"I give you my solemn oath, Miss MacLeod, that I will take far more care with your sister's welfare and contentment than my own."

For a moment, Isobel thought Maggie was going to snap at him again. But something in the gold eyes must have satisfied her, for she nodded instead. "Aye, well then, I wish you both happy." She reached out to give Isobel's hand a quick, fierce squeeze. "With all my heart."

Knowing she was close to shattering, and hating the weakness, Isobel embraced her father and other siblings. "I'll miss you," she murmured to a determinedly dry-eyed Tessa. "Don't you dare change a whit 'til I see you next."

Then, without looking back, she allowed her husband to assist her into the carriage. Her resolve lasted only until they reached the stone gates. She leaned out the window, just in time to see Tessa scampering easily up a towering oak where, Isobel knew, she would remain until the coach was out of sight.

Nathan allowed her her silence as long as he could. She would be grieving, he knew, for the family she loved so deeply. He knew, too, that she would rally. Self-pity was simply not in her nature.

"Your sisters are welcome to visit any time," he said at last.

"I'm glad. Thank you."

"In fact, I was thinking Margaret could stay with us next year, have a Season . . ." His voice trailed off; he was unable to think a year ahead.

"I doubt she'll want one," was Isobel's soft reply, "but 'tis kind of you. I'll mention it to her, when next . . ." Her voice, too, trailed away. She was no more able to contemplate the months ahead than he.

As the carriage made a turn in the road, the interior, which had been in shadow, was briefly flooded with bright spring sunlight. Nathan could make out Isobel's form as she sat across from him and thought he could see the faint outline of her left hand against the dark seat. He was reminded of the thin gold band on her third finger. Her mother's ring. Guilt assailed him. The ring was one more shabby link in the twisted chain in which he had snared her.

"Isobel," he said softly, and saw the copper halo shift as she turned to face him. "I am sorry."

"Sorry for what?"

"For, well, for today."

"Good heavens, why?"

"Why? My God, it was your wedding day! You should have had . . ." *What?* The list seemed unimaginably long. "A proper courting, roses, a ring of your own. Instead, you have had a three-day betrothal, a harsh, hurried wedding performed by an unwilling clergyman, and a god-awful banquet."

He was shocked to hear her musical laugh, more still when she reached out to cover his hand with hers. "I never in my life expected to be courted, my lord. We're a month away from roses yet, and I am more than content with my mother's ring. Luncheon was no worse than any I've had at your table and, as for the good reverend . . ." She laughed again. "Well, the MacLeods have never had much luck with the clergy."

Nathan listened for any hint of bitterness or sadness. He found none. Of course she had wanted to be courted. Not by him, certainly, but by someone. She must have, even if only in girlish dreams. He wanted to press, to demand that she not be so *accepting*, damn it, to make her share some of her dreams with him then and there as they rolled their way toward London and into marriage.

Instead, awed anew by her spirit and unable to stop himself, Nathan turned his hand so it met hers, palm to palm. It took more will than he thought he possessed, but he resisted the urge to link his fingers through hers. She did not pull away.

Her hand was so small against his, warmer now than it had been in the chapel, and the slight connection had his own skin heating. "Matters change," he said. "Luck first among them."

"Aye. I've always believed so."

He might have imagined it, the tiny tremor that rippled from her palm to his, imagined, too, the slight breathy catch to her voice. Then she pulled her hand away, a quick slide that had her fingertips skimming across his sensitive palm. Elation fierce as fire swept briefly through him, followed immediately by the cold wash of reality.

Fool, he reproached himself, *to think she might desire . . .*

Better to think of the practical reasons he had married her. She was serious in her tasks and had unquestioningly written the four letters he had dictated to her. The first had been to his London house, to make certain that it would be ready for their arrival. The second had been to Matthew Gerard, informing the man of Nathan's return to Town. The third and fourth had been to the *Times* and his parents. Those had not been sent ahead. He would wait until they were in London before sending out announcements of their marriage. It was a situation for which he needed to be well prepared.

He had to deal with Gerard first. And carefully. Nathan did not want to get the man's hopes too high. He had formed a plan of sorts, one that might very well allow him to move among the ton with no one the wiser about his disability. There was no guarantee, however, that he would ever learn the true circumstances of Dennison's death, or any connection to Gabriel's. As far as he was concerned, the whole matter was only so much coincidence and nonsense.

Isobel had made no comment on his terse letter to his parents, nor his pained hesitation in choosing the words for Gerard. There was so much he could not tell her, but, Nathan thought, she deserved some explanation, at least, something that was perhaps a warning.

"Isobel, we must talk about my . . . responsibilities in Town."

"Of course."

"There will be social engagements, invitations to answer. We will decide together which to accept."

She made a small sound of distress. "But I know so little of Society."

"The rules are simple." He smiled humorlessly, reluctant to so much as taint her warm, forthright nature with the absurd games of the ton. "Title and wealth are all that matter when it comes to being accepted. You now have both, and grander than most. All you need to remember when among Society is to never show fear, never trust, and never be honest."

"Really, my lord!"

"Yes, I know. But you are already a worthy hand at the first. You will master the others soon enough." He shrugged. "Even if you cannot lie, and I do have my doubts as to your abilities there, you will be fine. As long as you speak your mind with great pride, none will slight you."

"I am not—" He heard her sigh. "Nay, I *am* proud.

'Tis a strength and failing at the same time. But I like to think I am never proud at the expense of others."

"Ah, Isobel. I cannot imagine you doing anything at the expense of others." It was one of her glories. "My mother will, no doubt, take it upon herself to turn you into some sort of stiff, infernally dull paragon. Your job is to prevent her from doing anything of the sort."

He heard an agitated rustling of skirts. "I am afraid your mother will find me somewhat lacking."

"Only at first. You are who you are, Isobel. Only the worst of fools could ever find you wanting in anything." Of course, he mused grimly, the ton was comprised of the worst fools the world had to offer. "Now, if I may, I would like to talk of other matters—of what I will require from you."

"Aye?"

He had thought it all through. There were chinks in the plan, to be sure, but he was armed with something in which he was willing to place all his trust: his new wife. "I will ask you to take notes for me at times and to read them back. They will seem odd to you, as will various items of correspondence you will read. I will explain what I can, no more, and you will not ask."

He paused at his own arrogance. "You have come to expect officious statements like that one from me, no doubt. There will be more. I . . . no, I have no excuses to make. Trust me when I say I make my choices with fore-thought and reason. Now, let me explain how I think we will best manage life in Town . . . ."

It was slow going, in a heavy coach with frequent stops to change teams. By the time they reached the city, it was dark. Isobel, her head spinning from hours of detailed instructions and her body stiff and weary from the long ride, still could not suppress her awe at the spectacle of London.

Despite the hour, the streets were teeming with vehicles and people. She caught glimpses of elegant couples, garbed in rich fabrics, heading to or from glittering soirees. There were soldiers, sailors, gaudily dressed women who she imagined were prostitutes, and rag-clad creatures who, she thought sadly, were the city's lost souls.

Whirling thoughts and stiff joints forgotten, she pressed her nose to the coach window and kept it there, determined not to miss a thing. Under the dancing flames of the streetlights, London had the flickering aura of a dream scene—unformed and foretelling something larger than life. She was slightly frightened and completely entranced.

Eventually, the coach made a series of turns through more quiet streets lined with large, ornate townhouses. This was where she would live. She, a country girl raised in sea air and heather, with a knowledge of city life built only on those fleeting months in Edinburgh and Manchester, would live here.

The carriage turned another corner onto a park and rolled to a stop in front of an elegant brick house. The front door flew open almost immediately, and light flooded onto the cobblestones. Within moments, footmen were surrounding the carriage. Isobel could see more servants through the open door.

Before she could comment on this notable change from the solitude of the Hall, Nathan was descending to the street. His stick skittered against a stone, and she could see him fighting for balance. She reached out instinctively to steady him, but it proved unnecessary. He stood straight and turned, strain and concentration etched into his face. He offered her his hand as she had leapt to offer hers.

Mutely, she allowed him to lead her up the stairs and into the foyer. Not once did he falter, and his gaze swept from side to side as if assessing the state of the home he had not occupied in more than a year. It was an impressive show. The Marquess of Oriel had returned to Town.

"My lord. Welcome home."

Isobel blinked at the figure before them. The attire was that of a butler, but the countenance was that of a rotund elf. The man stood no higher than her own shoulder, had a beaming, moonlike face, and a fringe of white hair that looked no more substantial than a Highland mist.

"Thank you, Milch," her husband replied. "It is good to be here."

Milch? Certain he had made a mistake, Isobel waited for the beaming face to stop beaming. It did not.

The small man bobbed cheerfully. "Welcome to Oriel House, my lady. We've been waiting far too long for you to arrive."

While Isobel stood gaping, astonished by the odd, if charming, reception, her husband chuckled. "We made poor time from Hertfordshire, to be sure."

"Roads. Well, I wasn't referring to the wait tonight, my lord, but clear roads are always a blessing."

Oriel nodded at this sage pronouncement, then said to Isobel, "This is Milch, my dear, brother to my estimable Hertfordshire factotum and prince of London butlers. This house would have ceased running decades ago were it not for him. I assume all is in readiness for our occupation, Milch?"

The butler stopped glowing from the compliments just long enough to pout. "As if I'd have it any other way, my lord."

"Good. Now, Isobel, I imagine you are fatigued from our travels. I will have someone show you to your suite and have a supper tray sent up to you."

"I-very well."

She could never have imagined such a reception. Her husband had been all but bantering with his butler, who seemed more like family than a servant. She found it all but impossible to believe he was related to the dour man who plodded through Oriel Hall. This Milch chattered amiably as he guided her up two flights of sweeping stairs.

"The house was built in 1679 by the fifth marquess," he announced, pointing to a portrait of a somber figure with a notably red nose. "Didn't become a duke 'til eighty-four. Folks say he sent the king a barrel of Highland whiskey. Old Jamie Second did love his drink. Now this urn was a gift to his lordship's grandfather from old Marlborough. If you'll look up to the right, you'll see the picture of them drinking claret from it . . . ."

For the first time in a week, Isobel actually thought she might have found herself a new home.

The sitting room and bedchamber were smaller than those she had occupied at the Hall, but just as exquisitely appointed. A pink-cheeked little maid was waiting for her. Though more reserved than Milch, she still managed to fill the silence. She clucked over the long drive and the dusty state of Isobel's single trunk. And, amid the clucking, she got her new mistress in and out of a warm bath, into night garb, and settled in front of a roaring fire with a supper tray.

By that time, Isobel's head was whirling anew. All but certain she had fallen asleep and was now gliding though a bright, colorful dream, she barely resisted the urge to pinch herself. But no, she was awake. The maid's frequent, knowing glances at a door in the bedchamber wall were all too real.

When the maid finally departed, Isobel found her own gaze straying constantly to that door. No doubt it connected her rooms to those occupied by her husband. *Her husband.* He would be there, on the other side of the paneled wood, preparing for . . . Her hands tightened in the folds of her dressing gown. Preparing for . . .

When the knock came, she released her hold on the worn cotton and clenched her hands over her heart, which threatened to leap from her chest as the door slowly swung inward.

CHAPTER 9

Enter these armes, for since thou thoughtst it best,
Not to dreame all my dreame, let's act the rest.
                    —John Donne, "The Dreame"

Nathan could all but feel Isobel beneath him, silken skin and welcoming arms that would twine like vines around him. He could hear her quickened breath, sense the rushing pulse that would pound beneath his fingers as they traced the hollow of her throat, the sensitive expanse of her inner wrist.

Ah, it was a heady dream he had while standing in the doorway between their chambers, and it had not limited its effects to his head. He was well heated, hard as stone, and at an utter loss as to what he was going to do about it.

He could, he knew, enter her chamber with all the arrogance of both lord and husband and demand his marital rights. He did not think she would refuse him. But that was not how he wanted Isobel: reluctant and obligated. No, he wanted her willing and fiery with the passion that blazed so clearly under the surface of everything she did.

Isobel would not be having her own erotic thoughts about him, Nathan knew. He had no doubt she was a virgin. And no doubt the sight of him fell somewhat short of driving her mad with desire. He wondered just how distasteful his appearance was. The wavering, indistinct sight of her, of her pale gown and bright hair glowing in the firelight, was enough to make his tongue go thick in his mouth. But she, with her perfect vision, was most likely considering the possibility of jumping headfirst out the window.

Nathan forced calming air into his tight chest. It did little to cool his body but served to clear his head somewhat. He would sit with her, talk with her a bit. Calm her nervous breathing. Then, if he had to, he would leave her alone.

"G-good evening, my lord," he heard her offer, and watched as she rose to her feet.

"And to you," he replied, thinking how ridiculous their words sounded. Certainly there must have been a greeting more appropriate to her feelings at the moment. *I bid you unwelcome, my lord. Take yourself right back through that door if you would, please, my lord.* "I trust everything is to your liking?" He grimaced at the further inanity even as he added, "I, ah, the chamber is acceptable?"

"Aye. Thank you. 'Tis lovely."

He imagined he could see her hands, pale and clasped together with knuckle-whitening force against the folds of what was quite probably a nightgown. He forced his wandering mind away from the contemplation of precisely what his wife was wearing. Knowing what he did of Isobel, he imagined prim white muslin with a high neck and lots of buttons.

His body leapt in response.

"Ah, God . . . er, *good!* You have only to ask if there is something you need." He floundered again. "I . . ." His hand closed over the door frame. "May I come in?"

There was only the slightest hesitation before she replied, "Of course."

Determined to move slowly, smoothly—although his instinct was to storm forward and drape himself over her—Nathan entered. Isobel stood, framed by the blazing fire in the hearth. Like moth to flame, Nathan thought a bit hazily as he walked toward her. She was drawing him, with her soft scent and her silence, luring him as surely as if she had cast a net.

Slowly, he commanded himself as he strode forward. *Smoothly, damn it!*

He might have succeeded had he been in more familiar surroundings. He rarely had a reason to be in this bedchamber, however, and did not know all the obstacles. The tip of his cane caught on a chair leg. His weight shifted dangerously, and before he could do more than curse, he was falling forward.

He saw a blur of motion, and decided, in the split second, that perhaps a continuously bruised ego due to his clumsiness was not such a terrible thing—especially when compared to being embraced by his wife.

Isobel did not think. She acted. Rushing forward, she managed to get her arms around him before he fell. As remembered, he was heavy enough to make her stagger. As remembered, too, the contact sent the oddest warmth coursing through her.

The first flash was like wildfire, fierce and fast. What followed, as they both went still, was like coals. The end of a fire—or the beginning. It pulsed and warmed, and made her feel far more weak than Oriel's mere weight against her.

She had intended for him to do something to find his own balance again. At least she thought it had been her intent. He did not relinquish his hold on her, however. Instead, he settled one large hand at her hip. And she did not think to object. It was disturbing, this instant response to his touch, deeply unsettling, but she did not find it unpleasant at all.

She lifted her gaze from his loosened cravat to his face and saw something vivid in the depths of his eyes. It was a flash, a light, an emotion trapped, she thought, as a shard of life might be trapped in amber. Her nerves jittered at the sight, and she braced her hands against his chest.

Even through his waistcoat, she could feel the muscles of his torso. They were iron hard and taut. As if by a will of their own, her fingers itched to slide under the silk and linen to find the heat. It was a crazed impulse. Isobel knew in that instant, as her gaze held steady to his, how a doe must feel when cornered by a wolf. She was breathless, her heart pounding madly. She was mesmerized—and terrified.

She could not move, could not even flinch, when he lifted his hand from her waist to cup her jaw. His fingers rested lightly against her cheek, his thumb on the hollow of her throat where she could feel her pulse beating rapidly. His touching her face was, she realized, somehow every bit as intimate as the full press of his body against hers.

His thumb moved from her throat to slide slowly over her lips, tracing the swell and leaving her trembling in its wake. "Isobel?" he murmured.

She did not know what he was asking. Not until he spread both hands over her face. His touch was unbelievably gentle as he explored the contour of her jaw, the arch of her brows. When one fingertip ran downward from the bridge of her nose, she tried to drop her head. It was an instinctive motion, an attempt to hide what she saw as only one of her flaws.

She opened her mouth to tell him to stop, but the words died on her tongue. His hands held her face still. The touch feathered on gently, over her slightly-too-broad nose and rounded chin. His fingertips slid back to her ears, tracing the curve of her lobes. Then, as she gathered the strength to pull away, he thrust both hands into her hair.

Isobel gasped at the tug, again when pins scattered. Freed from its bonds, her hair tumbled down, covering his hands to the wrist and falling heavily over her shoulders. She felt his fingers threading through the thick mass.

The last of the neat knot uncoiled with the persistent tug of her husband's hands to flow halfway down her back. It was a heady sensation, the feeling of his fingers combing gently through the length and, unable to help herself, she sighed with the pleasure of it.

"Like silk," he murmured. His grip tightened again as he lifted a heavy skein to his face. One hand curved around her neck, the other held her hair. Then he whispered something low and harsh, something that sounded like *"Mine."*

She saw his nostrils flare as the honey and chamomile scent of Maggie's soap wafted upward. Then his mouth curved into a faint smile. Suddenly all Isobel could think of was hunter and prey, those slight feral twitches of his face reminding her of how very fierce he could be. Aye, his gentleness had all but melted her, but she could sense it slipping away. Heart lodged in her throat, she edged backward on shaky legs, half expecting him to tighten his grip in her hair as she did and bury his face in her throat.

He let her go. She watched as her hair slid through his fingers to fall over her breasts. And then he was not touching her at all.

Isobel darted a furtive glance around the room. There was nowhere to go. She did not truly understand this need to run from him, nor the faint compulsion to step back into his grasp.

Even as she struggled to speak, to say anything, she heard him murmur, "Thank you."

Of all words, those were not what she had expected. "I-I beg your pardon?" She was still edging away and found herself trapped against the satin-draped mattress.

A new smile flitted across his lips, this one far more

wry than feral. "I said thank you. For allowing me that liberty. It was impertinent, I know, but . . . satisfying. I have been curious."

Of course he had been. In their time together he had never seen her face. He had trusted and married her without ever looking into her eyes. She raised trembling fingers to her warm cheeks. "I would have described myself to you at any time had you asked."

Now he chuckled. "And what would you have said, Isobel, had I asked?"

"I would have told you—"

"You would have told me that you have red hair and green eyes. They are green, are they not?"

"Aye."

"*Mmm.* Yes, your father mentioned that. I suppose, had I pressed, you would have gone on to say that your green eyes are spaced too far apart, that your nose is too broad at the tip, and that your mouth is too wide. Am I correct?"

She felt her jaw go slack. Then, resigned to honesty and to his dismaying perception, she muttered, "Aye, I probably would have said just that."

"And you would not have listened for an instant had I told you it was all nonsense."

"I beg your pardon?"

"Ah, Isobel. The words of a blind man . . . They would have meant nothing to you before, and I shall not distress you with them now." He shrugged. "It hardly matters. I have seen for myself, in my own way."

He bent over and felt about his feet for his fallen cane. Retrieving it, he gestured to the chair on which he had stumbled. "May I sit down?"

For the time being, Isobel set aside her confusion and her undiminished nervousness at his presence in her chamber in favor of propriety. "I am sorry. Of course."

He lowered himself into the delicate chair, dwarfing it

and making the idea that it had all but reached out and felled him completely absurd. After a moment, he said, "I will have to rise again should you choose to remain standing, my dear, and that might prove dangerous for us both." She hurriedly dropped into the facing chair. "Thank you. It might have proven difficult to go on as I wish while standing."

Isobel's throat constricted. She knew enough of what happened between man and wife in the bedchamber. The thought that Oriel might want to do those unfamiliar, intimate things to her was every bit as terrifying as it was reasonable. "Of course. You wish to . . ." Her eyes were drawn unwillingly to the bed. "We are to . . ."

"Talk."

"I . . . what was that?"

Nathan was torn between the urge to laugh and to howl. He could feel the tension vibrating from her, even a good five feet away. "I though we could talk for a bit before bed." He heard her shift nervously in her seat and sighed. "Would it reassure you at all were I to tell you that I have no intention of forcing myself on you tonight?"

"It might."

He had the impression that Isobel was as taken aback by her retort as he was. Despite the awkwardness of the moment—and the persistent throbbing in his groin—he laughed. "You consistently amaze me with your candor. It is a mighty struggle for you—is it not?—the war between honesty and courtesy."

"I am sorry. I did not mean to—"

"Rot. You meant precisely what you said. It is, as I have said before, a great strength of yours."

As always, he wished he could see her face. Or, hold it again in his hands. He imagined her smooth brow was furrowed. Her voice was strained when she said, "You have every right to expect . . . certain things from me, my lord. And I will endeavor to be a proper wife to you."

"You have not disappointed me yet." He was disappointed, certainly, but he could not blame her for it.

"Nay? I am not sure I believe that." He heard her sigh. "This is all very new to me, my lord. And very unsettling. I would ask that you be patient."

"Ah, Isobel." Nathan leaned back in his chair and crossed his legs lest she see precisely how impatient he was. "This is new to me, too. I would ask the same patience from you."

"But our union . . ."

Yes, their union. He could imagine joining himself fully with Isobel, burying himself so deeply within her that he would cease to feel where he ended and she began. He knew the smile he managed was just a hair's breadth away from a pained grimace, but he knew, too, that even the worst attempt at humor was better than the primal howl swelling in his chest. "Are you telling me you are impatient to claim your wifely rights, then?"

"Dia's Muire, nay!"

Oh, it hurt, that vehement denial. Not that he had expected it to be any other way, but still it hurt. "I said I would make no demands of you tonight. I hope your fears will be allayed entirely by my vow that I will *never* force you into my bed."

"Thank you."

It was no good. Nathan could not ignore the sting. "Have some care for my male pride, my dear. There is no need to sound so relieved."

"I am relieved, my lord."

Perhaps her damnable frankness was rubbing off onto him, or perhaps it just needled at both his pride and desire, for the rest of the calming assurances he had planned melted on his tongue. "I have not said we will not share a bed, Isobel."

"But—"

"I said I would not demand that you enter it, and I will honor that. There are more ways onto a mattress than by force."

He left her to ponder that concept and turned to the reason he had entered her chamber originally. Oh, he had hoped he might be lingering for another reason, but necessity as much as desire had motivated him.

"We will be paying a call on my parents tomorrow," he announced. "I thought it best to prepare you."

"I cannot possibly meet your parents."

He could hear the distressed tone in her voice. "Whyever not? I assure you, Isobel, they will accept you regardless of your birth."

"I did not mean that." She grew still suddenly. Then, "There is nothing wrong with my birth, my lord. My father, clown though he may be, was born a gentleman."

He felt himself smiling again. His wife's pride was a fierce thing, nearly as fierce as her devotion to her family. "I apologize. That was unforgivably arrogant of me."

"Ah. Well. I was actually thinking of my appearance."

"And I have told you, Isobel, there is damned well nothing wrong—"

"You cannot see me! *Och*, I'm not referring to my face, Oriel. I'm thinking of my apparel."

"I do not understand."

"Nay, I suppose you don't. You couldn't see that I became Marchioness of Oriel wearing a gown that is faded, five years out of fashion, and has a spot on the bodice. Not that you would have seen the spot in any case. Maggie covered it with a posy."

No, he had not seen. But he would have eagerly allied himself with the devil for eternity to have a good look at her bodice.

"And," she continued, "what little else I own is no better. I cannot meet your parents looking like, well,

looking like just what I am: a poor, plain, country spinster with no beauty and no fashionable follies with which
to compensate for that lack. Your mother would most
likely shriek on first view, and none would blame her."

Nathan scolded himself for not considering the matter
of her wardrobe before. He was an intelligent man with
vast experience of the world, but it appeared he was far
behind his wife when it came to the basics of social
necessities.

"My mother has never, to my knowledge, shrieked at
the sight of anything."

"That is not my point."

"I fully comprehend your point. And I will see to the
matter. No," he said when she started to interrupt, "you
will simply have to trust me. As for who you are, it
appears we have vastly different ideas. You are not a poor,
country spinster, Isobel. You are the very wealthy wife of
a marquess, which means you are a very wealthy duchess-
to-be. No one will ever see you as anything less."

He thought he heard her mutter something about *his*
money, *his* titles, but let it go. She was quite right, and he
did not want to argue the point. "Now, what I wanted to
tell you was that my parents might seem a bit contemp-
tuous and priggish at first." His mouth quirked. "My parents *are* a bit priggish. But they are decent people and
will, I know, welcome you readily into the family."

"Aye, so you say," she grumbled.

Despite the fact that he was still more than half
aroused, Nathan felt his humor improving. Amazing
what his promise not to bed her had done for Isobel's
delightful spirit. If she did not kill him with unrequited
desire, she would be the miracle of his life.

"I have but two warnings for you."

"The contempt and priggishness weren't warning
enough?"

"That was a brief character sketch. The first warning is

this: Do not ever, in their presence, ask my brother William about his experiments."

"His experiments?"

"We will discuss William's little hobby at another time."

"I see." Which, of course, she did not. "And the second warning?"

"The second," he said, repressing a grim laugh, "is that my father is rather fond of guns. Should you find yourself with one pointed at your chest, I would not advise any sudden moves."

He caught a flash of fire-touched red as she jumped to her feet. "What are you telling me?"

"I am not foretelling your doom, my dear." Nathan rose as well. He did not especially want to leave, but it seemed best. "I am merely arming you with a bit of useful knowledge. For the moment, we will leave it at that."

"Leave it at that? Are you daft?"

All he had to do was lean forward and give her a deliberately cold smile to still her tongue. It was a nasty trick and he knew it, but the very last conversation he wanted to have at present was a detailed one concerning his parents.

"I will bid you a good night, then, Isobel."

To her credit, she managed a reasonably even, "And to you, my lord."

"Nathan. I should like to hear you say my name, even if only when we are alone."

"Very well. Nathan."

He imagined she was relieved enough at his departure that she would probably call him Saint Augustine should he ask. He was smiling again as he headed, carefully, toward the connecting door. "Ah, one more small matter."

"Aye" She sounded wary again.

"For what it is worth, Isobel, you are the most beautiful woman I have ever known."

He entered his own bedchamber and closed the door firmly behind him.

It was sometime later when Isobel made her way to her bed on shaky legs. Never in her life had anyone said any words remotely similar to her, and their effect was diminished only slightly by the fact that they had been spoken by a blind man.

"Vanity," she muttered, annoyed at her reaction "and you've no right to it, lass." She was not a vain woman, but she was proud, and it irked her that she could be so moved by shallow, patently untrue sentiments. But oh, how nice the words had sounded.

Cursing, scolding herself, Isobel crawled under the covers and leaned back against the lush pillows. It had been a mad day, ending the maddest of weeks. She felt drained and battered, the best of her defenses gone. She had spent her life battling familiar enemies: her father's drinking, her brothers' carelessness, unending poverty. Now she was faced with a devil she did not know.

She was on foreign turf here in London, among an unquestionably foreign race of people. She could no more imagine herself moving with ease through the ton than through tribes of cannibals. And from what little she knew of those tribes, they had logical reasons for chewing on one another. English society did it for no reason whatsoever. She had a very good idea that this group of people whom she had never met would have a taste for simple Scot.

Above all, it would be folly to assume she knew the man she had married. He changed like the weather, alternating from saying words that made her melt to saying no words at all. And then there were those moments when he seemed more animal than man.

Shivering, she burrowed under the covers. "In for a pence; in for a pound" was but one of the axioms that tripped merrily from her father's tongue. He had never been much good at following it, but his daughters were. Not that she herself had had much of a choice, Isobel thought. She had made her promises, though, and she would keep them. Assuming, of course, the duke did not shoot her first or the ton devour her.

Wide awake and knowing there would be little sleep for her that night, Isobel stared at the ornate panels of the connecting door. She wondered, even as she did not really want to know, what was going through Nathan's mind as he slept in his lair.

Gabriel was whistling a cheerful tune about willing lasses and deep, waving grasses. Nathan was glowering into the Portuguese darkness, since glowering at his friend served no purpose whatsoever. "Idiocy," he muttered. "Told you the second bottle was too much. We'll be an hour finding our way to the docks."

"Can you not desist with the grumbling even for a minute? You are quite spoiling my tune." Gabriel slowed his weaving pace so they were walking even—or at least together. "I could have sent you off on your own, you know. I had an unmistakable invitation from that barmaid to stay."

"Don't know why you didn't," Nathan grumbled. But he did know. His friend was stumbling beside him for the same reason he had come to Lisbon. "Damn, but I'm going to miss you."

"Oh, I'll be joining you at home soon enough. Comfort yourself by thinking of all the splendid, uninterrupted time you'll have with your new bride."

"You are still being altogether too glib about the matter."

"Just glib enough, I think. I do not envy you your shackles, my friend."

"Gabriel . . ."

"Plenty of time for me to forge my own chains." Indicating the subject had been pounded into the ground, the man commenced with a new tune, singing instead of whistling this time, about two sisters, four breasts, and twenty roaming fingers.

Nathan shook his head wryly. God only knew who was writing this drivel. Then he found himself humming—then singing along. Gabriel paused long enough to give an approving laugh, which carried above the tune and into the still night.

They never had the chance to complete the chorus.

Two figures erupted without warning from the shadows, dark specters whose blades flashed even in the darkness. Nathan's reflexes saved his life. He'd turned and the saber sank into his thigh rather than his side. The pain was instant, blinding, and he went down. As he did, he saw the black stain on his friend's shirt—and his white astonished face.

"Rievaulx!" he gasped. *"Oh, God. Gabriel!"*

Then Nathan was dealt a crushing blow to his temple. With fire behind his eyes and pain screaming along his leg, he could not tell whether he had been hit with a blade or cudgel. It did not matter. Desperate, in agony, he fought the blackness, screaming his friend's name.

"Gabriel!"

Nathan came awake with a start, his chest slick with sweat, his cheeks damp with tears.

CHAPTER 10

Isobel flinched as another hurriedly placed pin bit into her skin. She accepted the flushed modiste's apology with far more grace than she was feeling. It was not the woman's fault, after all, that Nathan had swept into the establishment with all the officiousness of Wellington himself, demanding immediate and complete attention. Nor could the woman be blamed for the fact that none of the partially completed gowns on hand was a perfect fit for Lord Oriel's new wife.

Whoever had commissioned the pale green silk now draped over Isobel's weary form had been broader of hip, smaller of bosom, and would undoubtedly be less than pleased to learn her gown had been commandeered. Isobel decided the unknown lady could not be anyone of great title or fortune; the modiste had handed the garment over much too easily for it to have been intended for anyone of importance.

Even as she admitted it was a lovely creation, Isobel grumbled to herself over the inequities inherent in Society. How very irksome it must be, she thought, to have one's silk confiscated by a marchioness, even more so to have to take such theft with good grace.

"Voilà!" the modiste cried. *"Parfaite.* Do you not think so, my lord?"

She had yet to address much more than apologies to Isobel. Nathan's severe and decidedly looming manner had that effect on people. They all but performed acrobatics to satisfy him.

His presence in the fitting room was apparently disconcerting to no one but his wife. Even the knowledge that he could not see any of her exposed skin did not offer much comfort. He was sprawled in one of madame's delicate chairs, nodding occasionally at the comments shot his way while, Isobel thought, his mind was quite probably somewhere else entirely.

He tilted his head now and frowned. He had frowned nearly as often as he had nodded. At first the severe expression had frightened the modiste's assistants to the point that one had dropped several bolts of fabric on Isobel's foot. Now the frown merely engendered a few discreet flinches.

"I am not certain," he said gruffly, "that the style does justice to my wife's charms. What is your opinion, my dear?"

They had done quite well, really, at this particular charade, and Isobel played her part with ease. "I am rather fond of this shade, my lord. It brings to mind the first blades of spring grass, does it not?"

Describing the differences in the dresses had not been difficult. Color, fabric, trim. Other than the riding habits, all had been high waisted and softly draped. This one, however, possessed a feature Isobel was having some problem putting into words.

"The bodice is perhaps a bit, er, it . . ." *It what? Plunges? Skirts the edge of decency? Has created a very nice little shelf on which I can rest my champagne glass?*

Madame clucked her tongue impatiently. "The décolletage is the height of fashion, milady." She turned to Nathan. "And what do you think, milord?"

Without saying a word, Nathan all but erupted from his seat and, before Isobel could protest, was ascertaining the dress's edges for himself.

Isobel bit back a squeak as his hands slid up her arms, his thumbs flying quick and intimate over the silver gilt embroidery trimming the bodice. As before, her skin tingled in the wake of his touch, an insidious warmth spreading along the sides of her breasts. It tingled, too, in spots he did not touch at all. Mortified, she nearly lifted her hands to cover the visible signs before remembering he could not see the effect of his tactile assault.

He could not see. Odd, how easy it was to forget between one moment and the next. And she always forgot when he was touching her.

The disturbing perusal was over in an instant, done under the guise of turning her to face him. Still, the sensation lingered even after his hands dropped away. Perhaps she would have relaxed had he stepped back. But he remained less than an arm's length away, frowning down at her. There was an intentness in his unseeing eyes, and Isobel felt her own chin rising.

A ball gown did not a marchioness make. Nor did strange sensations bring her any closer to understanding the odd connection between her and Nathan. But she would dress in sackcloth and ride a goat down Piccadilly, she thought, rather than allow this situation to defeat her.

"It is a beginning," Nathan said at last.

He had, it seemed, somehow comprehended her thoughts. And Isobel understood, without a doubt, that he was not speaking of green silk.

"I will have it delivered this evening." The modiste, understanding nothing at all, clapped her hands at her assistants. "The rest will follow."

"Indeed," Nathan murmured. Then, blinking as if in

sudden light, he demanded, "What is available for Lady Oriel now?"

"Décolleté armor," Isobel answered, and wished Nathan could see madame and her assistants scrambling to find a dress appropriate for launching Lady Oriel into London Society.

"Gray," she muttered sometime later as the carriage wended its way through Mayfair. "It would be gray."

"Madame said it was all the rage," Nathan replied, unable to resist mimicking the modiste's Paris-via-Yorkshire whine. "Madame la Marchioness weel resemble nossing less than a dove, weel she not?"

Isobel snorted. "With my hair? Madame la Marchioness weel resemble nossing less than a pin with a rusted head. A dove." She sighed then. "Doves are nossing but pigeons with delusions of grandeur."

Nathan wanted to touch her. Well, he always wanted to touch her, but this time it would be to offer some small measure of strength. He clenched his hands more tightly around the knob of his walking stick. "You look lovely, Isobel." She snorted again. "Yes, yes, the blindness. Do us both a great service, my dear, and do not underestimate me. I can feel your presence, you know. It is lovely."

There was a softness to the following silence. Astonishing, Nathan mused, how he actually *could* feel her. She was pleased with the compliment and annoyed with her pleasure.

"I do wish I could have given you more time," he offered after a moment, "but the announcement will have been in the morning's *Times*, and my parents would never recover should they have to face the certain hordes of well-wishing friends without having seen you first."

He thought he heard her mutter something about first blood.

He had sent his announcement to his parents. What he

had not told her was that he had timed its arrival to beat the newspaper by minutes. The duke and duchess would be able to say, with complete honesty and hauteur, that they had known of their son's marriage before the public. They would not, however, have had time to do much more than gape and stutter.

His father would do the gaping and stuttering, actually, Nathan thought. His mother would sigh, square noble shoulders, and immediately begin mapping out her own strategy.

He had great faith in his mother's ability to master the situation. He had complete faith in Isobel.

"Have you any last-minute instructions for me, my lord?" she was asking now. He could sense her hands fluttering, smoothing dove gray skirts and copper curls.

"Have you any last words?" he shot back, knowing instinctively that humor would aid both of them.

Her silvery laugh was both comfort and torture. "Aye. If I do not walk away from this skirmish, Maggie is to have every last one of the dresses for which you just emptied your pockets. I'll not have you slipping 'round that one simply because your strategy proved poor."

"You have my solemn oath on the matter, madam." He, too, was smiling "Have no fear. It will all be over in no time."

Well, that was not precisely true, but he had chosen the element of surprise. She would forgive him. It was simply her nature.

The carriage rolled to a stop. In the moment before a footman rushed forward to open the door, Nathan satisfied his urge to touch his wife. Reaching forward, he grasped her hand with strong and surprising ease. It seemed there was no fumbling when his skin met hers. "You are all I could ask for, Isobel. You will be fine."

As seemed only natural to him now, her fingers tightened briefly around his.

As they made their way, arm in arm, up the townhouse stairs, he was strengthened by her presence at his side. Oh yes, they would be fine.

Nathan could hear his father's voice the moment they entered the hall. Waving off the butler, he guided Isobel toward the dining room where he knew his parents would be found. Had not the bellowing announced his father's location, the hour would have. London could set its clocks by his father's eating habits.

"Steady on," he murmured, and pulled his now lead-footed wife toward the lion's den.

The Duke of Abergele was holding a gun. It was not a big gun, perhaps, but a gun nonetheless. Isobel noted this very important fact well before the next: The Duke of Abergele looked very much like his son. There was more silver in the dark hair, and the amber eyes were clear, sharp, and shrewd. They were also now fixed directly on her face.

She swallowed, half convinced there was a lead ball in her immediate future. As she watched, one black eyebrow, so much like Nathan's, rose a fraction. The hand not holding the gun tapped a quick pattern on the tablecloth.

"I expect you're damned proud of yourself," he growled.

"Now, Frederick . . ."

Isobel darted a quick glance at the other figure in the room. The duchess, she noted, was tall, fair, and impeccably garbed in a turquoise dress. *The peacock and the pigeon,* Isobel thought as she considered her own appearance. Much as she wanted time to ascertain just how regal her new mother-in-law was, she turned back to the duke: A wise woman never took her eyes off a pistol.

"Well?" he demanded. "What have you to say for yourself?"

Isobel swallowed, having nothing whatsoever to say at

that moment. She would have preferred a more traditional form of greeting, but she could not fault the duke. His question, rude though it might have been, was fair. A penniless Scottish spinster would be damned proud indeed to have snared a marquess. She wondered how Nathan's father would react to the truth.

Well, Your Grace, it happened this way: My father is a thief, you see, and your son caught me with a pouchful of gold.

"Well . . ." she began.

"I apologize for not alerting you sooner, sir." Nathan addressed his father evenly. Isobel sighed. Of course the duke had been speaking to his son and not to her, but it was rather difficult to think clearly while that disconcertingly familiar bronze gaze was fixed on her. "If I may be allowed to remedy the matter now, I would like to present my wife, Isobel."

"Ah, yes. Isobel MacLeod, late of Skye, Scotland, daughter of James MacLeod." The duke's brows snapped together. "We've seen the *Times*."

"Frederick, please." The duchess moved forward then, hands extended. "Nathan," she said softly, a wealth of emotion in her pale blue eyes. Her pain was evident as she watched her son limp across the rug toward her. "We are so very glad to have you back. And Isobel. Welcome."

Perhaps that greeting was a bit stiff; perhaps the perfect brow was now marred with a faint frown of confusion. Perhaps the very beautiful, very elegant Duchess of Abergele was engaged in a mighty struggle as she tried to comprehend just what her son had brought into her palatial home, But Isobel's own heart opened to the woman instantly. She had no doubt that this was one mother who was, ridiculous aristocratic reserve aside, stirringly glad—and grateful—to have her son back.

"Your Grace," Isobel said gently, "this must be quite a shock to you."

"A . . . not-unpleasant one," the duchess managed. "We are delighted that our son has married."

A plain Highland nobody? Of course you are.

Isobel allowed herself a silent sigh, then allowed herself to be led to a seat at the massive table. The beginnings of a meal were spread there, and a footman hurried in to lay two more places.

"Now, Frederick, put the gun away." The duchess, cool as water, settled herself in her chair, her eyes still soft on her son's face. "I do wish you would refrain from bringing it to the table."

Nathan took a seat. "How gratifying to see things have not changed in my absence."

"House could've crumbled to dust in that time," the duke muttered, but he thrust the pistol at the footman. The servant, clearly accustomed to such a task, discreetly tucked it away. "A damned year, boy, with not so much as a visit. And now what do you do? You show up on our doorstep with a wife in tow."

"Frederick, please," the duchess said again. Then, to Nathan, "You are . . . well?"

"Splendid, madam. As you can see, my injuries bother me little."

"Oh, I am pleased to hear it." Quietly, the duchess added, "So pleased. Now, you will not rush off again, will you? We would so like the chance to see you—and to become acquainted with Isobel."

"As it happens, we will be passing the Season in Town. You will have ample time with us both."

"Ah. Good."

Isobel looked from the duchess, with her transparent hope, to the duke, with his fierce scowl, to Nathan's unreadable mask. There were ghosts of old wars here, and she could only imagine what the battlegrounds had been. She could only trust there would be some advance warning should cannonballs start flying again.

"Your Grace," she addressed her mother-in-law, "Lord Oriel has spoken much of you." It was a lie she was certain would be forgiven. "He has been so looking forward to being with his family in Town."

"Has he? I am so glad."

The duke grunted.

"Tell us something of yourself, my dear." The duchess actually smiled at her. "I understand you are originally from Skye. That is just north of the border, is it not?"

A choice comment or two came to mind, but Isobel wisely dismissed them. It did not matter that the only acceptable Scot was one who had once been allied to the English at the borders. She wanted this woman to accept her, if only to make Nathan's life easier.

"Nay, madam. Skye is a western isle, somewhat to the north of the Borderlands." Again, she was confident that the matter of a few hundred miles would be divinely forgiven. " 'Tis a lovely place."

"I am certain it is. You must tell me all about it and about your family. Your father is a gentleman, I assume?"

Oh, aye. By birth, perhaps. By nature . . .

Her response was stalled by Nathan's movement. Confused, she watched as he pushed back his chair and stood. "You may quiz Isobel all you like, madam. I entrust her to your care."

"I beg your pardon?" the duchess asked.

"What?" Isobel gasped.

"I am afraid this must be a brief visit on my part. I have an appointment. If you would be so kind as to escort my wife to Lady Winslow's this evening, I will meet you there."

Isobel leapt to her feet. "You are leaving me here?"

"In capable hands, my dear. I arranged for Madame

Hervey to send some of your purchases here. I will join you at the soiree this evening."

"But you cannot . . . I cannot . . . Concern for his well-being, wherever he was going, was fast lost to images of bloody murder. "My lord, this is not what we had planned."

"Oh, did I not inform you of my change of plans? How careless of me. Forgive me, my dear." While Isobel gaped, Nathan bowed to his mother. "Until later then, madam. Sir." Then, with a wholly insolent wink at Isobel, he headed for the door.

She regained her wits just in time to see him exit, not so much as clipping his sleeve against the doorway.

"Well, dearest, it appears we are to have time to become acquainted sooner than expected." The duchess nodded to a footman, who approached with a wine decanter. "Now, you must begin at the beginning. How did you and my son meet?"

Isobel, trapped as surely as if by steel, sank back into her chair. She aimed a weak smile at the glowering duke, then turned to the duchess. The urge to spite her husband, curse his sneaky hide, by telling the whole miserable tale was strong. But not strong enough.

"We met, Your Grace," she began, wondering if there was a spot in heaven set aside just for Scottish martyrs, "soon after he returned from the Peninsula . . . ."

Nathan, upon hearing about the death of yet another member of the Ten, had to resist the urge to slam his fist into the nearest wall.

"Damn it, Matthew, he should not have been there!"

Behind the familiar desk, in the very familiar office, his former superior was slumped in the deep chair, well into a bottle of brandy. "Don't you think I have been telling myself that since yesterday?" Gerard lamented. "He was so intent on going to Barcelona. I never thought—could not have imagined—he would be followed."

Brooke. Quiet, studious Brooke, had been meant for the Church before the lure of serving king and country had brought him to spy-hunting, into the Ten. Brooke, not yet thirty and dead in a Spanish alley.

Nathan paced the expanse of Gerard's office, each inch having been paced before so many times. "Why was he alone?" he demanded. "I thought Montgomerie and Brandon were still in Spain."

"They are. I do not know why he was traveling without them. I have been unable to contact Brandon since March." There was an audible clink as Gerard plied the bottle again. "God, Nathan, I should have brought Brooke home after Dennison's death."

"You couldn't have known what would happen to him, and it would not have been the right decision in any case." Nathan spoke reluctantly, even as he knew the words were true. "We all take risks. *Took* risks. We knew that, coming into the corps." Weary now, he lowered himself into a chair. "Have you any information at all? Anything that might be of use?"

"Nothing. No one could . . . or would tell Montgomerie anything." Gerard's distress was palpable. "Whoever got to Brooke appeared like a ghost and disappeared just as completely. I hoped you would be able to . . ."

"What, Matthew? Realistically, what can I do here?"

"I don't know. Perhaps I should not have asked you to return to Town. After Brooke . . ." There was a pause as Gerard emptied his glass. "They know who we are, Nathan, who you are. You would be safer in Hertfordshire."

"Rubbish. No one is coming after me."

"How can you be so bloody certain?"

In truth, Nathan wasn't quite so certain, not now. "I understand Rotheroe is back in Town."

"He is. I called him back in April. And I'll be damned if I'll let him die in his own land!"

Nathan thought of the Earl of Rotheroe with his quick smile, quicker mind, and useless right arm. "I'll find him."

Glassware rattled as Gerard slammed his glass onto the desk. "I will not have you setting yourself up like some wooden duck, damn it! Nor will I allow Rotheroe to put himself in danger. You've both been injured as it is. Nothing will be served by having you dead."

"That, my friend, would depend on point of view. If, as you believe, someone is intent on dispatching the Ten, he is serving his aims well indeed."

"I was speaking of the active Ten," was Gerard's sharp retort.

"You activated me when you came to Hertfordshire. This was all your idea, bringing me back to Town. Don't go weak on me now, Matthew."

"You're married now, man, and are making a life for yourself."

Nathan grunted. "None of our lives ever made a difference before."

"Your lives were never as overtly threatened before. Oh, hell, Nathan. I have selfish reasons for my concern as well. You were a good soldier and damned good at gathering intelligence. England cannot afford to lose more of your kind and still hope to win this infernal war."

Nathan could imagine what he could not see: Matthew Gerard with his bloodhound's face and wiry gray hair, made wilder by constant tugging. He could envision the always wilted cravat and misbuttoned waistcoat. No one looking at the man would recognize the brilliant mind.

"Matthew, I sat back for nearly half a year, doing nothing. Brooke was my friend, Rievaulx more like a brother. You called me back, and it's too late for me to return to hide in my lair."

Too late, perhaps, but he was a mere day away from Hertfordshire, and he already missed it. Missed the days he had passed there—once Isobel had climbed through a window and into his life.

He recalled a proverb from his childhood, something about God opening a window when He closed a door. Nathan could not quite decide how it applied. By gaining Isobel, he had also been given a chance to close his own door, the door left ajar by Gabriel's death. The question, of course, was whether he was capable of turning his back on the past and looking only to the future.

Just think how jolly we will be once we're both back home. No limits, Nathan, my friend. Damn but we'll take a good bite out of life in days to come.

"How did they know, Matthew? How did they know Rievaulx and I would be in Lisbon that night?"

The question had plagued him endlessly in the past months. None of the possible answers sat well at all.

"That is the question of the hour, isn't it?" Gerard muttered.

Names and faces flashed through Nathan's mind. There were few to choose from now. "Where is St. Wulfstan? Have you located him yet?"

"As a matter of fact, I've heard rumors he is on his way back to England."

"He hasn't contacted you?"

Gerard sighed. "Remember you are speaking of St. Wulfstan. His communiqués are, at best, sporadic." As if reading Nathan's mind, he added, "He is the very best at what he does. I cannot complain if ordinances fall somewhat low on his list of priorities."

Only a man who did what St. Wulfstan did best would be allowed to flout regulations as he always had. What St. Wulfstan did best was make himself completely invisible when necessary. He would disappear for months on end, only to surface with information no one else could come close to obtaining. He was irresponsible, irreverent—and invaluable to the unit.

Nathan had never liked the man, but he respected his uncanny abilities. "Should he deign to check in, I trust you will let me know."

"Of course." There was a rustling of paper. "The Winslow ball is tonight, is it not?"

"It is. I have arranged to meet my family there."

"Good, I have an invitation here somewhere."

While Gerard fumbled, just a bit drunkenly if the noises were any indication, through the piles of papers that were always on his desk, Nathan wondered what sort of greeting he could expect that night. Oh, Lady Winslow would be happy enough to see him. It was Isobel whose welcome would be questionable.

It had been expedient to leave her with his parents, even as it seemed cowardly. He knew her, far better than she thought, and knew she would have been uncustomarily quiet had he stayed. Family, to Isobel, was sacred. She would have felt like an interloper and done everything in her power to stay in the background.

As it was, she probably felt like a cornered fox in hunting season.

She would see to herself. And, in the process, she might very well succeed in blazing a place for herself in the cool, controlled Paget clan. Then again, she might already have fled for the relative safety of Mount Street, if not all the way back to Oriel Hall.

No, Nathan decided. Isobel would never take flight that way. Nor, he knew with utter, satisfying certainty, would she leave him alone. There was probably a Highland gale coming his way, but it would rise fast and blow hard, then whisper away.

From habit, he turned to face the window. He knew

that Pall Mall was below, the Carlton House Gardens not more than a stone's throw away. If he remembered correctly, the Princess of Wales had insisted that yellow roses be planted there during the brief time she spent in residence. He wondered if the plants had survived her fall from grace.

He would have to ask Isobel the meaning of a yellow rose. That was, of course, if she was still speaking to him.

Restless, he turned back to face Gerard. "Let's get on with what we have, then. Back to Almeida. No, before that."

"I don't know if it will help. We were so confident then, so convinced of our cleverness."

Nathan smiled humorlessly. "And wholly ignorant. Take heart, Matthew. We might be just as blind, but we are infinitely wiser. Now, before our garrison at Almeida fell . . ."

"The Ten was still intact then, all somewhere on the Peninsula. Dennison and Rotheroe were at Almeida. St. Wulfstan had yet to go into France. You and Rievaulx were working your way to Lisbon. Brooke, Montgomerie, and Brandon were at various points in the south, Harlow in Lesaca, and Witherspoon in Coimbra."

"All scattered," Nathan mused, "and constantly moving. What is the link, Matthew, other than that we each had to the others?"

"That *is* the link. The Ten."

Now there were five left: himself, Montgomerie, Brandon, Rotheroe, and St. Wulfstan. "All on the Peninsula," he repeated quietly, "all constantly on the move and not always where we were supposed to be."

Nathan had come to several realizations the first of which he knew he must share with Gerard, even though the man would, no doubt, refuse to believe it. If it was really true that someone was after the Ten, the most likely person to have known their identities and location was one of the members himself. If, in fact, someone was really after the Ten, one of the remaining five was quite possibly a traitor. And a murderer who had been able to get close enough to four men on the Continent to attack them, close enough in London to dispatch Dennison.

The second realization had come to Nathan fast on the heels of the first. In coming to London, blind and essentially helpless, he could very well have placed himself in danger. Worse, he had been stupid—blindly stupid enough to drag Isobel right along with him.

CHAPTER 11

O, how full of briers is this working-day world!
                                    —Shakespeare

Idiot! Nathan cursed himself as he navigated the foyer of the Winslow townhouse. *Witless, foolish, idiot!* He had no idea what had possessed him to create this particular plan. It had seemed such a good idea at the time.

Now, as he gripped his walking stick with unnecessary force and hoped he would not encounter anyone requiring more than a polite nod, he tried to remember if Lady Winslow was the sort to fill her house with ridiculous china objects and chattering, prying people. Yes, he thought, she was.

Damn Gerard. Nathan had planned on his superior's being by his side. Instead, he was at present where Nathan had left him, sprawled in his chair, the worse for too much brandy.

Gerard had been coherent enough until that second bottle. In the end, Nathan had had no choice but to leave him slumped behind his desk. Not that he begrudged the man one good escape into numbness. He had certainly had a few himself. But there was work to be done, and one of them lost to sentimental reminiscences was one too many.

What a pity he could not get his own image of Brooke's wide, earnest face from his mind.

He muttered something between prayer and curse as he made his way down the hall toward the ballroom. At least he hoped it was the ballroom he was approaching. The multitude of brightly colored skirts and bobbing appendages surrounding him were, no doubt, absurd feathered fripperies and would seem to indicate he was going in the correct direction. Of course, it was entirely possible he was about to stumble into the ladies' retiring room. He had no idea how he would be able to explain that gaffe.

Arriving late was helpful in more ways than one. Even those people who had decided upon fashionable tardiness would have been present for some time, which meant he could likely reach the ballroom without meeting anyone he knew. Also, the later he was, the sooner the evening would be over. He was counting on having Isobel out of this place and home within an hour. London would have had its look at both the absent marquess and his surprise Scottish bride, and Nathan would have determined just how simple, or impossible, it would be for him to navigate another familiar haunt. He had done well enough that afternoon at Gerard's, treading halls he had trod a thousand times before.

With Isobel at his side, he was convinced he could navigate Hell. But Isobel was not presently at his side. No, she was somewhere among the sea of blurry revelers. The problem, he knew, was getting to her without falling on his face. Proverbially or quite literally.

He gritted his teeth and, cursing the faint sheen of sweat he could feel on his brow, took the first downward step toward the dance floor. He saw her before he took the second. There was no mistaking the fiery halo, even in the midst of a crowded ballroom. Isobel had seen him and, contrary to protocol and expectation, was fighting her way to him through the crush.

Nathan had a very good idea that more than a hundred

heads were turning to watch the new Marchioness of
Oriel all but sprinting her way across the floor to her
grim, reclusive, and crippled husband.

Then she was there at the bottom of the stairs. Caution
be damned, Nathan released the rail and, cane barely
touching the steps, strode down to her side. "I am here,"
she murmured as her hand slipped through the crook of
his arm.

"I could s—" Nathan silently cursed the near slip. He
wanted to tell her, wanted so much to reveal what he
could see. But she'd said there would have been no marriage had he not been blind. Foolish it might be, but he
could not fight the feeling that she might leave him if she
knew—if she felt herself no longer needed.

He cleared his throat. "I could only assume it was my
wife being so forward with my person."

"You told me you would not arrive alone."

"My companion was unable to attend."

"You ought to have informed me."

"I managed, Isobel, and will thrive now that you have
found me." He gently pressed her arm against his side.
"You have fared well, I take it?"

She gave something between a laugh and a snort.
" 'Twas a nasty thing you did, my lord."

"Throwing you to the wolves of the ton?"

Now she gave his arm a fleeting, warm squeeze. "Not
at all. Throwing me into your father's company for such
a time."

Damn. Nathan had expected some reticence on his
father's part in accepting Isobel, but he had not expected
any true unpleasantness. Of course, she had spoken the
words lightly. And he knew his wife. It would take a great
deal more than one impossible old snob to wither her.

Unfortunate that Nathan knew they were surrounded
by no less than a hundred impossible snobs of every age.

"Has it been so bad for you?"

Again the squeeze. "Judge for yourself."

No one stopped them as she guided him through the crush. Her grip was firm, her stride confident, allowing Nathan to move with far more ease than he had expected. Only once did his stick catch on someone's foot, and even then there was a muffled, "So sorry, my lord, before the offending appendage was hurriedly pulled out of the way."

Nathan thought he could pick out a few acquaintances in the crowd. He aimed a terse nod at a towering, dark head that could only be Rotheroe, caught a trilling laugh that was unmistakably Maria Sefton's, and guessed that one exuberant, flailing wave from a decidedly round little form was his welcome-home from Sedgwick.

He heard his father well before Isobel announced, "Here he is, as promised, Your Grace."

"Hmph," was the reply. "Took his sweet time, didn't he?" Abergele then deigned to address his son directly. "Lost your mother to that old biddy Winslow. She'll want to have a few words with you." The duke leaned forward, so close that Nathan could very nearly believe he could see the familiar, sharp amber eyes. "Damned shoddy business, young man. Damned shoddy."

Nathan tried to read Isobel's stance through her hand. Oddly, she seemed perfectly at ease. No small feat considering what jabs her new father-in-law would have managed, even unintentionally, to aim at her. And it was his own fault she had been forced to face them alone.

"Sir, I cannot allow you to—" he began tersely, breaking off as his father's hand thumped like a mace onto his shoulder.

"Rotten business all around, leaving your wife to her first night in Society while you hied off to God knows where! But she's done splendidly. Haven't you, girl?"

"I was in the very best of company, Your Grace," came her cheerful reply. " 'Twas a tense moment there when Lord Allenham began his lecture on the ills of Scotland, but you were the most gallant of rescuers. I daresay he will be prepared for your greeting next time. I have rarely felt so well protected as when your grip nearly brought him to his knees."

From the garbled noises that followed, Nathan could only surmise his father was speechless. And, if the gruff chuckle that followed was any indication, the old coot was smitten on top of it.

"Well, my boy," the duke said at last, cuffing Nathan's arm, "I must say I'd all but given up on you. After Cecily . . . er . . . dash it all. Bloody well about time. You've brought a jewel into the family coffers with this one."

"I am glad you approve, sir."

"Approve? Damn me, boy, you've made me bloody proud!"

It was on Nathan's tongue to inform his father that making him proud had not been among the first ten reasons for marrying Isobel. Pleasing the man had always been a task of Sisyphean proportions. Every milestone Nathan had rolled upward toward the ducal peak seemed to have been tipped right back at him. Marrying Isobel had been the one thing he had done purely for himself.

Sarcasm would serve no purpose. Still, he could not resist saying, "I have always done my best to see to your pride, Father."

He could not believe his ears when the duke replied, "You are my pride, Nathan. Always have been, even when you're breaking my heart." This time, when the hand descended onto Nathan's shoulder, it was gentle.

A distinct lump formed in Isobel's throat as she watched. Brusque and rough as the duke might be, there was no question that he did have a heart that ached for his son's plight and rejoiced in his return. She had seen, in both his eyes and his wife's, how Nathan's life had pained them. They had been forced to watch him ride off to war and then been denied the simple pleasure of having him come home to them.

It was time, Isobel decided, to fetch the duchess. Perhaps this family reunion would better have been conducted in more private surroundings, but the sight of father and son, dark heads close together as they talked, made it a moot point.

"If you will excuse me," she murmured, stepping away before Nathan could grasp her arm.

"Where are you going?" he demanded.

As she opened her mouth to answer, the duke slapped affectionately at her cheek and announced, "That's right, girl. Go off and find your friends. My son and I have a bit of talking to do." Then he all but shoved her off into the melee.

Friends, was it? Isobel smiled a bit sadly. With the exception of Nathan and his parents, she did not know a soul in the very crowded room.

It was simple enough to make her way through the crush. As predicted, no one had dared snub her in the obviously approving presence of the Abergeles, but it was equally obvious that the ton was still reserving judgment on the new marchioness. Lord Allenham's gaffe had been but a taste of Society's idea of welcome. After several hours of audible sniffs and countless perusals through awful quizzing glasses, Isobel was quite convinced she had the ton understood. It was not a particularly heartening comprehension.

She paused for a moment, straining to locate her mother-in-law's towering turban among the multitude of towering turbans. It was a ridiculous fashion, as English in its absurd popularity as it was Eastern in origin. How very like the *Sasunnach*, she mused wryly, to revile those persons they conquered while making a perfect spectacle of their garb. No doubt tartans were due a turn in English high fashion sometime soon.

She found herself wondering if turbans were forbidden to the peoples who had invented them. After all, if Bonnie Prince Charlie's uprising had caused such terror of bits of plaid that wearing them had constituted treason for nearly forty years, there was no telling what fear of silk head wraps might bring about.

As she was scanning the crowd for the duchess, the crowd was scanning her. Most of the gazes aimed her way were frankly curious, but more than one bore the distinct stamp of disapproval. And she wasn't even wearing her MacLeod tartan.

"Pompous toads," Isobel muttered.

She jumped as a voice very near her ear replied, "A kind assessment, I would say."

Isobel spun about, the tart retort dying on her lips. The man standing there was as unlike the rest of the pale, preening crowd as she was. And a good deal more disconcerting. The right side of his forehead was bisected by the puckered crescent of a massive scar. Curving from hairline to eyelid, it had the rather frightening effect of holding the lid at half-mast while drawing the brow upward in a fixed arc.

The slightly diabolic smile did not help in the least. This man was not quite as tall as Nathan, but he was imposing. His broad shoulders and torso were more than a bit intimidating. All the more so as he seemed intent on leaning onto her breasts.

Isobel took an instinctive step backward. "Have we met, sir?" Shared assessment of the assembled revelers aside—and Isobel was not at all happy to have been overheard even if he agreed with her—she could not help but feel this was not a man she particularly wanted to know. There was something altogether too forward in the vividly blue eyes.

"I would say we are meeting now," he announced.

Irish, Isobel mused, hearing the almost exaggerated

cadence of his speech. Having taken to broadening her own brogue that evening, she could nearly appreciate another intruder in the fold. Almost.

Not bothering to step away, he swept into an elegant bow. Unruly auburn hair brushed Isobel's arm, and she stepped back again. "Trevor Robard at your service, Lady Oriel."

So he knew who she was. That was no great surprise, really. Judging from the softly rippling wave of whispers that preceded her, everyone at the ball knew who she was.

"Mr. Robard." She darted a quick glance over her shoulder. Several other men had joined Nathan and his father. Not that she would have been able to catch his eye in any case, but a rescue now would have been most welcome.

"Worried your husband wouldn't approve of your conversing with me, my lady?"

Isobel's chin went up a notch. It was one matter to be skittish in this man's presence, another entirely for him to see it. "My husband is an intelligent man. Are *you* worried he would not approve?"

Robard's flashing smile was far more attractive than his smirk, but it quickly turned cold. "Not at all. Oriel and I have been acquainted since our days together at school. 'Tis no secret that he doesn't care for me much. Are you after testing his patience, then?"

"You are presuming I know who you are, sir. Other than your name, which has rung no bells, I know nothing of you save that you've a bit of wit and, quite likely, a dearth of manners. Now, if you will excuse me . . ."

His hand shot out to lightly encircle her wrist. "Skittish, are you? I'd never have thought it of Oriel. He's always tried to marry dash in the past. Never had much success, plodding old bugger, but damned if he didn't make the effort."

This very personal and offensive comment caused

Isobel to snap, "You presume to know much of my husband, yet clearly do not know him at all. I find this conversation distasteful, sir."

"And I find you somehow irresistible, my dear. I see the beginnings of a marvelous friendship at work here."

Isobel wanted nothing more than to smack him soundly on his grinning mouth. Instead, she opted for prudence. Deciding her mother-in-law could stay precisely where she was, she jerked her arm from the man's grasp, gathered up her skirts, and hurried back to Nathan's side.

She could feel Robard's speculative gaze on her back with every step she took.

Nathan glanced down, eyebrows lifting slightly, when she all but attached herself to his side. "I was wondering if we had lost you to Lady Winslow as well."

"Nay, I did not . . . Your mother . . . I . . ."

"Isobel? Has something happened?"

She struggled to put her encounter with Robard into words. It was not as simple as it should have been. And she was further stalled by the appearance of yet one more towering turban.

"Oriel!" the lady bellowed. "How very vexing of you"—she rapped Nathan's arm with her fan—"to surprise us with a new bride this way. Why, we are all just aflutter with the news."

"I, er . . ." It was obvious to Isobel that Nathan did not recognize this person.

Isobel lifted her chin as she stepped forward. An evening spent at the Abergeles' side had been invaluable, just as Nathan had predicted. She had been introduced to this woman and had no problem whatsoever remembering her name.

"How kind of you to have taken such an interest, Lady Mewell. Your felicitations are most appreciated."

Lady Mewell, who had clearly meant to be anything but kind and congratulatory, huffed a bit. "I am certain they are, Lady Oriel." Then, all but freezing Isobel from the circle, she had another go at Nathan with her fan. "You must come to supper, Oriel. You will no longer be able to play the gallant to my darling Julia, poor boy, but I daresay you will be ever so pleased to be once again in her lovely presence."

"Please give my regards to Miss Mewell, my lady. Lady Oriel and I would be delighted to attend one of your famous supper parties." Nathan nearly choked on his words. If he remembered correctly, Miss Julia Mewell's lovely presence had, since her last debut two years earlier, involved yards of transparent fabric that had a way of insinuating itself into a man's lap and a decidedly copious amount of rosewater. It was amazing how such an innocuous substance as rosewater could affect a man like a pike between the eyes when applied with an overly liberal hand.

If he could find anything kind to say about his former fiancée, Cecily Bronnar, it was that she had mistrusted her very dear friend Julia to the extent that she had always placed herself between the girl and Nathan.

At his side, Isobel was standing tense and silent—too silent. Nathan aimed a last nod in Lady Mewell's direction and turned his wife away from the group. "Something has distressed you."

"Aye." It was she who drew him a few feet away now. "I made an . . . unfortunate acquaintance."

It was on the tip of Nathan's tongue to say she had made a great many unfortunate acquaintances that night. Instead, he waited for her to continue.

" 'Twas a man who said he knows you well. A Mr. Robard. He was a bit . . . forward."

The name did not register immediately. Then Nathan found his head snapping around as if he could possibly locate the man in the crush.

"Where is he?" he demanded harshly.

"Well, I . . . 'Twas not so very awful, my lord." Her hand tightened on his sleeve. "I would not want you distressing yourself on account of it. He was merely somewhat—"

"Forward. Yes, I am certain he was." Nathan cursed softly. "Do you see him, Isobel?"

She was silent as she scanned the room. "I don't. He might have left."

"Yes, I imagine he did." Although he was ready to shout in frustration, Nathan tried to be gentle as he tucked her arm through his. "We shall follow his example."

"What of your plans for the night?"

"They've been completed. You did very well, my dear."

"Thank you." She resisted as he tried to guide her away. "Your parents—"

"Wave to my father, Isobel," he commanded tersely, "and then direct us toward the door."

It took a bit more doing than that to leave the affair. The duke insisted on cuffing both his son and daughter-in-law a few more times, and the duchess, having arrived as she always did just when Nathan wanted to be away from her, insisted on holding him there by his free hand.

"Nathan, you are not leaving!"

"We are, madam. It has been a long day for both Isobel and myself."

"Oh, Nathan." His mother sighed, and her hand gripped his tightly for a moment. "Well, if you must. But you will come for supper tomorrow night. Please."

He opened his mouth to decline, but Isobel, curse her, was quicker. "We would be delighted, Your Grace," she announced firmly. "Wouldn't we, my lord?"

The light jab to his side was somewhat less than subtle. "Delighted," he agreed between clenched teeth. "Until then, Mother. Father."

He hustled Isobel away before she could commit them to a week in Abergele House.

"Really, Nathan, there is no need for us to depart. Your parents would like so much to have more time with you. There's so much they want to say."

"Oh, I'm certain there is." He settled her firmly in front of him and pushed her in what he hoped was the direction of the stairs.

"Nathan."

"Enough, Isobel, please. My parents will have ample time to quiz me about my disappointing behavior."

She sighed but fell silent as they made their way out of the house. The night air was unseasonably chilly, and he felt her shiver at his side. Without thinking, he wrapped an arm about her and held her close. She fit so perfectly.

He did not particularly want to think of how very right she felt tucked against him, wanted even less to contemplate having her warm and willing beneath him. So, clearing a voice gone annoyingly husky, he demanded, "What did Robard say to you?"

With rising fury, he listened to her recount the meeting. "Stupid bastard, trying to seduce my wife!"

"Well, I hardly think seduction was his true intent, my lord."

"Oh? And why do you say that?"

He heard her soft snort. "Really, Nathan. I am not the sort of woman whom men try to seduce."

She was so terribly wrong, Nathan thought. He forgot his anger as he mused how very much he would like to seduce her. He suppressed a sigh. "Should he approach you again, you will let me know immediately."

"I tried."

"Yes, I know." A carriage rolled toward them. "Is this ours?"

"Aye." Isobel guided him forward. "Do you really believe he would try anything truly unseemly?"

Another man might have been angered by the wistful tone in his wife's voice. Nathan knew better. Isobel really did not believe a man could desire her so. She would never stray; he was completely confident on that matter. But she needed to know her own allure.

He could only hope he would have the opportunity to educate her.

"My dear, he is a reprobate of the worst kind. He will try *anything* unseemly."

"I am sure you are mistaken. He was merely—"

"Yes, yes. Somewhat forward. Do not fear. I will deal with the matter."

He hoped she would not pry further. Splendid creature that she was, she did not. Instead, she was silent as he helped her into the carriage, then grasped his hand to assist him. Nathan, however, pulled back.

Something held him still. He strained his ears for the sound that had seized his attention. He could not hear anything above laughter, conversation, and rattling carriage wheels that signaled the departure from a ball.

Reluctantly he climbed in beside Isobel. But even as the vehicle rolled away, he could not shake the feeling that, for the second time this evening, he was being watched.

The first had been upon leaving Gerard's office. He had felt eyes upon his back. The sensation had sent a chill of foreboding— and memory—rippling down his spine.

He was still pondering the matter sometime later as he bade Isobel good night and retired to his chamber. There was very little chance he had imagined both occasions. Experience had honed his instincts and taught him to trust them. Someone had been watching him closely. A curious gaze directed at the reclusive Marquess of Oriel, or something more ominous?

As he removed his clothes and slipped into a dressing

gown, he wondered if he ought to mention the matter to
Isobel. He abandoned the notion quickly. He did not
want to answer the questions that would, quite rightly,
follow. Nor did he want to frighten his wife unneces-
sarily. Should he sense any real danger, he could have
her back in Hertfordshire within hours.

He paced the room, driven by restlessness and vague
disquiet. He found himself first at the brandy decanter,
glass in hand, then within arm's reach of the connecting
door. He could hear the faint sounds of the fire being
stoked. Isobel would be in her nightgown, making final
preparations for bed.

The urge was too strong. He had to be with her again,
if only for a moment. Even as he tapped lightly at the
door, he was searching for a good excuse. Another compliment for her handling of the night? More questions
about her unpleasant encounter with Trevor Robard?
Comments on the upcoming Paget family circus? Yes,
that would do nicely. He pushed the door open and
entered Isobel's chamber.

Perhaps had she not just stoked the fire, he would not
have seen. But leaping flames and a brace of candles
were more than enough. Isobel stood near the hearth,
and, for the briefest moment, Nathan could not tell where
the flames ended and she began. Then, in that scant
second before she scrambled for her dressing gown, his
heart nearly stopped beating in his chest.

Tumbled copper hair and pale satin skin were, fleet-
ingly, as clear to him as if he had his vision back. Perhaps it was only that his imagination was far more
powerful than his failed eyes, but he had received a glorious gift.

The vision was gone already to wavering colors and
hazy curves, but Nathan had seen it. He had seen his
wife in all her fiery glory. He had seen the gentle
sway of her breasts, the curve of lush hips, the flash of

sun-fire curls at the juncture of her soft thighs. For the second time, he found himself offering thanks heavenward for those beautiful images he could still perceive.

CHAPTER 12

Isobel struggled to get her arm into the sleeve of her dressing gown, only to discover that she was shoving her right hand into the left sleeve. Blushing and fumbling, she reversed the gown and quickly put it on. All the while, Nathan stood in the doorway, face not averted in the least. Of course he would not look away, she thought. He had no idea he had just walked in on her stark naked. The knowledge offered some comfort, but not enough.

"My lord, I did not hear you knock."

"I apologize. I assure you I did so."

Somewhat calmer now that she was covered, Isobel suggested that he sit. He did not.

"Thank you, but I won't stay. I only came to remind you that we are dining with my family tomorrow."

"I remember."

"Ah, yes, well, good."

For a moment, he looked very young and slightly lost, hands thrust into his dressing-gown pockets. Isobel deliberately kept her own gaze averted from the dusky, hair-sprinkled skin visible below the hem. Well, averted after that first glance. He had lovely feet.

Feet? *Dia*, she must be more rattled than she thought to have noticed. But then, she was fast coming to the conclusion that Nathan was far more handsome than she had first thought. Still frightening, yes, when he was not charming her into witless stammering, but not at all hard on the eyes.

Clearing her throat, she managed, "Was there something specific you wished to discuss about tomorrow night?"

One of his lovely feet brushed against the other as he shuffled. "I-I suppose I ought to tell you about my siblings. I thought you would meet my sister tonight, but she was not in attendance."

"Nay. Your mother said she is at a party in Surrey."

"Inconsiderate," Nathan muttered, and Isobel smiled.

"She could not have been expected to know we were arriving in Town. No one did."

"*Mmm.* True. She will be there tomorrow, no doubt." There was a moment of silence, then he announced, "My brother will be there, too."

"William. Aye, so your mother said. He is in Town with his regiment."

"Ah . . . yes."

Isobel had never seen Nathan quite so awkward, and while she searched for an explanation, she found herself smiling with the unexpected pleasure of the moment. "Do you perhaps wish to tell me of William's mysterious experiments now?"

"*Hmm?* Oh, no. No. Another time." He shook his head bemusedly, sending a lock of hair falling onto his forehead. "Well, then, I will bid you a good night. Again."

"And to you, Nathan. Again."

He turned as if to enter his chamber, then stopped. "How did you manage it, Isobel?"

"Manage what?"

"My father. I have never seen him take to anyone as he clearly has to you. Not even his own children."

She wanted to tell him just how very taken the duke

was with his own children, but it did not seem quite the
right moment. So she gave an airy laugh and answered,
"Trout."

"I beg your pardon?"

"Trout," she repeated. "The fish. There's a strapping
grand one mounted in his study. I merely mentioned my
own fishing experiences. I've a fair hand with a rod, you
know."

She thought she saw his chin jerk. Obviously fishing
was not an activity in which proper English ladies partici-
pated. How very predictable. But he did not comment on
her talent at all.

"You were in my father's study?"

"Aye, for a good hour."

"He *invited* you in?"

She smiled. "Nay, I invited myself. Your mother and I
were passing by on a tour of the house. I daresay she
wasn't planning on my darting into the study, but I saw
your father at his desk and thought it would be a good
time—"

"Isobel," Nathan interrupted, a rueful smile softening
his features, "you are a wonder."

"I am glad you think so." Driven by some odd impulse, perhaps from that smile, Isobel crossed the room
and, rising to her toes, brushed a light kiss over his jaw.
"I am continually impressed by you, too." She retreated a
few feet. "Sweet dreams to you, Nathan."

He muttered something in response and disappeared
into his chamber. One hand, she noticed as he went,
drifted upward to touch the spot she had kissed.

Warmed and somehow giddy, Isobel wandered toward
the window. She had discovered there were few stars to be
seen in the London night, but she thought she would look
anyway. There had been enough gratifying surprises in her
day that she was ready to chance one more. She drew the
curtain aside and peered out. It had rained since their

return, laying a glossy sheen over the street. Under the streetlamp, the moisture glinted faintly. Not stars, certainly, but a pleasing sight nonetheless.

A slight movement caught her eye. Following it, she saw a shadow slipping into the darkness. Had someone been there, across from the house? But nay, there was nothing now.

"If you can see stars on a rainy night, lass," she chided herself, "to be sure you'll be seeing ghosts next."

Amused with herself, she let the curtain fall and retreated to the warm comfort of her bed.

The duke was muttering again. Nathan, well used to his father's temperament, kept his attention fixed on his trout. He had not cared much in the last few months, but Isobel's entrance into his life had made him determined not to resemble some ravenous beast at meals. Besides, he did not think he would be able to explain a trail of spots and crumbs to his mother. She had drummed the importance of impeccable table manners into her children at a very early age and would certainly not countenance a lapse in her thirty-two-year-old son.

The duchess, however, was not paying attention. She was too busy explaining to Isobel, for the third time no less, that dearest William had been expected but was unavoidably detained.

"Detained by some high-stepping filly," the duke muttered. "What think you of that, Isobel? Damned poor excuse, if you ask me."

Nathan smiled into his wineglass. Isobel was at a rare loss for words. He took pity on her. "He means that quite literally, my dear. William has an unfortunate affinity for the Turf."

"Ah. I see." She was, no doubt, blushing. It had been an honest mistake, thinking the duke was referring to a filly of the two-legged variety. Nathan had seen other people do the same.

"Ain't the affinity that is unfortunate, boy; it's the gambling!"

"As you say, sir." Nathan turned back to Isobel. "I stand corrected. And I daresay the wagering would not be unfortunate, either, should he have a modicum of sense in the matter. My brother has a knack for picking any horse guaranteed to come in dead last."

Isobel, it seemed, had nothing to say about William's poor judgment. The duke had a great deal to say, of course, but was forestalled by his wife's stern reproof. "This is hardly proper discussion for the table. Isobel, dear, you must tell us how you are finding London."

Nathan thought he heard Isobel mumble something in Gaelic. He would have to ask her to teach him some of the language. No doubt she had just given an amusing commentary on Town, and an astute one.

Aloud, she replied, "I've yet to see much beyond the house and the modiste's establishment, Your Grace."

"*Mmm.* Yes. Well, that dress is most . . . becoming."

Isobel assumed the duchess would have much preferred another word. *Bright,* perhaps. The older woman would never stoop to saying *garish.* In truth, the vivid emerald crepe with its daffodil trim was a bit bright, but the modiste had assured her it was all the rage. And she liked bright colors.

"It is a lovely dress," came from across the table.

Isobel sent a grateful smile in her sister-in-law's direction. Lady Mariah was as much the image of her mother as Nathan was of the duke, but she had none of the cool reserve that accompanied the duchess's pale beauty. She had welcomed Isobel with open arms and not hesitated to express what her parents could not.

"You have brought Nathan back to us," she had

announced firmly, "which proves you are, quite simply, perfect."

That, apparently, was that.

"You must introduce me to your modiste," she was saying now. "Mine does not do nearly so appealing a trim."

Isobel glanced down at the pretty, if rather ordinary embroidered ribbon trimming the bodice of her dress and smiled. Mariah's own gown was a delicate confection of gilt tissue and lace, and put one in mind of fairies. Her compliment was little more than nonsense. Her kindness, however, was sincere and irresistible.

The duke's muttering increased in volume. He had clearly had enough of this particular subject. "Man can't even eat without having his ears filled with rubbish about flounces and feathers. Bad for the digestion, I say."

"We have mentioned neither flounces nor feathers, Papa," Mariah returned pleasantly, "and I feel compelled to mention that women cannot seem to have a peaceful meal without talk of horses, guns, and warfare. If you must have such conversation, you shall have to appeal to Nathan. We women find such things unsettling."

Her bright eyes convinced Isobel that very little would be unsettling. Like her brother, Mariah was made of sterner stuff. It must have been difficult, though, for her to hear any talk of the war. Her husband was an officer, serving somewhere on the Peninsula.

"I must confess I am perfectly content to hear about fashion." Nathan's hand brushed Isobel's as he set aside his glass. "Isobel has given me new interest in the matter. Tell me, Mariah, what color would *you* call my wife's gown?"

"Green," was the pert retort.

"Bad for the digestion," the duke muttered, and tossed back his wine.

Supper was over soon enough, and the duke seemed

no worse for the discussion. On the contrary, he patted his belly contentedly and glanced toward the sideboard with its port decanter. His gaze then slid to Nathan. Isobel could see the contentment there, and the pleasure at what would be their time alone.

She would have very much liked to kick her husband soundly when he announced, "Since there are just the two of us men here, perhaps we could forgo formalities and accompany you ladies to the drawing room now."

Disappointment to one parent, joy to another. The duke's eyes closed wearily even as the duchess's lit up. "Of course, my dear. We should be delighted."

She led the way, chattering all the while. "We moved your Great-uncle Horace's painting from the drawing room, Nathan. No matter that he was a general in the nasty little spat with the Colonials; it was simply too grim a visage to have scowling down on one during tea."

"And to where did you move it, madam?"

"Oh, merely upstairs."

"To the darkest depths of the attics," was Mariah's cheerfully whispered addition.

"I felt it was time for a change." The duchess swept into the grand, and decidedly yellow, drawing room, the rest of the party behind her. "I covered that hideous paneling and moved the—"

"Furniture," Nathan muttered as he encountered some object that most certainly should not have been there.

Isobel was quick to his rescue as always, her shoulder fitting as if by nature under his. "Ottoman," she whispered. As he righted himself, she added softly, "A very ugly, very orange ottoman."

He laughed a good deal louder than he had intended. The dry pronouncement, in that soft Scottish voice, had done him in.

"What's the matter, boy?" the duke demanded. "Too much wine for you?"

"I beg your pardon, sir. It must have been." As Isobel discreetly led him to a settee where, if Nathan remembered correctly, the pianoforte had once been placed, he leaned down and whispered, "Can you see a small, painted table, the base of which is a trio of cherubs?"

"*Mmm* . . . oh, aye, near the windows. 'Tis the same green as my brothers' faces when they've had too much wine."

Nathan smiled. "An improvement, no doubt. It used to be purple."

The pianoforte had found a new home across the room. Mariah settled herself there and launched into a pleasant minuet. Mozart, Nathan decided, and wondered how long it would take for his father to begin snoring.

It was less than five minutes. Mariah, sighing in fond resignation, joined the family. "He never snored when you played the violin, Nathan."

"With good reason, sprite. No one could sleep with the dogs howling in misery."

"You play the violin?" Isobel was clearly amazed.

"Extremely badly, my dear. It was a short-lived musical career."

"Do you play, Isobel?" the duchess queried, raising her voice slightly, since the duke's snoring had taken on symphonic proportions.

"A little, but not well. We had a harpsichord on Skye. 'Tis my sister Margaret who—"

"You must play for us now!"

"Oh, I do not think—"

"There is ample music on the stand." The duchess was either ignoring her protestations or could not hear them.

"Yes, my dear, you must play. I have not yet had the pleasure of hearing you do so." Nathan, it seemed, was enjoying the exchange far too much.

"With good reason," Isobel mimicked quietly, then

rose to her feet. "Very well, then, but you'll be seeing to your own shins when we leave."

"Whatever did she mean by that, dearest?" the duchess inquired.

Nathan chuckled, then lied easily. "Madam, I have no idea."

Isobel took her seat at the pianoforte. She did not begin playing immediately, but instead took a long look at the Paget family tableau. They were a stunning group, to be sure, even the duke as he sprawled in his chair, mouth wide open. Stunning, and a wee bit complacent. Too complacent, she thought.

She knew precisely what she would play, and it would certainly not be found among the sheets of Bach and Haydn before her. Grinning, and offering a silent request for forgiveness, she struck the first chord.

"What?" The duke came awake with a jerk.

Mariah, on the verge of accepting a cup of tea from her mother, covered her smile with her hand. The duchess bobbled the china. Nathan laughed aloud.

Never had "The March of the MacLeoid," in the absence of pipes and drums, been played with such gusto. Never had Isobel enjoyed it nearly so much.

She finished with a flair—to complete silence other than Nathan's chuckling. Mariah, eyes bright, still had her hands clasped over her mouth. Feeling rather smug, Isobel returned to her husband's side. His hand found hers, and he squeezed it warmly.

The duchess broke the silence at last. "Well, my dear, that was . . . lively."

The duke muttered something about digestion.

"It was marvelous, Isobel," Nathan announced.

"Good heavens, we've been invaded!"

All four swung to face the door. Lounging there, with tousled brown hair, a red uniform that looked as if it had met with a stiff wind, and a very familiar smile that left no doubt as to his familial affiliations, was the elusive, unlucky William.

"The Scots have arrived," he said cheerfully, and flashed that grin at Isobel. "I daresay the Pagets will never be quite the same."

"William!" His mother's greeting was a good deal more delighted than berating. "How good of you to come after all."

"How much did you lose, boy?" the duke demanded.

"Oh, a trifling amount." The young man swept in and bowed in front of Isobel. "Fifty pounds. What a great pleasure to meet you, madam." While his father sputtered over the fifty pounds, William turned to Nathan. "You're looking well, old boy."

"He looks like hell!" the duke muttered.

"Ah, well, good to have him back regardless." With the ease of a circus juggler, he kissed his mother, deftly pulled a pin from his sister's hair, and dodged her batting hands to take a sip of tea from her cup. "I must say, what a day it has been."

The duchess launched into a halfhearted and ineffectual harangue against William's manners. Nathan found himself grinning. It was impossible to be angry with William. Isobel, laughing quietly at his side, seemed to agree. Nathan was ten years older than his brother, and it was only recently, now that William was an adult, that William's idolization and his own benevolence had melded into mutual affection. When his brother reached out to clasp his shoulder, Nathan felt an odd trembling in his jaw.

He was home, among his family. With Isobel's warm presence at his side, he was fully convinced, if just for the moment, that all was well.

William cheerfully ignored his mother's harangue and turned to his father. "I say, Father, I've arranged to have something delivered here, and you mustn't appropriate it for yourself."

"Oh, William, you haven't bought more of that nasty Welsh ale, have you?" Mariah shuddered. "Stephen was ill for days after that last batch."

"Stephen," her brother shot back, "loved the stuff. I've half a mind to send him a keg in Portugal. But no." Delicate teakwood groaned as he dropped heavily into a chair. "This isn't potable stuff. As a matter of fact, it's gunpowder."

"Gunpowder? Oh, *William*, not again!" The duchess's weak protestations were lost. William was off again.

"Stopped by Brooks's on my way here," he informed Nathan. "Heard you haven't been about since your return. Sedgwick was most blue-deviled about it."

"I . . . no. I haven't had the time. Perhaps—"

"Had an interesting encounter with another old schoolmate of yours. Can't say I ever much liked the fellow, but he was blasted eager to hear of your welfare. We shared a damned fine bottle of Madeira. You really must talk to your cronies yourself, Nathan. It's bloody embarrassing for me to have to tell them I haven't the foggiest idea what you've been up to all these months."

"Was it Rotheroe?"

"Was Rotheroe what?" China rattled as William bounded to his feet, no doubt in search of something to put into his belly.

"Was it Rotheroe who provided the Madeira?"

"Good God, no. Rotheroe still thinks I'm in short pants. Stodgy old coots, your friends. What a terrible tragedy, Rievaulx's going. He was always a step above the rest. They can't seem to accept the fact that I'm an adult now and can handle my liquor perfectly well."

"Debatable," Mariah commented.

Nathan sighed, both in sadness at the mention of his lost friend and in exasperation. "I cannot be expected to field questions, Will, if you refuse to tell me who is doing the asking."

"*Hmm?* Oh, yes. It was St. Wulfstan. Seems he just got back to Town himself." Having ascertained there was not, in fact, anything edible in the room, William plunked himself down next to Isobel. "Skye, was it? Splendid Scotch whiskey there."

Nathan was a step behind. "St. Wulfstan?"

"He's Irish, man, not Scottish. Though I can't imagine why he insists on using that god-awful accent. He was at Eton and Oxford with the rest of the lordlings."

"St. Wulfstan was quizzing you about me?"

"I just said so, didn't I?"

"I've never much cared for Lord St. Wulfstan," the duchess commented primly. "He has always seemed rather coarse to me."

"He seems that way to everyone, Mama," Mariah replied. "It is, I believe, deliberate."

"Damned fine shot, St. Wulfstan," the duke muttered. "Never misses. Good to have about during a hunting party."

As far as Nathan was concerned, this particular party was over. He needed to get away from his family so he could think. It was impossible to manage a clear thought with William rattling on. He assumed Isobel, too, would be ready to depart. She had certainly had her moment. Why not give her time to gloat quietly.

"You cannot mean it!" the duchess protested when he announced his intentions. "Why, we have had so little time with Isobel. And you—you have been missed, Nathan."

"We are not making a run for the Scottish border, madam. We are simply going home. I assure you, you will see plenty of Isobel. I am an appalling shopping companion for her. If you are especially pleasant, perhaps she will even allow you to make a recommendation on a pelisse or two."

Mariah pouted prettily but brightened when a shopping expedition was, in fact, planned. The duke grunted something about not understanding what was the hurry to be off. Oriel House was only around the corner, after all. William was more philosophical. "Suppose you newly wedded do need time alone." He gave Isobel an enthusiastic kiss. "I daresay we'll get along smashingly, you and I. Never did fancy that Cecily chit. Too toplofty by half. You seem a simpler sort of girl."

"William!" the duchess chided.

Nathan hustled Isobel out the door.

She was silent during the short ride. Nathan found himself muttering vague curses under his breath. Too much time in his father's presence tended to have that effect.

He ought to have known Isobel would not remain quiet for long and that when she did speak, it would be to home in on his concerns unerringly. "Nathan," she said as they crossed their foyer, "who is this Lord St. Wulfstan to you?"

He did not reply as he navigated the first set of stairs.

"Nathan."

"St. Wulfstan is an acquaintance. We knew each other at school and served together on the Peninsula."

He hoped she would be satisfied with that. Of course she was not. She did, however, wait until they were up the second flight before pressing. "An acquaintance, is it? Not a friend. Yet he was asking about you."

"Natural curiosity, I suppose. We have not met in many months. Good night, Isobel. I trust you will sleep well."

Instead of trotting obediently off to bed, she planted herself squarely in front of his door. As much as he might wish it—and oh, how he did—she was not waiting for an invitation to enter.

"Ah, no, you don't! I'll not be dismissed so easily."

He gave a faint smile. "Trust me, my dear, dismissing you would be very difficult indeed."

Isobel was fast losing her patience. She understood Nathan's pride, the foolish pride that made him think he could handle all matters on his own, but she was having none of it now. "Well, then," she said firmly, "suppose you tell me why this man is snooping about, first me and then William. Really, Nathan, you cannot think I wouldn't be able to put two and two together. It was St. Wulfstan who accosted me last night, was it not?"

"It was."

"Curious. And you don't like him. What is his interest in you?"

"Really, Isobel. St. Wulfstan and I go back some years. It is only natural that he would have an interest in my present state."

"Rubbish." She blew out her breath in an exasperated huff. "Don't tell me, then. But you cannot go on keeping me ignorant of matters you find unpleasant. I am your wife, Nathan." As seemed only natural to her now, she reached up to plant a quick kiss on his cheek. "I'll bid you good night, and trust you will sleep w—"

She broke off with a soft gasp as his cane clattered to the floor, again when his hands clamped around her upper arms. It was far from painful, but it was not a gentle touch, either.

"Yes, Isobel. You are my wife. If you believe nothing else I tell you tonight, believe this: I never for a moment forget who you are to me."

Had she been prepared for the kiss, expected it, she might have moved away. But he took her by surprise, his lips finding hers swiftly and unerringly. In fact, they fitted to hers so well that they might have been molded just for that purpose. He tasted of brandy, smelled lightly of sage, and completely overwhelmed her senses. The kiss was quick, hard, and so sweet that she sighed with the simple pleasure of it.

Then it was over.

Nathan's hands were still clasped on her arms, and he moved her easily from in front of his door. "Good night, Isobel. I will see you at breakfast." He released her abruptly. Then, with the grace of a man in complete control of every faculty, he entered his chamber and closed the door behind him.

Isobel stood where she was, one hand pressed lightly to her mouth, unable to tell if it was her fingertips that tingled, or her lips.

CHAPTER 13

Hold embers to the breast of thy lover
Against the sting of the rain
And the changing of the wind,
And I will vow and warrant thee
That lover shall never leave.
                    —Highland love charm

"And I say you're not ready to attempt any such thing!" Isobel snapped.

Nathan smiled over the rim of his coffee cup. "What a protector you have become, my dear, jittery whenever I am out of your sight."

Isobel's snort meant far more than the string of Gaelic words that followed. He decided he really would have to ask her to teach him some of the language, if only so he could curse right back at her.

"I assure you, Isobel, I shall be fine. I have spent more time at Brooks's than anywhere else in London. Each chair, each umbrella stand is as familiar as any in my own home."

"They could have moved."

"The mountains of Wales would move first. Trust me when I say change is as horrific a prospect to gentlemen's clubs as a plague."

"Well, then, you might give yourself away by misaddressing someone."

She was nothing if not persistent. Nathan smiled anew. She did not mean to destroy his confidence. On the contrary, he knew she had a great deal of faith in him. Isobel was simply being Isobel, used to her own indispens-ability and determined to be of help.

"In the past sennight, my dear, I have attended enough balls, soirees, and supper parties to satisfy even the worst of high-sticklers. Few acquaintances have been able to resist the opportunity to come close and ascertain just how mad I have become in my solitude. Or just how mad was my marriage. Between my ears, my father, and my wife, I have been able to identify most of the persons I will encounter in Town."

"Aye. I cannot imagine a single *Sasunnach* noble was missing from last night's circus."

The previous night's circus had been a bash at Carlton House. Isobel was quite right in assuming everyone who was anyone in the ton had been there. She had been pinned down, perused, and quizzed by Sally Jersey, Alvanley, and the Duke of York, among countless others. The pinch-lipped Sally had pronounced her "tolerable." York's more eloquent assessment had included the words "damned spicy piece indeed." Isobel had been impressed with neither.

"Ah, well, perhaps a member or two of the gentry was not in attendance." Nathan reached for another slice of bacon. "I will be back in plenty of time to don my armor for tonight. You have made quite an impression on Society, my dear. We could not possibly miss Lady Cowper's concert."

Another snort made Isobel's opinion of this honor quite clear. "I vow if I must sit through one more hour of a quartet sawing and squeaking its way through Bach, I'll do something rash."

"Yes, no doubt you would prefer the whining and wailing of bagpipes." Nathan grinned as she chucked her napkin at him. "Very well. Enough of that. You, I believe, are engaged with the modiste this morning."

"More pins," she grumbled. " 'Tis a wonder I've not bloodied every gown. Or a few noses."

Nathan slid his hand across the table until it met hers. "Just remember, sweetheart, how much Scots blood has been surrendered to the depraved English. You are merely adding your chapter to history."

"Well, I've a mind to alter the path of history."

"There is every chance you might do just that, Isobel. Every chance."

She left the table then, with one more admonition for his care at Brooks's. When she had gone, trailing vague Gaelic invectives and her honey-and-rosemary scent, Nathan lifted her napkin to his face. It was an absurd gesture, he knew, but he couldn't help himself.

He had not kissed her since that one time, a night that seemed years past rather than days, nor had she repeated those innocent good-night brushes of her lips that had been so unexpected and so welcome. No, they had been cordial enough with each other, affectionate even. But they had not touched beyond the necessary linking of arms.

Sleep had become damnably difficult. Nathan had taken to adding a shot of whiskey to his bedtime preparations. It did nothing for the continually aroused state of his body, but did serve to dull his mind somewhat. It was a shame he could not drink his way through the days as well. Isobel's presence never failed to set nerve to attention. But he had business to see to, and a dull mind made for poor work.

He had arranged to meet Rotheroe and Gerard at Brooks's. As for St. Wulfstan, he seemed to be everywhere Nathan was not. He had heard nothing of the man in days.

Rievaulx, Harlow, Witherspoon, Dennison, Brooke . . . five gone. Of course, in times of war, such things happened. Entire regiments died. Certainly, more often than not, intelligence agents died, for they were inevitably the ones who got the closest to the enemy. Nathan wanted to find a connection between the deaths, something more tangible than war and the cleverness of Napoleon's own spies. But as the days passed and he pondered the same, sketchy information over and over, he was left frustrated and no closer to any answers than he'd had on that night when he had lost his sight and his closest friend.

Rotheroe, with his useless arm, seemed as likely to have orchestrated a series of fatal attacks as Mad King George himself. He had never been much of a soldier but had been useful to the Ten for his knack with languages and his uncanny ability to decipher French communiqués. He had returned to England only a few weeks ago and, as foolish as it seemed, could not be eliminated as a suspect.

Sighing, Nathan set Isobel's napkin aside and rose from the table. Most likely, he and Rotheroe would do no more than reminisce about a time better left unremembered. Gerard would remain firm in his belief that none of his men could have turned against the others.

If Matthew felt guilt-ridden about the deaths, Nathan felt worse. Five good men were gone, and he could concentrate on only one matter: that of bedding his own wife.

Isobel had assumed her sister-in-law was developing an affection for her. Apparently she had been wrong. Mariah was clearly of the opinion that torture by pins had not been enough. She was now herding Isobel, rather like some mindless animal, into the milliner's.

"Do not be absurd," she chided, "every woman likes hats!"

"I did not say I disliked them." Isobel wondered if it

would be too childish of her to grab onto the door frame and cling there. "I said I had no need of more."

"Nonsense."

Mariah gave her a shove and got her into the busy shop. Isobel offered a weak smile to several familiar faces. Mariah glared resolutely and set to examining the stock with a serious and critical eye. She selected a hat, placed it on Isobel's head, then stood and silently regarded her.

When she finally did speak, it was with a weary sigh. "Can you not smile a bit, Isobel? It is so very difficult to tell what becomes you when you are scowling."

Isobel shoved an encroaching spray of papier-mâché cherries from her brow. "I look ridiculous. Were I to smile, I would look witless."

"Well, perhaps the fruit arrangement is a bit much."

" 'Tis no arrangement. 'Tis a breakfast bowl."

The cherries were soon replaced by a profusion of silk lilies. "There! Much better."

"Than the cherries?" Isobel muttered. "To be sure, but an improvement like going from pan to fire."

Mariah stepped back and planted her hands on her hips. She, of course, looked utterly charming, Isobel thought, with a feathery creation that resembled a swan perched atop her pale curls. "You are hopeless!"

"Aye, well, I've been telling you that for days now." Isobel returned the lilies to the counter. "I've an appalling taste for the unacceptable." Turning to the shopgirl, she pointed to a simple, high-crowned bonnet and said, "Leaf-green silk, pleated within the crown, ivory ribbon."

"Yes, madam." The woman hurried away in search of the fabric.

"Really, Isobel. I am doing my best to put you in fashion, and you insist on thwarting me at every turn. Why, that red silk at the modiste's—"

"Made me look like a lobster with a carrot garnish." Isobel gave the other woman an unrepentant grin. "I am very much afraid you're destined to be disappointed by me."

Mariah's frown quickly turned into a smile. "I could never be disappointed by you, dearest. I never would have thought—that is, none of us . . ." A delicate flush stained her cheeks, and she turned back again to forage among the flowers and fruit.

"Mariah?"

"Hmm?"

" 'Tis all right. I understand. But it would help me if you were to talk about it."

"About?"

"Oh, don't, please. About Nathan and what happened to him, to your family."

For a moment, she thought her sister-in-law would refuse. Then Mariah gave a small sigh. "We thought we had lost him for good after he returned from the Peninsula. He went straight to Hertfordshire with no more than a brief message telling us not to come. William went, as soon as he could. Nathan would not . . . would not see him."

Isobel's heart ached for her husband's siblings, for his parents who still did not quite know how to reach him. "His pride is a fierce thing," she offered gently. "It pains him even now to be seen with the cane."

"I know that. We all do. But it's more than pride. Nathan has never quite been like the rest of us. He has always taken so much upon himself, responsibility for things beyond his control. Has he spoken of Anne?"

"His first fiancée, aye."

"We all adored her. We all suffered when she died. But Nathan . . ." Mariah shrugged, her eyes sad. "Nathan blamed himself and would not allow any of us near enough to tell him how foolish that was, nor to comfort him. Dear God, Isobel, after the funeral he stood by her graveside for hours, so straight and silent, even when it began to rain. We all tried to get him to come away, but it was as if he were deaf and blind in his grief. No, in his guilt."

"He loved her," Isobel said softly. And she thought, irrationally, that this Anne had been a weak woman indeed to die when she'd had Nathan's devotion to live for.

"We were so frightened when he left for the Continent," Mariah continued, "sure he would take the country's future onto his shoulders alone. We were so frightened, yet none of us dared ask him not to go."

"He's back now." Isobel had no idea what else she could possibly say.

"He is, yes. But he is still distant around us. There's still that reluctance in his eyes. Except when he looks at you."

"Mariah."

"I think my brother can't help but be touched, perhaps too much, by those around him. It's his nature. It frightens him, though, so much that he closes himself off." Mariah gripped Isobel's hand tightly, desperation in her touch. "Don't let him go away again, Isobel. Please. Don't *you* go away."

Saddened and overwhelmed, Isobel could only give a silent shake of her head. How could she explain that her role was practical, nothing more? And that, should Nathan perceive himself unable to function in Society, he would close himself off again—from all of them, herself included. Even after mere weeks in Nathan's presence, she was aware it would hurt beyond comprehension if he should turn away from her.

She was both confused and frightened by her conflicting feelings. Each night, her knees went to jelly at the thought he might come again to her chamber. He would not break his promise, she knew, but her nerves skittered nonetheless each time she heard a noise through the connecting door. If it had been mere apprehension, she would have scolded herself and been done with it. But there was more: a vague anticipation that bewildered her. He charmed her at times, set her heart to rabbity jumps, and then made her so wary that she could have screamed.

Worried that anything she might say would cause more damage than solace, she stepped away from her sister-in-law to survey a display of beaded bandeaus.

She did not look up when the door opened, but could not resist a peek when a clear, soprano voice demanded attention. The new arrivals were, she decided, precisely what Mariah was hoping to make her. The shorter woman was fair, delicate, and bore a lovely resemblance to a china doll. The taller was, to Isobel, nearly perfect. Slender and raven-haired, she had a face that belonged on a cameo and a voice that belonged on the stage.

"Why, Mariah! What good luck to find you here!"

From her vantage point several yards away, Isobel watched her sister-in-law replace a length of spangled ribbon with unnecessary care. "Good morning, Lady Bronnar."

Lady Bronnar, ignoring the coolness of the greeting, moved forward in a swirl of pristine white muslin and violet scent. She seized Mariah's hands and demanded, "You must set my mind at ease on a particular matter. I have heard your brother has married."

"He has, yes."

"So the report was true. We have just returned from Bath, you see." She leaned in, quite dwarfing the diminutive Mariah. "I arrived home to hear . . ." One slender hand went to her bosom. "Oh, it cannot be true, my dear. I have heard he married the daughter of a Highland *crofter*!"

Someone coughed. Someone else giggled. Isobel swallowed a sigh, stepped behind a display of military-style hats, and wondered if she ought to have a sign made to wear about her neck. *Lady Oriel*, it would read. *Scottish. Domesticated. References available through Her Grace, the Duchess of Abergele.*

"My brother," Mariah said evenly, "married the daughter of a Scottish gentleman, cousin to Lord MacLeod of Skye."

Isobel winced. They were related, to be sure, to the chief of Clan MacLeod, but it was a distant connection at best. Most of the ten-thousand-odd MacLeods in Scotland could claim as much. Beyond that, to call him Lord MacLeod of Skye was not quite accurate. He was MacLeod of MacLeod, and was about as likely to be found in any English book of the peerage as her "gentleman" father.

Sighing, she decided she'd best correct the mistake. She had taken no more than a step, however, when Lady Bronnar's companion chanced upon the green silk that the milliner had brought out for Isobel's bonnet.

"Oh, Cecily, look! Would this not be perfect with your new morning dress? I daresay it is precisely the same color!"

Cecily. The title alone had meant nothing to Isobel. The name Cecily set her teeth on edge. She had heard it just a tad too often, whispered just loudly enough in her presence so she would be certain to hear. And understand.

This was the woman to whom Nathan had been engaged, the one who had broken their attachment with a careless letter while he lay wounded in a Portuguese field hospital.

The door opened again, admitting enough giggling ladies to make the shop crowded and to convince Isobel that someone had orchestrated this event and sold tickets. Such was the way of London, she was learning. All potentially unpleasant encounters must be had with at least a dozen gawking people in attendance.

Perhaps a good Highlander would never turn away from adversity, but a wise woman always retreated from an uneven battleground. Had Bonnie Prince Charlie and his hapless Scots been a bit less thickheaded, they might have avoided the slaughter at Culloden Field. Of course, there had been no women in their ranks.

Isobel was presently surrounded by the English, on their turf. What she had to say to Lady Bronnar would be much better done in a dark alley with a claymore. Pelting the woman with fake apples in the midst of a crowded millinery shop would not suffice.

"Mariah," Isobel called, relinquishing her hiding place, "I believe it is time to go."

"But the bonnet . . ." The modiste, arms full of silk, saw her sale heading toward the door.

"The green," Isobel announced coolly, "is bilious."

Doing her best to forget that her periwinkle sarcenet was a bit mussed from a day's shopping and that Mariah's ministrations with the papier-mâché fruit had left her hair in wild disarray, she gave Cecily Bronnar an even glance.

Mariah, clearly torn between dread and gleeful anticipation of some stinging Scottish wit, performed the introductions. Isobel vaguely registered that the other woman was Miss Julia Mewell. She would very much have liked to offer her condolences on having such an unpleasant mother, but stifled the urge.

"Lady Bronnar." She would have chewed on glass before expressing any pleasure in the meeting. "My husband has spoken of you."

This was clearly not what the divine Cecily had expected. Isobel had the impression that she herself was not what had been expected, either. Quite probably, this ravishing creature had expected the Highland crofter's daughter to be another ravishing creature. How else, after all, could she have snared a marquess?

One thing Isobel could say with some affection for the English was that they were amazingly easy to read. She had, in mere moments, been perused and dismissed. Lofty MacLeod connections or no, she was clearly not worthy of the lady's concern.

"Has he?" Cecily queried archly, flashing a smile that might have been truly dazzling had it not been so false. "I am gratified to know he still remembers me upon occasion. How very kind of him."

Isobel gave Cecily an equally false smile. "Oh, the recollection wasn't particularly kind."

The woman's eyes narrowed at the insult, but her smile did not falter. What a picture they must make, Isobel thought: smirking at each other. It was all just too silly. And rather entertaining.

"We have all been much concerned for Oriel's health, my lady," Cecily announced.

"Have you? How kind."

That particular gauntlet remained down.

"His friends were much distressed. Why, he disappeared so completely from Society after his return, we could not help but comment upon the gravity of his injuries. I have since heard the physical wounds were not so very terrible, after all."

So you think he has a broken heart, do you? Isobel wondered if Cecily fancied that Nathan was shattered beyond repair. How very vexing it must have been, if so, to hear he had married—and married a woman whose appeal could not have been money or position. "As we are in Town now, I imagine you will have ample opportunity to see how fully he has recovered."

"*Mmm.* We shall see, shan't we?" The woman gave an elegant shrug. "Men must expect a bit of discomfort, traipsing off to war like that. I am sure he, like so many others, regrets his decision to enlist."

Isobel tilted her head and hoped her smile read as much of pity as distaste. "I believe, Lady Bronnar, he has no regrets at all on *that* choice. His regrets lie in others. Now, if you would excuse us, we must go in search of some color. Come along, Mariah. I have a lovely bit of tartan in mind."

Her knees were shaking by the time they reached the street. It was bad enough to have been forced into a confrontation with a woman from her husband's past; far worse for the woman to have possessed everything she did not. Beauty, elegance stature.

"Insufferable conceit!" Mariah shook out her parasol. "I cannot tell you how delighted I am she took another man rather than my brother. That was very well done, Isobel."

Isobel darted a quick glance back into the shop. Cecily, head thrown back, was laughing. Her own victory soured with the taste of lies. "Was it? I'm fast coming to the conclusion, Mariah, that there isn't a whit of honesty to be found in this town."

Her sister-in-law patted her hand. "Don't fret, dearest. You have yet to visit Parliament."

Isobel turned in surprise. Mariah's clear blue gaze was guileless; only a single twitch of her lips betrayed her. A moment later they were walking arm in arm down the street, laughing loudly enough to turn heads.

Nathan was heartily regretting this particular decision. Thus far, he and Gerard had done nothing more useful than compare the merits of several different brandies. He was contemplating excusing himself to slosh his way home when Rotheroe, an hour late, sank into the empty chair.

"Ah, a breath of old times," he announced, pouring himself a brandy, then clinking his glass against Matthew's.

Nathan could not help but smile. Their breath in past times had indeed been much as it was now. Flammable. "It has been a while."

"Damn me, a year at least. How is Town treating you, Oriel?"

"As well as ever. It is . . . good to be back."

Rotheroe muttered something noncommittal. The return to Society could not have been easy on him. He had arrived from the Peninsula with a useless right arm and empty pockets, returned to the same lofty title and debt-ridden estates he had left. "Well, here we are again."

In vastly depleted numbers, Nathan thought. Aloud, he said, "A toast to the fallen."

"To Brooke," Gerard added. Rotheroe said nothing.

"Rievaulx."

"Dennison."

"To Brandon." Rotheroe plied the bottle.

Nathan's fingers tightened around his own snifter. "Brandon? Has something happened to him?"

The earl gave a humorless chuckle. "I have no idea, but he is the only one still on the Peninsula. It wasn't a peaceful place for the lot of us." He tapped his fingers on the table. "I hear you've been asking about Dennison. You really ought to spare yourself the effort."

Nathan leaned forward. "Oh?"

He could imagine the man's lean face closing, his often comically mobile features going stiff. "Come now, Oriel. Don't tell me you've forgotten. He was with me at Almeida."

Gerard coughed, shifted awkwardly in his seat. Yes, Dennison had been there that day, a day seldom mentioned among the Ten. It could never be proven that Dennison had fled his post, leaving English forces with no idea where their aid was needed most. Nor had anyone ever dared to ask Rotheroe if the vague rumors were true—if he had, in fact, been happily ensconced in a Portuguese brothel when the fatal attack began and had arrived belatedly at the garrison.

Whatever the reasons, the French had demolished the pitiful defenses. Almeida, its garrison long regarded as indestructible, had fallen. Rotheroe, half-dressed and bloody, had fought well but ended with arm and reputation shattered. Dennison, hale and far too corpulent for a man stationed in a city under siege, had eventually been quietly shipped home.

"Did you encounter him often in Town?" Nathan asked, as casually as he could.

Rotheroe snorted. "Everywhere. The man had a knack of appearing in whichever place he was least welcome." There was another clink as bottle met glass again. "Let me guess; he died owing you money. Take my advice and cut your losses, my friend. He died owing *everyone* money."

"Including you?"

"Hah. I am beginning to suspect your time away has affected your memory, Oriel. Remember me? The earl with four houses, five sisters, and not a bloody cent to my name? The last person I would have sat down at the card table with was Dennison." Then Rotheroe sighed. "It really isn't sporting of me to speak so ill of the dead. Forgive me." He leaned forward and placed his good hand briefly over Nathan's. "It is good to know where you are, Oriel."

"Well, well, what have we here? 'Pon my word, it seems to be a sentimental reunion, and I wasn't invited. Breaks me heart, it does."

Nathan instantly recognized the voice. He felt his jaw, relaxed with brandy and Rotheroe's words, go stiff. "St. Wulfstan."

"Ah, as lavish a welcome as any man has ever had!"

ENTWINED 195

Unasked, St. Wulfstan dragged up a chair. "Lest I over-
stay my welcome, I'll join you but for a moment.
Damned if the three of you don't look like the business
end of a mop. Marriage not suiting you, Oriel?"

"It is suiting me perfectly well."

"Grand. I had a bit of a chat with your wife at the
Winslow bash."

"I know. She told me."

"Did she now? Well, I must say you've made an
intriguing choice there, man. Not a bad one, though. Not
at all. All spark and flame. I look forward to continuing
my acquaintance with her."

Nathan was halfway from his seat when Gerard's hand
on his arm drew him back. "Stick with your empty-headed
debutantes, St. Wulfstan," he growled. "Isobel is far too
intelligent to find you remotely interesting."

He could almost see the man's flashing, insolent grin.
"Why, I do believe I have just been warned off the lady.
How diverting." There was a creak as St. Wulfstan lev-
ered himself from the chair. "Take care you don't amuse
me too much, Oriel. I've been known to howl at the
moon. Gentlemen, we simply must do this more often.
Auld lang syne and all that."

Nathan, still simmering, wondered if he really had to
let the man walk away so easily. Foolish as it might have
been, his fingers itched to grasp a handful of cravat and
stuff it into the smug mouth.

Beside him, Matthew Gerard cleared his throat. "I trust
you will come see me, St. Wulfstan. When you have a
moment to spare." His voice held the old steel thread of
authority. "We have matters to discuss now that you are
returned."

St. Wulfstan gave a short laugh. "Of course, sir. You
may be sure I'll not shirk my responsibilities. When I
have a moment to spare."

Gerard waited until St. Wulfstan had left before offering, "You really mustn't let him provoke you, Oriel. He is, after all, being no more than himself."

Nathan grunted. "Tell me, Matthew, why we have always been forced to accept that excuse for him. Should Rotheroe here have behaved as St. Wulfstan does, you would have had him on the carpet in an instant."

There was a moment of silence before Gerard replied, "It is wrong of me, I suppose. But St. Wulfstan was asked to do tasks the others of you never were. I always felt it best to let him go about as he saw fit." He gave a heavy sigh. "Beyond that, I have never once felt that I had complete control over him. St. Wulfstan is so good at what he does because he enjoys it. I honestly don't think honor or loyalty has ever played the smallest part in his service."

That, Nathan decided, was as disturbing as it was impressive.

Later, as he made his way home, two sheets to the wind and decidedly dull of mind, he replayed St. Wulfstan's insulting words. Damned if the blackguard hadn't been right. Isobel was indeed all spark and flame. The question, of course, was how he was going to get her burning beneath him.

CHAPTER 14

Nathan could not find his wife. She had been by his side not five minutes past, but William had arrived and, when Nathan reached for Isobel, had earned himself a stinging comment from the elderly Mrs. Harrington. She'd had a perfectly good reason for scolding him; he had taken a rather intimate grip on her arm.

His quick apology, including a ridiculous comment about having mistaken her youthful presence for that of his wife, had apparently satisfied the lady. He had then heard her remark to some unidentified companion that perhaps the Oriels should show a bit less affection toward each other in public.

The general consensus of Society seemed to be that the Marquess and Marchioness of Oriel were utterly enamored of each other. One London rag had recently printed a quip about a certain lord all but tripping over his own feet in his efforts to be always at his adored bride's side. Nathan found being mocked by a newspaper far preferable to having his eyesight questioned. It would have been nice, however, to have been portrayed in a less ego-pricking manner. His adored bride had laughed and read the section aloud a second time, just to be sure he'd heard properly.

At present, his adored bride was not at his side, nor could he find her. He could hear her, though, that soft Scots voice taking some poor fellow to task for having placed Skye off the coast of Yorkshire. Isobel was having the damnedest time accepting the fact that, for most of the benighted ton, the earth ended at England's borders.

"A pity 'tis not so," she had muttered on a previous evening. "Had your ancestors believed they'd drop into the sea should they venture north of Galloway, we'd be a jollier lot in the Highlands now."

Well, Nathan thought, England had done her empiric best at overrunning lands northerly. Now it seemed Scotland had come back to captivate London.

"She's made quite a mark, your Scottish wife."

"Hmm?" He turned back to face his brother. "Yes, Isobel appears to have brought the Highlands into vogue."

"She's in fine looks this evening. To think Alvanley called her plain. Absurd."

Nathan had not heard Alvanley's remark. He wondered if he ought to set the man straight on the matter of Isobel's beauty, perhaps with a fist to the jaw. He reluctantly decided against it. Should he miss and Alvanley strike back, there was every chance he would end up flat on his back. It would be embarrassing beyond measure to be felled by such a soft creature and would do Isobel no good.

Of course, she would likely come to his defense and flatten the baron with one swing. Oddly, such an act would probably raise her to mythic status. The ton already considered her something of a luminary. Like her country-woman Flora MacDonald, renowned for risking her life to spirit Bonnie Prince Charlie away from British troops, Isobel held a definite fascination for the descendants of those bumbling soldiers. The Scottish Woman, according to current opinion, was not at all what one might expect.

In fact, whispers declared, there must be a good dose of English blood running through the MacLeods.

Isobel, to her credit, expressed her opinions on that matter in Gaelic. Her audience, having no idea what she was saying, was invariably charmed.

While William rattled on, Nathan scanned the colorful blur nearby. He could hear Isobel, but he still could not see her familiar red curls.

" 'Tis not an island, my lord," she was saying. "Scotland is joined to England by land."

Nathan could not hear the response to that, but Isobel's explanation was more than audible. "I expect the moat confused you, sir. 'Twas dug by English slaves and runs from Locherbriggs to Pittenweem."

A figure promptly detached itself from a nearby knot and rushed off, no doubt to explain to still ignorant cronies that it was the slave-dug moat that made Scotland appear an island. Grinning, Nathan made his way toward his wife, her brilliant hair now visible in the midst of the circle. Obligingly, people moved out of his way. Oriel, current opinion dictated, was too besotted with his wife to notice whose feet he trod upon.

"Who was that, my dear?" he asked when he reached her.

"Mr. Ellsworth."

"You really must stop sporting with the savages, Isobel. They will believe anything."

Her laugh, as always, served to set his every nerve ending on fire. The easy slide of her arm through his did not help. Damn William. Damn every well-sighted, fawning fop present. They could see precisely how well Lady Oriel looked in her brilliant yellow gown. He could only imagine.

Isobel watched Nathan's expression grow stormy and wondered at it. Only moments before, he had been grinning, looking inordinately pleased. Now he looked pained.

"Is your leg bothering you?" she asked softly. "We can leave, if you like."

"*Hmm?* Ah, perhaps a bit. Are you certain you do not mind?"

"Not at all." It was quite true. She tired of performing for the ton and was looking forward to some time alone with her husband. They had had so little of late. "Shall we go, then?"

It took them far too long to reach the door. They were forced to pause as countless people bade their good-byes, expressed belated or repeated felicitations on their marriage, or merely stood in their path and stared. Isobel's pleasant smile wavered at the sight of Ellsworth bearing down on them, his round face washed with vivid pink. She really ought to have resisted the impulse to make up that story, but he had been so easy to dupe.

The young man, it was clear soon enough, bore no grudge. "I must say, Lady Oriel, that was a deuced good one. A moat." He actually seized her hand and bent over it. "Deuced good. I might just use it myself. With your permission, of course."

Isobel managed to grant his request while maintaining a straight face. After a few more *deuced*s and another sweep at her hand, Ellsworth trundled off.

"Careful, my dear, or they will be constructing a monument to you in Hyde Park."

"*Cuist!*" she scolded Nathan and pushed him toward the door.

Their footman spotted them as they reached the street and ran to fetch the carriage. Isobel, idly scanning the arrivals, thought she spied St. Wulfstan. She released Nathan's arm and stepped forward to get a better look, but try as she might, she could not find him again. It was no loss, she decided. She would be more than content not to face the man again any time soon.

She turned back just in time to see her husband struggling with a portly figure garbed in a tight blue coat and straining brocade waistcoat. The man's heavily ornamented watch chain, pushed outward by his belly, yet caught firmly at the watch end in the waistcoat pocket, had snagged on one of Nathan's sleeve buttons. Nathan, in his blindness, and the other gentleman, no more coordinated as the clear result of too much drink, were all but pummeling each other in an effort to solve the matter. Nathan was muttering vague invectives; the other man laughed with abandon.

Isobel stepped in and, with a deft twist, disconnected them. The man patted her cheek with force worthy of her father-in-law and bellowed, "Splendid girl, splendid!" Then he gave Nathan an equally approving cuff.

Nathan grumbled something rude.

It was lost to a shouted, "Good man, Oriel! My regards to both of you!" The figure tottered up the remaining stairs.

Isobel turned back to Nathan to find him scowling fiercely, recognition clear on his face. She laughed and patted his cheek. "Dinna fash yourself, laddie. He's too drunk to have heard you."

He grunted. "Very amusing. You might have warned me."

"I was too busy enjoying the scene." Isobel took his arm and guided him toward their carriage. She paused at the step to face him. " 'Tisn't every day a woman sees her husband wrestling with the Prince Regent. 'Twas too—"

Her breath went out of her lungs in a whoosh as Nathan's fist landed hard on her chest. The carriage shuddered; someone shouted. Isobel's only coherent thought, as her husband's weight shoved her backward through the open door and onto the floor, was that as she had been the one struck, there was no call for another woman to be screaming. Then Nathan was cursing and covering her body with his.

The entire scene was over in seconds. There were more shouts, the carriage rocked again, and Nathan's weight was lifted away. Isobel glanced up, gasping for breath, to see several gentlemen supporting him. One was examining the back of his coat.

"Did you catch him?" Nathan rasped. "Damn it, somebody stop him!"

Bewildered, Isobel looked past him. The crowd on the steps had turned to face them. Several faces were decidedly pale.

"Happened too fast," one of the men answered. "He just struck and ran."

Another let out a low whistle as he poked at Nathan's coat. "Someone above was looking out for you, Oriel. The blade sliced right through the tail."

Blade? Isobel struggled to sit up. "Nathan?"

He was in front of her in an instant, his hands finding her shoulders with unerring ease. "Dear God, Isobel, are you all right?"

"I am fine. What happened?"

"Footpad," someone offered. "Must've been going for the purse. Bloody scoundrel could've killed you."

Nathan's hand did not go to his pocket. Instead, he pulled Isobel tightly against him. For a moment, she could feel his heart, beating hard, against her breast. Then he released her and stepped back, face taut. "Did anyone get a decent look at him?"

Everyone had. Only no one had gotten the same decent look. According to those present, the man had been monstrous, average, and the size of a young boy. He was blond, raven-haired, and hooded. The only matter on which everyone could agree was that he had moved extremely quickly.

There was little to be done, Nathan thought. The man was long gone. Running after him was not an option. Nathan climbed into the carriage, bitterly cursing both his blindness and his leg, which ached from the event. No, he could not chase the blackguard, but he could get Isobel away from the scene. He might not be capable of protecting her, but brick walls would. He rapped his cane against the roof, willing the driver to get them away as quickly as possible. He wanted to get Isobel home— immediately.

"Nathan?" Her soft voice beckoned him and, heedless of pride, he shifted from his seat to hers, gathering her tightly against his side. "Nathan, he did not cut you?"

"No. He did not."

Nathan knew that the near miss had not been for lack of intent or effort. It had been pure luck the knife had not found its target. He had felt a shove at his shoulder, causing him to lose his balance. As he was falling he had felt a tug, clearly from the blade, at the back of his coat. The fall into the carriage had, in all probability, saved his life, and possibly Isobel's.

His heart was still thudding. It had been a bold act, attempting such an attack in public, and a clever one. It was a simple matter for a man to approach his target unobserved in a crowd that size—and then to disappear just as easily.

"Disgraceful," Isobel was saying, "to be attacked just outside a ball!"

Belatedly, he realized that he had hit her rather hard. "My God, I must have nearly shattered your ribs!"

He lifted his free hand and held it, uncertainly, above her lap. She reached up to clasp it tightly. " 'Tis no matter. You merely knocked the breath out of me for a moment."

"But—"

"You might have wanted to go about it a different way, Nathan, but you protected me. I'm grateful for it."

The soft assertion nearly undid him. Protected her? He had dragged her into this bloody mess, all under the selfish assurance that she would care for him, help him get about while he humored Matthew Gerard on a fool's quest.

He was the fool now. Someone had just tried to remove one more member of the remaining Ten and had very nearly succeeded.

The carriage rattled to a halt. Nathan descended immediately and stared hard, for all it was worth, up and down the street before allowing Isobel to follow. It was there again, the feeling of eyes upon him. He knew that a man on foot could easily have moved as quickly as the carriage over the few blocks. Nathan hurried Isobel up the stairs. Clumsy in his haste, he nearly stumbled twice, his thigh protesting each jarring step.

Once inside, he let out a shaky breath. For the first time since Portugal, he felt fear sliding cold down his spine. This was not the war-torn Peninsula; this was London. Pride had kept him from admitting just how vulnerable he really was. And it was not merely his own sorry neck at stake. He had a wife, a smart-mouthed, warmhearted wife, whose value was well above his own. If he had not been jostled into Isobel, if the knife had been thrust in her direction . . .

"Nathan?" Isobel was gently urging him toward the stairs. "Come along. I've a feeling some brandy would be welcome."

He was moving, she noticed, more stiffly than she had ever seen him move before. He leaned heavily on the bannister as they ascended. His face, too, was weary. Distressed, she trailed behind him.

He paused at the entrance to his chamber, ostensibly to

bid her a good night. She was having none of that. Reaching past him, she opened the door and scooted into the room. He turned, frowning.

"What are you doing?"

She had never been inside his bedchamber and took a moment to glance around. It was richly appointed, very masculine, and stark in its neatness. Other than a single wrinkled cravat that had been tossed, in frustration she assumed, onto the massive bed, there was scarcely a single personal possession to be seen. She thought of her own room, neat but quickly filling with the small items that made up her life, and ached with the knowledge that Nathan had cleared his life out of necessity.

"Have you no brandy here?" she queried with forced cheer. "I thought gentlemen always kept a bottle near to hand."

He stepped through the door and gestured toward a Chinese cabinet. She found a bottle and several clean glasses. On impulse, she removed two and poured a generous shot into each.

"I'll join you, if I may," she said, trusting he would not refuse.

He remained standing just inside the door. "Isobel, this is my bedchamber. If you wish . . ."

"A delightful room. These chairs are Hepplewhite, are they not?" She made certain her silk skirts swished audibly as she sat. She wanted him off his feet. " 'Twas one of those bits of knowledge my father thought necessary to impart. We can all identify furniture at fifty paces." He did not move. "Oh, do sit down, Nathan, or I will be forced to get up again."

His mouth twitched faintly. "I believe that should be my line."

"Well, what's good for the goose and all that. Will you sit?"

He did, walking slowly but unerringly to the facing

chair. She pressed a glass into his hand. "I am really not certain you should be in here, my dear," he said.

"Whyever not? I assure you"—she leaned forward and lowered her voice—"my husband is the most understanding sort of man."

He gave another brief smile. "Then he is a fool."

"Oh? Why?"

"Some treasures are not to be shared."

Warmth curled through Isobel's stomach. She took a hasty sip of her own brandy and coughed as it burned its way down her throat. Now she felt even warmer.

Nathan did not touch his drink. Instead, he sat stiff and upright in his seat, gold eyes fixed on her face. For once, she did not drop her own gaze. He could not know she was studying him intently, and she took full advantage of the situation.

More than a week of good food had filled out the hollows somewhat. His face was still lean, the cheekbones sharp, but he no longer looked gaunt. Isobel had not yet offered to trim his hair, so it waved dark and glossy over his ears and the back of his collar. But he looked better, she thought, much better.

Then he lifted his glass, and her gaze centered on those wide, perfectly curved lips. His mouth had fit so well against hers. So well. She pushed herself slowly to her feet. It had seemed like such a good idea at the time, coming into this room.

"Isobel? Are you leaving me so soon?"

Are you leaving me . . . ? As if she could. As if she ever could. Nay, MacLeods were good to their word. And he needed her.

"I am merely . . . restless, my lord. Nay, don't get up." She turned and, clasping her glass tightly in one hand, wandered across the room, trying to put some distance between herself and whatever it was she was feeling.

She had not noticed before, but there was something

spread over the top of the writing desk. It appeared to be some dark fabric. Approaching, she loosened her near-painful grip on her glass and set it down on the glossy surface. The fabric was black velvet. Resting upon it were three miniatures, each small enough to fit into the palm of her hand.

Isobel touched a fingertip to the first image, that of a young woman. She was lovely: pale, large eyed, and honey haired. "Who is this, the woman in pink?" She turned as Nathan's chair creaked. He was still sitting, but he must have moved suddenly. "Ah. I am sorry. I was nosing about your things."

He leaned forward, resting his elbows on his knees. "No, it's all right. That is Lady Anne Kedwell. I told you about her. We were . . . childhood sweethearts and were meant to marry."

The woman at whose graveside Nathan had stood, inconsolable, in the rain. "I am sorry," Isobel said again. "She was very lovely."

"Yes, she was. In character as well. Anne was the sweetest girl I have ever known."

Something very close to pain lanced through her. Of course Nathan's first love had been beautiful and sweet. Of course he mourned her still. His wife was neither. "It must have been a terrible loss for all."

"Yes." He gazed off toward the window. "It would have been a disastrous marriage in the end, I think, but we were young and could not see beyond each day."

"Why do you say it would have been disastrous? She seems perfect."

"Perfectly lovely, yes, and perfectly good-natured. But Anne was not . . . sharp. I don't mean to say she was simple. It's just that she would never have understood my moods, would have been unable to strike back at my poor wit. I would have made her miserable."

He smiled humorlessly. "Amazing—isn't it?—what self-ish beasts young men can be. I thought she would wait for me forever, would forgive my carelessness. I was away for a year, doing my damnedest to consume all of Britain. God only knows the reports she received while I was gone, and never a denial or confirmation from my own lips."

"You're hardly responsible for idle gossip, Nathan."

"Perhaps not, but most of what was said was perfectly true. For my part, I knew Anne was ill, had been for months. She wrote, her mother wrote, my own father summoned me. I returned home only to find she had died two days earlier."

Isobel did not know what she could possibly say. She did not think he would appreciate her telling him that he had been young and could not be held accountable for his sweetheart's death, no matter how selfish his behavior had been. So she left him to his remorse and lifted the second miniature. It was of a man, tawny haired and handsome, laughter clear in the gray eyes. "The gentleman?"

"Rievaulx," was the terse response.

"A relative?"

"My closest friend."

Isobel mentally reviewed the men she had met in the past days. The name was vaguely familiar, the face not at all. "He is not in Town?"

"He died. On the same night when I . . ." He gestured abruptly at his leg, then raised his fingertips to brush just above his right cheekbone. His mouth was drawn into a pained line now. Isobel barely resisted the urge to cross the room and embrace him. Only the feeling that he might push her away kept her in place.

She had never asked how he'd lost his sight, assuming it had been in the same Peninsular battle in which his leg had been damaged. Now it appeared he had lost something equally precious that day as well.

"Too many good men have died," she said softly. "I thank God some survived."

For a moment his features softened. Then the harsh mask returned. "He should not have died that night. He shouldn't have been there at all."

"Nay?"

"He was meant to remain in the hills. I was on my way home. He insisted on accompanying me to port. Damned fool. No man should die for—for—"

"For friendship? For love? Oh, Nathan." Isobel sighed. "It seems far nobler than dying for power, if you ask me. I would imagine he felt as strongly for you as you still do for him. And I daresay you would have done the same."

Nathan snorted. "Unlikely. Gabriel—the bloody archangel. Stayed with me even after I—" He cursed, low and vehemently. "You see the third miniature?"

Isobel neither looked at nor touched the third. " 'Tis Lady Bronnar. We have met."

His head snapped up. "You did not tell me."

" 'Twas a brief meeting. I didn't think you would want to hear of it."

"*Mmm.* So, what did you think of our Cecily? Beautiful, is she not?"

"Yes," Isobel agreed sadly. "Incomparably."

"That is precisely what I thought the first time I saw her at her debut. She dazzled me. She dazzled everyone. Especially Rievaulx. He had met her in Bath during the winter and had every intention of offering for her."

"Oh."

"A telling syllable, my dear. Yes, I set out to steal the woman my best friend wished to marry. And she came willingly enough. I would be a duke someday, you see. Rievaulx was but an earl." The bitterness in his voice was nearly tangible. "It appears a dukedom was not enough in the end. When she learned I might not return home whole, she decided she did not want me after all."

"Oh, Nathan."

"He forgave me, you know. Gabriel, the archangel. He forgave me freely and completely, and died for his generous heart. So now you see why I keep the miniatures."

"As a reminder of those you have loved?"

His breath hissed between his teeth. "As my penance."

It was no use. Isobel could no more have held back than she could have controlled the tide. Heedless of his response, she rushed to kneel before his chair. She took both his hands in hers, tightening her grip when he made to pull away. "I don't think I could change your feelings of guilt if I tried, but I can tell you one thing with full certainty. There is no coldness in your heart, Nathan. A wall around it, perhaps, but no coldness. I've seen you with your family, seen what you do for your tenants."

"Isobel . . ."

Impulsively, she lifted his hands to her lips, kissed each palm and, when he tried again to pull away, all but dug her nails into his wrists. He made a harsh sound deep in his throat. "I am sorry, Nathan. I didn't mean to hurt you."

This time, the sound was almost a laugh. "You meant to comfort me. I know that. But you are hurting me, Isobel, terribly, and not for the first time."

"What?" She gasped as he broke from her grasp and captured her shoulders, nearly pulling her across his thighs.

"As I said, those I desire wound me. God, Isobel, if you only knew how I ache."

Her mind was whirling far too fast for her to find a coherent thought. "I—you—you desire me?"

"More than anyone before. Can't you tell?" He seemed to realize how tightly he was holding her and released her arms with a self-deprecating snarl. "I want nothing more than to bury myself within you, Isobel, and never withdraw. I want it enough that it's killing me. So, unless you fancy being carried across the room and tossed onto that bed, madam wife, I suggest you remove yourself from this chamber. Quickly."

Isobel sat back on her heels, stunned, shaking. And knew she had to move. She took a steadying breath and placed one trembling hand on his knee. "Very well," she said.

"Very well what? You are not moving as I told you to."

"Nay, I am not." She darted a quick glance behind her. "And I meant very well, you may take me to bed, Nathan, if you really wish to."

CHAPTER 15

Where the virgins are soft as the roses they twine,
And all, save the spirit of man, is divine?
                                                    —Byron

"What did you say?" Nathan asked hoarsely.

Isobel's hand slipped from his thigh, and he nearly groaned with the loss. "I said," she replied, her voice barely above a whisper, "that you may take me to bed. If you truly wish it."

"If . . ." Breathing had become difficult for him, speech almost impossible. "Isobel. I wish it so much I fear it will consume me whole."

"Well, then." She rose to her feet.

He threw his hands out and somehow captured one of hers. "It isn't enough, my wanting you. I . . . cannot bear the thought of your being unwilling."

"Nathan." Her free hand drifted, quick and trembling, over his cheek. "I want to be a wife to you, in every way possible. I want you to be a husband to me."

Husband to her. *God,* he thought, he wanted to be nothing more. And at times it seemed to him that he'd been made for that very purpose.

"Isobel, are you certain?"

He remembered the wedding, how her responses had come neither eagerly nor with hesitation. Her quiet affirmation now was the same. "Aye, I am certain." Then she

212

added, more softly still, "I would have us as the roses, Nathan. Entwined." And he was lost.

His control more an effect of his injuries than his will, he slowly rose to his feet. He shrugged out of his ruined coat, letting it drop to the chair along with all thoughts of anything but her. "I can do that for you, sweetheart," he vowed, releasing her hand to slide both of his gently into the heavy silk of her hair. "I can bring us so close that we will not know where you end and I begin."

Pins scattered as he loosened her fiery curls. Her hair spilled warmly over his wrists, her shoulders, and he smiled as he lowered his lips to hers.

Her mouth was warm and still. Gently, he tilted her face to meet his fully. His hands itched to drop lower, to move fast and hard over the pliant curves now just brushing his chest and thighs. But he would wait.

He tugged at her lower lip with his teeth until she opened to him. His first deep taste of her was incomparably sweet. He cursed himself twice; once for not having given himself this pleasure far sooner; and a second time for the fact that all this was new to Isobel. He could have, *should* have begun nights before, giving her the chance to experience each step and to blossom with it.

She sighed into his mouth. It was a soft, wondering sound, and it thrilled him. There was so much, too much he wanted to give her. And right away. He could only hope he would not kill them both in the process.

She lifted a hand to his jaw. Slowly, hesitantly, her fingers unfurled to spread over his skin. He broke the kiss for a moment and pressed his cheek into the warmth of her palm. He drew a deep breath, allowed his eyes to drift shut, closing off the last vestiges of hazy sight, and surrendered to the soft acceptance of her touch.

"Oh, Isobel," he whispered then, overwhelmed, and all but crushed her mouth beneath his.

The velvet sweep of his tongue against hers was too

glorious to be real. It was odd, Isobel realized in a fleeting moment of clarity, how such a touch, only mouths meeting, could register so deeply elsewhere. She was aware of a faint swelling, almost like an ache between her thighs. It was so very strange, almost frightening, and she hoped it would never end.

She parted her lips more for him, inviting him deeper. He growled low in his throat, took what she offered. His hands slipped from her hair to her shoulders, down the outside of her bare arms, leaving a path of tiny embers in their wake.

Why? she thought hazily. Why had she not asked him to do this before?

The answer came all too quickly. She had not asked because she had not really known. All she knew of this business between man and woman could be written in one shaky line.

"Nathan," she managed, drawing back. "Nathan, I—"

"Hmm?" His head dropped, and the silken brush of his hair across her cheek shook her nearly as much as that of his lips over the hollow of her throat.

"Nathan, I do not know how to go on from here."

He straightened slowly, his eyes molten bronze. She could see the pulse beating at his temple, the rigid set of his jaw, hear the ragged edge of his voice when he replied, "I do. And I will teach you all I know."

"But I am so completely ignorant."

"Innocent, sweetheart, not ignorant. The teaching is my pleasure, and my task. Yours will be to trust me and to tell me as we go on if there is anything you do not like—and anything you do. Can you do that?"

Isobel knew she could stop him now, that he would let her go if she asked. "Aye," she whispered. "I can do that."

He nodded once. "Good." Then he offered her one hand. "Take me to bed, Isobel."

She guided him, stopping when their legs brushed the high mattress. Uncertain what to do next, she bit her lip and studied the massive expanse. The covers had been turned back to expose snowy sheets. She should lie down, she knew, but could not seem to manage the feat.

Nathan did it for her. In one smooth motion, he stretched out on his side and took her with him. They faced each other, his arm curved loosely under her head, cradling her. She could feel the strength of his thighs where they barely touched hers, knew if she took a deep breath her breasts would be brushing against his chest. She found herself staring into his shadowed face. He looked intent, dangerous, and utterly beautiful. She hesitantly reached up to trace a fingertip over his generous mouth. She liked it when he kissed her with those lips, liked it a great deal.

"Do you wish to extinguish the light?" he asked.

She peered at the single brace of candles on the desk. Aye, perhaps darkness would be easier, but it would involve getting up, and she was reluctant to break the warm contact of his lean body against hers.

"Nay. 'Tis fine as it is."

"As you wish."

He slipped his free arm around her shoulders as his tongue slipped again between her lips. She knew to kiss him back now, heard his whispered approval of her ready response. She curved herself into the embrace so they were chest to chest. He was hard against her, all muscle and sinew. She ran her hands over the textured brocade of his waistcoat, feeling the pattern of the fabric, flattening her palm above the strong beat of his heart. She might have stayed like that forever, absorbing the reassuring, steady rhythm, but he was soon urging her softly to release the buttons.

Nathan felt his muscles leap at her halting exploration. She burned him, even through the fabric of his shirt. His own fingers ran along the fastenings at the back of her dress. He should have been clumsy, perhaps, inflamed as he was. But he could feel each button, imagine it slipping free of the placket to expose one more inch of her pale skin.

The last one gave way. He spread his hand flat over Isobel's back, feeling fine linen and satin skin against his palm. *Slow!* he cautioned himself, but could not resist the need to feel more of her. He broke the kiss and, whispering nonsensical, soothing words, drew the dress over her head. The chemise and petticoats followed. His fingers were sure and deft, guided by his imagination. Her shoulders were bare now—the curve of her waist, the soft expanse of her thigh. It nearly killed him not to pause and touch every exposed inch.

Nathan drew back to tug at his own shirt, wanting that first full meeting to be his skin against Isobel's. He felt her shifting, lifting her arms from her sides to cover what he had bared. He imagined her: all milk-pale skin and blazing hair, a combination as alluring and elemental as fire and water. And more beautiful than anything he had ever seen with his undamaged eyes.

"Oh, Isobel," he whispered, keeping his hands away but brushing his lips over the soft hair at her temple, "you are exquisite."

There was a moment of complete silence. Then she gave a soft, whispery sigh and relaxed against him.

He sat up to shed his boots and shirt, clumsy now in his haste. His erection strained against the placket of his breeches, near painful in its pressure to be free. But Isobel was not blind and she was a virgin. His hands itched to tear at his breeches, to send them flying after his shirt. Instead, he stifled a groan and lowered himself as gently as he could back onto the mattress.

That first contact of skin to skin nearly undid him. Her breasts were even fuller than he had thought, her belly and thighs soft and gloriously welcoming. Isobel had a body meant for loving, all lush curves and gentle hollows. One long leg slipped between his, instinctively twining to pull him closer. Nathan, overwhelmed by the warm generosity of the act, offered up silent and humble thanks.

Awed, aching, he reached up to cup her breast. It more than filled his palm, the nipple hardening quickly. "Perfect." He sighed and took the peak into his mouth.

Isobel felt her body quiver with the feeling—little licks of fire teasing at her senses. *Wicked.* It had to be wicked to feel this way. But she could only think of the delight. All last doubts were sliding away in the wake of Nathan's touch. She whimpered as his mouth lifted from her breast, only to gasp anew as his tongue laved the other. Pleasure like an arrow lanced through her, and she wound her fingers into his hair, holding him as close as she could.

All the while, his hands roamed hot over her skin, missing not an inch as he explored: along her side, over the curve of her hip, to her knee. There was awe in his touch, his appreciation of her as clear by his touch as if he had spoken. It was as much a gift as the very physical sensations assailing her.

His palm drifted to the inside of her leg, paused, curved warmly around her thigh. When his fingertips skimmed upward, trailing more embers, Isobel moved against him. There was no thought of embarrassment at all now, no question. When he reached the juncture of her thighs, she hesitated only for a moment, then opened to his touch.

This was Nathan, her husband. It seemed only natural that she would give him her body. She had known forever, it seemed, that she would give him her loyalty and care. And known for hours that she had given him, without being aware it was happening, a piece of her heart.

He had told her to inform him of what she liked. Oh, she liked this, this incredibly intimate touch, but could not find the breath to tell him. She tried. Gasping, searching for speech, she tried. It was no use. So she simply accepted the caress, her own hands fluttering over the broad expanse of his shoulders.

He stroked her, gently, rhythmically. She could hear the faint ticking of the mantel clock, the pendulum swinging in time with the steady slide of Nathan's fingers.

It came slowly—half hum and half pulse, rising from where his fingers caressed to swell like an aura around her. She felt her own hands clenching, as if to grab onto the feeling. "Nathan," she managed at last. "I cannot . . ."

"Feel it, Isobel," he commanded, his voice threading through the sensations. "Feel me touching you."

Oh, she did. She felt each delicious stroke. Then the pad of his thumb flicked over an exquisitely sensitive spot, and an intense flare of pleasure swelled and rippled through her core. It swept like a wave, inside and out over her skin. Trembling, breathless, she let it carry her unresisting over a peak never imagined.

"*Ah . . . Dia . . .*" She gasped as the wave crested, numbing and exhilarating at the same time. When it subsided, slowly, sweet tremors rippled away with it. "Oh, Nathan."

He gathered her to him and held her close. "That was part of my vow to you," he whispered against her temple. "A husband's gift to his wife."

Still struggling to catch her breath, Isobel rubbed her cheek against the hair-sprinkled roughness of his chest. " 'Tis a grand gift, Nathan . . . I'd not imagined . . ."

"I don't expect you did. But now you know."

Aye, now she knew. "And for you? There must be more."

"For both of us. But we can wait for it. I want you to remember this . . . this first night."

"As if I could possibly forget. 'Twas a wondrous thing you did to me, Nathan. I'll remember it well."

"Good," he murmured, and shifted against her.

"I want you to remember, too."

His laugh sounded pained. "Believe me, Isobel, I could never forget. You bloomed like the rose, so very beautiful in your release."

Isobel's heart swelled anew. "But it was me alone." Hesitantly, still unsure of how to go on, she slipped one fingertip into the waist of his breeches. "I would have you feel pleasure, too, Nathan."

"I did, sweetheart. Oh, I did." Nathan thought to pull away, to break the contact until his erection had faded—or at least stopped threatening to burst through the placket— and he could take her back into his arms to sleep. But her touch, that gentle tug, was drawing him straight into the flame. "I, ah, Isobel, perhaps—"

"Perhaps you ought to be off with these. I expect they're in the way."

He meant to ask once again if she was certain, but the good intention was lost as he all but tore his breeches from his legs. He could feel each pulse of his blood in his veins, in the tip of his rigid penis. And, as he stretched out again above his wife, he felt each inch of her skin like warm silk against his.

He braced one arm next to her head, his hand sliding into her mass of tumbled curls. With his other hand, he traced downward, past the curve of her breast and hip to curve around her thigh. She parted her legs beneath him, welcoming the brush of his thumb against her damp core.

"Isobel. This will—I will—hurt you. I would give all I am to avoid it, but—"

"I know. I do know that." She reached up to stroke his

jaw, her fingertip caressing his lips as his did between her legs. "*Tha gradh agam ort,* Nathan."

He could not hold back the laugh, painful though it was. "Cursing me, are you? I do not blame you in the least."

" 'Tisn't a curse." She shifted, cupping him with heat and softness.

Nathan could not have spoken then if he had tried. She was still slick from her climax, ready for him. He slipped his hand under her thigh, shifting it to rest against his flank. Then, spreading his palm at the back of her knee, he pressed upward, opening her fully to him.

He pushed forward, slowly, his entire frame shaking with suppressed need and the intense pleasure of sliding into her tight heat. "Isobel," he whispered as he met the fragile barrier. "Hold onto me. Please."

As her arms clasped about his neck, he surged forward, filling her completely and shattering that last vestige of control. Panting, muttering vague, sweet words, senseless in the glory, he stroked once, twice, then emptied himself into her in a long, shuddering release that no one could convince him was not an earthly view of heaven.

He allowed himself the pleasure of lying still, his face pressed to hers, their bodies linked as intimately as could be, while his heart slowed to something approaching a normal pace. It was, he knew even as it was happening, perhaps the only time in his entire life when he had felt completely whole.

Thank you, he offered silently, uncertain where the words were meant to go. He had been given the incredible gift of his wife, but it was Isobel and Isobel alone who had given herself. "Thank you," he said aloud, turning his cheek so it rested in the satin flow of her hair.

Her hands drifted like air down his sweat-slicked back. "You are welcome," was her soft reply as, for a moment, she tightened her thighs about his. It was a giving, and a welcome, and it humbled him anew.

"I'll move," he said, taking his weight again onto his arms. "I'm certain you are . . . not comfortable."

She was not certain just how she felt. Sore, a bit, and pinned by his much larger body. But she was still reluctant to let him go. Her legs clung to his as if by their own will, her arms loosening but not dropping from his sides. She sighed as he eased from her, and she smiled as he took her with him when he shifted to his side. There, her cheek pressed to his chest, she could feel the beat of his heart. Strong and steady, it soothed like the distant waves on an autumn Skye night.

They lay like that, silently, for countless minutes. Isobel let one hand slide down his side and over his hip. It was amazing, she thought, how very different their bodies were, his hard angles and hers soft curves. Each inch of his skin, taut over firm muscles, felt unspeakably wonderful.

She traced her fingertips down the depression in his upper thigh where those muscles met, then stopped as she felt the scar. Nathan did not move as she hesitantly explored the puckered line that ran nearly to his knee. Her heart twisted at the notion of what he must have suffered.

Thinking he had fallen asleep, Isobel turned to look at his face. His eyes were wide-open and fierce.

"Does it still pain you?" she asked softly.

"No. Does it repulse you?"

Startled, she stared into the dark, unreadable gaze. Then, slowly, she placed her palm flat over the scar. "It grieves me," she said, stroking her hand back and forth as if she could erase the mark. "Nothing about you could repulse me. Oh, Nathan, you're lovely. All of you."

He grunted. "Really, Isobel."

"And don't you be telling me otherwise. I'm the one

here who can see." His silence at that unnerved her. "Nathan . . . ?"

"I was remembering the night we met."

She shuddered. " 'Tis something I would prefer you forget."

"Really? It seems to me you taught me an important lesson or two."

"To be sure I did. Not to trust your secretary."

Now he chuckled. "I was thinking more along the lines of second chances. You will give me one, won't you?"

"Good heavens, at what?"

"At making love to you. It will be better the next time."

Stifling her own laugh, Isobel teased, "Oh? Is this another husbandly promise?"

He stiffened then, and she knew he had mistaken her tone. "I am sorry. The pain was unavoidable. I do promise—"

Grinning, she stretched to plant a quick kiss on his clefted chin. "So English, hearing slights where none were meant. What I am saying to you now, Lord Oriel, is that I've no complaints about the first time. But if you've a mind to prove yourself, who am I to tell you nay?"

She felt him stir against her, then felt the full pressure of his arousal as she once again found herself flat on her back. Above her, his cat's eyes glittered. "Tell me aye, then, Lady Oriel."

"Oh, I suppose I—"

"Twice, is it? Very well, then. Your wish is my command."

Her pleased laugh turned into an even more pleased gasp as his hands began their clever exploration once again.

She woke to bright sunlight and an empty bed. Well, almost empty. Nathan was not there, but the indentation in his pillow where his head had rested was now occupied by a profusion of red and white roses, each stem clumsily woven to the next.

Isobel reached out to touch a petal, wondering whose hothouse he had raided and how much he had paid to do it. It was still early in the season for such blooms, and she knew the young Town bucks all but dueled with each other for what was available each day.

"Daft man," she said aloud as she lifted one white flower to her face. A red came with it. "Daft, marvelous man."

She smiled her way through her bath, splashing and startling her maid by launching into one of her father's bawdy Highland songs. It was a splendid day, and she knew precisely how she would spend it. She would seek Nathan out wherever he might have closeted himself and make him sing with her. She had no idea if he could sing, but she was determined to find out.

She chose a pale pink morning dress and, after pinning two of the smaller roses to the bodice, did a cheerful twirl in front of the cheval glass. Aye, it was still the Isobel she knew, solid and far from beautiful, but the vision bothered her not at all. Whatever it was Nathan saw when he touched her was also in that reflection, and it was enough.

"Where is his lordship, Betty?" she asked the maid, who was busily tidying up the room.

"I don't know, milady, but the two gentlemen are in the breakfast room."

Isobel stopped in the doorway. "What gentlemen?"

The maid stopped working long enough to give her a quizzical look. "Why, your brothers, milady. I thought you knew. They only just arrived an hour ago . . ."

Isobel was already racing out of the room. With any luck, she would be in time to prevent Nathan from caning the foolish, feckless pair into the street. With more luck, she would have ample time to do a bit of scolding herself. After she had hugged them and gotten all the news from home, of course.

Her brothers were indeed in the breakfast room, and neither looked at all as if he had met with the knob end of a walking stick. In fact, they both looked impossibly hale and handsome. Rob was sporting a new hairstyle that looked rather as if it has been fashioned by a small child's hands, and Geordie was wearing a blindingly yellow waistcoat under his tight and obviously padded blue superfine. Both leapt to their feet as she entered the room.

"Izzy!" Geordie cried, enveloping her in a crushing embrace. "How we've missed you at home."

"You're looking uncommonly fine!" Rob added as he sent her hair into a disarray similar to his with his enthusiastic hug. "Town seems to agree with you."

As always, Isobel's annoyance was no match for her affection. She returned the embraces, listened to the various greetings from her father and sisters, and tried not to laugh when Rob's eyes drifted off to the side as he recounted Maggie's message. No doubt she had tried to prevent them from skipping off to London, and he was too poor a prevaricator to hide it.

"What are you doing here?" Isobel asked as they settled back at the table. They had already taken full advantage, she saw, of Cook's morning spread. "I was under the impression you were to stay in Hertfordshire and behave yourselves."

"What, miss the opportunity to check on your well-being?" Geordie added an ample serving of kippers to his already full plate. "We had to see for ourselves that Oriel was treating you well. I must say"—he paused long enough to consume a mouthful of sausage—"you seem happy enough."

"I am perfectly happy." She refrained from making a tart comment about his obvious approval of the provisions. "So you may return to the country with the best of tidings."

"Oh, we'll do that, to be sure," was Rob's assurance. "In a few . . . days."

"*Och,* Robbie." Isobel sighed but was unable to hide her smile. "Tell me, where is Lord Oriel? I daresay he'll have a few choice words for the pair of you."

"Already did," Rob replied, not at all abashed. "Not half bad, actually. I expected him to be a bit of a beast about it, but he merely muttered a few words about the park and staying where he'd left us, then hobbled out."

"Quite a man, your husband," Geordie added. "Saw him ride past the window a minute later. For limping along so with that stick, he sits a horse damned well. Splendid coat, too. Weston, no doubt."

All thoughts of lecturing the boys vanished. "He went out riding?" she asked. "Alone?"

Rob shrugged. "S'pose there could have been someone with him. The streets here are so dashed crowded."

Isobel was out of her seat like a shot and already into the hall when Geordie called, "I say, Izzy. Do you think Oriel would mind if we were to pay a visit to his tailor? We don't need much, really, just a few items to see us about Town."

She skidded to a halt. "Absolutely not! You'll not put so much as a button on his tab!"

"Oh, but, Izzy—"

"Do you hear me, lads? Not a button! You will stay precisely where I've left you. I'll deal with you when I return."

Leaving the pair to their grumbling, and, no doubt, Nathan's liquor cabinet, Isobel hurried up the stairs. She winced as she struggled into her new riding habit. She was a bit stiff. Hardly surprising, as Nathan had kept her well occupied until near dawn.

What a surprise was the instant warmth that spread through her as she remembered those hours.

" 'Tis a fair hussy you've become," she muttered as she shoved her feet into a pair of boots. "And shameless, too."

For she could feel no embarrassment in her memories, nor in the new longing they produced. Perhaps Nathan would want to make love to her again that night. She smiled and warmed anew with the thought.

Aye, 'twas a lovely thought. Of course, should he ride his hell-horse in front of a rushing town coach, it would all be a moot point. Bootlaces flapping, Isobel rushed down the stairs and out of the house.

CHAPTER 16

Hyde Park, Nathan had decided some years earlier, was God's revenge on man for having forsaken Eden. What had been originally designed as a simple, green paradise for the peaceful enjoyment of city dwellers had quickly become a showplace for poor taste. Beyond the ridiculous presence of several gaudy pavilions, one dirty false lake, and countless ornate gates, there were the crowds.

It was barely noon, but the paths and promenades were already jammed. By the fashionable hour of five, Nathan imagined people would be resorting to climbing the trees for a bit of space. A flashily painted tilbury bounced past, causing his mount to sidestep quickly. Another rider, for some reason turning his mount in tight, repeated circles, was forced to jerk away to avoid a collision.

Grumbling to himself, Nathan calmed his horse and scanned the surrounding vistas for a clear spot. All he could see was an oscillating blur of gilt and rainbow-hued fabrics.

"Hasn't London anything better to do?" he muttered. "I am certain there is a new cravat knot to be discovered and a frippery or two as yet unsold."

William chuckled. "Activities for poor weather. Such

a sunny day is by divine decree intended for display of yesterday's cravat knot and Prussian bonnet."

They had been riding a slow circuit for nearly an hour now, and Nathan was ready to be gone. His brother's spontaneous invitation to ride had seemed a good idea. He wanted very much to encounter Rotheroe and St. Wulfstan. He doubted either would openly admit any knowledge of the previous night's attack, but if there was one skill he had learned during his tenure of ferreting out spies, it was how to conduct a subtle interrogation.

Of course, both of the men he meant to interrogate were just as skilled as he.

So far that morning, he had encountered countless acquaintances who had heard of his near encounter with a knife. None had been able to offer any information whatsoever. There had been numerous comments on his luck at avoiding a nasty attack from a petty thief, more welcomes on his return to Town, and felicitations on his marriage—some made even without the sly commiseration common to both bachelors and other married men.

There had not been an intelligent comment among the lot.

"Nathan?"

William's voice cut into his musings. *"Hmm?"*

"You haven't heard a word I've said, have you?"

"Of course I have. You were talking about . . . about . . ."

"Ostrich plumes."

"Ostrich plumes. Yes."

His brother grunted good-naturedly. "Really, Nat. As if I would be bothered to discuss anything so absurd. No, I was telling you about my latest experiment."

"Ah, yes. The Welsh ale. Have you taken it upon yourself to improve this batch, too?" He vaguely remembered a three-day-long stomachache and winced at the memory.

"It wasn't half bad!" was his brother's indignant retort. "You downed a full tankard."

"So I did."

"Oh, I recognize that face, old man. You inherited it from our sire. But I shall let the slight pass. As a matter of fact, it isn't ale at all, but gunpowder . . ." Nathan's attention flitted off again. "Bother that. You don't want to hear it." William waved off his brother's halfhearted demurral. "I don't suppose you'd care to share whatever matters are occupying *your* mind."

"I . . ." *I'm blind as a bat, little brother, and there is the distinct possibility that someone wants me dead as well.* For a fleeting second, Nathan debated telling Will everything. Pride, and the knowledge that he would only be dragging the rest of his family into the mess, killed the impulse. "It is nothing of importance."

"If you say so." William seemed content to believe him. "Shall we have a bit of a gallop?"

Nathan peered dubiously at the collision course that was the Row. "I am not sure that would be such a good idea." But William was gone, his scarlet coat a blurry beacon as his horse wove in and out among others. "Well, damn," Nathan muttered, and followed.

Chiron, Nathan's stallion, was up to the task, dodging obstacles with ease. Nathan himself was not quite so secure, however. Keeping his seat was not his real problem. Keeping his seat while holding his brother in his poor sights and tossing vague apologies to those persons dusted or pushed from the path was the challenge. Finesse was optional.

Even as he began to enjoy the hell-for-leather ride, Nathan knew he must make an odd sight indeed: the Marquess of Oriel, careening along a park road, bobbing about like a buoy in the saddle and muttering "sorry," "so sorry," "I do apologize," as he went. His only hope was that he would not address his regrets to more than one or two bushes.

He swore as something slapped at his arm. He had not

seen the branch—or whatever it had been. It was near impossible to see anything when his already impaired eyes were being rattled about in his skull.

Ahead, William shouted something that sounded distressingly like "Water!" and, indeed, veered away toward the Serpentine. Nathan could only hope he did not have some impromptu bathing in mind. It would be entirely like William to ride his horse right into the lake.

On his own part, any submersion would be unintentional. Jaw set, Nathan tightened his grip and managed to stay mounted when Chiron followed William's horse over a low bench. All in all, demonstrating his ability was proving to be decidedly hard on his bones.

He kept his eyes on the sun-speckled water as they thundered along the bank. Not that it would make much of a difference should he go sailing toward it, but he knew that a wise man always did his best to know the position of the enemy. When William reined in suddenly, Chiron jolted and came to a shuddering halt. Nathan bounced a few times in the saddle, bruising both his posterior and his pride.

"If you want the title, Will," he grumbled while regaining his balance, "why not just shoot me and be done with it? There is every chance I would survive a fall."

His brother laughed. "I shall keep that in mind." Then, "I say, Nat, whatever happened to that demon horse you bought at Tattersall's last year?"

Nathan frowned. He had purchased the ill-tempered, wild-eyed chestnut gelding mere days before his voyage to Portugal and had completely forgotten about it since. Now, with embarrassment born of regret, he found himself hoping it had not killed whichever unfortunate groom had been assigned to exercise it.

"I suppose it is still in the stables. Why?"

"Well, I could be mistaken, but I do believe it is coming toward us at a rather impressive clip."

"Impossible." Nathan's chin jerked around, but all he could see was a blur of oscillating color.

"Oh, my. Look! It has just sent the Richmond sisters scattering like hens. And there goes Allenham. Serves him right, putting racehorses to his phaeton. I daresay they'll stop before they reach Brighton. And out the gate they go! I must say, Nat, she has a dashed fine seat. Not a woman in fifty could manage that beast. Still, whatever were you thinking, giving her the chestnut?"

"William, what are you blathering about?"

"Your wife, of course. Can you not see her?"

Nathan concentrated on looking for copper hair and finally saw a bright flash. Yes, it was Isobel, and it appeared she was riding with the speed and carelessness of one fleeing the devil. Of course, she could not be fleeing the devil. She was riding him.

"I think," Nathan said, "I will have to throttle her."

"I wouldn't advise it, old trout. She's become quite the thing. Your estimable peers would hang you in an instant."

"Oh, cork it, William," Nathan snapped, and turned Chiron in Isobel's direction. He had no idea what she was doing riding alone through Hyde Park, but he was certainly going to find out.

Isobel watched him ride toward her, greatly relieved to see him in one piece. Her pleasure dimmed, however, at the sight of his expression. His features, harsh on most days, were drawn into a scowl guaranteed to terrify small children, indolent servants, and recalcitrant wives. Isobel, not placing herself among any of the three, smiled as she reined her mount to a jerky halt.

"Good day, my lord, William. What splendid weather we are having!"

"Where is your groom?" Nathan snapped.

"I haven't one. Where is yours?"

Apparently blithe insolence was not the correct choice. Nathan's scowl deepened.

"Why are you not at home? You are supposed to be at home."

"I heard you had come to the park and thought I would join you." She saw William's eyes darting between them and read the surprised speculation there. "I am sorry," Isobel said, as confused as her brother-in-law. "Have I interrupted a private brotherly interlude?"

"Not at all," William insisted. "We are delighted to see you."

"Damn it, Isobel, have you any idea what sort of beast you have there?"

She raised one eyebrow. "What sort of beast *do* I have, my lord? A surly one, from what I can tell."

She thought William's cough was meant to cover his laughter. Nathan aimed a steely glare in his brother's direction, and he blinked and turned in the saddle, apparently finding the tree to his right especially fascinating.

"Isobel," Nathan growled, "that horse is a menace. He is mean, unpredictable, and liable to bite without the least provocation."

She sighed. So that was it, was it? As pleasant as it was to have him concerned for her, it was absurd. "It seems I've an affinity for such creatures." She reached down to pat the horse's lathered neck. "As it happens, Aingeal and I have found a meeting of the minds."

"Ankle? You named my horse *Ankle*?"

"I did. The groom said he had no name, so I gave him one."

"But *Ankle*?"

She could not help grinning. " 'Tis Gaelic, Nathan." She spelled it for him. "It means 'angel.' "

He snorted. "Your humor escapes me, Isobel. This *angel* is likely to be the death of us both."

Actually, she was rather pleased with the name. "It means 'fire,' too, so you may cease with the scowling."

"Name aside, you should not be on that horse. In fact, you should not be here at all, alone. I'm going to sack that damned irresponsible groom the minute we get home."

"*Och*, Nathan, you'll do no such thing. 'Twas the only horse suitable for riding in the stable, and I couldn't see why I should drag a groom away from his more important duties merely to escort me to the park."

"Escorting you *is* his duty!"

He was blustering now, and she wondered just what would happen if she were to comment on the unmistakable resemblance he bore to his father. She didn't think he would be flattered. "You haven't had your breakfast, have you?"

"*What?*"

"I daresay the lads chased you out before you could eat. 'Tis an empty stomach venting at me."

William's laughter rang out. Apparently he had expended the aesthetics of the tree. "You know my brother well indeed, Isobel. Yes, Nathan, do tell us. *Have* you eaten today?"

For a moment, Isobel thought they were both in for a blast of temper. But after a tense moment, Nathan's face relaxed into a faint smile. Then he chuckled. "The devil take you both. It is wholly unfair to gang up on a fellow before he has dined."

"Ah, I knew it!" Isobel said, and laughed with him.

The sound sent memories of the night before sliding sinuously into Nathan's mind. Any pique he might have been able to stubbornly maintain was lost to images of Isobel, her hair spread like fired silk against the pillows and her body liquid flame beneath him.

He shifted edgily in the saddle and managed a stern "You will not ride that beast again, Isobel."

"Will you supply me with an alternative beast to ride, then?"

That voice, that husky, lilting voice, left him with no illusions of what she meant. His Alba rose had not merely opened; she had blossomed with a glory that took his breath away.

"It will be a husband's gift to his wife. Will that suit you?"

"You know it will."

Every nerve ignited, Nathan shifted again and wondered what would happen if he were to haul her out of her saddle into his and take off at breakneck speed for home. Public spectacle aside, he would probably end up breaking both their necks. Aroused, frustrated, and as gloriously content as he had ever been, he eased Chiron around a prancing Aingeal and led the way along the path. The gelding did indeed seem to have calmed a bit, whether by time or Isobel's influence. He should not have been surprised. She had a way with stubborn, anti-social creatures.

"Nathan tells me your brothers have arrived from the country," William offered a few minutes later. Nathan had forgotten he was there. He wondered just how much the insolent sod was enjoying himself.

"Aye, they have," Isobel replied. "Their visit was—"

"Unexpected," Nathan said grimly.

"It was that. But Rob told me how very warmly you welcomed them, my lord. I vow they'll have settled in by now."

The image set his teeth on edge. The only person less welcome in his home than Geordie and Rob MacLeod was their father, and Nathan was still not convinced, even though both boys had denied it, that the man was not hot on their heels.

"I should very much like to meet them," William was saying.

"What a grand idea. Don't you think so, Nathan? Your brother can take mine under his wing, show them about Town."

"Isobel," he began.

"Aye, a grand idea. I can trust you to keep them away from the tailors, Will, can't I? They've a penchant for awful waistcoats."

"Isobel . . ."

"Trust in me, madam. I vow there will not be a single waistcoat added to your household during their stay."

Nathan gave up. He wondered at the precise moment when he had lost control over his life. A month earlier, he would have said it was in Portugal. Now he had a very good idea that it had occurred somewhere in the middle of his wedding vows.

Oddly, the concept bothered him not at all.

Half an hour later, he was ready to tear out his hair. When in God's name had his life slipped completely out of his control? He had nearly gone tip over tail on entering his very spacious, very familiar foyer. Sometime during his brief absence, it had sprouted a frightening abundance of boxes.

"Milch!" he bellowed.

"Yes, my lord?" The butler scuttled forward. At least Nathan thought it was the butler. He seemed to have grown decidedly stocky since morning. He guessed the man's arms were full of more parcels. "What is all this?"

"Ah, Nathan." Isobel slid her hand intimately along his arm.

"Well?" he demanded.

Milch cleared his throat. "We have had a delivery, my lord."

"So I see. Did the East India Company decide to deposit its monthly cargo here?"

"Nathan," Isobel said again.

"This arrived for you, my lord." Milch awkwardly pushed a small, wrapped parcel toward Nathan's hand. Then he gave a slight rattle to the boxes he held. "These others, I believe, are from the glovemakers. And the ones near the wall are from the milliner."

"Hats, my dear?" Nathan queried blandly.

Isobel sighed. "It began as one, you see. But Mariah was there, and—"

"I believe I understand." He turned in a slow circle until he came to face the pile that had nearly felled him.

"Shoemaker," Isobel said.

"Shoemaker," he repeated.

"And the modiste," she said weakly.

A dozen or so dresses had already arrived in the past sennight. "Mariah again?"

"Your mother."

Behind them, William let out a low whistle. "I believe we have our answer as to the crowd in the Park, Nat. No one is shopping as there's not a ribbon left to be found in Town."

Isobel gave a martyred sigh. Nathan felt his own lips twitching. He knew precisely how she felt. Arguing with his mother was as useless as trying to fight the tide. "Well, my dear, have you left me a guinea or two to pay our beleaguered staff?"

"Oh, Nathan, I did not mean to—to—"

He clasped his hand over hers. "Dinna fash yourself, lassie. We'll only be on ale and bannocks for a quarter or so."

She gave a soft laugh and repeated the fond curse from the night before. "*Tha gradh agam ort,* Nathan."

He meant to ask her how long before he turned into a frog, but did not have the chance as he heard an ominous thump upstairs. "What was that?"

"I believe, my lord," Milch volunteered mildly, "the young gentlemen are in the library."

"*My* library?"

"Indeed, my lord."

Nathan, heedless of boxes scattering at his feet and his wife stumbling along at his side, stormed up the stairs and toward his sanctuary. William, chuckling loudly, trotted right behind.

It was, Isobel decided as they entered the room, a very good thing indeed that Nathan could not see. The liquor decanters had been removed from their cabinet, and one rested sideways on the low table, dry as a bone. The others were lined up in crystal splendor beside it. The unfinished game of vingt-et-un spread among them nearly completed the picture.

Isobel's brothers were the finishing touch. Rob was sitting on the floor next to the table, one hand wrapped around a glass, the other holding a bent queen of hearts. One of the heavy wing chairs was upended, its legs pointing toward the door, and Geordie was in it, sprawled on his back, limbs going in several different directions. Isobel was uncertain just how he had managed to tip over, but she knew this was the source of the thunderous noise.

"*Och*, Geordie," Isobel lamented, and stepped between the chair legs.

He waggled a foot in her direction. "Izzy! We were wondering where you'd gone off to. No, don't apologize for deserting us. We've had a dashed splendid time without you."

"So I can see," she muttered.

"Don't suppose you'd consider keeping your husband out of the room for a time. We've some straightening up to do before he arrives. He might be a wee bit irked by the mess."

"That is one way of phrasing it, MacLeod."

Isobel had not heard Nathan approach and groaned. Had Geordie not mentioned the matter, he might have been none the wiser. Geordie, for his own part, was now making a concerted effort to raise himself. He was doing a very poor job of it, as his own legs kept getting in the way.

"Perhaps we should go upstairs and freshen up for luncheon," Isobel suggested. "I am certain Cook could have something ready in a few minutes."

"Oh, I fully intend for us to go upstairs," Nathan said quietly. His words sent delicious shivers down Isobel's back. More loudly, he announced, "After I see your brothers into a carriage. They can be home by evening."

"Now, Nathan, they did not intend—"

"Oh, we're not leaving," Rob said cheerfully from his spot on the floor. "Only just arrived, you know. But it's ever so kind of you to offer."

"Robbie, *cuist!*" Isobel cautioned. She really ought to have known better than to bother.

"Very kind, indeed!" Geordie agreed. He had managed to get up and was standing reasonably upright on the other side of the fallen chair. "But there's no need to put yourself out yet. We thought to pass a fortnight or so here in Town."

"A *fortnight?*" Nathan repeated. "You intend to stay here for a fortnight?"

"Aye, or two. We had a bit of a jaw about finding rooms elsewhere, but—" Geordie gestured expansively, nearly clipping Isobel with his flailing hand. "Grand digs you have here, Oriel."

"I am so glad you approve," was the dry response.

Thinking now might be a very good time to avert further disaster, Isobel beckoned her standing brother out from behind the chair. Rob was still doing his best to get up from the floor. There was a tearing sound as he put his heel on the hem of his coat.

"So these are the famous MacLeod brothers!" William

strode across the room, hand extended. "I say, what a great pleasure to meet you at last!"

A bemused Rob accepted the hand and, in no time, was on his feet. William's ostensibly welcoming grasp on his shoulder steadied him enough that he did not go down again. "William Paget," he announced.

"Robert MacLeod."

"Of course. And you are . . ."

"Georàs MacLeod. Geordie." Geordie was already grinning, having sensed, with unerring MacLeod instinct, an ally and potential playmate.

"Ah, splendid." One arm firmly settled over Rob's tilting shoulders, William turned his own blinding smile toward his brother. "Off with you now, Nat, old man. I am going to get acquainted with Isobel's brothers. I daresay we have a great deal in common and will get on smashingly."

"God help us," Nathan muttered, but he did not protest as Isobel gently led him away from the carnage of his library.

"Thank you," she mouthed at Will. He winked and guided Rob toward an intact chair.

"You must let me tell you both about my latest experiment," she heard him say as she and Nathan reached the hall. "You begin with a dash of gunpowder . . ."

"A fortnight. They intend to stay a fortnight."

Isobel gave her husband's arm an affectionate squeeze. "William will take care of them."

"God help us," he said again, and started up the stairs, shoulders slumped in defeat.

"Thank you."

"For what? Not booting them into the street?"

"Aye. I wouldn't have blamed you for hauling them out by their padded coats."

He actually chuckled. "A wise man never gets that close to two drunkards at once."

"Wise, indeed. They'd have just bocked up the brandy all over you."

"Isobel, that is disgusting." But he was grinning. "Bocked, *hmm?* I'll remember that one. I suppose it would be one way of getting some of my liquor supply back. Did they leave anything in the bottles?"

"A bit."

"Well, there's a comfort. At least I know I'll have a bit available when they drive me stark raving mad."

Charmed by this side of her husband, but feeling the need to support her brothers, Isobel said, "They're good lads at heart."

"Made all the better for your defense of them, sweetheart. Have no fear. I won't cast them out yet, drunk or sober."

"I might," she muttered, and stopped outside his chamber door. "I'll join you downstairs in half an hour, then? We can both have something to eat."

"Still concerned with my mood, are you?"

"Nay. You've improved tremendously."

"Ah, well, then, perhaps luncheon can wait awhile."

She glanced at him curiously. "Are you not hungry?"

"Immensely."

"So why . . . ?" Her question ended in a breathy gasp as she found herself flat up against his chest.

"I did not have food in mind." His hand was rubbing a very interesting pattern down her back. "Are you hungry?"

Familiar heat was spreading through her limbs. Aye, she'd become wanton indeed. "Immensely. So much that I believe luncheon can wait awhile."

"Ah, Isobel. A wife after my own heart."

Moments later, tangled with him on the massive bed and not quite certain how she had come to be there, Isobel gave fleeting consideration to his words. Was she after his heart? A little piece of it would not be unwelcome. But he was unlikely to give even that, so why distress herself with the possibility. . . .

She stopped thinking altogether when his hand slipped under her skirts to curve around her thigh.

"I believe the months of bannocks and ale will be well worth it," he murmured, "if all of madam's creations are as pleasing as this one. They afford me such delightful access with so little beneath to get in the way."

She could feel the fine wool of his breeches against her bare inner thighs, felt the strength of corded muscle beneath. She slid back a few inches, then forward again, reveling in the textures. "Ah, Nathan." She caught her breath as his fingers unerringly centered and slipped inside her.

"With you so appropriately attired, I feel compelled to keep my promise."

"And what was that?"

"How quickly you have forgotten, my dear. I promised to provide you with an alternative mount."

"Oh, aye, you did." Isobel felt his free hand beneath her, tugging at the placket of his breeches. Her breath caught again as the full splendor of his erection rose boldly. "Nathan, can we . . . Ah!"

She had her answer as he surged upward, gripping her hips at the same time and pulling her tightly against him. She felt herself stretching, warming, shifting to accommodate him. His breath, in concert with hers, hissed between his teeth.

"Yes. Ah, yes. Dear God, you undo me, Isobel!"

But she was no longer listening. Guided by his hands, she began to move above him, rocking with a rhythm as old as the tide and just as elemental. His hands lifted from her hips then and reached to cup her breasts, teasing her nipples through the soft fabric of her bodice.

"Oh Dia," she whispered. As if in answer to a prayer, the glorious warmth caught like a spark, spreading

through each flammable inch of her body. Too fast, it was coming, too fast. She wanted to capture each second, savor it, draw it out until she could stand it no longer. But his hand was between her thighs again, his fingers sliding exquisitely and relentlessly inward.

His thumb centered, circled, and she was lost. Gasping, laughing, she went to flame. One after another, the tremors coursed through her, each more splendid than the next till they flowed away.

Nathan writhed beneath her. The hand still gripping her hip tightened, pulled her that scant bit closer than she could have thought possible. Even as the last wave receded within her, he tensed and cried out her name.

Then his hands dropped away. Left without this brace, imagined though its support might have been, Isobel slid bonelessly forward. Her cheek ended up pressed against a coat button, and her first coherent thought was that they were both fully dressed. Her second was that he smelled truly wonderful, potent and wholly male.

She mumbled something to that effect. Her face bounced on his chest when he laughed. "I probably smell like a horse."

" 'Tis part and parcel of a role well played, I suppose, if you do." Yawning slightly, she rubbed her cheek against the soft wool of his coat. "I can say one thing for you, my lord."

"And what is that, my lady?"

"When you make a promise, you keep it. And grandly." She thought she felt him stiffen, but then his arms folded around her, and she smiled at the comfort of the simple embrace. "I don't suppose I can get you to promise we'll not have to leave this room for the rest of the Season."

There was genuine regret in his voice when he replied, "You cannot imagine what I would give to be able to promise you that."

"I was hardly being serious, Nathan."

"I was."

"Aye, well, we've plenty of time to spend lazing about in bed." She ran one hand along his arm, stopping when her fingers reached a tear in his sleeve. "Whatever did you do to your coat?"

He reached across her to touch the spot. "It must have been a branch. I was trying to keep up with my crack-brained brother."

Isobel leaned up to look. "Quite a branch. I'm surprised it didn't knock you right out of the saddle."

"Ah, a direct blow to my ego. I have been lauded for my splendid seat."

Grinning, she let her hand slide between his hip and the mattress. She gave a firm squeeze. "You may add my commendation to the list."

"I am delighted you approve, my lady. My return compliments." And he squeezed right back.

CHAPTER 17

Isobel was in her chamber singing something slow and sweet and, if Nathan's ears did not deceive him, about kisses. Abandoning his hapless attempts to fashion a cravat knot, he crossed his own room and quietly opened the connecting door.

She was at the window, her face turned toward the glass. Nathan thought he could make out the soft curve of her hip beneath green silk. It amazed him how much he had learned to see since she had entered his life, details that might otherwise have been lost to him. He knew the luster of silk in a well-lit room, the ripple of fire as Isobel's hair flowed over her shoulders.

His wife had brought him nuances. As the glint of silver caught his eye—the stroke of her hairbrush—he wondered how he had managed before her and wondered, too, if a man could be taught sight when the God-given had been taken away.

His hands itched to take the brush from her hands and to feel the water softness of her hair sliding through his fingers as he brushed it himself. He could not, however, think of a way to explain the action, to explain how he knew where she was and what she did. So, instead, he stood in the doorway, content with the sound of her singing about a fond kiss.

The words were in that lilting Scots English that teased the ear and often defied translation. With her untempered brogue, Nathan missed a good deal of what she sang. Until the words became a clear farewell: "Ae fond kiss and then we sever; ae farewell, alas, forever . . ."

He must have made a sound, for she turned, the music ending abruptly. "*Och,* Nathan, you move like a cat!"

"I wanted to hear you."

"Without my knowing it? You know I'll sing for you if you ask."

Yes, he knew she would, but not the songs she chose for herself. "Melancholy words."

"Aye, perhaps, but grateful, too."

"In parting?"

" 'Tis all a matter of what you're left with when the door closes," she said lightly. Then, before he could press her further. "You're sporting quite an interesting arrangement about your neck this evening."

Nathan reached up and ruefully fingered the botched knot. "You do not think Brummell will approve?"

"As if the thought would ever cross my mind. The man always looks as if he's swallowed a pole and only got it halfway down." There was a click as she set the hairbrush down, the swish of silk as she walked toward him. She batted his hands away and tugged at the cravat. "Aye, well, you've ruined this one. And with all the starch, I'm surprised you didn't shatter it in the process."

"Feel free to speak to the laundress, madam wife."

"Oh, and have you bleating because you can actually move your chin about? Thank you, nay."

He found himself grinning as she led him back into his chamber in search of a fresh cravat. "Bleating? I do not bleat." She ignored him, tugging free the wilted linen and replacing it with new. "Are you listening to me? I do

not"—she efficiently, and tightly, made the first tie—
"bleat."

"You're doing it now, lad," she said tartly. After a few
more twists and tugs, she patted his chest. "All done."

She gasped as his hand snaked out to tangle in her
loose hair, halting her departure midstride. As his thumb
stroked feather-soft over her nape her gasp turned to a
breathy sigh. "Ah, I take it back, then."

She felt rather than heard his chuckle when his lips
traced the line of her brow. "Wise woman."

He was barely touching her, yet still her entire body
hummed with the contact. Wondering how long she
could remain standing on knees gone weak, she peered
over his arm. The bed was still touseled from their romp
that afternoon and looked excessively enticing.

"Nathan, we'll be late."

"Mmm." his teeth closed over her earlobe and tugged
gently.

"I . . . people are expecting us."

He grunted and let his free hand slide upward from her
shoulder to cup her jaw.

"Well, bother." She sighed and leaned in. "Whatever it
is you do to me, Nathan, you ought to put it in a bottle
and sell it. You'd be a rich man in days."

"Sweetheart, I've been a rich man for years."

"Oh, well, then, save it for me only. You'll hear no
complaints from me on that score."

His lips curved against hers. "Isobel?"

"Aye?"

"We'll be late."

"So we will."

"People are expecting us."

"So they are." Her eyes fluttered open when he pulled
back. Oh, but he looked bonnie with his night black hair
and devil's smile. Her heart gave a cheery thump just at

the sight of him. "What are you waiting for, you great daft man?"

"I have a gift for you."

"Of course you do. Get on with it, then."

She tried not to be offended when he laughed aloud. "Ah, Isobel, I wonder if you will ever appreciate the irony of this situation." In a motion as quick and graceful as the beginning of a Highland dance, he guided her toward the bedside table. A wrapped parcel sat there. "Open it."

Thinking she would much rather be unwrapping him, and muttering something to the effect, she obeyed. The paper fell away to reveal a flat velvet box. "Oh, nay." She promptly shoved it at his chest. "I'll not accept this, Nathan."

He made no move to take it from her. "Perhaps if you were to look inside . . ."

"I'll do no such thing. I know full well what this is, and I'll not have you buying me jewels. I've no wanting for them and no use!"

"Isobel, you have not even opened the box."

Exasperated, and still jittery from his assault on her senses, she poked him again with the unopened case. "Are you telling me there's not an ungodly expensive, glittery something inside?"

"No, I am not telling you anything of the sort."

"Well, then, I've no need to open it." She wouldn't have it, would not have him wasting his money in such a way. "You're a good man, Nathan Paget, but a fool sometimes. Now what *are* you laughing about, you great, daft beastie?"

"Isobel, you are a wonder. I had a feeling you might behave so. You are more than accepting when the gift is my humble person, yet you won't even look at jewels."

"Pearls before swine and all that."

This time, he did not move quite as quickly when he reached for her. There was a bit of a scuffle as he tugged and she twisted, but the end was a foregone conclusion. She was sitting in his lap, and he was still chuckling.

"You will be sorry you said that, my dear." With a flick of his thumbnail he released the catch and the case sprang open. "And not a swine in sight."

She had expected emeralds or rubies, something bright and glaring, and suited to the row upon row of previous marchionesses with their perfect features and cold portraits. As inappropriate for her as sackcloth and ashes.

He had given her pearls.

It was a simple set, a double-strand necklace and drop earrings. The glory was in the pearls themselves. Large, perfectly matched, they held the luster of sea and sunset, a glow that seemed almost unearthly.

"Oh," she breathed, awed. "*O Dia.* Nathan, they are glorious. But I cannot accept them."

"Why? Tell me what it is that frightens you about this gift."

She struggled to find the words. " 'Tis too much, Nathan. Too much."

Still, she could not resist the urge to run a fingertip reverently over the strands. His hand slid over hers a moment later, their fingers linking. "I would say not quite enough. I could feel them, Isobel, even though I could not see. They felt like your skin. Please," he said so softly she barely heard, "do not reject this." And she was lost.

"I've never had anything nearly so beautiful." She turned in the circle of his arms and softly, slowly brushed her lips over his.

"Neither have I," was his murmured response.

He waited some time before reaching for the other box, in part because he was still afraid she would turn a gift away, but also because the gentle clasp of her arms about his waist was incomparably sweet.

"There is one more piece," he announced at last, and tried not to sigh as she dropped her arms.

"Nathan! No more."

He found her hand, slipped the ring onto her finger before she could protest. "I was hoping you could wear this with your mother's ring. It belonged to my grandmother. The one who planted the roses."

It, too, was a pearl but a unique one. A deep, luminous pink, it had come, family history said, from the crown of an Eastern princess dead a thousand years. A long-ago Paget had brought it back from an ill-fated Crusade. Through succeeding generations, the pearl had gone to other estates, a part of bribes and dowries, but somehow, it had always come home to Hertfordshire.

It was set now within a circle of diamonds. Nathan could remember seeing it on his grandmother's hand and could imagine it on Isobel's. He told her as much of its history as he could. "Wear it," he said gruffly, as much plea as command, "so you won't forget where you belong."

"That, my lord, seems to be a matter of debate."

"Oh, Isobel, don't—"

She stilled his growl with a finger on his lips. "I know what you meant."

"Do you?"

He wanted her to understand her own value, never certain she did, but he could not find the right words to tell her. Perhaps, he thought, if he knew what his value was to her, it might have been easier. But she had never spoken about it. She had given him her body, to be sure, freely and with as much passion as he had known she possessed. He had her loyalty; of that there was no doubt.

He would ask no more, regardless of what he wanted.

"Thank you, Nathan," she was saying now, "for trusting me with this. I'll take care with it." Then she gave a heavy sigh. "You've a way of tromping right over my better judgment, you know. 'Tis a spell, I think."

"Oh?"

"Aye, and one of these days I'll wake up and find myself married to an ordinary man."

"I will do my best to see it does not happen."

"*Mmm.* That, I fear, is the problem."

With a last gentle, fleeting kiss, she slipped from his lap and returned to her chamber.

Isobel stood near the wall of the crowded ballroom and fingered the pearls at her throat. The speed with which they had warmed to her skin astonished her. They had been so cold at first, and she imagined they would turn cool again once she took them off.

All in all, they were just like her husband.

When Nathan was with her, he seemed an entirely different man than the one she had first met. He smiled, teased, and set her nerves sparking with the simplest glance. Then something outside would touch him, and the cold light would return to his eyes.

His face was stony now as he talked to the Earl of Rotheroe. Isobel could not hear what they were saying, but it worried her. She had seen that expression on Nathan's face altogether too often since their arrival in London. Now, as usual, she wanted to go to him, to do anything within her means to relax those deep grooves beside his mouth. But, as happened frequently now, she sensed he did not need her presence, did not want it.

She wondered if perhaps she had completed her duty. There was not a man in a thousand who would be able to do what he had. He was back in Town, easy and comfortable around his peers, his blindness still a secret. She had aided him in that—less, to be sure, than she had expected. His will and ability were staggering. Of course, she had always known as much. She had simply not expected to become obsolete so quickly.

"Isobel, dear, you are not listening to a word I say!"

"*Hmm?* Oh, I am sorry, Your Grace. I was—"

"Preoccupied." Her mother-in-law sighed, then gave Isobel an approving smile. "I understand. I was much the same when I was first married." Her eyes drifted to her son, softened. "You have made all the difference, Isobel. To all of us."

"You overestimate my import, madam."

"Unlikely." The ice blue gaze sharpened again. "That is not to say, dear, that you should make a habit of galloping through Hyde Park alone. I cannot think my son has grown so soft that he has lost all sense of propriety."

Isobel suppressed a smile. The mother, unlike the son, could always be counted upon to behave precisely as expected. " 'Twas an impulsive act, Your Grace."

"I should say so. And the tale is all over Town."

"It must have been a quiet week in Parliament," Isobel murmured. It never ceased to amaze her what the ton found noteworthy.

"Sarcasm," the duchess said quietly but firmly, "is decidedly unbecoming for a marchioness. So is being the subject of flapping tongues."

Mariah, for her part, was taking this new disaster with her usual good-natured calm. "Oh, Mama, really! Everyone finds Isobel utterly dashing."

"Dashing is not among the adjectives Lady Bronnar and Allenham are using."

"Cecily Bronnar," Mariah said succinctly, "is a witch. And Allenham is a fool. It is hardly Isobel's fault he overturned his phaeton."

"Perhaps not, but he seems to disagree." The duchess gestured to the rotund baron holding court across the room. His right arm was encased in a sling.

Isobel winced. Mariah laughed. "According to Sedg-wick, that great mass inside the sling is not bandages but a bottle of brandy. Note how he passes it over his glass every so often." She winked at her sister-in-law. "Lady Hampden is not known for the quality of her refreshments."

True enough, Isobel thought. The champagne was quite sour. Of course, it could have had more to do with the fact that everyone seemed to be discussing her yet again than with the wine itself.

"Perhaps I ought to go apologize to Lord Allenham. I *was* a bit reckless."

"Oh, pish." Mariah rolled her eyes. "You are being hailed as a unique spirit, dearest. Don't spoil it with something as tame as an apology. I only wish I could have been there to see you handling the beast. We all told Nathan he ought to have had it shot when he purchased it. I'm surprised he didn't do it himself yesterday."

"Don't think he wasn't tempted. But I was as safe on Aingeal as on any horse."

Allenham was waving his constrained arm, but it was impossible to tell if he was tippling or merely adding drama to what was undoubtedly his commentary on Lady Oriel's deplorable behavior in the Park.

"Ankle?" Mariah was asking.

Isobel sighed. " 'Tis Gaelic. I think I really must go offer my apologies."

The duchess was now plying her fan with ladylike gusto. "If you must, dear, perhaps you'd best start with the Misses Richmond. They have just arrived, and if I understand correctly, you quite disrupted their promenade."

Isobel had no idea who the Misses Richmond were. "Are any of them sporting plasters or slings?"

"I do not think so."

"Aye, well, they can wait, then. I've but one apology to spare a night."

Mariah was still blathering something about unique spirits as Isobel moved away. She had, over the past weeks, done her best to explain the honor of being labeled an Original. To Isobel, it sounded like calling an infant "engaging," which was, of course, merely a polite way of saying "ugly."

She was not at all certain she wanted to be labeled either a unique spirit or an original one. She simply wished Society would tire of its Scottish novelty and ignore her. As far as she was concerned, the attention was no more than a nuisance, but Nathan was clearly becoming a bit tired of the gossip, especially that in print. Perhaps if she could diffuse Allenham's ire, they would be spared another mention in the papers and Nathan's public face might lose some of its stoniness.

He had not smiled when his brother remarked on the most recent cartoon. Isobel had tried to keep Nathan from learning about it. William, of course, had taken great pleasure in describing, in detail, the etched image of the haughty Marquess of Oriel's head poking out from a bagpipe.

Aye, she would have to apologize to Allenham, but the words stuck like dry oats in her throat.

"He is not worth the effort, you know."

Isobel blinked as Lord St. Wulfstan appeared at her elbow. She was too startled to be wary. "I beg your pardon?"

"Allenham. It won't do you any good to speak to him, you know, and from your expression, I daresay the effort might do you some serious damage."

"Eavesdropping is hardly a worthy trait, my lord," she snapped, wondering how someone with such a poor reputation in the ton could move so freely within it.

"Neither is ignorance, my lady," he shot back. "Why don't we dance? I have some things to say to you."

"Spare your breath. I've nothing to say to you."

His scarred brow rose, and he flashed his stunning smile at the same time, reminding Isobel of an ancient two-sided mask: good and evil together. It was not a soothing thought. "So they've gotten to you, have they? Pity. I cherished the hope you might be able to resist joining the mindless flock."

"A wolf looks the same to a lone sheep as to a hundred."

"Ah, the clever tongue. But has it never occurred to you that I might not be such a bad creature after all?"

Perhaps it had, but there was something in the depths of his eyes, something cool and secretive, that said more than his teasing words. "I haven't spent much time thinking on the matter, my lord. Nor do I plan to in the future. Now, if you will excuse me."

"Ah, yes. I am interrupting your encounter with Allenham." The cobalt eyes narrowed. "You really are a naive little thing, aren't you? It pains me to think of the things your husband is not teaching you."

Isobel nearly snarled at him. "You—"

"*I* am just the sort of tutor you need, Lady Oriel. You might be amazed by what you could learn from me."

"I'd sooner take loyalty lessons from Judas!" she spat, and watched as he smiled again, this time an eerie parody of his easy grin.

"Bold words, and reckless. Take care, *Albanach*, that you don't confuse righteousness with wisdom. You might end up regretting it." After bowing mockingly, he strutted off.

Isobel watched him go, unspoken curses left to simmer on her tongue. She heartily regretted having talked to him at all. Besides being unpleasant, her encounters with St. Wulfstan made all the sense of fool's riddles. Proud as she might be of her own quick mind, she knew his was a game she simply did not comprehend.

He moved easily through the crowd until he was standing just behind Allenham. A moment later, the baron let out a startled yelp as his elaborate sling slipped from his shoulder. He flailed about with two perfectly good arms, but was not adept enough to keep a large flask from hitting the floor.

Isobel's eyes flashed from the now red-faced Allenham to the spot behind him. The viscount, perfectly visible a moment before, was nowhere to be seen. Warily, she scanned the crowd but caught not so much as a glimpse of him.

"One more bit of wisdom, my lady." St. Wulfstan was right beside her. "Next time you think to ride that hell-horse through the Park, think again."

Nathan should have been stunned by the news. He should have been, but he was not. Instead, he was bone weary. "I had forgotten all about Henry Stone."

"We all had." Rotheroe's voice was harsh. "Damn it, Oriel, he was all but on my steps! He was shot within sight of my bloody house!"

Stone. Nathan barely remembered him. The man had not been one of the Ten. He had been a very early member of the corps, but had been demoted into the ranks of lesser operatives a good two years before the Ten was formed. By the time they had sailed for the Peninsula, Stone had been long gone.

Now he had been shot in Hyde Park, within sight of Rotheroe's house and just as close to where Nathan had been riding with Isobel.

If what Rotheroe said was true, the matter was being expediently if not wisely hushed up by His Majesty's Army. The military's reputation was of great importance; it would hardly look good that members of its forces were being gunned down right in the midst of Hyde Park. Tomorrow, people would stroll past the hedge where Stone had been hidden, none the wiser for the blood that had been shed there. Only an old man whose hound had found the body would know, and Rotheroe, whose home had been quietly commandeered. Money would serve to silence the first; duty would silence the latter.

"Has Gerard spoken to you?" Nathan did not need to ask whether Matthew had been notified. There was no doubt of that.

"Gerard," Rotheroe replied wearily, "told me absolutely nothing. He just had Stone wrapped and sent away to the surgeon, then swore me to silence."

"Wait. Stone was alive?"

"As far as I know. He was still breathing. Please, Oriel, don't be as silent as Gerard. I need to know what is happening."

Nathan thought for a moment before replying. If Rotheroe was the one responsible, he would already know the situation. If not, he might be of some help. Either way, Nathan felt he had nothing to lose.

"Someone is going after the Ten," he said calmly, "one by one. Gerard called me back to Town."

"But Stone was not one of the Ten."

"No, but he was still privy to much of what we knew—and did." Once again, Nathan repeated the sad list. "Harlow, Witherspoon, Rievaulx, Dennison, Brooke. Three gone would merely be the carnage of war. Four could be a matter of very bad luck. Five . . ." He shrugged. "Someone knows who we are, Rotheroe, and has thus far done a very good job at cutting down our number."

If Nathan had expected a revelation, even so much as a careless word, he was disappointed. Rotheroe was silent. At last, he demanded, "Why didn't Gerard enlist my aid?" A moment later, he answered his own question with a sharp laugh. "Of course. Almeida. Since he believed I failed so badly there, he couldn't possibly trust me now."

"He trusted you enough to leave you on the Continent."

"Oh, to be sure. Sitting in a dark garrison in Lisbon with Montgomerie leaning over my shoulder, reading French missives of little importance."

The man was bitter, Nathan thought. Was it guilt—or anger at having been misjudged? "Where is Montgomerie now?" he asked.

"Calais, I assume, or—" Rotheroe drew in his breath, then released it with a grim chuckle. "You think it's me, don't you? Of course. I was at Almeida when the fort fell, away from my post and in the arms of a Portuguese whore. Congratulations, Oriel. You have now single-handedly won the war."

"Rotheroe . . ."

"No, none of the comradely denials, if you please. We are men of experience and action. Well, I have but one thing to say to you."

Nathan felt the man lean in, felt Rotheroe's good hand jab at his chest. "And what is that?"

"You'll have to prove it, Oriel. And damned if you can!"

Then he was gone.

Prove it. Nathan's chest felt hollow suddenly. Rotheroe. Always eager and solid, even when the disaster at Almeida had deprived him of the use of his right arm. There had never been any actual proof that he had been in a brothel; he had been in the wreckage when the last of the smoke had cleared. There had only been Dennison's babbled suggestions. And Dennison had saved his own sorry hide from the sudden French attack on the fort by fleeing himself.

Prove it. Nathan silently and violently cursed his lost sight. He had no way of looking into Rotheroe's eyes, no way of knowing if the man even met his when he spoke. All he had was his suspicions, and the gut feeling that his conversation with Rotheroe had served him badly.

He had either just antagonized someone who already wanted him dead or lost a valuable ally.

CHAPTER 18

Isobel was asleep when he came to her that night. He had been so forbiddingly silent on the ride home that she had left him to his thoughts and gone alone to her bed. Now, drawn by the shifting of her mattress from an uneasy dream filled with thorns, she whispered, "Nathan?"

"Shh." His mouth brushed over hers. Soothed by the kiss and by the gentle stroke of one hand through her hair, she closed her eyes again.

There was no urgency in his touch. His fingers traced tantalizing patterns over her skin, long strokes up her arm, teasing circles at her nape. He took equal care with the kiss. It feathered from her parted lips to her cheek and upward to her brow. Warmed, lulled into boneless contentment, Isobel lazily twined her arms around his neck and turned fully into the hard length of his body.

He was all solid heat and gentle strength against her. He circled one arm under her shoulder, drawing her even closer, and she reveled in the play of his muscles against her ribs. He surrounded her, covered her, and she sighed with the wonder of it.

"Nathan," she murmured as he parted her legs, again as her body softened and opened to welcome the unhurried press of his erection.

He slipped his other arm beneath her then, holding them chest to chest as he moved slowly within her. Each stroke was measured, deliberate, touching every sensitive nerve along its path. When he lowered his cheek to hers and whispered vague, husky words, she answered with her own sighing breaths. For countless, wondrous minutes, all she heard were those soft whispers and the rhythmic brush of linen against linen. Then, as the first wave of her climax lapped at her senses, she heard nothing at all.

Later, when he rolled onto his side, taking her with him in a tangle of limbs and rumpled sheets, she recalled her dream. "There were only thorns in the garden."

Nathan shifted and rubbed his jaw against her hair. *"Hmm?"*

"I was dreaming of the roses. Your grandmother's roses. They should be budding now, but in my dream they weren't. There were only thorns."

"It was a dream, sweetheart."

"Aye." she curved around him, sliding one leg between his. This time, the slow stroke of his hand along her back did not still her restless thoughts. "We'll miss the buds."

"Is there an omen in that?"

He was humoring her, she knew, with his drowsy participation in a discussion that could not interest him. "Would you believe me if I were to say there was?"

She saw his eyes glitter in the moonlight, felt him come fully awake. "No. But it might be an interesting tale."

"It might at that, if there were one. Nay, there's no omen, just the meanings of the buds."

"And they are?"

"Och, you don't really want to hear this." She did not really want to tell it, regretting her hasty words.

"Try me."

"Very well. A yellow rosebud means 'Let us forget.' " She hoped he would do just that for her.

"I don't remember yellow roses in my garden." He prodded her shoulder when she did not respond. "Red. Tell me about red buds."

"A red rosebud signifies a heart inclined to love."

"Ah. And the white?"

"A heart without it."

He grunted and closed his eyes again. "The wonder of folklore. How empty was my life before it."

"Don't be rude," Isobel muttered, but tempered the words by rubbing her hand in a lazy circle over his heart. " 'Twas my dream."

Nathan said nothing, just held her close and berated himself for making too much of simple words. She had been repeating something older than either of them, older than his grandmother's roses. A legend. Folk wisdom. She had not been speaking of either his heart or hers.

Unfortunate that he knew better.

Oh, his heart was indeed inclined to love. He had loved far too easily in the past, seldom wisely. But never completely, until now. Somewhere in the brief time he had known Isobel MacLeod—probably in the earliest days—he had given her his perhaps guarded, certainly battered, ever-hopeful heart. And, in uncharacteristic carelessness, he had not bothered to hold onto even a piece of it for his own protection.

Isobel had given him everything he had asked her to give: her freedom, strength, and silence. When she had learned how much he desired it, she had given him her body, and with it her inherent passion. He had never asked for her heart, perhaps because it would have shattered him to hear he could never have it.

Had he been stronger, smarter, he would have remained aloof, would have put an end to the curse that caused him

to lose those things he cared for most. Of course it was too
late for self-protection now.

He lowered the hand that curved around her waist to
cover the soft swell of her belly. Even now, his child
could be growing there. He imagined Isobel, round and
rosy in pregnancy, her fire tempered to an inner glow. He
moved his touch upward to cup one full breast, imagining a dark-headed infant suckling there.

Isobel mumbled something incoherent and moved
against him, her nipple hardening as she turned fully into
his hand. His own body responded, as it always did. He
stroked the tight bud until her own hand lifted to cover
his. " 'Tis lovely, that."

"Isobel."

"Hmm? Ah, don't stop."

"Isobel, listen to me."

"Aye?"

He drew a shaky breath. *You return to Hertfordshire
tomorrow. I'm sending you away because I can't bear to
think of what might happen to you if you stay.* He found
he could not force the words past his tongue. "Are you
content here?"

"Well, that's an odd question, isn't it? Should I moan a
wee bit louder for you next time?"

"I did not mean here in bed. I meant London."

She sighed and propped herself on an elbow. "Middle
of the night," she complained to the wall, "and the man
goes soft-headed. Nathan, *cagairean*, you've no desire to
hear my opinions of your city now."

"What does that word mean?"

"It means m'darlin', darling. What, did you think I
was calling you something foul?" She nipped at his ear.
"I've told you I never curse at you in bed." She feathered
kisses downward then, over his throat to the hollow
where his heart was beating—harder now than moments
before. "Ah, 'tis the pelt of a selkie you have."

Thoroughly distracted from his less pleasant thoughts, he covered her hand as it caressed his chest. "And what is a selkie?"

"A selkie is a beast of enchantment, half man and half seal. We've a fair number on Skye."

"Oh? They must be an odd sight, flipper and foot."

She laughed. "Nay, you'd never know a selkie but for getting close enough to look into his eyes. Whether in form of man or seal, the eyes are the same. Longing."

"For?"

"For whatever they don't have; the land if they're in the sea and the sea if they're on land. 'Tis the fate of a selkie never to have what he yearns for most. The enchantment won't let him. So sad." Her voice had gone soft, serious.

"Why, Isobel, one would think you actually believed in such things."

This time he yelped as she tugged at his chest hair. "I'm an islander, Lord Oriel, and would be a poor one indeed if I were to deny the existence of selkies. As a child I always believed I might capture one. You see, they shed their sealskins when they come to walk among us and if you hide the skin, they must stay on land. 'Tis said a woman who takes a selkie for a husband will have a mate with a magic touch and faithful heart, but a wandering soul."

Even as he knew she was teasing, he fell into the lure of the tale. "And if they hide their skins, how do you know you have a selkie on your hands."

"I told you, 'tis the eyes. There's wanting there, for what they cannot be or have." She rubbed at his cheek then. "Of course, they've fierce whiskers, too."

Nathan reached up to finger his jaw and the scratchy growth there. Both the act and his expression were so wistful that Isobel nearly laughed. Next time she would tell him the myth of the kelpies, dark, wild-eyed horses who were guardians of the water. Any woman foolish enough to be lured onto a kelpie would soon find herself on a reckless ride.

"Now, what was it you were asking me? About London, was it?"

His hand stilled on his jaw. "It doesn't matter. I—" He fell silent, his muscles going taut against her.

"Nathan?"

"*Shh.*" He peered intently toward the door. Then, in a move so sudden and smooth she had no time to object, he slid from the bed.

The sudden crash in the hallway had her all but leaping to join him. On her knees, she groped about for her dressing gown, which had fallen to the floor, and found herself with a faceful of linen when Nathan shoved her down again.

"Stay there!" he snapped, and moved into the hall.

She was not about to obey. An ominous thump sounded as she quickly donned her dressing gown, an eerie moan as she scrambled for the tinderbox. By the time she got a candle lit, there had been more banging, several yelps, and finally a frightening silence.

Gripping the heavy silver candlestick to use as much for a weapon as a torch, she stepped into the hall. And almost tripped over an arm. "Nathan?" she whispered, her heart thundering as she followed the line of an unfamiliar sleeve up past a padded shoulder, to bloodshot green eyes and wild auburn hair. "*Geordie?* What?—"

"Think it was your husband," he mumbled. "Can't be sure. Great, hulking, naked man with a fist like a mace?"

There was one final thump from somewhere down the hall. Isobel turned just in time to see her great, hulking, naked husband step over a fallen table. He limped toward her, gripping a strip of white cloth in one hand.

"I believe," he said as he groped for his door, "your brother has lost his cravat."

"Dia s'Muire." Isobel hurried toward the stairs. Rob was sprawled there, his chin resting on the top step. "Rob?" There was no response. "Robbie?"

He slowly turned his head, squinted. "Ah, Izzy. Be a good lass and give me an arm. I seem to have been felled by something."

That something, she decided as she leaned down to help him, had been as much liquor as Nathan. In the faint candlelight, Rob's skin was the palest green, and he smelled like a still. Hoping he would not be ill all over her, she alternately pushed and tugged until she had him upright and weaving his way down the hall. Geordie was still flat on his back, contemplating the shadowed ceiling.

Nathan reappeared as they passed his door. He was somewhat better covered, having donned breeches and a shirt, which he hadn't bothered to button. Rob's cravat still dangled from his fingers. "I am going to kill them," he growled.

"Seems to me you've got the job half-done already." Isobel staggered a bit under Rob's weight. "What were you thinking, going after them like that?"

"I was thinking to save— Oh, never mind that." He moved down the hallway, and his foot connected with the arm of the prostrate Geordie. "Can you walk, MacLeod?"

" 'Course," was the fuzzy reply. "Soon as I can get up." Nathan gave a lurid curse, then hauled the younger man up by the collar. "Thank you," Geordie said solemnly. "Much obliged." Then his knees buckled and he was down again.

"What should we do with them?" Nathan demanded as he got a good grip on Geordie's coat.

"Put them to bed. I assume 'tis where they were heading when you thundered out and flattened them."

"Isobel," he said wearily, "if you could possibly hold the sisterly indignation for a few minutes . . ." He tried to find the most productive manner of holding onto his burden without getting too close. "I don't trust your brother not to bock whatever he was drinking all over me."

"Let him go, then. I'll tend to him in a minute."

It took a bit of effort, but Isobel eventually got Rob settled across a guest-chamber bed. Nathan, handling Geordie very carefully, managed to get him as far as the bedroom, where he left him on the floor. As he was turning to leave the room Geordie got a weak grip on his ankle. "What is it?" Nathan growled.

"Forgot Will," Geordie mumbled, then hiccuped. Nathan sighed, then leaned closer to hear the rest.

Moments later, he was on his way down the stairs in search of his own brother. Heeding MacLeod's garbled instructions, he slowed near the bottom and saved himself a tumble. He encountered a shoulder first. He bent and, running his hand downward, located the rest of his brother. Will was facedown at the base of the stairs, one arm threaded through the spokes of the bannister.

Nathan prodded him with a toe. "William!" His brother mumbled something unintelligible. Resigned, Nathan crouched down, wondering how he was going to get the bounder untangled and up the stairs without causing injury to either of them. In the end, he settled for looping Will's arms over his own shoulders and essentially crawling upward.

In typical fashion, William awakened when they reached the top. "Ah, Nathan. Didn't mean to wake you, old trout." Nathan merely grunted. "MacLeods are somewhere behind me. Do let them in."

"They're in."

"Ah, good. Good. S'pose they'll have to leave Town in the morning. Damned shame. Splendid fellows."

Nathan paused in the process of disengaging himself. "What do you mean?"

"In deep, you know. Haven't the foggiest how they'll pay up." Will's head lolled against Nathan's shoulder.

"Ah, 'course. You'll lend 'em the blunt, won't you, Nat? Always good for a few pounds . . . few hundred. Good man." Apparently reassured, he was out again.

Nathan left him there, snoring. Having a very good idea what had happened, and at the tail end of his patience, he made his way back to where he had left the three MacLeods. Isobel had managed to get the second onto the bed beside the first and was struggling with what appeared to be a boot, muttering a string of Gaelic invectives all the while.

"Wake them," Nathan commanded.

"Why? 'Twould take a cannon blast."

"Isobel. Since you are no doubt vastly experienced in such matters, I am giving you the opportunity to rouse them. Otherwise, I will do it, and I daresay you would not approve of my methods."

Some ten minutes later, courtesy of a good deal of coaxing and a few splashes of water, the brothers were propped up and reasonably alert. Nathan had sat silently through the operations. Now he demanded, "Where have you been tonight?"

"Why, they were out with your brother, Nathan—"

"Isobel, please. Your brothers will answer for themselves. *Where*, MacLeod?" He had no idea which brother he was addressing. It didn't matter. "And how much did you lose?"

This got a response.

"How much of what?" one mumbled.

"Haven't the foggiest what you mean," said the other.

"Are you looking for something, milord? 'Fraid we can't be of much help. Had a drink or two, you know."

Nathan had a strong urge to stalk over and bang the two auburn heads together.

"Enough!" He aimed what he hoped was a suitably intimidating glare in their direction, flexing his fists at the same time. "I am in no mood for games."

No doubt their vision was as blurred as his, but they apparently saw the gesture, for Nathan heard a distinct scuffling.

Isobel reached over and gently touched his arm. "Nathan, perhaps I—"

"Perhaps you will trust me with this."

She withdrew. "More of that, is it? Oh, very well."

"Thank you. Now, gentlemen, how much did you lose?"

There was a long silence before one replied, "How did you know?"

"Which one are you?"

"Rob."

"Rob. I will ask the questions from now on. Is that clear?"

He received a sullen "Aye."

"Again, how much? Why don't you be the one to tell me, Geordie?" He could not quite hear the response. "Don't toy with me, damn it! *How much?*"

This time, the amount came loud and only slightly slurred. "Four . . . hundred."

Isobel was on her feet like a shot. "Four hundred pounds? *Mac Muire*, have you no sense at all?" She let loose with a harangue in Gaelic. Nathan had no idea what she was saying, but he knew her brothers certainly did. He could imagine them shrinking against the headboard.

He waited patiently for her to finish. "I quite agree, my dear."

"*Och*, Nathan. I have no idea what to say."

"I am certain you said it all quite well." He addressed whichever brother still remained upright after her tirade. "Where were you playing?"

"Watier's."

"Watier's?" Isobel repeated. "How did you get in there, Robbie? You've no—" She let her breath out in a slow hiss. "William."

"You'll not blame him!" Geordie came quickly if clumsily to his new crony's defense. "He instruc— insect—taught us quite thoroughly on the matter of club play. And he lost but a hundred."

Nathan cursed. He really was going to have to do something about his own brother. But first he had to see to Isobel's. "I sincerely hope it took you more than one hand to lose four hundred pounds."

"A good deal more than one," came the glum answer. "Damn me if the fellow didn't string us like trout. Showed up late at our table, bottle in hand and looking as if he'd already put a goodly amount away. He'd lose a few hands, we'd be up a tenner then, well . . ."

There seemed to be no end to the male MacLeod's stupidity, Nathan thought. They had fallen for the age-old ploy of a man arriving at the gaming table ostensibly drunk. No doubt they themselves had been well sotted and had had no excuse for continuing to play.

"Thought we had him plenty of times, my lord," the other offered. "Then he'd draw a flush, and we'd be out the ten. Devil's own luck."

"Devil's own skill," the other corrected.

Nathan leaned forward. "Are you saying the man cheated?"

"Wouldn't say it to his face! Damned scary brute. We might be unlucky, Oriel, but we ain't stupid!"

Difficult as it was, Nathan held his tongue. There were more important matters to be considered than helping idiots see their own idiocy. He could think of any number of damned scary brutes who might be found at Watier's tables. Quite a few of them would be more than capable of fleecing a pair of green cubs out of four hundred pounds.

He had the distressing feeling he would soon be parting with that very amount. And cursed inwardly. He could have bought the pair a cottage in the northernmost reaches of Scotland for that, with enough money left to employ a keeper to watch them for a decade.

On the bright side, he now had an irrefutable reason for sending them home with their sister.

"Very well. You will give me the fellow's name. Then you will obediently, quietly, sleep until morning. And if you so much as stick a toe outside this house before I've spoken with you again, you will find yourselves making your way back to Hertfordshire tied *behind* the coach. Have I made myself clear?"

"Damn it, Oriel, you cannot order us—"

A sharp Gaelic phrase from Isobel put an abrupt stop to that sentiment.

"Who was it, Rob?" Nathan demanded.

He should not have been surprised, really. But he still felt his jaw clenching when he heard the reply. "A viscount. Lord St. Wulfstan."

Well, there it was. And how simple it must have been. All St. Wulfstan had to do was find the connection between the brothers and Nathan, cast out a lure, and draw the line taut. Mutely, Nathan rose to his feet and limped from the room. He needed to be away from the MacLeods, needed to clear his own mind and still the new churning of his gut. *St. Wulfstan.*

"Nathan?"

He had not heard Isobel follow him into his bedroom. "Not now."

"But . . ."

"Not *now*, damn it!"

Isobel shrank back, startled by his tone and by his expression. Standing by the mantelpiece in his bedchamber, only the faint light of a single candle to illuminate him, he looked much, too much, as he had that very first night.

Uncertainly, she reached out one trembling hand. "Nathan, I—"

"For God's sake, Isobel, leave me be! I cannot speak with you now."

Stung anew, she let her arm drop. Nay, she wasn't leaving, but she needed more light to stay. She busied herself with stoking the fire, then moved about the chamber, lighting several braces of candles. When she had finished, she drew a deep breath and tried again. "My lord, I am sorry the lads allowed themselves to be fleeced. They are foolish, but—"

He slammed his palm hard against the mantel, sending a silver holder with its unlit taper toppling. Isobel flinched, waiting for the sound of metal clanging against the tile hearth. But with his free hand, Nathan managed to catch the candlestick as it dropped. "They were chosen!" he shouted. "St. Wulfstan chose them."

Bewildered by what she had just seen, all she could manage was a faint "Chosen?"

"A pair of sheep in a landowner's pen. No more important than that."

"I—do not understand."

His harsh laugh sent a shiver through her. "Come now, Isobel. You are a Highland Scotswoman. Don't tell me you are unfamiliar with the expansive curse: 'May your well run dry, your crops wither, your debts fall into the hands of the devil . . .' "

"Nathan, please. You are frightening me." And he was. There was an unholy light in his amber eyes, a deepening harshness to the lines around his mouth. He looked bitter, distant, and slightly mad. "You are speaking nonsense."

"Nonsense. If only it were so." He faced her fully now, his eyes burning. "You were meant to be my redemption, Isobel. My saving grace. God, look at you, the brilliant halo above the celestial white. I should have known you would prove to be my greatest weakness."

He set the candlestick back on the mantel, right in the

center, right where it had been. Then he reached for her. Isobel took a shaky step backward, prevented from taking another when her heel landed on the hem of her dressing gown.

"H-how did you know?"

"What, that St. Wulfstan chose—"

"How did you know," she interrupted, her voice shrill, "that my dressing gown is white?"

"Isobel . . . Ah, hell."

"How did you catch that candlestick and put it back precisely where it had been?" Images flashed through her mind, one atop the next and sharp as steel. "*Dia s'Muire.* All along. You've seen all along."

"Isobel . . ."

"How much, Nathan? Everything?" Cursing him, cursing herself more, she gasped, "Was it all a lie?"

She nearly went down, trying to back away as he came at her. For the first time, it was his hands that did the steadying. He pulled her to him, and she fought against him. "Listen to me!" His repeated pleas came through her helpless fury, but meant nothing. When she went limp, it was simply because she knew it was no use to struggle. He was too strong. "Isobel, there have been no lies. I have not lied."

"You can *see*!" she raged, blind herself now with hot tears.

"Only blurry shapes and colors in a well-lit room. The glow of firelight in your hair, for instance. So beautiful, my love. So beautiful."

She did not move when he buried his lips in her hair. She stood, rigid against him, silent, until he released her. "Isobel, please."

"Why, Nathan?" Then she shook her head. "Nay, I've no heart to hear you now."

He answered anyway, and his eyes were fierce and pleading as he told her, "You said you would never have accepted me had I been able to see. I thought you would leave me."

"I was *jesting*, you daft fool. You knew full well I was jesting!" Chilled now, Isobel pulled free of his grasp. He let her go. "Perhaps when you've readied your tale, I'll listen. Perhaps. But for now"—she turned away and headed for the door—"I cannot."

"I love you, you know. More than my own life."

She froze, wondering why she had not realized how much she had longed to hear those words. Yearned for them. And now that she had heard them, they were bitter to her ears.

"You must believe that," he continued, his voice rough and low. "If you believe nothing else."

"I read novels, my lord. More than you, no doubt, though perhaps you ought to try your hand at writing one. You certainly have the words ready."

"Damn it, Isobel!"

"I know I'm meant to turn now, listen and forgive. Perhaps next chapter."

For the first time, she bolted the connecting door between their chambers.

CHAPTER 19

Had we never lov'd sae kindly,
Had we never lov'd sae blindly,
Never met— or never parted—
We'd hae ne'er been broken-hearted.
  —Robert Burns, "Ae Fond Kiss"

Nathan let the string of pearls slide through his fingers to pool on the desk. Then he lifted the necklace and let it slide through his fingers again. He had been doing it for so long now that the act had become automatic. He had long since stopped feeling the satin ripple of the pearls, stopped hearing their rhythmic clicking against each other and the desk.

He looked up, startled, when the string was jerked from his fingers.

"Stop that!" his brother snapped.

"How long have you been there?"

William snorted. "Five minutes. I knocked, you know, but you're so immersed in your rosary and solitude that you didn't hear me."

"She left me, Will."

"I know. The entire household knows. Damn, Nat, I expect all of London knows."

Perhaps he had not been quiet on finding Isobel gone, but even as he had stumbled through the house, scattering small pieces of furniture and nervous servants, he had thought he might yet find her. In the morning room, the attics, the wine cellar.

Only when he had calmed down enough to talk to the

staff did he learn that a pale, red-eyed Isobel, weaving brothers in tow, had climbed into the traveling carriage just after dawn and driven away. She would be halfway to Hertfordshire by now, gone as he had planned. Only not as he had planned, after all. He had not been able to ask her to go, not been able to countenance being in his home without her.

His need to have her with him had been selfish, he knew, and potentially dangerous. Perhaps her leaving was, in fact, an act of divine intervention. Perhaps it was really punishment for his selfishness—and his refusal to tell her the complete truth.

It was some consolation to know precisely where she was going. He was relieved to know she was removed from danger, but his guilt-ridden loneliness was every bit as powerful as the comfort.

"Nathan." William's voice drew him from his grim musings. "Tell me something, would you, old chap?"

"If I can."

"What in damnation are you still doing here? You should have gone after her, should bloody well be tearing up the Cheshunt Road now!"

"Thank you, William, for that very helpful opinion."

"Well?"

Nathan sighed and held out his hand for the pearls. "Go away, William."

"But, really—"

"I mean it, William. Take yourself elsewhere."

"Very well." His brother plunked the pearls onto the desk. "At least tell me what you plan to do about St. Wulfstan. The man isn't going to react too kindly to the news that the MacLeods and his four hundred pounds left Town."

Nathan threaded the pearls through his fingers again and felt marginally better for it. "Give me a small amount of credit, if you would. And trust me to deal with the matter as I deem best."

"As you did with your wife's departure?" was the snide retort.

"William!"

"I'm going. But I have to say, Nat, you married a smashing woman, and you're a bloody fool to let her get away."

Nathan heaved an inkwell. It came nowhere near its mark, but William slammed the door with unnecessary force as he left.

A few minutes later, the door opened, and Nathan heard the swish of skirts. His heart leapt. But no, the hazy image before his eyes was too small to be his wife. "Good morning, Mariah," he offered wearily.

"It is hardly a good morning, you great oaf! How could you do it?"

Before Nathan could respond with a few choice and not particularly loving words, he heard the swishing of more petticoats. They were not Isobel's this time, either.

"There are moments, Nathan, when I am forced to contemplate the possibility that I did something horrendously wrong as a parent!"

"Good morning, Mother. Where is—"

"Damn me, boy, what have you got inside that thick head of yours? Sure as blazes ain't the brains you were born with!"

"Father," Nathan finished wryly.

"William has given us the most distressing news!" The duchess's voice was the tiniest notch above normal volume, signifying her emotional state. "He says Isobel left you this morning!"

"She—"

"Well, son, what are you doing still here? Get on that bloody horse of yours and get her back!" The duke,

whose vocal volume never signified much of anything at
all, pounded the desk in rhythm with his words.

Mariah, bless her heart, merely snapped, "Idiot!"

His own patience frayed, Nathan rose slowly from his
seat. "If you would be so kind," he began, then gave up
the fight when William bounded back into the room,
muttering new insults. In an instant, his entire family was
scolding at once.

And Isobel had been concerned they would not accept
her. How surprised she would have been to know what a
storm her departure was causing, Nathan thought. He
rather suspected that had he been the one who disappeared, there would have been a comment or two at
supper, then nothing save a brief mention at holidays.
Isobel, despite having been a Paget for less than a month,
had left a hole as large as Scotland itself in the family.

Pearls gripped in one fist, cane in the other, Nathan
limped from behind the desk and toward the hall. He was
immediately surrounded by his parents and siblings, all
growling and snapping like mad dogs. A fist, owner
uncertain, shook in his face, a hand tugged at his sleeve.
When the duke actually called him "a damn fool *Sasunnach*," his patience shattered.

"Enough!" he bellowed. "Enough. I appreciate your concern. Isobel, were she here, would appreciate your concern.
But it was not requested and it damn well is not wanted!"
With that, he cleared his path with a sweep of his cane and
headed for the stairs.

"I beg your pardon, my lord . . ."

"For God's sake, Milch! She left. Yes, she left. I know
the staff does not like it. *I* bloody well hate it! But if I
hear one more word from anyone on the matter, I will not
be responsible for my actions!"

There was a moment of complete silence. Then the
butler hesitantly cleared his throat. "Yes, my lord. I quite

understand, my lord. I meant, however, merely to inform you that Mr. Gerard is here to see you."

"Where is he?"

"He is in the morning room, my lord."

Brandishing his cane as a clear warning to all and sundry, Nathan turned and made his way back across the hall. There was no question in his mind why Gerard was there; he wanted to discuss Henry Stone. Nathan did not want to talk about Henry Stone. In fact, he did not want to talk about any facet of the hopeless Gordian knot that had brought him back to Town in the first place.

"I know about Stone," he muttered, without preamble, on entering the morning room.

"Ah." Gerard cleared his throat. "And I know about your wife. I am sorry, Oriel."

"It isn't permanent. I am considering driving to Hertfordshire this evening."

"You are certain that is where she went?"

"I am. Her brothers are with her."

"Of course. I know about St. Wulfstan's encounter with your brothers-in-law as well."

Nathan wearily lowered himself into a chair. "How quickly good news travels in this blighted town."

"It was hardly a quiet scene in Watier's last night, and I am well informed. As for Lady Oriel, I am afraid I could not keep from hearing you when I arrived. I had not meant to be listening."

"Oh, leave off, Matthew. Of course you heard me. According to my brother, all of London heard me. But as I said, it is merely a misunderstanding. Isobel and I will be reunited soon." He found Gerard's sympathetic murmuring a good deal less than welcome. "How is Stone?"

"Still alive, but barely."

"When can I speak with him?"

"I wish you could. I wish anyone could. He has been

unconscious since he was found. The surgeon does not expect him to live, nor to speak again before he dies."

Nathan cursed under his breath. "It would have been too much to ask, perhaps. But he could have given us a name. Not that we need one."

"You know who shot him, then?"

"Ah, Matthew, you know as well as I do."

Gerard muttered the name that had been taunting Nathan all morning. "I cannot believe it."

"Yes, you can. You do." Nathan leaned back and rested his head against the chair. "Will you be able to forgive yourself?"

"For?"

"For not seeing it earlier? For not preventing Brookes's death, quite possibly Stone's. You couldn't have, you know."

"And you are wrong, Nathan. I could have prevented both. Dennison's, too. That is for me to bear."

Nathan suspected the man had already dipped into the brandy that day. Danger had never affected Gerard in the least, but any failure for which he blamed himself sat like the weight of the earth on his shoulders.

"I will deal with the matter, Matthew," Nathan said. "I will leave it to you to explain, should the War Department ever ask, but I will deal with it."

"Nathan, I will not have you—"

"Don't waste your breath, man. I have already begun. Go home. Go anywhere. I will send word to you when . . . when it is done."

"I am sorry, so sorry I drew you into this." Gerard leaned forward, gripped his arm. "I could have left you in peace in the country, but my suspicions weren't enough. You were always the best at finding the rats, Nathan. I needed your certainty."

"I understand. I ask but one thing of you now."

"Anything."

"Cut me loose, Matthew. Promise me that when this is over, you will not summon me again."

There was a moment of heavy silence. Then, "Of course. This will be the end of it."

"Thank you."

Much later, as he sat in the library waiting for a message, Nathan tried to remember the man he had been at the beginning of this cursed war. He had come eagerly to Gerard's service, a bold young buck with visions of heroism, driven by the desire to please his father and make amends for having failed his fiancée. The promise of action, of serving his country, had been irresistible. Before enlisting, he had never been much good at anything other than riding fast, playing hard, and dressing well.

Rievaulx had followed him, lured too, by the possibilities. And what a pair they had made in those early days: brash, careless, always treading that narrow line between clever and brilliant. Rievaulx. Somewhere deep in the Portuguese earth now.

"We'll have our vengeance, Gabriel," Nathan muttered, "tonight if all goes as it should. Will you be content then?" There was something mocking in the silence, and he gave a harsh laugh. "Of course. It really has nothing to do with your peace, does it? It is my own conscience. So, will *I* be content?"

He realized altogether too quickly that his contentment had very little to do with vengeance. It was waiting for him in Hertfordshire.

"I am sorry, Gabriel," he whispered, unsure of precisely what the apology was meant to solve.

It was nearly dusk when Milch appeared, bearing the message that Nathan had been waiting for. If the butler thought it odd that the master asked him to read it aloud, he did not show it. Nathan, face all but pressed to the window overlooking the house's garden, did not turn. He merely listened.

"That is all, my lord."

"Thank you, Milch. You will see the carriage is ready at the appropriate hour."

"Of course, my lord."

When he had gone, Nathan remained at the window. The cards were down, and he had nothing to do but wait.

Isobel turned from the glass. "The garden has grown so since I left. I could smell the rosemary as I came in." She managed a faint smile. "Savoury, sage, rosemary, and thyme. You could never leave the legend behind, could you?"

Maggie sat still and serene at the table, but her concern was evident in her eyes, hard as she tried to conceal it. "We're to have chicken with rosemary for supper. 'Tis there but for practical use."

Isobel tenderly patted her sister's shoulder as she walked past to her own seat. Wherever they went, Maggie planted the four herbs. "I'll tell you, darling, if I never believed in that sorry tale, I'm inclined to now. Highland women and English men are not meant to marry."

"Oh, Izzy . . ."

"No, don't say it. I daresay Nathan and I will find some way of managing together. I'll certainly not push him off a cliff. Is it in the blood, do you think? Deception, I mean, and a talent for it. Perhaps my man is related to the other, the one who came to Skye in hopes of toppling the king."

"Izzy, please. It grieves me, hearing you talk so. 'Tis but a legend, the Englishman who came to Skye. I cannot believe Oriel had such devious intent."

Isobel raised a brow. "Nay? You were the one reluctant to accept him, Maggie Líl. What makes you so certain of his good intentions now?"

"I can see how much you love him," her sister said gently. "Your heart would know."

"I imagine our long-departed island maiden felt the same," Isobel shot back with a snort. "And look where it got her—a dirk in the breast and an unmarked grave."

"Isobel!"

"*Och*, Maggie, pay me no mind. I'm bitter and past weary now. I'll be better for a decent supper and good night's rest."

Tessa bounded into the room then, hair wild over her shoulders and nothing at all on her feet. "They walk the cliffs, you know, searching for each other. She has the dirk sticking from her chest; he has a deep gash in his head and seaweed wrapped about his throat. I've seen them!"

"You have not!" Maggie scolded. " 'Tis only a bedside tale meant to keep foolish young lasses from casting their hearts away and reckless children from walking the cliffs."

" 'Beauty and the Beast' is a bedside tale. Our dead lovers are history. I only wish I'd gotten a closer look. I daresay you can see his brains through his skull."

"Tessa!"

The girl shrugged, then skipped across the room to poke among yesterday's sugar biscuits. "Will you stay, Izzy? Robbie says your husband will be along soon enough to drag you off to the Hall, but I said I would plant him a smashing facer should he try."

Isobel forced a grin, her strength sapped all the more for the girl's boundless energy. "I'll bide a while, *pigidh bheag,* but I expect I'll have to go again sooner or later."

"*Mmm.* I will smack him for you, if you wish, should he show up. Have we no gingerbread, Maggie? I'm peckish."

"Supper will be ready soon enough. You should have

just enough time to make yourself acquainted with some soap and water."

"Oh, Maggie."

"Off with you now! Another day like today and I'll be able to plant seeds on your neck. 'Tis nearly enough dirt there now."

Tessa grumbled all the while, but disappeared with a towel and filled pitcher. Isobel watched her go, a genuine smile blooming. "I think she's grown, too."

"Perhaps, but you've only been gone a month."

" 'Tis amazing what can happen in a month's time." She rose to help Maggie set the table. "Look at what the lads did in a mere day."

"Aye, which reminds me. What of their debt, Izzy? I've a bit put by, but not nearly enough."

"*Cuist!* As if I would take your money or allow them to! Nay, I sent a note to St. Wulfstan, telling him I had taken over the debt and would settle it upon my return."

"Are you going back, then?"

"I'll have to eventually."

"And this St. Wulfstan will sit patiently and wait?"

" 'Tisn't the money he wants, Maggie, but some sort of satisfaction against Nathan. He'll have it in his own way now, whether I'm there or not." Isobel forced herself to set the knives gently on the table. "You shouldn't be too hard on Rob and Geordie. They were merely being their usual witless selves. They had no way of knowing they'd come up against and between two men with old wounds."

"Aye, well, forgiveness is only good 'til the next time they go empty heads first into deep water."

"I don't think they'll be so quick to fall into deep card-play next time. Nathan put the fear of God into them last night."

Maggie snorted. "For all the good scaring them has done in the past."

"Oh, you've never seen my husband in a rage. 'Tis enough to send the devil himself running for cover."

"Yet you love him. That frightens *me*, Iseabail Roís."

Isobel set the plates aside to catch her sister's hands. "He has reasons for his deception, Maggie. I'll not pretend to understand why he did what he did, but I'll not condemn him completely, either. There's a nobility in him, and honor. Hidden and slippery, aye, but there."

"You've already forgiven him for lying to you about his sight."

Isobel stepped back, drew her shawl closer about her shoulders. "I suppose I have. But I don't understand and I'm still hurting. Rob's right; Nathan will come here sooner or later. I'll be here when he does, and perhaps we'll be all right in the end." She shook her head, uncertain of anything at the moment. "The worst part of it, Maggie, is that from the beginning he told me there would be secrets."

"*Och*, Izzy, it hardly matters," Maggie shot back. "You did all he asked of you with a good deal more honor than he showed."

Perhaps Maggie was right, but for now, all Isobel wanted was to be in the midst of her family again. Aye, they had faults, but they were beyond obvious. What one saw on the surface was precisely what one got.

How much easier things would be if the same was true of Nathan. It would be simple, hardening her heart against a man whose core was as harsh and damaged as his shell.

"Izzy, lass! You've come for a visit!"

Jamie MacLeod, red-faced and weaving, appeared at the kitchen door. "And looking quite the lady. London must suit you."

She returned his clumsy embrace, cherishing the familiar smell of wine and sage soap. In the end, she was forced to concede that there was indeed some comfort in knowing certain things would never, ever change.

"Oriel's back at the Hall, is he? Well, you'll have your darlin' family over for supper soon enough. Daresay we'll have a grand spread. Splendid cellars, your husband has. Endless." He tottered over to the stove and banged a few lids. "Good lass, Maggie. I've an appetite like the sea." Then he headed, far more steadily, for his own meager cellar.

His daughters sighed in unison, then laughed aloud.

Whether it was the smell of food or the promise of drink that attracted the boys, they appeared almost immediately. Both still had a shade of green to their skin. Isobel, warmed by the pleasures of home, managed a twinge of pity. It could not have been easy for them, being bounced for hours along country roads so soon after their encounters with too much brandy, a loaded deck of cards, and Nathan. She even patted Geordie's head consolingly when he slumped into a chair.

"You'll feel better for a meal," she offered, and went off to summon the perhaps cleaner Tessa.

It was a supper like so many before. Jamie fell to snoring as soon as his belly was full, Tessa spilled the milk, and Rob ended up rushing from the table midway, face the color of grass. Through it all, Maggie presided with serene disapproval, slipping away for a bit—furtively, as if no one would notice—to prepare a soothing tisane for poor Robbie. Calmed, feeling far removed from London and what had happened there, Isobel sat back in her chair and reveled in the simple scene.

It ended all too soon, with Tessa bounding off to dig for worms or some such activity, the boys slinking off, no doubt, to Harris's. Jamie, for his part, stayed just where he was, rattling the china with his snores.

Isobel and Maggie cleared the table in companionable silence. Maggie was quite vocal, however, in her refusal to let Isobel help with the rest of the cleaning. "Not in that gown, lass," she scolded, "or with that boulder on your hand. You sit and play the grand lady for one more night." Her voice softened. "There will be time enough for all the old tasks."

Isobel glanced down. She had not thought about the fine muslin, nor about the ring. Now she tugged at the latter, thinking to put it aside during her stay. It would only be in the way and serve to remind her of things better set aside as well, at least for the time being.

The ring resisted, sliding no farther than her knuckle. Cursing it, Isobel twisted it one way and then the other, hoping to pull it free.

"*Isobel . . .*"

"Aye?"

Maggie was busy with the pots. "I said naught."

"Papa must have wakened."

Maggie peered over her shoulder. "Nay. He's still out."

"*Isobel!*"

"What is it?" She turned in her seat. Maggie was staring at her now, brow furrowed. "You didn't hear that?"

"Hear what?"

Nathan's voice. It had sounded so like his voice that time. Of course she was thinking of him. She'd thought of little else since creeping from their home. Wearily, she closed her eyes.

And saw him.

He was sprawled on a dusty floor, limbs thrown out and eyes shut. There was a tear in his sleeve, another in his white shirt, and a dark stain, spreading slowly across the floor.

"Oh, *Mac Muire!*" Isobel's eyes sprang open.

"Izzy?" Maggie's face was pressed close to hers. "Isobel?"

She was huddled in her seat, her right hand clasped

over the left, pressing the pearl and diamond ring deeply
into her palm. And seeing nothing. "Please," she begged,
having no idea where the plea was meant to go. "Please
help."

"Isobel . . ."

"Nay, Maggie." She pulled away from her sister's
embrace and struggled to her feet. "I must go."

"Go? Go where?"

"Back to Town." Isobel was already out of the kitchen
and on her way up the stairs. She stopped, then rushed
back down. All she needed was her cloak; the rest could
stay. "I cannot explain now, but I've no choice."

" 'Tis nearly dark! You wouldn't arrive 'til the middle
of the night. Wait, go in the morning if you must."

Isobel gave her a fierce hug. "Gather sage for us,
Mairghread, for love."

And Maggie, her own eyes seeing as much inside as
out, did not try to stop her. Instead she nodded, held
Isobel close for a moment, and let her go.

Nathan navigated the steps slowly. It had been more
than a year since he had last been to this place, the house
where the Ten had gathered whenever a quiet meeting
was needed. The door opened at his touch, creaking
slightly as it swung inward. He could smell dust, dampness, the odors of disuse.

It was more than appropriate that it should all end
here, where it began.

He moved slowly, trying to tread silently on the
marble floor. It was as dark inside as out—not that it mattered. Cursing his helplessness, Nathan peered around
the foyer and listened. He couldn't hear anyone moving
about, but with his vision poor as it was, he was an easy
target.

It was earlier than arranged, only half-past eleven. He
had taken the chance that he would arrive first. Not that it

was much of an advantage, but any little bit helped. He had every hope of walking away from the encounter.

Heart thundering in his ears, he took a few hesitant steps forward. There was a coatroom to the left, stairs straight ahead—and any number of doors he had never seen behind. There had been no reason in the past. Now, each was one more possible snare.

The pistol was heavy in his hand. He had not fired a gun in months, not even held one since leaving Lisbon. What use would it have been? Hitting an elephant in broad daylight would be a challenge. A slick, shadowy figure at midnight was all but impossible.

Still muffling his steps, he headed for the stairs. The first floor was smaller than the entry, only three rooms. One, he remembered, did not have a window. That was where he would wait—and hope that the other man had decided against carrying a lantern.

He reached the landing, and turned down the hall. It seemed his instincts had been accurate. He was as yet alone in the building. Again, surprise was only worth so much when a blind man faced a seeing one, but a wise man took what he could.

Second door? Third? He could not remember which was the windowless chamber. He took a chance on the second and, as he stepped inside, knew he had made a terrible mistake.

"Clever, Oriel, but you should have remembered that we all learned our trade at the same knee."

Nathan took a shallow breath as he felt the gun barrel dig deeper into his abdomen. "Until you took further lessons from the French."

"Oh, please. Could you not have left the dramatics at the door?" The barrel poked at his ribs. "Hand over your weapon, if you would be so kind. Slowly."

Helpless to do otherwise, Nathan obeyed. Much of his bravado slipped from his grasp with his gun. Some small voice deep within him cried for mercy, called Isobel's name.

He quashed it. "Will you keep at it until we're all gone? Is Rotheroe next? Montgomerie? Brandon?"

"Give me a bit of credit. Montgomerie is already dead. Brandon, too. They've been dead some weeks now."

Nathan's gut twisted. "And Rotheroe?"

"Rotheroe. Rotheroe could have walked away from all this none the wiser. Damned fool had to get himself involved with you."

"Stone."

"What of him? He was a rodent."

"You don't deny it, then." Nathan's mouth was dry. He still held his cane, had climbed the stairs with it tucked under his arm. Perhaps if he could get one good swing . . .

"Deny what?"

"That you shot him."

St. Wulfstan's harsh laugh echoed through the empty room. "And deny myself credit for perhaps my best aim ever? Of course I shot Stone." He lifted the gun and pushed the barrel into Nathan's chest. "Dead center."

CHAPTER 20

Isobel leapt from the carriage just as a distant bell chimed one o'clock. Driven past exhaustion into numb terror by the rattling ride, she rushed up the stairs and pounded on the door. She had left her key in Hertfordshire.

It seemed an eternity before Milch appeared, hurriedly buttoning his coat as he pulled the door in. His heavy eyelids shot up as he saw her. "My lady!"

She shoved past him, ran for the stairs. "His lordship—"

"Is not here, madam."

"What?" She skidded to a halt.

"He went out before midnight in the carriage."

"Where? Where did he go?"

"I don't rightly know, my lady. He received a message, instructing him to meet at Ten House."

"Ten House?" She racked her brain but could not remember ever having heard of such a place. "Ten what?"

The butler flushed miserably. "I really can't say, my lady. I . . . assumed it was a private residence."

Truly frantic now, Isobel all but knocked the diminutive man off his feet when she rushed back and seized his lapels. "Is there a pistol in the house, Milch?"

"A pistol? I, ah, believe his lordship keeps a pistol in

his desk. If I may say so . . ." But Isobel was already running for the stairs again.

She emptied every drawer in Nathan's desk. There were countless papers, a wealth of long-dried ink bottles, several pouches of coins, but no gun. Breathing heavily, her mind blank, she pounded her fists against the blotter, sending the single sheet of foolscap sliding off the far side and onto the floor. She went after it.

Midnight, it read, *Ten House.* It was signed with a scrawled *St. W.*

St. Wulfstan.

"Dear God," Isobel whispered and, note clasped to her breast, rushed from the room.

She overturned all the drawers in Nathan's bedchamber but found nothing save his clothing, his toiletries, and the three miniatures. There was no pistol. A few minutes later, she shoved past the sputtering Milch again and ran out the door.

She lost precious minutes hauling an unwilling Aingeal from his stall, more in fighting him with saddle and bridle. By the time they rounded the corner of Grosvenor Square and stopped in front of Nathan's parents' home, both horse and rider were wild-eyed and winded.

Isobel pounded relentlessly with the brass knocker on the Abergele door, not caring if she woke the entire family. She was greatly relieved to find Will in the upper hall when she finally got inside. He was in his dressing gown, hair standing in dark licks about his head.

"Isobel?" he said vaguely. "What on earth . . . ?"

"I need a pistol, Will. Now."

"A pistol? Whatever for?"

"William, please. No questions. Where do I find one of your father's guns?"

He gestured toward the duke's library. "But, Isobel . . ."

Will made it into the room as Isobel was tossing a

pistol aside. There were several more on the desk, a legion on the wall.

"These are not loaded!" Isobel reached for another, and William grabbed for her hand.

"None of them are. Mother will not allow ammunition in the townhouse."

Not quite believing her ears, Isobel slumped into the massive desk chair. "None at all?"

"I'm afraid not. She's always worried he'll shoot someone. Probably wise . . ."

He broke off as Isobel seized him by the collar. "Gunpowder. Your experiments. You must be able to load a pistol for me."

"Wet."

"I beg your pardon?"

He raked his fingers through his already wild hair. "The gunpowder is wet." He flushed. "Mother again. After I caused a bit of an, er, explosion in the cellar last year, she had all my gunpowder soaked with water. She did the same with the gunpowder I bought recently. Now I am experimenting with it wet. Could be of great use to the navy, you know."

"Dear Lord." Isobel dropped her head into her hands. "I have married into a family of clowns!"

"Now see here, I have made great progress in the past weeks. Genius is always destined for derision."

"William." She got a new, tighter grip on his dressing gown. "Where is Ten House?"

"Ten House?"

"Aye! Where is it?"

Now he was looking at her as if she had a cog or two loose. "I have no idea about any Ten House. Isobel, you are clearly distraught. Perhaps a warm glass of brandy . . ." At her responding snarl, he took a wary step back. "I, ah, you might want to ask Rotheroe. I believe

I've heard him and Nat muttering once or twice about a ten of something."

He reached out as she shot past him but ended up getting tangled in his own dressing gown. Isobel ignored the thump and groan and, not even bothering to wave to Nathan's pale parents or her sister-in-law, who had now appeared in the hallway, Isobel headed for the street. In her hand was one of the duke's guns. It was useless, of course, but no one need know that but her.

It was a moot point unless she discovered just what and where Ten House was. Finding Lord Rotheroe was the only place to start. He lived in one of the narrow houses just off Hyde Park. Which one was another matter.

Well, she would simply pound on each door until she found him.

It never occurred to her to question the horrible vision she had had in the cottage. She was a practical woman, but she was also an Island Scot. No one raised among the lore and tradition of the Highlands would ignore so vivid an omen. None would dare.

Aingeal was where she had left him, against the cast-iron rail in front of the house. There was someone with him now, one of the duke's grooms, she assumed. Isobel offered silent thanks to the man's staff. She had not bothered to do more than toss the horse's reins over the rail. All things considered, had someone not intervened, the animal would have been back in his own stable by now, happily tucking into the oat bin.

"Thank you," Isobel panted, reaching for the reins. A hand shot out and encircled her wrist. Stunned, frozen, she tried to scream, but another hand clamped over her mouth.

Struggling was no use. The man subdued her easily and, Aingeal trailing behind, dragged her quickly away from the house. As she watched, helpless, Abergele House, and the help that was just inside its walls, disappeared behind a hedge. On they went, she dragging her heels and thrashing uselessly against the iron arm, he cursing and tightening that grip. In seconds, they were deep within the shadows.

"Now, my lady, I will remove my hand. But if you so much as open your mouth to scream, I will be forced to silence you again. Is that clear?"

Isobel nodded, planning even as she did to scream the Square down as soon as he released her. She twisted against the restraining arm, trying to get her bearings for flight. In that fleeting second, her attacker's features were visible.

The scream died, forgotten, in her throat.

"Dia s'Muire," she breathed. "You."

Nathan's eyes fluttered open. He groaned with the resulting pain and let them close again. Scattered sensations flashed through his mind. A gun at his chest, a shove, flaring pain.

St. Wulfstan.

Had he been shot? He could see nothing but blackness. No light, no hazy shadows. Numb, he tried to move and realized he was lying on the floor, his cheek pressed into the wooden floor, his arms behind his back. He moved his fingers, felt the heavy twine binding his hands.

"Welcome back, Sleeping Beauty," a voice mocked from nearby. "I thought I might have to kiss you and damned if the idea didn't turn my gut."

With the words, memory came rushing back. The air had erupted suddenly with a whoosh. St. Wulfstan had grunted, gone down, his weight knocking Nathan backward. Before he could regain his balance, he had felt the first blow to his temple. Lights exploded behind his eyes. He remembered falling, remembered a second blow. Then nothing.

"St. Wulfstan?"

"Who did you expect? Some benevolent fairy?"

"You—someone—"

"Someone indeed. I don't suppose he left your arms free."

"No. Legs, either." Nathan tested the bonds, giving up with a moan as his head protested.

"Don't bother. He's a fair hand with the rope. And the cosher. My head feels as if it's been bashed with a mace."

Gritting his teeth, Nathan rolled over onto his elbows. An agonizing few minutes later, he was sitting up. The ropes were tight about his wrists and ankles, tight enough that his feet were numb and his fingers fast getting there. "Tell me this is all part of your depraved plan."

St. Wulfstan snorted. "Well, that would be handy, wouldn't it? Come now, Oriel, I never took you for stupid. Full to the brim with naive nobility, perhaps, but not stupid."

"I would be careful, calling me stupid. You're the one who has been double-crossed here."

"Double-crossed? What are you blathering about now?"

No, Nathan was not stupid. And he was having some extremely disturbing thoughts. "Why did you choose this place to meet?"

"*I* choose? It was your choice. I simply arrived early."

"You did not send the note."

"What note?" St. Wulfstan swore, low and harsh. "I take it back, Oriel. We're a fine *pair* of idiots."

They had been duped, brilliantly, each turned against the other. "Were you at Watier's last night?" The MacLeods would not have known St. Wulfstan, Nathan thought. Someone else could have easily used his name.

"Oh, I was there."

"You drew my wife's brothers into deep play?"

"I did."

"For God's sake, why? Surely not for the money."

St. Wulfstan grunted. "Don't go all dense on me again, man. Same reason I sniffed about your wife. I wanted to get to you. There was no question of those carbuncle-faced fools having the funds to pay up, nor of your letting the matter go quietly. I knew you would contact me."

"I did, this morning. I assumed the message was your response."

"All I got from you was a note tonight, telling me to meet you here."

Nathan didn't want to believe him. But he had seen too much strategy and deceit to reject obvious truth. "What of Montgomerie and Brandon? Are they really dead?"

"I would imagine so. Who knows? I thought you—"

"You thought I was responsible." Of course. "What of Stone? I thought you said you shot him."

"Damn it, man, I *did* shoot Stone. He'd made one attempt too many on me in Spain. I didn't expect him to come back here, but when he did . . . He had Rotheroe in his sights. Or at least I thought he did. Now, of course, it appears he was working *for* Rotheroe. He got Brooke, Montgomerie . . ."

Rotheroe.

"I was in the Park that day," Nathan said dully, remembering a torn coat sleeve, which quite probably was not the fault of a low-hanging branch after all.

"I know. Not ten feet from where Stone was hiding when I first saw you."

"You didn't kill him."

"Stone? Of course I did. The ball struck dead center."

"Yes, so you told me. But he did not die. Gerard got him to a surgeon."

"Well, splendid. I should be ecstatic, I know. But his

talking won't be worth a damn to us. We'll be dead by then."

Nathan considered mentioning that Stone probably would never talk again, but it hardly seemed worth the effort. St. Wulfstan was absolutely right. They would be dead anyway. He tried again to slacken the rope around his wrists and succeeded in doing nothing more than chafing his skin and setting his head pounding anew.

"Rotheroe," he muttered. He heard the man's indignant words, thought of his ruined arm. Ruined arm. How simple it would have been for the earl to exaggerate his injury, make himself seem harmless. "What has he to gain from allying himself with the French?"

"Money," St. Wulfstan snapped. "Power. What does it matter?"

Nathan felt movement to his right. He doubted the other man would have any more luck with his bonds than he, but it gave him an idea. "Move toward me, toward my voice. If we get back to back . . ."

He did not need to explain further. St. Wulfstan was scooting quickly in his direction. It took a few minutes, but soon enough each had access to the knots binding the other's wrists. Nathan felt his fingers chafing, then bleeding. The knot turned slippery.

"Any luck?" he asked, panting.

"No." St. Wulfstan's hands would be bleeding, too. "Keep at it, boyo. We've nothing to lose."

At first, Nathan thought he imagined the faint give. Another tug and he felt it again. The knot had loosened— just a little, but it was a start.

"I think," he said through clenched teeth, "I think perhaps—" He froze as he heard the door swing open.

All he could see for a moment was the hazy light of a lantern. Then, slowly, the shadowy outline of a figure appeared behind it. He squinted, trying desperately to see any identifying feature. From his vantage point on the floor, and with his vision, it could as easily have been the queen as Rotheroe.

St. Wulfstan let out a low whistle. "Well, I'll be damned."

Nathan knew they had been fooled again.

"It occurred to me you might try something like this." There was a clink as the lamp touched the floor. "Careless of me. After all, I taught you—"

"Everything we know." Nathan closed his eyes for a moment and allowed himself a single sigh. "Why, Matthew?"

"Silly question, Oriel." Gerard bent over him. "Money, of course. You wouldn't have any idea how poorly His Majesty pays a lowly corps commander. All for king and country, you know. Pride over pocket." He chuckled, an eerie sound. "Fools."

Nathan heard a heavy thud, heard St. Wulfstan gasp. Felt him slump over sideways. Gerard must have struck him. Hard, if the resulting tremor had been any indication. He steeled himself for a blow. It did not come.

"I never liked you, St. Wulfstan." Gerard had moved off again. "Always gave you the worst assignments, but damned if you didn't prove resistant to killing. I should have known you would come close to being my downfall here." To Nathan he said, "You, on the other hand, were my favorite. It was painful, arranging your death in Portugal. I was almost relieved when you survived."

"But you're going to kill me now."

"Of course I am, dear boy. I can't have any loose ends lying about."

Gerard was still bent over, arranging something on the floor. Nathan inched his arms back and groped for St. Wulfstan. His fingertips brushed the man's still wrists, then the knot binding them. Praying Gerard would not look up, Nathan tugged and again felt the rope loosen.

"Tell me, Oriel." There was a rustling of paper. "You never did receive any communiqués from the Continent, did you? No, I didn't think so. I wonder if there ever was one. Wouldn't it just be too unfortunate if there never was? All these deaths for nothing. I really thought I had been discovered."

"By one of the Ten?"

"I assumed so. I must say, it gave me quite a start, hearing an Englishman there was asking too many questions about me. Brandon, I imagine. He always seemed to be in contact with Dennison here. Well, I don't suppose we'll ever know." Gerard sounded almost cheerful.

"You killed him, too. And Montgomerie?"

"Oh, not with my own hands. I had Stone do that. The guilt would have been the death of me." Gerard laughed again, then gave an altogether too familiar groan as he mockingly repeated a familiar lament. "God, Nathan, if only I had known. I could have done something, anything—" He stopped abruptly. "Convincing, isn't it? You never suspected. Shame on you. A good agent never dismisses the obvious. Ah!"

Nathan cried out as a boot heel came down heavily on his fingers. St. Wulfstan did not move at all.

"We can't have that, now." Gerard crouched and pressed his face close. "All in good time, Nathan. All in good time."

"Why didn't you kill me while I was in the country?" Nathan forced the words past clenched teeth. Gerard must have broken fingers on both hands, the pain was so severe. "I was an easy target there. Few would have questioned it should I have had an accident." Perhaps, if he could just keep the man talking, there was a chance . . . "Why go to all the trouble of reactivating me, luring me back to Town?"

"Oh, Nathan. Always with the endless questions. It is quite simple, really. I needed to know how much you knew, if anything. And then it occurred to me that if someone were to try to contact you, he would be easier to track in Town. Kill two birds with one stone, so to speak." Again the shrill laugh. "But Stone got careless. Never was terribly clever, but corruptible as the devil himself. And goodness, didn't he have a grudge against the War Department for removing him from the corps. Stupid man never realized it was my order."

Nathan bit back a cry as Gerard seized his arm and forced him onto his stomach. Then, with surprising strength for his age and condition, the man dragged him several feet away from St. Wulfstan.

"*Hmm.* I really did hit our friend here hard that second time, didn't I? I wonder if I ought to wake him, thank him for his splendid showing at the tables last night. I will pay a visit on your wife, of course. Oh no, nothing like that. Shame on you for thinking any such thing, Nathan. No, no. It will merely be to offer my condolences at your untimely death. It will be her fault, you know."

"Damn it, Gerard, if you go near Isobel . . ." Nathan choked as the man's foot came down heavily on the back of his neck.

"Save your breath. You have so little of it left. Did you not know she sent a letter to St. Wulfstan, taking responsibility for her brothers' debt and vowing to clear it? In some manner. Oh, I have no doubt the offer was perfectly chaste, but just think what people will say when they find her note near your bodies. Really, I couldn't have planned it better myself. Oriel and St. Wulfstan kill each other over a woman. Perfect."

"You honestly believe," Nathan growled, despite the pressure on his throat, "no one will notice ten men dead and all connected?"

Gerard removed his foot, then bent down and patted him on the head. "Naive to the end. We were a clandestine operation, my boy. Only *we* knew the names of the others. And as soon as I deal with Rotheroe, there will be no others. Now, let's see. How best to arrange this. I'll move the pair of you to the bigger room, of course. You will be found with a clean shot to the heart. Everyone knows St. Wulfstan has perfect aim."

He chatted on, as calm as if he were arranging a dinner party. "I think I'll just put a ball in St. Wulfstan's gut. Your dying shot. Damned awful way to die, you know, takes hours. Be grateful I like you, Nathan." There was a loud click as Gerard cocked his gun.

"No!" Nathan bellowed and, using every ounce of strength he possessed, rolled over and lashed his legs toward Gerard. At the same time, St. Wulfstan coiled, coming up in a blur of motion.

Nathan could not be certain of exactly what happened next. His feet struck something; he thought he felt Gerard stumble. There was a blast, a flash of fire, and St. Wulfstan went down again. At almost the same moment, there was a crash from the doorway. He heard the sound of a hard object meeting bone. Then he fell back again, landing heavily on his injured hands. He cried out once with the pain before everything went black.

Isobel was sobbing as she threw herself down beside him. He was so still, and there was blood all over the floor. "Oh, Nathan, please . . . Nay!"

From the corner of her eye, she saw the older man coming to his knees, saw him go down again as the pistol butt cracked once more against his skull. She saw St. Wulfstan, too, lying a few feet away. But her attention was centered on her husband.

"Nathan," she coaxed, his name mingling with fervent prayers as she ran her hands over his body, searching for wounds. "Nathan, come back to me. Please."

Near blinded now by her own tears, she struggled to shift his weight. Then she cradled his head in her lap. His beautiful face was bruised, his overlong hair tangled on his brow. And his mouth, that glorious, generous mouth, was marred by a jagged cut in the lower lip.

She jerked off the gentle hand that rested on her shoulder. "Nay! He will be fine!"

"Lady Oriel . . ."

"Nay!" Tenderly, she brushed the dark hair from Nathan's brow. "Hear me now, my love. I am so sorry I ran away, but I'm back now, and I'll not leave you again. *Tha gradh agam ort, mo cridhe.*" Her loosened hair flowed forward, falling like a curtain around his face. *"Tha gradh agam ort."*

"You pick the damnedest times to curse me, madam wife."

Heart in her throat, Isobel blinked the tears from her eyes. Then she was sobbing and raining damp kisses over his face.

It was some time before she was calm enough to draw a deep breath. " 'Tis not a curse, you great daft fool."

"No? I always meant to learn Gaelic, but never quite got around to it."

She laughed, then hiccuped. *"Tha gradh agam ort.* It means *I love you."*

He gave her a shaky smile. "Do you promise? I won't find out later that it means stinking, three-legged cur?"

"Och, Nathan, I do love you!" Ignoring the fact that his hands were still bound and that the assault was no doubt doing nothing good for his cut lip, she kissed him deep and hard.

"Isobel . . . Isobel." His voice was rough with emotion. "You came back. Why?"

She smiled, feeling the ring on her finger as surely as if it were infused with heat. "That is a tale for a cold winter's night. I think now is a good time, though, to give a bit of credit where it's due." She leaned back then, giving him a view of her companion. "It might help if you were to say something, my lord."

Nathan frowned, confused. "Say what? How would it help?"

"Ah, not you, my lord. The other 'my lord.' "

Nathan sensed another figure leaning in. The man removed the bonds at his wrists, then his ankles. "I must say, Oriel, this was not quite how I had planned our reunion."

Nathan cursed his ears for playing cruel tricks. It could not be. . . .

"Rievaulx? *Gabriel?*" Then he reached up and wound his arms around the neck of his oldest friend. Laughing, choking on his own tears, he clung tightly. "Dear God, I thought . . . I saw . . ."

Rievaulx returned the embrace, then drew back slightly. His voice hoarse with emotion, he explained. "They left me for dead in the alley behind the tavern. *I* thought I was dead. By sheer luck, I was found by a local shopkeeper. He saw money in saving the English soldier and carried me to his home."

"But it was over six months ago, so long not to hear a word."

"It took me more than two months to recover, still longer to find Brandon. I was with him when he died, just ten steps too far away to save him. I saw the man who killed him, Nathan. It was Henry Stone."

As Isobel and Nathan sat silently, he continued. "Brandon had intercepted a fragmented French message. It mentioned Gerard. After Brandon and Brooke were . . . gone, I had no idea who I could trust on the Continent. And I didn't want to put you in danger by contacting you. I got passage on a Dutch merchant ship, then I stayed as close to you as I could get without attracting attention."

"How long have you been back?" Nathan asked quietly, his hand tight around his friend's.

"Three weeks."

"Gabriel has been keeping an eye on us, Nathan," Isobel said softly.

"Stone nearly got to you that night in front of the Hampdens'," Rievaulx muttered. "Damn it, man, I almost didn't make it through the crowd in time to push you away."

"You should have come to me," Nathan insisted, "to us."

"And put your new wife in danger, too? I had no idea how closely you were being watched by Gerard or Stone. If they'd learned I was still alive . . ."

"We would have seen to each other's backs."

"As we did in Lisbon?" Rievaulx sighed at Nathan's curse. "Yes, I know. You blame yourself. Isobel told me. Don't you see, Nathan? I survived because I was with you. Had Gerard gone after me in the hills, there would have been no distractions. We would both have died. With no one knowing I was alive, *I* had the advantage."

Nathan wanted to argue, but he couldn't. "How did you find me here?"

"I was watching Gerard's house. He wasn't there. But then I went to yours and followed your wife. She had a note from St. Wulfstan that mentioned Ten House, and she allowed me to tag along." Rievaulx leaned forward, as if Isobel could not hear. "I like her, Nathan. A damned sight better than our Cecily." To Isobel, he said, "I don't suppose you have a sister."

Her laugh was magic, and Nathan absorbed it like sunlight. "I have two. Perhaps someday, when I've come to know you a bit, I'll introduce you."

A faint groan from across the room caught their attention. "Gerard?" Isobel asked.

Rievaulx was already moving. "Good God, he's still breathing! Wulf? Wulf, can you hear me?"

St. Wulfstan, despite having a lead ball lodged deep in

his chest, said something very clear and very rude. He followed it by grumbling, "Should the three of you wish to continue your oh-so-heartwarming reunion, you can bloody well do it later!"

It was much later, when the sun was just peering over the horizon, that Nathan found himself heart-and-body warmingly entwined with his wife in bed. Rievaulx had seen St. Wulfstan to the surgeons, Gerard into official hands, and was himself comfortably settled down the hall. His reintroduction to Society would, no doubt, take the last curious eye from the Marquess and Marchioness of Oriel.

"Tell me again," the marquess demanded.

"Ah, clever attempt," the marchioness countered, "but 'tis your turn."

Nathan chuckled. "I cannot fool you, can I?"

"I'd say you did a good enough job with your sight."

"Isobel, I was wrong and I am sorry."

"Cuist!" She kissed his chin. "I've forgotten."

"Mmm. Why do I not believe you?"

"Because you're a naturally suspicious, unsocial creature."

"Oh, is that the reason?" Nathan tightened his grip on her and grimaced. Only one of his fingers was broken, the physician had said as he set it, but Nathan was not certain he believed that, either. "What if I promise to change?"

"Into what? *Nar leigeadh Dia!* God forbid. One magical transformation ought to be plenty for a man in his life."

"I would agree. Now, tell me how much you adore me again. In English."

"Nathan."

"Oh, very well. My turn. Once upon a time, a man went astray onto the land of a poor, cursed beast. In what he considered fair recompense, the fellow handed over his daughter, a sharp-tongued, iron-fisted Scottish wench—"

"Nathan!"

Laughing, he told her precisely what she wanted to hear, using plain English words. And then no words at all.

EPILOGUE

Faire fire, faire fire,
Thou art not the beast of burden.
Faire fire, faire fire,
Thou art the man of dreaming.
My treasure and my delight,
By theft I won thee,
In the dead of night,
Without glimmer, without light.
Faire fire.
—Lullaby of the MacLeoid

May 1812

Nathan could not find his wife. While this was a common occurrence during their time in London, it frustrated him to no end in the country. Grumbling as he navigated the slick steps behind the house, he wondered why, with eighty-six rooms to choose from inside, she inevitably turned up in the garden.

She was there, on the bench below his grandmother's roses. Her red hair blazed at him as he approached, a fiery beacon that warmed him more with each step. As always, his frown turned into a smile. By the time he reached her, he was grinning like an idiot. Isobel had that effect on him.

She looked up to find him looming over her. Oh, but he was a bonnie fellow, she thought, all bright eyes and smile. She wondered if the sight of him would ever cease to set her heart thumping. She suspected it never would.

"Out to enjoy the fresh air, are you?" she asked.

With ease born of much practice, he lowered himself to sit beside her. "I am out," he answered with a resigned sigh, "because I wish to be with my wife and she does not seem to realize how bloody cold it still is."

307

"Oh, nonsense." She took one of his hands and rubbed it between hers. " 'Tis spring and I like being among the roses."

Nathan turned to view the wall. Not that he could see any more than he could a year before, but he damn well knew there wasn't so much as a bud in sight. He had seen the blooms, though, the red and ivory glory of summer. As a belated wedding gift to Isobel, he had taken a flower from each plant and had it gilded. The pair rested now, forever entwined, beside their bed.

Paper rustled. "Writing to Margaret again? She has only been back on Skye for a fortnight."

"Aye, I've much to tell her."

Nathan grinned. "Since last week? Your letters, my dear, are keeping the mail coaches running."

"Well, I thought she should know Gabriel is on his way to Scotland."

"*Mmm.* Forewarned is forearmed."

"*Cuist!* She'll find him as delightful as I do."

"Perhaps. I must say, Isobel, you are being rather blithe about the concept of Gabriel getting near your sister. He has a poor history and poorer reputation with women who find him charming. If I were you, I would be horrified by the prospect of their meeting."

"Shame on you, speaking of your friend so." Isobel shook her head in amusement. "Besides, Gabriel and Maggie . . . No, I cannot see it. Oil and water."

"Some would say the same of us, love."

"Ridiculous. We're fire and . . ."

"Dry twigs?" he offered, grinning.

"Well, 'tisn't what I might have chosen, but it suits."

Yes, flame and kindling they were, Isobel thought. One at its best with the other. Isobel sighed in contentment and snuggled closer to Nathan. "I've decided you're good for me, *Sasunnach*."

"After only ten months? Careful you don't rush into a

statement you'll regret." He caught her hand as she smacked his shoulder. "Tell your sister how good I am for you, if you would. I still don't think she trusts me not to savage you."

"Oh, Maggie likes you well enough. She'll like you all the more when she hears she's to be an auntie."

Awed still, Nathan slid his hand under Isobel's cloak to rest against her stomach. It humbled him to think part of him was growing there. Each night since she had told him—six times now—he pressed his lips to her still-flat abdomen and murmured, *"Tha gradh agam ort,"* to his child. Isobel giggled at the brush of his day's growth of whiskers and laughed harder still at his pronunciation. When done insulting him, she would kiss him with sweet passion and deepest love, then reassure him that seven months was ample time to get a wee Gaelic phrase right.

As long as she said the words several times a day, was his response, and he repeated them back, he thought he could have it mastered—oh, in sixty years or so.

"So, about Margaret and Rievaulx . . ."

"Och, Nathan, will you stop with that!"

"I should think you'd be happy to see my wildly romantic nature running amok."

"Oh, to be sure, but not at my sister's expense." Isobel hummed thoughtfully. "My wildly romantic nature points to Trevor as the next one to lose his heart."

"St. Wulfstan? The man hasn't got a heart."

"So you say. I would venture to disagree."

Nathan grinned. "Care to make a wager on it, madam?"

"I would indeed. What are the stakes?" It was Isobel's turn to laugh as Nathan whispered his reply into her ear. "I accept, though it seems a shame to wait until I win."

"Bold words, my love, especially since it will be my victory."

"Perhaps we ought to go make certain it's a worthy

wager. I'd be vastly disappointed to find my winnings aren't as grand as I'd thought."

Nathan's eyes sparked. "I agree completely." He gauged the distance to the house. "I think I should carry you inside immediately so we can find out."

"Ah, I think not, lad." Isobel laughed and batted at his hands. "I think we should walk."

"Will you at least hold my hand?"

"Of course," she said, and twined her fingers with his.

Love Letters

Ballantine romances are on the Web!

Read about your favorite Ballantine authors and upcoming books on our Web site, LOVE LETTERS, at **www.randomhouse.com/BB/loveletters**, including:

- ♥What's new in the stores
- ♥Previews of upcoming books
- ♥In-depth interviews with romance authors and publishing insiders
- ♥Sample chapters from new romances
- ♥And more . . .

Want to keep in touch? To subscribe to Love Notes, the monthly what's-new update for the Love Letters Web site, send an e-mail message to **loveletters@cruises.randomhouse.com** with "subscribe" as the subject of the message. You will receive a monthly announcement of the latest news and features on our site.

So follow your heart and visit us at **www.randomhouse.com/BB/loveletters**!

"It isn't enough, my wanting you. I cannot bear the thought of your being unwilling."

"Nathan." Her free hand drifted, quick and trembling, over his cheek. "I want to be a wife to you, in every way possible. I want you to be a husband to me."

Husband to her. God, he thought, he wanted to be nothing more. And at times it seemed to him that he'd been made for that very purpose.

Her mouth was warm and still. Gently, he tilted her face to meet his fully. His hands itched to drop lower, to move fast and hard over the pliant curves now just brushing his chest and thighs.

She sighed into his mouth. It was a soft, wondering sound, and it thrilled him. There was so much, too much he wanted to give her. And right away. He could only hope he would not kill them both in the process. . . .

Books published by The Ballantine Publishing Group
are available at quantity discounts on bulk purchases
for premium, educational, fund-raising, and special
sales use. For details, please call 1-800-733-3000.